THINKING THROU

Ralahine Utopian Studies

Series editors:
Raffaella Baccolini (University of Bologna at Forlì)
Antonis Balasopoulos (University of Cyprus)
Joachim Fischer (University of Limerick)
Michael G. Kelly (University of Limerick)
Tom Moylan (University of Limerick)
Phillip E. Wegner (University of Florida)

Volume 35

PETER LANG
Oxford - Berlin - Bruxelles - Chennai - Lausanne - New York

Miguel Sebastián-Martín

THINKING THROUGH HIGH-TECH HELL

A THEORY OF THE NEW MEDIA DYSTOPIA

PETER LANG
Oxford - Berlin - Bruxelles - Chennai - Lausanne - New York

Bibliographic information published by the Deutsche Nationalbibliothek.
The German National Library lists this publication in the German National Bibliography;
detailed bibliographic data is available on the Internet at http://dnb.d-nb.de.
A catalogue record for this book is available from the British Library.

Library of Congress Cataloging-in-Publication Data

Names: Sebastián-Marfín, Miguel, 1995- author.
Title: Thinking through high-tech hell: a theory of the new media dystopia
   / Miguel Sebastián-Marfín.
Description: Oxford; New York: Peter Lang, 2024. | Series: Ralahine
   utopian studies, 1661-5875; 35 | Includes bibliographical references
   and index.
Identifiers: LCCN 2024012582 | ISBN 9781803744629 (paperback) | ISBN
   9781803744636 (ebook) | ISBN 9781803744643 (epub)
Subjects: LCSH: Dystopian television programs–Great Britain–History and
   criticism. | Dystopian television programs–United States–History and
   criticism. | Digital media on television. | LCGFT: Television criticism
   and reviews.
Classification: LCC PN1992.8.D97 S43 2024 | DDC
   791.450941–dc23/eng/20240402
LC record available at https://lccn.loc.gov/2024012582

Esta publicación ha contado con el apoyo económico del "Programa propio V: Difusión de resultados de investigación" (Vicerrectorado de investigación y transferencia, Universidad de Salamanca).
This publication has had the economic support of "Programa propio V: Difusión de resultados de investigación" (University of Salamanca).

Esta publicación ha sido realizada al amparo de un contrato de investigación predoctoral co-financiado por la Junta de Castilla y León y el Fondo Social Europeo (ORDEN EDU/601/2020).
This publication was realized under a pre-doctoral research contract co-funded by the Junta de Castilla y León and the European Social Fund (ORDEN EDU/601/2020).

Cover image: "Digital mise-en-abyme," by Miguel Sebastián-Martín,
digitally edited photograph, 2024.
Cover design by Peter Lang Group AG

ISSN 1661-5875
ISBN 978-1-80374-462-9 (print)
ISBN 978-1-80374-463-6 (ePDF)
ISBN 978-1-80374-464-3 (ePub)
DOI 10.3726/b21834

© 2024 Peter Lang Group AG, Lausanne
Published by Peter Lang Ltd, Oxford, United Kingdom
info@peterlang.com - www.peterlang.com

Miguel Sebastián-Martín has asserted his right under the Copyright,
Designs and Patents Act, 1988, to be identified as Author of this Work.

All rights reserved.
All parts of this publication are protected by copyright.
Any utilisation outside the strict limits of the copyright law, without the permission of the publisher, is forbidden and liable to prosecution. This applies in particular to reproductions, translations, microfilming, and storage and processing in electronic retrieval systems.

This publication has been peer reviewed.

A mi tía y más que tía, Leonor Martín Vicente, esa persona tan fuerte y constante en mi vida, que tanto me cuidó, y que supo transmitirme su humor y su espíritu crítico desde que era niño.

Leo: creciste en pleno franquismo con todo lo que ello conlleva para una mujer de clase trabajadora, viviste la precariedad de una familia de periquines charros que volaron por toda España, y por esas y otras circunstancias, no estudiaste formalmente. No obstante, hay algo que hiciste mejor que casi cualquier profesor, investigador o académico: me animaste (o, mejor dicho, me picaste) a dudar y preguntar. A imaginar e indagar. A interesarme por la historia, y por supuesto por las historias.

Gracias por todo eso, y por tanto más que no viene a cuento, pero que igualmente cuenta.

Contents

List of Figures — ix

Acknowledgments — xi

List of Abbreviations — xiii

Introduction: Feeling Dystopian? — 1

CHAPTER 1
Our Hopeless SF Times: Contemporary Capitalism as a New Media Dystopia — 23

CHAPTER 2
New Media Reflexivity: Self-Referentiality and Self-Consciousness in the Audio-Visual SF of Digital Platforms — 117

CHAPTER 3
Between Critique and Mystification: The Aesthetic and Ideological Ambivalences of New Media Dystopias — 189

CHAPTER 4
New Media Quixotism: Satiric and Utopian Characterizations of Digital Subjectivity — 265

Conclusion: Exit Dystopia? — 339

Bibliography — 347

Index — 375

Figures

Figure 1.	Anonymous meme.	3
Figure 2.	Anonymous meme.	27
Figures 3–7.	*Black Mirror: Bandersnatch* (directed by David Slade, 2018).	169
Figures 8–9.	*Westworld* (created by Lisa Joy and Jonathan Nolan, 2016–22).	233
Figures 10–14.	*Devs* (created by Alex Garland, 2020).	249
Figures 15–17.	"USS Callister" (directed by Toby Haynes, *Black Mirror*, 2017)	293
Figures 18–21.	*Mr Robot* (created by Sam Esmail, 2015–19).	309
Figures 22–25.	*Maniac* (created by Cary Joji Fukunaga and Patrick Somerville, 2018).	321
Figure 26.	A *Black Mirror* mock-advertisement.	346

Acknowledgments

The research required for this book was realized as part of a research contract with the English Department of the University of Salamanca, granted and co-funded by the Junta de Castilla y León and the European Social Fund (ORDEN EDU/601/2020) within the framework of the research project *El Quijote Transnacional* (Ref. PGC2018-093792-B-C21, <https://quijotetransnacional.es>). Were it not for that contract, obtained in mid-2020 after a year of juggling with part-time jobs, I might have joined the ranks of aspiring researchers who are frustrated (or directly excluded) by the structures of neoliberal academia. So let this be a thank you note to all those who fought for a more inclusive academia and to those who fought for the existence of funding opportunities like the ones I have enjoyed. Without them, the offspring of the working classes wouldn't stand a chance—even if, of course, grants and scholarships alone may be nothing but tiny band-aids on deeper social wounds. For this reason, let this also be a reminder—for those in a condition to do so—to keep on working towards democratizing access to higher education, towards democratizing the learning process itself and—more generally—to keep on resisting fighting against the commodification of everything and everyone, in academia and beyond. Things may look rather dystopian—as they indeed do from a book like this one—but even so, the simple but radical ideal of *public education* is still worth fighting for and worth pursuing in deeper ways.

As a young researcher under the infamous "publish or perish" imperative, I also want to express my gratitude for the anonymous work of those reviewers and editors who helped me to pursue and polish my ideas. This book is inseparable from the careful feedback that I received in the journals *Science Fiction Studies*, *Utopian Studies* and *Science Fiction Film and Television*, as well as in the Spanish journals *Hélice* and *452ºF*. Even when these and other journal articles and conference papers were—initially, partly, undeniably—written out of the necessity to get practice on the field, throughout these many experiences I have learnt to value even more the importance of sharing ideas and criticisms in constructive and respectful ways. For if anything is contained in blind review processes and open conferences, it is the utopian potential of an academia constructed upon *open dialogue*—a place where one can grow and learn from and with a plurality of voices. Because of this, I can only hope to contribute towards working conditions where we all have *more quality time* for dialoguing and thinking collectively and I can only thank and celebrate all those people who, in their daily practices, favor a *slower, collectively-minded* academia: one where publishing and conferencing are not done compulsively or just out of necessity, but for the sake of having some meaningful dialog, some stimulating exchange of ideas which might contribute to collective human knowledge.

More personally, this book is also the long-term product of ongoing conversations with many teachers and colleagues and I should thank them all here for being part of the journey. Firstly, Javier Pardo, my doctoral supervisor at Salamanca, who a long time ago introduced me to the field of SF studies and who has since then supervised much of my work, from undergraduate to doctoral. Thank you for inspiring this academic project and for accompanying me to its completion. Thank you too to the admired colleagues, teachers and researchers who evaluated this book when it was still a PhD thesis: Alfredo Moro, Paula Barba and Maite Conde, in person, as well as Jesse J. Ramírez and Liz W. Faber, remotely. Thank you all for your kind appreciation and your useful suggestions. Another thank you goes to all the colleagues-turned-friends who accompanied me in the years of researching and writing and often read my work, encouraging me and commenting on my ideas. Specifically, thank you, Lucía Bausela, Lucía López and Marta Bernabéu, for being that odd, more-than-academic group of colleagues. Thank you, too, teachers of the English Department at Salamanca and teachers of the Centre for Film and Screen at Cambridge, for being part of the most formative and intellectually stimulating periods of my life. Thank you, too, mamá, papá, for the political common sense and the sense of humor that I inherited from you both, because that too is visible in this work and has helped me live and laugh through it. And thank you too, Sara, above everyone else, for being my first and most critical reader, my most patient supporter and the best life companion.

Abbreviations

AI   Artificial intelligence
GLH   *The Grasshopper Lies Heavy*
MHC   *The Man in the High Castle*
SF   Science fiction/speculative fiction
VR   Virtual reality

Introduction: Feeling Dystopian?

> It's all gone sour. It's all gone a bit "Black Mirror," in fact. Which is bad for human civilization, but publicity for our little TV show. Every cloud, eh? I sometimes wonder if I'm well equipped to cope with our terrifying dystopian present because having worked on the show for all this time, I've already repeatedly experienced what it's like when *Black Mirror* stories slowly manifest themselves in the real world. Not sure that's going to be much comfort when I'm being chased by an autonomous robot bum-on-legs with the Facebook logo etched on its perineum and a Make America Great Again hat perched up top, but you can't have everything.
>
> —Charlie Brooker, *Inside Black Mirror* (6)

It has become a cliché to say that reality has become dystopian, to say that we live in science-fictional times, or that "it's all gone a bit 'Black Mirror,'" as *Black Mirror*'s co-creator Charlie Brooker ironically puts it.[1] Taking this logic to a caricaturized extreme, one anonymous meme proposes that You Are Here, at the center of a Venn diagram, in the very

---

1 Writing in the mid-1980s, in a historical situation where making this claim was (perhaps) more transgressive and provocative than today, Donna Haraway based her "Cyborg Manifesto" upon the premise that "the boundary between science fiction and social reality is an optical illusion" ("A Cyborg Manifesto" 149). Throughout the years, echoes of these claims have been heard among SF scholars especially, as in Sherryl Vint's 2010 claim that we now "inhabit a cyberpunk future" ("Afterword: The World Gibson Made" 228). And today, this analogy continues (and will probably continue) to be echoed by theorists who invoke SF to critically re-imagine the present and, at the same time, the analogy also has (and will probably continue having) echoes in corporate marketing and aesthetics—perhaps to a point in which one can speak of a "futures industry" (see Vint, "Introduction to 'The Futures Industry'") or of "business SF" (see Ramírez). Thus, given the comparison's reduction to a formula that can fit into almost opposite discourses—as Charlie Brooker cynically acknowledges—it seems necessary to reconsider the ambivalent potentials of taking this SF look at the present, especially when the estranging effect of re-imagining reality as SF is now (partially) undercut by the sheer omnipresence of "science-fictionality" as "a mood or an attitude" that informs contemporary cultures (Csicsery-Ronay Jr, *The Seven Beauties of Science Fiction* 2).

worst place of all, where several famous dystopias overlap and converge (Figure 1). Even in our everyday life, many of us have surely heard complaints about new technologies or the media which evoke—or even explicitly refer to—dystopian narratives and imagery. Whether we are talking about the numberless amount of conspiracy theories online, or about the occasional witticisms of some acquaintance of ours, it seems that we now live in what could be called a new media dystopia—a world in which new media technologies appear as one of the most popular scapegoats for broader socio-political problems.[2] With this popular imaginary in mind, my proposition here is the following: what if we took this collective feeling as the point of departure for a critical theory of the present? What if, more specifically, we proceeded by examining fictional new media dystopias such as Brooker's *Black Mirror* and, through them, we tried to arrive at a better understanding of the high-tech hell that we supposedly inhabit?

---

2 My words here might be taken as an implicit suggestion that this popular logic is neo-Luddite in a sense and, in some instances, this might very well be the case. Nonetheless, I would want to avoid the term Luddite for the derogatory connotations of a (supposedly) inherently reactionary and mystifying form of critical thinking. As opposed to that common caricature, it would be worthwhile to consider Cory Doctorow's argument that SF is inherently Luddite literature, but in a way that recognizes the ambivalences of Luddism. In Doctorow's account, Luddism is to be re-evaluated as much more than a reactionary mystification of the power of technology, but rather a form of politics that, like SF, asks "not merely *what* the technology does, but who it does it *for* and who it does it *to*" ("Science Fiction Is a Luddite Literature" n.p.).

Feeling Dystopian?

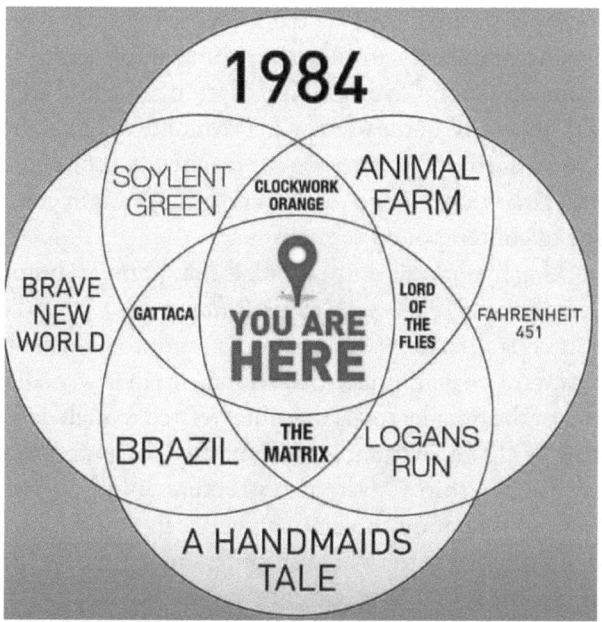

Figure 1. Anonymous meme widely circulated online, with an untraceable origin.

On the one hand, there is a degree of truth and a seed of critical thinking in the truism that the present is a dystopia; yet, on the other hand, to reiterate this clichéd complaint can contribute to reinforcing and further reifying hegemonic ideas and ideologies. To say that we live in a dystopia can be a subversively critical gesture, but it can also be a cynically disempowering one—and this is probably the core ambivalence of a popular logic that, as of yet, does not seem to be losing traction. During the 2010s in particular, the decade of the emergence and consolidation of what has alternatively been called "surveillance," "platform," or "digital capitalism" (see, respectively, Zuboff; Srnicek; Pace), the words "dystopia" and "dystopian" have grown in use considerably, becoming trendy buzzwords just as the world witnessed how "new media" technologies were becoming irreversibly interwoven with the fabric of everyday life. The rise in usage of "dystopia" and "dystopian" may be observed precisely (and ironically) thanks to one digital platform, Google Ngram: here we find that the occurrence of both noun and adjective has been growing even faster than before, at some points quasi-exponentially, after around 2007–8. Therefore, with their rising popularity and the deepening ambivalence that comes with such popularization, "dystopia" and "dystopian" could and should be examined as "keywords" of the present, in Raymond Williams's sense of the term. Thus seen, the dystopian may be approached as a common-sense but contested imaginary, one which reflects and reifies certain contradictions and conflicts of contemporary capitalism.[3]

The working hypothesis of this book is that popular dystopian series such as *Black Mirror*, *Westworld*, *Devs*, *Mr Robot*, *Maniac* and others can be grasped as crystallizations of hegemonic (and, to an extent, counter-hegemonic) ways of imagining recent developments in new media technologies, as well as of the broader social dynamics related to such developments. Also adopting Williams's terminology, Tom Moylan has proposed to think that we now dwell within a "dystopian structure of feeling," which highlights the central role of dystopian imaginaries in how we map our position as individuals within the whole of contemporary reality.[4] Specifically, Moylan's argument is that "the currently popular dystopian structure of feeling tends to foster passive resignation rather than stimulate engagement [...] in the sense of the diminution of the 'political' as linked to an increased interest in commodified entertainment" (Moylan, "The Necessity of Hope

3   Raymond Williams's *Keywords* proposed and demonstrated the idea that the "keywords" of a certain historical moment should be examined as sites of contested, shifting meanings, as crystallizations of broader historical trends.

4   Although Moylan's essay was published at the onset of the COVID-19 pandemic and there is an undeniable temptation to read it as prophetic, Moylan's critique is more of a decidedly *longue-durée*, systemic view that considers the present's dystopian structure of feeling as something derived from the pre-existing trends of global neoliberal capitalism and the impending climate crisis.

    In Raymond Williams's *Marxism and Literature* (128–35), "structure of feeling" is defined in opposition to static and monolithic notions of "ideology" and instead, defined as a complex of

    meanings and values as they are actively lived and felt [...] over a range from formal assent with private dissent to the more nuanced interaction between selected and interpreted beliefs and acted and justified experiences. [...] a 'structure of feeling' is a cultural hypothesis, actually derived from attempts to understand such elements and their connections in a generation or period, and needing always to be returned, interactively, to such evidence. (132–3)

Feeling Dystopian?

in Dystopian Times" 182). Probing into Moylan's hypothesis from a Marxist perspective, this book theorizes and analyzes *new media dystopias* with an eye on *their ambivalence within and against* that structure of feeling.[5] Whether or not one agrees with this hypothesis on the social function of popular dystopias, it nonetheless seems clear that "the fantastic" has definitively moved "from counterpublic to public space," as Jesse S. Cohn puts it (449), so, for better or for worse, SF narratives and images weigh heavily upon the popular imagination. Paraphrasing Karl Marx ("The Eighteenth Brumaire of Louis Bonaparte" 482), now it is not only the tradition of all dead generations, but also the dreadful futures of all dystopias which weigh like a nightmare on the brains of the living.

Out of the innumerable, intertwined elements of this seemingly hopeless global situation, which could include the anthropogenic climate crisis, the deepening of inequalities on a global scale, or the revival of reactionary political programs, the central focus of this book lies on one dimension, the "new media" dimension of this dystopian structure of feeling.[6] Specifically, this book examines how the conflicts and contradictions of

---

5   This book is conceived as a contribution to Marxist thinking, in sympathy with both the theoretical framework and the political motivations, although this should not be mistaken with an endorsement of everything done in the name of Marxism. My book is, in some ways, very orthodox, at least in the sense that it often relies directly on the writings and concepts of Marx himself, but this is, evidently, not necessarily antagonistic to re-interpreting and re-contextualizing. If I am dogmatic in following something that Marx ever said, it's in respecting his claim that "All I know is that I am not a Marxist" (Engels). Thus, being "orthodox" means approaching everything critically, including Marx.

6   This book's focus is on new media dystopias is not meant to overshadow the fact that the reasons why our societies may be considered dystopian (in the broadest, popular sense of the word) transcend considerations of media technologies *sensu stricto*. On the contrary, my belief is that the reasons for speaking about the contemporary moment as a new media dystopia are *intersectional*—in Patricia Hill Collins's broadest and most politicized sense of the term—and these reasons would also require thinking about our global "media ecology" in Sy Taffel's sense—that is, we would also have to consider how "digital media are deeply politically, materially and culturally implicated in the production of contemporary ecological crises and are necessary components of collective mobilizations designed to substantively address them" (Taffel 2; see also Parikka, *A Geology of Media*).

digital capitalism have been imagined through the lens of *new media dystopias* produced by the Anglo-American culture industry.[7] With the concept of "new media dystopia," I refer to certain dystopian narratives that both (1) represent (and problematize) the emergence and spread of new media technologies and (2) are themselves produced, distributed and/or consumed within new media platforms. Although dystopias that conform to this definition could be found in a diversity of media, this book centers its attention on audio-visual series, considering these as an art form that—especially in the SF genre—synthesizes the narrative complexity of literature with the spectacular aesthetics of cinema, allowing us to grasp certain dialectics between the two.[8] Besides, audio-visual series could also be taken as an emblematic site of the "media convergence" characteristic of the epoch (Jenkins), especially when these products, still conventionally called "TV" series, are now most commonly produced for, distributed through and/or consumed in digital platforms like Netflix, HBO, Disney+ or Amazon Prime and, therefore, they can indirectly shed light upon the spectatorial and consumer logics of the contemporary culture industry.[9]

7   Even if Hollywood's power has been to some extent affected and renegotiated after the emergence of new corporate actors that originated in Silicon Valley (such as Netflix), these are mostly intra-national conflicts and the US is still by far the hegemonic cultural producer on a global scale, so it can be safely assumed (as this book does) that its productions are broadly representative or at least symptomatic of hegemonic cultural trends. For overviews of how Hollywood and television have been reshaped by the emergence of digital capitalism, see Smith-Rowsey or Jenner.

8   In this theorization of the audio-visual series, I am essentially operating on the observation that contemporary "complex TV" (Mittell) of the dystopian kind illustrate the "aesthetics of ambivalence" of audio-visual SF (Landon), as a genre that has always had a problematic, if not directly conflictual relationship between its literary and its cinematic expressions. Thus, although in a more genre-specific way, this book could be read in dialog with other contemporary approaches to the "TV" series that emphasize both/either their narrative complexity and/or their aesthetics (see the volume by Winckler and Huertas-Martín; or the *Open Philosophy* special issue on TV series, esp. Shuster).

9   In this sense, this book echoes and engages with critiques of the capitalist culture industry across historical epochs: from the Frankfurt School's landmark critique (see Adorno and Horkheimer; Adorno, "Culture Industry Reconsidered"), going through the Situationists' critique of the society of the spectacle (see Debord,

Feeling Dystopian? 7

Hence, although my corpus is medium-specific, my theorization is clearly oriented towards a larger transmedia field and my concept of the "new media dystopia" has, I believe, relevance and resonance beyond the study of digitally-distributed "TV" series.

From that definition, this book's exploration of the fictional sub-genre pays special attention to the *reflexivity* of new media dystopias—that is, to the formal means whereby these narratives reflect upon their medium, which is usually the digital platform, itself accessible through a multiplicity of devices that are often thematized by these narratives.[10] From this formal perspective, the Anglo-American culture industry's "content" is, in turn, ideologically examined as *both symptomatic and subversive of its own platforms of distribution and consumption*. In other words, I approach this kind of medially reflexive "entertainment" *both* as a form of commodified, ideological mystification that is enabled by capitalist media technologies *and* as an SF form of (self-)critique that goes against capitalism's ideologies of technological progress. In taking this dialectical approach, I aspire to move beyond a theoretical standstill whereby the omnipresent reflexivity of postmodern culture tends to be seen as either radically subversive—as in some theories of so-called metafiction—or as thoroughly symptomatic of the logics of a capitalist culture industry—as in some Marxist theories.

Instead, my assumption is that—just like most postmodern audio-visual culture, but perhaps more acutely—new media dystopias should be examined with a clear eye on their *ambivalences*, which emerge not only from their ironic contextual position, but also from their narrative reflexivity, their visual aesthetics and their ideological implication. In essence,

---

Society of the Spectacle) and all the way to critiques of the culture industry in the age of digital new media (see Beller; Fuchs, *Critical Theory of Communication*; Briziarelli and Armano).

10 In speaking of "reflexivity," I am following Pedro Javier Pardo's definition of it as "the process or at of reflecting upon the medium" (Pardo, "Hacia una teoría de la reflexividad fílmica" 47, my translation) and I am also following in the steps of several scholars of SF film have argued that audio-visual SF is at least potentially (if not essentially) reflexive. Annette Kuhn, for instance, posits that SF is "the most cinematic of all film genres" and "a perfect example of the medium fitting, if not exactly being, the message" (*Alien Zone* 6–7).

I regard new media dystopias as both semi-autonomous artworks and fetishized commodities.[11] On the one hand, these are the products of an age in which even radical anti-capitalism is commodified. However, on the other hand, these are also tiny rebellious gestures against the logics of an age in which the consequences of expanded commodification and technological "progress" are becoming tragically obvious—as the worsening climate crisis of the Anthropocene (or Capitalocene) demonstrates.[12] We might be dwelling in a global new media dystopia, as some popular logics have it, but it is clear that we cannot afford to stay there any longer—at least not without causing irreversible human and environmental damage on unprecedented and unpredictable scales.

In pursuing such a holistic mode of analysis, it should be made clear that my intention is *absolutely not* to simply convey the idea of a "superstructural" mechanism—capitalism's media-technological apparatus—that would subordinate and subsume all aspects of cultural life, but rather to unveil the ways whereby contemporary hegemonies—like all hegemonies in the Gramscian sense—are subject to constant contestation and require re-negotiation if they are to maintain their legitimacy and sway over populations.[13] In any approach to dystopian apparatuses of power—fictional or real—one would do well to remember that, as Fredric Jameson warns us,

11   My approach sits within a strand of Marxist cultural theory that above all emphasizes ambivalence. Beyond the above-cited Raymond Williams and Fredric Jameson, Sianne Ngai's recent *Theory of the Gimmick*, for instance, revolves around the dialectics of—in her terms—"an *ambivalent* judgment tied to a *compromised* form" (Ngai 1, her emphasis).

12   For a comprehensive overview of critical approaches to the Anthropocene, the proposed new geological era in which human action becomes a central factor in environmental change, see Wark. Variations on the term abound, such as "capitalocene" (Moore), meant to stress the importance of capitalist dynamics for this geological turning point, or even "anthrobscene," meant to highlight "the environmentally disastrous consequences of planned obsolescence of electronic media, the energy costs of digital culture, and, for instance, the neocolonial arrangements of material and energy extraction across the globe" (Parikka, *The Anthrobscene* n.p.).

13   Antonio Gramsci indeed emphasized how, in liberal-bourgeois democracies, hegemony is established by securing the consent of the majorities and this requires that the ruling classes are flexible enough to adapt to any challenges and critiques coming from below. In his words: "The 'normal' exercise of hegemony […] is

Feeling Dystopian? 9

> the more powerful the vision of some increasingly total system or logic—the Foucault of the prisons book is the obvious example—the more powerless the reader comes to feel. Insofar as the theorist wins, therefore, by constructing an increasingly closed and terrifying machine, to that very degree he loses, since the critical capacity of his work is thereby paralyzed, and the impulses of negation and revolt, not to speak of those of social transformation, are increasingly perceived as vain and trivial in the face of the model itself. (*Postmodernism* 5–6)

As opposed to the possibility that this theorization may further contribute to the dominant hopelessness, my intention here is to insist on how even this structure of feeling is composed of innumerable ambivalences that may potentially be taken in utopian or subversive directions. Metaphorically speaking, my idea is that—despite well-founded fears of some emerging form of algorithmic "neo-fascism"—the whole networked machinery of our own global dystopia is still made up of potentially malfunctioning hardware and profoundly malleable software.[14] This machine may control us, but it can also be reprogrammed, or even broken. Thus, although this book immerses itself in an *a priori* disempowering imaginary, it is ultimately a "technoclastic" attempt to break with the widespread assumption that we live in an inescapable inferno.[15] On the contrary, even the seemingly "totalitarian" new media dystopia of some

---

characterised by the combination of force and consent, which balance each other reciprocally, without force predominating excessively over consent" (Gramsci 80). Of course, this is not to say that force is absent from the picture and one should not read Gramsci in that overly "culturalist" manner.

14 It is by now well-known and widely demonstrated that algorithms have tended to reinforce pre-existing axes of domination and inequality, as certain data-driven, seemingly "objective" uses of such technologies (in the US but also globally) end up reifying racism, police violence and the prison-industrial complex (see Noble; Wang). Besides, it is also clear that use of algorithmic technology by financial institutions (and speculators) have also tended towards an entrenchment of elite unaccountability and a growth of economic volatility (see Pasquale; Martin; Durand, *Fictitious Capital*).

15 I am borrowing this provocative neologism from Jesse J. Ramírez, who defines "technoclasm" as a Roland Barthes-style critique of capitalist myths about technology, a mode of critique that is ultimately intended as "a declaration of the [working classes'] right to exist as co-creators of the social world" (9).

fictions is shown to be—as any social formation—imperfect, instable and susceptible to transformation (even destruction) by diverse historical agents—human, or non-human. A better understanding of new media dystopias could humbly contribute to the intellectual efforts required in order to begin imagining the large-scale transformations demanded by our historical moment, because—although in a complexly mediated form—the narrative and aesthetic ambivalences of these kinds of fictions are in many ways echoes of the social contradictions and political challenges that confront this epoch.[16]

Overall, despite their technologically determinist and cynical appearances, my underlying hypothesis in this book is that new media dystopias *at least partially* challenge—or allow room for readings that challenge—the hegemony of pessimistic and defeatist ways of imagining past, present and future. Although contemporary capitalism—especially after the post-2008 Great Recession—has been the object of severe critiques and popular mobilizations, in practice, we still seem to bow to Margaret Thatcher's infamous dictum that "there is no alternative." There is little room for doubt that capitalism is still the world's dominant mode of production—and besides, the system seems to be thriving in its expansion into (or colonization of) the digital sphere. This is perhaps one key reason why—at least in the "global North," or in those regions where hegemony operates by consent more than by coercion—the contemporary epoch is characterized by a pervasive end-of-history fatalism with many names: "capitalist realism" (in Fisher, *Capitalist Realism*), "left melancholy" (in W. Brown, "Resisting Left Melancholy"), "the age of impotence" (in Berardi, *Futurability*) or "dystopian structure of feeling" (in Moylan, "The Necessity of Hope in Dystopian Times"). In fact, we do not lack ways of referring to the apparent inability of the whole political spectrum (anti-capitalist left included) to imagine alternatives to capitalism and, although naming this situation is

---

16   Of course, Marxist criticism, as Barbara Foley acknowledges, can "hardly occupy the frontline of the battle against the capitalist juggernaut," but it "can assist, however modestly, in developing an understanding of culture and society that has political value" (Foley xviii).

an invaluable step, overcoming it is a much tougher challenge, one that seems daunting even to the imagination.[17]

Overall, then, the main ambivalence to be pondered in this book is the following: even though it is undeniable that new media dystopias are riddled with ideological mystifications, especially insofar as they are, to all effects, *commodities* of the almighty Anglo-American culture industry, they can also function as SF allegories of contemporary capitalism that, to a certain extent, follow the logic of the "critical dystopia" (Moylan, *Scraps of the Untainted Sky*; Baccolini and Moylan). Contrary to the common-sense use of the word, a critical dystopia is not the same as an "anti-utopia"—the radically reactionary negation of the desirability and even the possibility of utopian transformations—; instead, it is a critical exercise of speculation that, despite its façade of negativity, is still guided by a "Utopian impulse" (Jameson, *Archaeologies of the Future* 1–9). By this definition, when the worst aspects of a historical epoch are denounced and satirized, it is often—though not always—by means of an implicit comparison with some utopian horizon of transformation that is implicitly inscribed in the text. The critical dystopia is, metaphorically speaking, like the photographic negative of utopia: a dialectical inversion, rather than a simple negation. Thus seen, what is to be gauged in this book is the extent to which and the ways whereby new media dystopias may function (or not) in this ideal way. My working hypothesis is that they do function as critical dystopias, but that this functioning is ambiguated and mediated by their medial reflexivity, their narrative-aesthetic ambivalences and their commodification

---

17 The sentence "It is easier to imagine the end of the world than the end of capitalism" is perhaps as popular (and clichéd) a saying as any version of the "we live in dystopia" trope, probably due to the influence of Mark Fisher's *Capitalist Realism*. The sentence origins are shrouded in mystery, however: Fisher attributes it to Fredric Jameson and Slavoj Žižek (*Capitalist Realism* 2) and Žižek himself seems to attribute it to Jameson (Žižek, *Mapping Ideology* 1), but then Jameson quotes it as something "someone has observed" (*Archaeologies* 199). And to muddle the puddle further, there is speculation that it could have originated from "remarks given by Donna Haraway during a 1995 talk" with David Harvey (Sadowski 207; cf. N. Smith).

within the circuits of digital capitalism—and all of these dimensions are our objects of theorization and analysis.

A Note on Methodology

In accordance with its historicizing hypotheses, the beginning of this book is an abstract survey of certain historical dynamics that were unfolding during "the long 2010s," broadly conceived as the period after the 2008 Great Recession, a decade that witnessed the consolidation of digital capitalism. More specifically, I begin by examining how the emergence and spread of new media technologies during those years connects and coheres with the pre-existing cultural logics of postmodernism, the socio-political logics of neoliberal economics and the newer "techno-logics" of the digital age. The first task of this book is necessarily to clarify what these phenomena amount to and how they relate to one another. Furthermore, such an initial survey is necessary insofar as one should avoid taking for granted such abstract notions as "postmodernism," "neoliberalism" or "the digital age"—and, perhaps, even the notion of "capitalism"—and all this is even more necessary when one aims at establishing a critical distance with such abstract hegemonies and with their cultural manifestations.[18] Accordingly, this book begins by *estranging*—in the manner of SF itself—those taken-for-granted but nonetheless unavoidable abstractions of historical dynamics in order to later descend into the hidden abode of textual and cultural ambivalences with a historically conscious perspective. Using a cinematographic analogy, one may say that

---

18 Regarding the concept of capitalism, McKenzie Wark provocatively asks: "Why have we become so comfortable with a way of describing an uncomfortable reality?" (*Capital Is Dead* 22)—and then proposes to entertain the possibility that "this is not capitalism anymore, it's something worse" (*Capital Is Dead* 29). Specifically, Wark's hypothesis is that there is an emergent mode of production based on the commodification of information and that this "vectoral mode of production" is subordinating pre-existing modes of production like capitalism.

this book begins with an aerial take of capitalism as *the real new media dystopia*, only to then zoom into the narrative-aesthetic details of *fictional new media dystopias*. Following Jameson, before probing any cultural phenomenon, one must "Always historicize!" (*The Political Unconscious* ix).

Methodologically, therefore, this book combines the contextual and ideological macro-analyses most associated with Marxist SF and utopian studies and the formal and textual micro-analyses most associated with narratology and audio-visual aesthetics, which gradually gains importance throughout this book's chapters, all in order to better understand ideological hegemonies through their fictional mediations. My approach, despite appearances, is not meant to imply that narratology and/or film aesthetics should be straitjacketed into a superstructure-infrastructure mode of analysis that would see culture and ideology as straightforward "representations" of capitalist logics, but rather to contribute to a better understanding of how and why there are many formal and ideological ambivalences in the act of representing.[19] Instead, I here attempt to treat each level of analysis with its own relative autonomy: that is, considering each level to be *inseparable* from the totality's dynamics, but also *never entirely subordinated or subsumed* by hegemonic logics.[20] If this book is interested in the narratological concept of *reflexivity*, it is precisely in order to arrive at a better understanding of the complexities of "reflecting" upon

---

[19] This seems to me like an unfair *reductio ad absurdum* of Marx's philosophy, but since it is still commonly heard, some clarification cannot be avoided. Even if such objections may make sense to criticize the economic determinism of those Marxists derogatively categorized as "vulgar," I would here concur with McKenzie Wark's idea that we should *avoid shaming the vulgar*, especially since that argumentative move—frequently made by Western "genteel" Marxism—tends to turn Marxism into an academic niche, thus potentially impeding much-needed dialogs with other theoretical fields and seriously hampering its popularization as a mundanely political way of thinking (see *Capital Is Dead* 143–63 especially).

[20] Louis Althusser famously schematizes the relationship between base and superstructure and specifically acknowledges two ways in which, for the Marxist tradition, "determination" can exceed the "traditional" from-base-to-superstructure unidirectionality: "1) there is a 'relative autonomy' of the superstructure with respect to the base; 2) there is a 'reciprocal action' of the superstructure on the base" (238).

new media platforms through fictional new media dystopias, especially insofar as these narratives tend to be (at least implicitly) self-conscious and/or self-referential with regard to their medium. Thus, although this book begins and ends with abstract historical speculations, at its core it consists of close analyses and meditations upon how the narrative and aesthetic ambivalences of new media dystopias echo (without equating) the ambivalences of neoliberal capitalism and postmodern digital culture. Across chapters, my focus moves from narrative reflexivity to ideological ambivalences, from audio-visual aesthetics to SF theory and from modes of characterization to modes of subjectivity, but always within the broader picture of such dystopias in their context. Like Marx once did in *Capital*, my hope is to eventually obtain a more lucid look into the present through a deep descent into inferno. Marx's (and Jameson's) favorite reference was Dante—so, now, why not descend into our own high-tech hell?[21]

On the whole, as a work of cultural, literary and film scholarship, this book evidently prioritizes the aesthetic, the narrative and the cultural over the social, the political and the economic—but, in spirit, it is still conceived as a critical theory of the present, one that speculates about the contradictions of our times via the imaginaries of the new media dystopia. However, this book is *not* meant to provide an exhaustive corpus nor a detailed history of a fictional sub-genre, *not* meant to examine in full detail every audio-visual narrative in its corpus and *not* meant to provide a sociological analysis of the present stage of capitalism. This book is meant to sketch *a theory of the new media dystopia* that allows an interdisciplinary dialog between all such dimensions and others that the concept may evoke—a theory that, hopefully, may be of academic *and* political interest for readers. Like the SF narratives that it examines, this book cannot be "totally totalizing" in its speculations, but, however tentative it may be, it should be read as a search for new utopian horizons of theory and—although more implicitly—praxis.

---

21 Jameson's recent work on allegory is probably the clearest case of the theorist's fondness for Dante (*Allegory and Ideology*), but then it has also been argued (B. Brown) that there were also significant echoes of the Florentine in Jameson's earlier *Postmodernism*, where passages describing postmodern disorientation invoke the Dantean *selva oscura*.

Chapter Outline

The first chapter, "Our Hopeless SF Times: Contemporary Capitalism as a New Media Dystopia," serves as historicizing prelude and theoretical entrance into the central concept. Here, the new media dystopia is approached in its broadest sense: not so much as an audio-visual sub-genre, but more as a science-fictional conceptualization of the present epoch—and, more specifically, as a conceptualization of the epoch's structure of feeling within cultural, economic and technological dynamics. In other words, here the term "new media dystopia" names *not a fictional construct, but an epochal reality*—a global situation in which new media technologies are pivotal within the generalized perception of the real as dystopian. If contemporary reality seems science-fictional and if new media play a hegemonic role in that perceived science-fictionality, then the logical next step is to theorize that new media are the hegemonic *novum* of our dystopian imagination. Therefore, besides delving deeper into the historical dynamics behind this structure of feeling, my main proposition is to conceptualize "new media"—an umbrella term that encompasses the ever-evolving global infrastructure of digital information technologies—as *the historical counterpart of fictional new media dystopias' nova*.

In these ways, this chapter is a historically holistic meditation focused on the role of new media technologies within the dynamics of digital capitalism, which necessarily requires examining the intertwined, semi-autonomous dynamics of postmodern culture and neoliberal political economy. Thus, in a sense, I here offer an overview of how "new media" are not so new, as they function by—borrowing Wendy Chun's phrase—*updating to remain the same*. This seems true especially insofar as the development and spread of new media has generally followed (and often intensified) both postmodern and neoliberal logics—perhaps to such an extent that one could be tempted with theorizing the former as a technologization of the latter. However, it is also conceivable that new media have led to the emergence of radically different logics—or at least, that they have generated some parallel, semi-autonomous dynamics. Thus, this chapter concludes by commenting upon McKenzie Wark's *Capital is Dead: Is This Something Worse?* In many ways interpretable as a nonfictional new media dystopia, this recent work of critical theory speculates with the possibility that digital technologies may be fostering the emergence of a *new and worse* mode of production that operates *on top of*—not in replacement of—capitalism. Therefore, Wark's hypothesis is here taken as *both* a paradigmatic illustration of the ideological ambivalences of thinking about reality as a new media dystopia *and* as an emblem of the pervasiveness of these kinds of imaginaries, which have echoes beyond fiction. Considering this and other critiques of the present situation, it appears that even when we dare imagining the end of capitalism, we are still left in a new media dystopia—or worse.

After this meditation on "the real new media dystopia," Chapter 2 is titled "New Media Reflexivity: Self-Referentiality and Self-Consciousness in the Audio-Visual SF of Digital Platforms." This second chapter serves as the theoretical bridge towards a closer examination of *fictional* new media dystopias, as it begins to approach them from a narratological perspective. Drawing from a range of theories of so-called metafiction and metareferentiality, but especially from Pedro Javier Pardo's theoretical model for the formal study of *reflexivity* in a broad, transmedia sense, in this chapter I conceptualize certain dynamics of *new media reflexivity*. Just as one might think, with Wark, that a new mode of production is emerging on top of capitalism, my proposition here is that new modes and levels of reflexivity are enabled within the new media architecture, especially if one considers how digital interfaces act as a mediating layer between the user and the diegetic worlds of those audio-visual narratives on offer in the platform. Although this interface or user layer is not a diegetic level in a traditional, literal sense, my proposition is that it might make sense to theorize the new media platform as though it were another diegetic level: as an all-encompassing digital-paratextual layer that contains and correlates a range of commodified fictions. Borrowing an SF concept recently re-appropriated by one infamous character, perhaps we should think of new media as an emerging *metaverse* in which any technical and cultural specificities are subsumed within a self-referential virtual space of constant consumption.

Feeling Dystopian?

In parallel to this theorization of new media reflexivity, this chapter takes a closer look at two audio-visual dystopias that provide a textual grounding for my theorization: Amazon's serialized adaptation of Philip K. Dick's *The Man in the High Castle* (created by Frank Spotnitz, 2015–19) and *Black Mirror*'s interactive film *Bandersnatch* (directed by David Slade, 2018). *The Man in the High Castle*, first, serves as an illustration of the possibilities—and the problematics—of projecting the notions of literary reflexivity onto moving-image media, especially as the series attempts—and partially fails—to translate the novel's reflexive structure into an audio-visual language and imagery. Secondly, *Bandersnatch* stands as an emblem of the potentials—and the paradoxes—of emergent new media reflexivity, since this is an interactive film that both satirizes and reproduces the dynamics of digital capitalism within the interface of a video-on-demand platform (Netflix, in this case). Throughout the two analyses, my interest lies in gauging the functioning of reflexivity in new media platforms from a dialectical perspective, with the guiding hypothesis that the technologically enabled omnipresence of reflexivity need not necessarily cancel out the critical and utopian potentials of art and culture—but perhaps, at times, reinforce them, entering a symbiosis with SF's own means of estrangement. New media may have paved the way for a widespread commodification of once-subversive reflexive devices, but they have also provided a platform for new forms of (self-)critique from within the culture industry.

Chapter 3, "Between Critique and Mystification: The Aesthetic and Ideological Ambivalences of New Media Dystopias," carries on investigating the ambivalences of new media dystopias, but focusing on the inherent tensions that derive from their narrative and visual dimensions—as well as from the interrelation of both. On the one hand, our sub-genre inherits and redoubles the ambivalences of SF and dystopian narratives and it combines them with the double-edges of audio-visual series' narrative complexity. On the other hand, as a specific kind of SF spectacle that is both estranging and mystifying, critical and beautifying, new media dystopias are structured around what I propose to call *a techno-ambivalent gaze*, a way of seeing technology that is integral to the epoch's dominant ideologies. In these ways, the ambivalences of our sub-genre are studied with attention to both narrative and spectacle, where there are, inevitably, both aesthetic and ideological ambivalences. In schematizing all these ambivalences, the underlying assumption of this chapter is that—because of their reflexive qualities and their status as commodities—new media dystopias both criticize and symptomatize the ideologies and dynamics of digital culture and media. As self-conscious critical allegories of the contemporary moment, new media dystopias oscillate between dystopian (self-)critique and anti-utopian mystification—and, indeed, most often they resist any kind of either/or binary categorization.[22]

Subsequently, as in Chapter 2, my theorization is illustrated by a more focused commentary of two dystopian series in particular: Lisa Joy and Jonathan Nolan's *Westworld* (2016–22) and Alex Garland's *Devs* (2020). My preference for these two serves the purpose of illustrating the sub-genre's ambivalences, but it is also meant to underscore how neither the "narrative" nor the "spectacular" side of these dystopias are free from ambivalences—instead, in my view, both sides deserve an equal valuation (and an equal skepticism) in any rigorous study of audio-visual SF. *Westworld*, on the one hand, is taken as a reflexive dystopia in which narrative complexity allows a myriad of subversive and critical interpretations, but also as a series in which narrative complexity is perhaps even more commodified than the usual suspect of commodification (that is, cinematic spectacle). *Devs*, on the other hand, is examined with a greater emphasis on its suggestive audio-visual aesthetics, which are the cornerstone of a deeply ambivalent narrative about the pseudo-religiosity of our techno-ambivalent gaze. To some extent, both series partake in both sides of the ambivalences, but together, they show how there is no "good" or "bad" side of the equation in the many dialectical tensions that undercut new media dystopias. On the contrary, often their value lies precisely in the tension, the short-circuits and the sparks that arise from the many conflicts and contradictions of

---

22   In this regard, my approach coheres with recent theorizations of utopian and dystopian fiction that propose to re-conceptualize the two as poles within a spectrum, rather than as locked in a binary opposition (see Ostalska and Fisiak). In this volume, Gregory Clays argues that "utopia and dystopia understood both as fiction and reality must be understood as lying on a spectrum which runs from friendship to fear and from consent to coercion" ("Foreword: A Utopian/Dystopian Spectrum: From Friendship to Fear, from Consent to Coercion" xxi).

the sub-genre, caught as it is between narration and spectacle, critique and beautification, estrangement and mystification.

Chapter 4, "New Media Quixotism: Satiric and Utopian Characterizations of Digital Subjectivity," takes a final, deeper dive into fictional new media dystopias by focusing on a peculiar mode of characterization that reflects and further problematizes the narrative, visual and ideological ambivalences discussed in previous chapters. Here, I develop my concept of *new media quixotism* as a way of theorizing a character type, with related narrative motifs, which seems of central importance in new media dystopias, especially for re-imagining the interaction between the human and the technological. Drawing from Pedro Javier Pardo's theorization of *the myth of Don Quixote*, understood not as Cervantes's novel but as an architext that was forged throughout the centuries since its publication, it is possible to trace quixotism across a wide range of narratives that do not openly adapt or rewrite the original *Don Quixote*, but nonetheless reproduce the defining, essential traits of the myth's quixotic subject. With the advent of postmodernity, what Pardo calls "accidental quixotes" now abound across media and cultures and, in my view, SF and digital culture are no exception to this "mainstreaming" of the quixotic. Therefore, in this chapter I explore how the ambivalences of new media dystopias are often refracted through the ambivalences of this kind of quixotic characterization, especially as both dystopias and the myth oscillate between satirical and utopian impulses. In so doing, my goal is not only to study a character type specific to our sub-genre, but also to sketch a theoretical basis for further studies of quixotism in contemporary culture more generally.

To flesh out these theoretical meditations, the chapter offers close analyses of three new media dystopias in which quixotism is central, although it also begins by acknowledging two works of postmodern SF that paved the way for such characterizations. Firstly, Philip K. Dick and Douglas Adams are identified as representations of two contrasting ways of re-imagining the quixotic subject: respectively, as the tragic, mediocre everyman of postmodern capitalism in Dick's *Time Out of Joint* and as the laughable stock character of postmodern reflexive fiction in Adam's *The Hitchhiker's Guide to the Galaxy*. Of course, all quixotic figures are at least implicitly tragicomic, but Dick and Adams illustrate how specific representations may feel the gravitational pull of one pole more than the other. Subsequently and most importantly, this chapter pays close attention to new media quixotism in three dystopian series, examining *Black Mirror*'s episode "USS Callister" (2017), Sam Esmail's series *Mr Robot* (2015–19) and Cary Joji Fukunaga and Patrick Somerville's miniseries *Maniac* (2018). In closely analyzing these three examples, which illustrate a range of possibilities for new media quixotism, this is proven to be a mode of characterization that suggests that—for good or bad—the use of new media fosters and reinforces quixotic personality traits. Just as it seems logical, within our hegemonic common sense, to believe that we live in a dystopia, it may be just as logical to believe that new media are making us all a bit quixotic, especially in the digital dimensions of our lives. In the end, therefore, the deeper, ideological question to be asked in this chapter is the following: how is new media quixotism mobilized with regards to our dystopian structure of feeling? Is new media quixotism presented as a symptom of the epoch's worst tendencies, or is it also, potentially, a vehicle for imagining utopian transformations from within deep in the digital milieu?

On the whole, throughout all these four chapters, I am valuing new media dystopias as a continuation of what Fredric Jameson most admired of cyberpunk: its functioning as a "representational shorthand for grasping a network of power and control even more difficult for our minds and imaginations to grasp: the whole new decentered global network of the third stage of capital itself" (*Postmodernism* 38). Thus, I am positioning new media dystopias under the shade of (post-)cyberpunk's legacy and influence, considering how that sub-genre's tropes and images have, in a sense, dissolved into cultural ubiquity, died of success. As opposed to cyberpunk, however, the key difference is that new media dystopias are much more directly and overtly about the present epoch, especially insofar as cyberpunk imaginaries have been re-appropriated—and some of its *nova*, materialized—with the advent of digital capitalism. Therefore, this book proposes a journey through a new, specific kind of dystopian narratives that allow us to re-assess our everyday use of new media technologies, as well as the broader historical dynamics in which these technologies partake. Like the narratives that it examines, this book too is conceived as a much-needed exercise of estrangement—an exercise of thinking not only *about* SF but also *through* SF in order to rethink our technologically mediated experience of reality and the social and political challenges that the present moment poses. The world may look hopelessly and irremediably dystopian, but how we think and what we do about it still matters and we should still care.

CHAPTER 1

Our Hopeless SF Times: Contemporary Capitalism as a New Media Dystopia

> We are living through strange days. Across Britain, Europe and America, societies have become split and polarised, not just in politics, but across the whole culture. There is anger at the inequality and the ever-growing corruption and a widespread distrust of the elites. Yet, at the same time, there is a paralysis, a sense that no one knows how to escape from this. [...]
>
> This paralysis is also fuelled by a technology, driven by the aim of giving you today another version of what you had yesterday ... and never a different tomorrow.
>
> —Adam Curtis, *Can't Get You Out of My Head*, episode 1 ("Bloodshed on Wolf Mountain" 0'26"-1'18").

Audio-visual series like *Black Mirror*, *Westworld*, *Devs*, *Mr Robot*, or *Maniac* are—from the standpoint of this book—the most interesting instances of what I will theorize as *the fictional new media dystopia*, but the ideologies and imaginaries that they evoke are, as I shall keep insisting, not exclusive to them. The fictional new media dystopia is a prismatic crystallization in an audio-visual SF form of broader ideological and historical dynamics that are explored in this chapter. They are all part of an epoch that I here call *the real new media dystopia*—a dystopian structure of feeling that is hegemonically haunted by the ghost of new media technologies.

Adam Curtis's documentary series *Can't Get You Out of My Head* (2021), for example, could be read as one attempt at narrating this structure of feeling.[1] A self-styled "emotional history of the present," it offers a view

---

[1] At the time of writing, this series is, by virtue of its length and its production date, perhaps the work of Curtis that best synthesizes and elaborates his vision of the present's hopelessness, although his previous documentaries already meditated upon the role of media technologies in such a situation, most notably

into the hegemonic sense of hopelessness and defeat in the face of new technologies, the rise of anti-democratic politics and the defeat of progressive popular movements. Throughout its chapters, Curtis's voice-over narration of doom and gloom (cited above) is accompanied with footage of police violence against street protesters across the globe, as well as short shots of drone-delivered bombings in a number of warzones, among other images of violence and repression. But more interestingly, some of the images that open and thus symbolically frame the series are eerily silent, long takes of massive, empty server rooms, as though networked media technologies were indeed the ghastliest ghost of the present epoch. Even though the series begins and ends by citing David Graeber's hopeful words that "the ultimate truth of the world is that it is something we make and could just as easily make differently" ("Bloodshed on Wolf Mountain" 15"-23"; "Are We Pigeon? Or Are We Dancer?" 1h54'39"-51"), one can seriously doubt that viewers would feel hopeful after eight hours of Curtis's storytelling.

Another interesting example is Russell T. Davies mini-series *Years and Years* (2019), which condenses the contemporary mood in a similarly explicit manner. Specifically, this SF series proceeds by extrapolating from 2019 into the future from the perspective of a British family and it primarily operates by assuming that the worst will happen and that there is not much to be done about it, except finding consolation in our closest friends and relatives. Indeed, the protagonist family is the collective spectator of a series of undesirably plausible future tendencies: neo-reactionary and authoritarian politicians shall continue seizing power; climate-related catastrophes shall become more intense and frequent; and media technologies shall allow more panoptic and intrusive kinds of surveillance upon our everyday. But ironically, as the family matriarch puts it in a moment of frankness, "it's a terrible, terrible world, but I want to see every second of it" (Mulcahy 18'01"-18'05")—a two-sided attitude, cynically casual and anxiously concerned, which concisely captures the ambivalent feelings

---

HyperNormalisation (2016) and *All Watched Over by Machines of Loving Grace* (2011). The latter, in particular, is tellingly introduced as "a story about the rise of the machines and why no one believes you can change the world for the better any more" ("Love and Power" 04"–19").

of the age. Of course, Davies's series has a utopian counter-narrative and it ends with utopian twists, with the dethronement of a neo-fascist UK government and the achievement of disembodied "digital immortality" by a terminally ill relative. However, these final drops of hope seem but two droplets that easily dissolve in an ocean of future-fearing hopelessness.

However, one need not go to series or documentaries in order to find signs of the epoch's structure of feeling: these signs abound and it suffices to be around the internet until finding certain kinds of memes. Although many could be mentioned, there is one, recently circulated online (Figure 2), which illustrates the present's dystopianism in a strikingly clear way.[2] A variant of the "Galaxy Brain" or "Expanding Brain" meme, which is often used to mock an assumed progression towards greater intellectual complexity, this meme focuses on ways of dealing with "all the bad things in the world going on around [us]."[3] The simple realization of the world's wrongness apparently leads to confusion, indignation, reformism, revolution, fatalism, mysticism and, finally, back to confusion. Thus, in this caricature of such a wide range of affective-ideological approaches to reality, it seems like the beginning and end of any attempt is confused screaming, a historicized version of the so-called primal scream—a helpless cry of desperation in the face of a seemingly unchangeable and ungraspable reality. Therefore, it would seem that even in cases in which dystopianism is approached with a degree of irony and/or with a critical intent, the epoch's structure of feeling is (inevitably?) reproduced and reinforced. We started

---

2 Tellingly, this meme was found in an online forum devoted to Mark Fisher's ideas—in particular, in a Facebook group that was already referenced by critic Mike Watson (54) as an example of how Fisher's critical diagnostics in *Capitalist Realism* have been popularized through memes. The "memeification" of Fisher's ideas stands as another index of the pervasiveness of this anti-utopian mood, a structure of feeling that is clearly not confined to the realms of "high" culture, fiction or theory.

3 The most popular wiki-site on the matter, *Know Your Meme*, defines the "Galaxy Brain" meme as "a multi-panel exploitable image series comparing the brain size of a person relative to other variables. Though the expanding brain is usually implied to showcase intellectual superiority over various objects, it is more often used in an ironic sense to imply the opposite, where objects of derision are implied to be of higher standard than objects that are usually highly regarded" ("Galaxy Brain").

with confused screaming and we shall end with confused screaming. But shall we, really?

Notwithstanding the nuances and ambivalences that one can find in each of these three cases, the underlying logic seems to be that historical "progress" keeps leading us into a dystopia of one kind or other. This is, therefore, a markedly *anti-utopian* logic that is characterized not only by a deep discontent with the present state of things, but also by an equally strong skepticism towards any future improvement. It appears as if, having renounced all pretensions to steer the wheel of history in order to avoid a catastrophe, the only believable historical narrative today is that the catastrophe is upon us.[4] Thus, while the postmodern distrust of utopia—based on a critique of the presumably "totalizing" teleology of Enlightened and/or Marxist notions of progress—often amounted to the idea that the road to hell is paved with good intentions, perhaps today one should rewrite and reverse this to claim that *the road to hell is paved with indifference or cynicism*.[5] Why bother? This is already high-tech hell, so there is not much

---

4   In this line of thought, Mark Bould's *The Anthropocene Unconscious* proposes that the present's political unconscious is dominated by the climate crisis, with potentially all culture being about the imminent collapse (in a more or less implicit way, of course). Because of course, some form of collapse is imminent and we are in all likelihood in the autumn (or rather—pun intended—in the fall) of capitalist civilization, as Bordera and Turiel put it.

5   Indeed, writing in the 1970s, Jameson diagnosed that "Utopia is a transparent synonym for socialism itself, and the enemies of Utopia sooner or later turn out to be the enemies of socialism" ("Of Islands and Trenches" 3). But this, of course, a reductionist understanding of both Utopia and Marxism as "teleological." Deconstructing a false caricature of Marx (and Marxism) that reduces his theories to certain propositions of *The Communist Manifesto*, Terry Eagleton's words are deeply clarifying in this regard:

> Marx had nothing but scorn for the idea that there was something called History which had purposes and laws of motion quite independent of human being. To imagine that Marxism is a teleology in this sense, which many postmodernists appear to do, is just as lurid a travesty as imagining that Jacques Derrida believes that anything can mean anything else, that nobody ever entertained an intention and that there is nothing in the world but writing.
>
> Socialism does indeed posit a telos of a kind the possibility of a more just, free, rational and compassionate social order. But so of course do radical postmodernists. Indeed some post-modernists seem to posit a teleology of a much more ambitious kind: the

Contemporary Capitalism as a New Media Dystopia

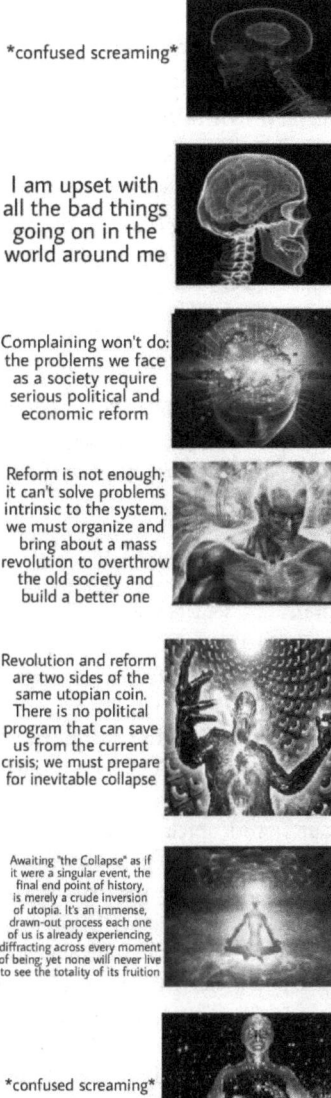

Figure 2. Meme circulated in <https://www.facebook.com/groups/2269060710041068/>.

we can do as human individuals in the face of the Machine (or the Earth). No matter what we do, what is already bad shall only get worse anyway. Of course, this is a self-consciously polemical caricature, but it nonetheless reflects a widespread mode of thinking and feeling—a mood fueled by an "output of dark narratives [that] has congealed in a 'dystopia porn' (as SF writer Vandana Singh puts it) that suppresses humanity's social anxieties through a fatalist, anti-utopian inoculation that normalizes pessimistic indulgence in this terrifying reality" (Moylan, "The Necessity of Hope in Dystopian Times" 166).[6]

Thus, if this is indeed an epoch in which new media technologies are "giving you today another version of what you had yesterday and never a different tomorrow," as Adam Curtis puts it, it seems that we live in the "end of history," though not in Francis Fukuyama's famously hopeful sense of the phrase.[7] Or, maybe, re-using Herbert Marcuse's old phrase, where

---

idea, for example, that the Enlightenment led inevitably to the concentration camps. But neither party believes that there is anything historically guaranteed about the goal of a more just society, or that it is somehow even now stealthily at work as the secret essence of the present. (Eagleton 45–6)

6 A similar hypothesis has been brought forward by Urraco Solanilla, who contends that young-adult dystopias encode certain "messages that, under a crude veneer of rebelliousness, reinforce the basic principles of twenty-first-century fluid capitalism." This hypothesis, however, as Urraco Solanilla himself acknowledges, is premised on focusing exclusively on "the messages intended to be conveyed," even though the audience can "rework or reinterpret them in a way that is completely different from the intentions of the creator of the work in question" (156–9, my translation). However relevant his hypotheses may be, Urraco Solanilla's study forcefully brackets narrative ambivalences and spectatorial autonomy within an ideologically one-sided focus on popular culture as a quasi-manipulative force. In this way, young adult dystopias are presented as deceitful, ideologically reactionary products that are marketed to confused young minds who mistakenly believe themselves to be rebels but are the system's puppets. There is a ring of truth in this, the partial truth of the polemicist, but academically and politically it would be better to examine dystopia (and popular culture generally) in a dialectical way, as both reification and utopia, following Jameson ("Reification and Utopia in Mass Culture").

7 At the very end of the Cold War, Francis Fukuyama famously proposed that "a remarkable consensus concerning the legitimacy of liberal democracy as a system of government had emerged throughout the world over the past few years, as it conquered rival ideologies like hereditary monarchy, fascism, and most recently

we are is in the "end of Utopia."⁸ Or, maybe, where we are is trapped in the "eternal present" of the "integrated spectacle" that was once theorized by Guy Debord.⁹ Weighed down by both past and future—or at least by images of them—the present epoch continues to attest to the dominance of what could be called "the reduction to the present in postmodernity" (Jameson, "The End of Temporality" 709) or more concisely "presentism"

---

     communism" (xi). In this sense, Fukuyama suggested that what "had come to an end was not the occurrence of events, even large and grave events, but History: that is, history understood as a single, coherent, evolutionary process," because this history had culminated, as Hegel had once speculated, in the global victory of liberal democracy (xii). For obvious reasons, Fukuyama's teleological and utopian narrative of the End of History has become the strawman antagonist of much leftist thinking, insofar as it unashamedly forecloses the possibility that there might be any political ideals better than those of neoliberalism. It is still interesting, however, to recall Fukuyama's proposition as one last rhetorically powerful attempt at breaking with how "The twentieth century ... has made all of us into deep historical pessimists" (3).

8   This "end of utopia" is the opposite of what Herbert Marcuse meant when he used the phrase in the 1960s: for him, the end of utopia was the historical moment in which utopia ceased to be a future horizon because it became realizable. In his view, the mid-twentieth century was already the moment "when the material and intellectual forces for the transformation are technically at hand although their rational application is prevented by the existing organization of the forces of production [...] in this sense, [...] we can today actually speak of an end of utopia" (*Five Lectures* 64).

9   Debord's idea of the "integrated spectacle" functions as a synthesis of "two rival and successive forms of spectacular power, the concentrated and the diffuse" that he associates with communist and capitalist media, respectively, during the Cold War era (Debord, *Comments on the Society of the Spectacle* 8). Specifically, Debord suggests that

     reality no longer confronts the integrated spectacle as something alien. When the spectacle was concentrated, the greater part of surrounding society escaped it; when diffuse, a small part; today, no part. The spectacle has spread itself to the point where it now permeates all reality. [...] The society whose modernisation has reached the stage of the integrated spectacle is characterised by the combined effect of five principal features: incessant technological renewal; integration of state and economy; generalised secrecy; unanswerable lies; an eternal present. (*Comments on the Society of the Spectacle* 9–12)

(Hartog).¹⁰ Besides the many possible names given to this narrowing of any utopian imagination, it might help to think that this whole predicament often has a readily graspable affective dimension: if confronted with a worsening dystopian future, one can only feel anxious and, confronted with a past of failed utopias, one can only feel depressed, then one's attention would "naturally" tend to focus on the terrible (but tangible) present.¹¹ This is precisely what fictional new media dystopias seem to do, insofar as—considerably more than speculating with the future—they examine their medium and their moment with a clear conscience of their horror and a fair fear of looking beyond.

Accordingly, the objective of this chapter is to offer a critical analysis and a schematic survey of the multi-dimensional dynamics and the core contradictions of the historical situation that gave birth to this hopeless mood. Striving towards conceptual clarity, I first pause to consider three

10   Jameson hypothesizes that "the end of temporality" is an existential part of the postmodern condition, which he contrasts with the modernists' sensibility towards time:

> I want to conjecture that the protagonists of those aesthetic and philosophical revolutions were people who still lived in two distinct worlds simultaneously; born in those agricultural villages we still sometimes characterize as medieval or premodern, they developed their vocations in the new urban agglomerations with their radically distinct and "modern" spaces and temporalities. The sensitivity to deep time in the moderns then registers this comparatist perception of the two socioeconomic temporalities, which the first modernists had to negotiate in their own lived experience. By the same token, when the premodern vanishes, when the peasantry shrinks to a picturesque remnant, when suburbs replace the villages and modernity reigns triumphant and homogeneous over all space, then the very sense of an alternate temporality disappears as well, and postmodern generations are dis- possessed (without even knowing it) of any differential sense of that deep time the first moderns sought to inscribe in their writing.

11   Although it falls beyond the scope of this book, one should note the indirect influence of affect theorists upon certain of my formulations here, namely Sara Ahmed, who places a crucial emphasis on the socio-political matrix within which affects come to be and (more often than not) become instrumentalized by the structures of power (see Ahmed). I thank my colleague Marta Bernabéu Lorenzo for bringing this field to my attention and for her explanations of Ahmed's and others' theories of affects—not least of them her own concepts, developed for her recently completed doctoral thesis.

contemporary conceptualizations of hopelessness: *left melancholy*, *capitalist realism* and *dystopian structure of feeling*. These three, in turn, provide an entryway into the twin periodizing concepts of *neoliberalism* and *postmodernism*, themselves windows into deeper dynamics. Subsequently, my attention turns towards considerations of *new media technologies*, specifying my conceptualization of them as this dystopian epoch's SF *novum* and examining their role as the infrastructural basis of so-called digital capitalism. Finally, after an analysis of McKenzie Wark's *Capital is Dead: Is This Something Worse?* as a paradigmatic "new media dystopia of theory," this chapter concludes with an initial definition of the new media dystopia, both real and fictional.

1.1. Three Ways of Thinking through Hopelessness

In order to begin comprehending this epochal predicament, the three concepts to be examined now have been selected because of the ways whereby they offer a glimpse into the historical becoming of the present mood: in chronological order, "left melancholy," coined in the late 1990s, "capitalist realism," from the late 2000s, and "dystopian structure of feeling," from the late 2010s. Some of their implications overlap and their concerns are interrelated, so they often supplement one another. My intention is to review them and to eventually subsume them into an expanded definition of the most relevant for my purposes, Tom Moylan's notion of the dystopian structure of feeling.

1.1.1. *Left Melancholy*

Although it rose to prominence with Wendy Brown's 1999 essay "Resisting Left Melancholy," the term was borrowed from Walter Benjamin, who coined it in his 1931 "Left-Wing Melancholy," a scathing review of a poetry book by Erich Kästner. Benjamin's usage of the term, which Brown would later follow, is meant to refer to a kind of left-wing or anti-capitalist radicalism that, despite an awareness of systemic suffering, has renounced the possibility of revolutionary-utopian transformations. In his words, this would be a kind of left radicalism that "has little to do with the labour movement," whose "political significance was exhausted by the transposition of revolutionary reflexes [...] into objects of distraction, of amusement, which can be supplied for consumption" ("Left-Wing Melancholy" 29). More specifically, Benjamin proposes that

> this left-wing radicalism is precisely the attitude to which there is no longer in general any corresponding political action. It is to the left not of this or that tendency; but simply to the left of what is in general possible. For from the beginning all it has in mind is to enjoy itself in a negativistic quiet. The metamorphosis of political struggle from a compulsory decision into an object of pleasure, from a means of production into an article of consumption—that is this literature's latest hit. ("Left-Wing Melancholy" 30)

Subsequently, left melancholy is further clarified (and further ridiculed) through a powerful bodily metaphor that closes the piece. Referring again to Kästner, Benjamin sentences that

> the fatalism of those who are most remote from the process of production and whose obscure courting of the state of the market is comparable to the attitude of a man who yields himself up entirely to the inscrutable accidents of his digestion. The rumbling in these lines certainly has more to do with flatulence than with subversion. Constipation and melancholy have always gone together. But since the juices began to dry up in the body social, stuffiness meets us at every turn. Kastner's poems do not improve the atmosphere. ("Left-Wing Melancholy" 31)

Elaborating upon Benjamin's caricature would amount to adding insult to injury, as his words suffice to explain the term—giving left melancholy a stench. What should be clarified is that here I am not interested in a moralizing use of the term, as a bullet to be shot at an unfortunate individual like Kästner. Rather, I am interested in how the notion of left melancholy can be used to characterize an epoch's structure of feeling. And this is precisely how Wendy Brown uses it.

Building upon Stuart Hall's previous diagnoses of the contemporary "crisis of the left" (in *The Hard Road to Renewal*; see also his later "The Neo-Liberal Revolution"), Wendy Brown proposes to explore one dimension of it: left melancholy. Brown first introduces the concept as being "attached more to a particular political analysis or ideal—even to the failure of that ideal—than to seizing possibilities for radical change in the present" ("Resisting Left Melancholy" 20). And as Brown herself makes clear, being attached "even to the failure of that ideal" clearly points towards a specific historical situation: the immediate aftermath of the Soviet bloc's collapse and the subsequent subordination of virtually all nation-states by the structures of neoliberal capitalism (so-called globalization). Surveying the landscape, Brown elaborates:

> Certainly the losses, accountable and unaccountable, of the Left are many in our own time. The literal disintegration of socialist regimes and the legitimacy of Marxism may well be the least of it. We are awash in the loss of a unified analysis and unified movement, in the loss of labor and class as inviolable predicates of political analysis and mobilization, in the loss of an inexorable and scientific forward movement of history, and in the loss of a viable alternative to the political economy of capitalism. And on the backs of these losses are still others: we are without a sense of an international, and often even a local, left community; we are without conviction about the truth of the social order; we are without a rich moral-political vision to guide and sustain political work. Thus, we suffer with the sense of not only a lost movement but a lost historical moment; not only a lost theoretical and empirical coherence but a lost way of life and a lost course of pursuits. ("Resisting Left Melancholy" 22)

The implications of this situation are complex, especially if one were to unpack how it affects any specific context—like the United Kingdom during and after Margaret Thatcher's tenure as PM, which is the paradigmatic example for both Hall and Brown. However, more globally and generally, the hegemony of left melancholy can be explained with one key: a shift towards defensiveness in the left, which (at least according to these theorists) no longer proposes a radically different future but instead struggles for the maintenance of rights and liberties that were already achieved in the past. Thus, although a defense of certain aspects of the status quo—such as the welfare state or liberal democracy—need not be incompatible with anti-capitalism, for better or for worse the fact is that

the left is now on a mostly defensive position *vis-à-vis* historical change.¹²
Because of this, Brown criticizes that

> the Left has come to represent a politics that seeks to protect a set of freedoms and entitlements that confronts neither the dominations contained in both nor the limited value of those freedoms and entitlements in contemporary configurations of capitalism. And when this traditionalism is conjoined with a loss of faith in the egalitarian vision so fundamental to the socialist challenge to the capitalist mode of distribution, and a loss of faith in the emancipatory vision fundamental to the socialist challenge to the capitalist mode of production, the problem of left traditionalism becomes very serious indeed. What emerges is a Left that operates without either a deep and radical critique of the status quo or a compelling alternative to the existing order of things. But perhaps even more troubling, it is a Left that has become more attached to its impossibility than to its potential fruitfulness, a Left that is most at home dwelling not in hopefulness but in its own marginality and failure, a Left that is thus caught in a structure of melancholic attachment to a certain strain of its own dead past, whose spirit is ghostly, whose structure of desire is backward looking and punishing. ("Resisting Left Melancholy" 26)

In a way, perhaps, while nineteenth-century capitalism was haunted by "the spectre of communism" and twentieth-century one by "actually existing socialism," the twenty-first century is again haunted by a specter—the specter of a specter, a specter of something that (depending on perspective) is either dead or was never born. In any case, it is clear that an alternative to capitalism does not appear so much as a future horizon anymore, but more as an irretrievably lost future past. As opposed to the nineteenth and twentieth centuries, each of them shaped in the wake of the French and Russian revolutions, "the twentieth-first century is born

---

12   Here I am echoing the argument made by Luis Alegre Zahonero and Carlos Fernández Liria's *El orden de* El capital, as well as by Antoni Domènech's earlier *El eclipse de la fraternidad*. These thinkers propose that Marxism as a political project should not be opposed to the Enlightenment's liberal-democratic project *tout court*, but rather seek to expand it by creating the economic preconditions for liberty, equality and fraternity. Thus, they reject the (only apparently radical) idea that "if capitalism was to be ended, the rule of law had to be overcome at the same time. The condemnation of capitalism had necessarily to go hand in hand with the rejection of 'bourgeois law' and the 'individualism' that lay at its basis" (Alegre Zahonero and Fernández Liria 21, my translation).

as a time shaped by a general eclipse of utopias. [....] The utopias of the past century have disappeared, leaving a present charged with memory but unable to project itself into the future" (Traverso 5–7).

Nevertheless, while the once-again-spectral quality of communism helps explain left melancholy and the broader mood of hopelessness and paralysis, the former does not automatically assure the latter. Indeed, as Jacques Derrida had proposed earlier in the 1990s, the end of the Soviet world meant that there was again a possibility for raising new "spectres of Marx," once again internationalist, potentially multiple and heterogeneous. In a correction to melancholics (and to Fukuyama's End of History), Derrida emphasizes the opportunity (and the imperative) of remembering and re-interpreting Marx(ism) in the new scenario of global capitalism:

> When the dogma machine and the 'Marxist' ideological apparatuses (states, parties, cells, unions and other places of doctrinal production) are in the process of disappearing, we no longer have any excuse, only alibis, for turning away from this responsibility. There will be no future without this. Not without Marx, no future without Marx, without the memory and the inheritance of Marx: in any case of a certain Marx, of his genius, of at least one of his spirits. (32)

Similarly and more recently, there are now voices that, explicitly rebelling against left melancholy, have been actively pushing for the re-imagination of a new "communist horizon" (Dean, "The Communist Horizon") or, in a more academic vein, for the development of "critical future studies" (Goode and Godhe). But clearly, these are all programs that propose to fight against hegemonic tendencies—so their very existence as *counter*-hegemonic projects attests to the enduring sway of what they oppose. Therefore, even if, in Derrida's own words, "no disavowal has managed to rid itself of all of Marx's ghosts," we are still in the "new world disorder" of "neocapitalism and neoliberalism" (34). Despite certain challenges, one can thus assume that, on the political left and elsewhere, melancholy still reigns—or at the very least, it weighs heavily upon this epoch's imagination.[13]

---

13 Enzo Traverso, in his 2016 book *Left-Wing Melancholia*, offers a complementary explanation of this post-Cold-War hegemonic mood, imagining left melancholy

1.1.2. Capitalist Realism

Even though left melancholy helps explain hopelessness within the anti-capitalist side of the political spectrum and, thus, it offers us a key about the ideological limits of anti-capitalist sentiments in contemporary culture, there is another concept that may clarify our dystopian structure of feeling in a way that is less associated with a political orientation. The melancholic situation in the left could and should be located within a broader phenomenon: what Mark Fisher theorizes as "capitalist realism." With this phrase, Fisher refers to "the widespread sense that not only is capitalism the only viable political and economic system, but also that it is now impossible even to imagine a coherent alternative to it" (*Capitalist Realism* 2).

One must insist, however, that unlike in the case of left melancholy, capitalist realism is not to be associated to the beliefs of an individual or a political collective—it is, therefore, not an ideological endorsement of or an affective attachment to the system. It is rather, as Fisher later explained in an interview with Jeremy Gilbert, to be understood as a "structure of feeling" in Raymond William's sense—or as a "political unconscious" in Fredric Jameson's sense—and this implies that

---

as the colonization of left-wing consciousness by a pre-exiting anti-communist narrative:

> The dialectic of the twentieth century was broken. Instead of liberating new revolutionary energies, the downfall of State Socialism seemed to have exhausted the historical trajectory of socialism itself. The entire history of communism was reduced to its totalitarian dimension, which appeared as a collective, transmissible memory. Of course, this narrative was not invented in 1989; it had existed since 1917, but now it became a shared historical consciousness, a dominant and uncontested representation of the past. After having entered the twentieth century as a promise of liberation, communism exited as a symbol of alienation and oppression. The images of the demolition of the Berlin Wall appear, *a posteriori*, as a reversal of Eisenstein's *October*: the film of revolution had been definitely "rewound." (2–3)

The main problem, then, is the void left in the collective imagination: where there was once an imaginable alternative, now there is nothing, perhaps only attachment to a bygone ghost.

> capitalist realism has effaced not only its own historicity and contingency, but also its own existence as an ideological constellation. You could say that effacement is what defines capitalist realism. The hegemonic field which capitalist realism secures and intensifies is one in which politics itself has been 'disappeared.' What capitalist realism consolidates is the idea that we are in the era of the post-political—that the big ideological conflicts are over, and the issues that remain largely concern who is to administrate the new consensus. (Fisher and Gilbert 90)

Subsequently, in a more self-aware way, Fisher continues by warning that

> there's something misleading about describing capitalist realism, as I myself often tend to, as the belief that capitalism is the only viable political economic system. Capitalist realism could perhaps better be seen as a set of behaviours and affects that arise from this 'belief'. The dominance of capitalism, the inability to imagine an alternative to it, now constitute a sort of invisible horizon. Few explicitly think about 'capitalism' as such—the disappearance of alternatives, even if only imaginary alternatives, make it much harder to apprehend capitalism as a specific, contingent system. Capitalist realism as I have understood it entails this deep embedding in a world—or set of worlds—in which capitalism is massively naturalised.
>
> Capitalist realism doesn't appear in the first instance, then, as a political position. It emerges instead as a pragmatic adjustment—'this is the way things are now.' This sense of resignation, of fatalism, is crucial to the 'realism'. (Fisher and Gilbert 90)

Effacement and naturalization, together with resignation and fatalism, are thus the keys to grasp our imaginative entrapment in the here-and-now of global capitalism.

However, the most perverse and most crucial consequence of the all-pervasive atmosphere of capitalist realism is that even explicit expressions of opposition against the system can contribute to its perpetuation. To make this argument, Fisher draws from Slavoj Žižek's *The Sublime Object of Ideology*, where the latter concept is redefined. As opposed to "the classic concept of ideology as 'false consciousness,'" which "implies a kind of basic, constitutive naiveté" whereby the dominated would be, so to speak, "fooled" by the elites, Žižek invites us to ponder whether this definition is tenable today. Acknowledging Peter Sloterdijk's argument that "ideology's dominant mode of functioning is cynical, which renders impossible—or more precisely, vain—the classic critical-ideological procedure" (*The Sublime Object of Ideology* 25), Žižek invites to re-consider ideology in the following way:

> If our concept of ideology remains the classic one in which the illusion is located in knowledge, then today's society must appear post-ideological: the prevailing ideology is that of cynicism; people no longer believe in ideological truth; they do not take ideological propositions seriously. The fundamental level of ideology, however, is not that of an illusion masking the real state of things but that of an (unconscious) fantasy structuring our social reality itself. And at this level, we are of course far from being a post-ideological society. Cynical distance is just one way—one of many ways—to blind ourselves to the structuring power of ideological fantasy: even if we do not take things seriously, even if we keep an ironical distance, *we are still doing them*. (*The Sublime Object of Ideology* 30)

This definition of ideology as a fantasy structuring reality—and not as a set of personal positions—is what allows Fisher to argue that capitalist realism relies on "the overvaluing of belief—in the sense of inner subjective attitude—at the expense of the beliefs we exhibit and externalize in our behaviour. So long as we believe (in our hearts) that capitalism is bad, we are free to continue to participate in capitalist exchange" (*Capitalist Realism* 13). In this regard, Fisher uses Žižek's framework to propose that even expressions of opposition can contribute to capitalism's perpetuation, especially insofar as ideology's power is not dependent upon an explicit ideological endorsement by the majorities, but rather upon unsaid presuppositions, naturalized habits and even ironic behaviors.

Interestingly for us here, Fisher refers to a dystopian film to insist on how

> capitalist realism is very far from precluding a certain anti-capitalism. [...] Time after time, the villain in Hollywood films will turn out to be the 'evil corporation.' Far from undermining capitalist realism, this gestural anti-capitalism actually reinforces it. Take Disney/Pixar's *Wall-E* (2008). The film shows an earth so despoiled that human beings are no longer capable of inhabiting it. We're left in no doubt that consumer capitalism and corporations—or rather one mega-corporation, Buy n Large—is responsible for this depredation; and when we eventually see the human beings in offworld exile, they are infantile and obese, interacting via screen interfaces, carried around in large motorized chairs, and supping indeterminate slop from cups. What we have here is a vision of control and communication much as Jean Baudrillard understood it, in which subjugation no longer takes the form of a subordination to an extrinsic spectacle, but rather invites us to interact and participate. It seems that the cinema audience is itself the object of this satire, which prompted some right wing observers to recoil in disgust, condemning Disney/Pixar for attacking its own audience. But this kind of irony feeds rather than challenges capitalist realism. A

> film like *Wall-E* exemplifies what Robert Pfaller has called 'interpassivity': the film performs our anti-capitalism for us, allowing us to continue to consume with impunity. (*Capitalist Realism* 12)

Here, Fisher's arguments fall dangerously close to that extreme of critical theory in which "the theorist wins [...] by constructing an increasingly closed and terrifying machine" but "to that very degree he loses, since the critical capacity of his work is thereby paralyzed, and the impulses of negation and revolt, not to speak of those of social transformation, are increasingly perceived as vain and trivial in the face of the model itself" (Jameson, *Postmodernism* 5–6). If capitalist realism is like a "pervasive atmosphere [...] constraining thought and action" (*Capitalist Realism* 16), how could we escape the air we all breathe?

Of course, it is undoubtable that Fisher's intention—like that of any critical theorist with hopes of emancipation—is to provoke a kind of political praxis that would lead to a social scenario in which his critiques no longer hold: that is, a post-capitalist world. Fisher's critique is not timeless, but a historical response to the (still enduring) hegemony of neoliberalism, which

> has sought to eliminate the very category of value in the ethical sense. Over the past thirty years, capitalist realism has successfully installed a 'business ontology' in which it is simply obvious that everything in society, including healthcare and education, should be run as a business. [...] It is worth recalling that what is currently called realistic was itself once 'impossible': the slew of privatizations that took place since the 1980s would have been unthinkable only a decade earlier, and the current political-economic landscape (with unions in abeyance, utilities and railways denationalized) could scarcely have been imagined in 1975. Conversely, what was once eminently possible is now deemed unrealistic. (*Capitalist Realism* 16–17)

Thus, even if the idea of capitalist realism suggests that there is an extremely limited horizon of possibilities for the contemporary imagination, the idea is also meant to highlight that what is "realistic" or "possible" is historically construed—and therefore open to contestation.[14] Nonetheless,

---

14 In this regard, Fisher's critique seems to live up to Alain Badiou's observation that "Emancipatory politics always consist in making seem possible precisely that which, from within the situation, is declared to be impossible" (121).

Fisher's concept is, probably, above all, an ambivalent emblem of our epoch: on one level, because of how—in criticizing it—the book often symptomatizes what Fisher himself calls "reflexive impotence" and, on another level, also because *Capitalist Realism* itself has been frequently "memed" as fuel for the cynical fires that it tried to put out.[15] As an ironically self-fulfilling prophecy, the popular prestige of *Capitalist Realism* thus shows how anti-capitalism can proliferate under capitalism, as even critical theory can be fed into its commodifying circuits. And in fact, I should say that the first time I came across *Capitalist Realism* was when Amazon's algorithm recommended buying it, at a time when I was especially discontent with labor prospects—and I did indeed buy it then. So let whoever is without sin cast the first stone: this is not a matter of anyone's individual hypocrisy, it is a matter of capitalism's structural contradictions.

1.1.3. Dystopian Structure of Feeling

It is a truth universally acknowledged that there has been a dystopian turn in SF, as scholars have been observing for decades. *Longue-durée* histories

---

15   Mike Watson's *The Memeing of Mark Fisher* repeatedly suggests how Fisher's authority in certain online communities (especially among so-called "doomers") attests to the enduring validity—and to the ironic co-optation—of *Capitalist Realism*. The potentially self-defeating character of Fisher's diagnoses, especially when decontextualized and quoted only at their most hopeless, was famously seen in the 2021 media "sensation" caused when US congresswoman Alexandria Ocasio-Cortez (AOC) wore a white dress to the Met Gala—with the inscription "TAX THE RICH" painted in red over and around it. Even though AOC was evidently successful in attracting attention to the cause of fiscal justice, there was a proliferation of memes that superimposed excerpts of *Capitalist Realism* on top of AOC's pictures. Such memes, which quoted those parts of *Capitalist Realism* that most cynically emphasize the potential uselessness of anti-capitalist gestures, seemed to be deployed in order to denounce the hypocrisy or pointlessness of AOC's act. Mark Fisher thus came to appear in fashion magazines (see Cartter) and the whole polemic led to curious headlines such as "Es más fácil imaginar un meme de Mark Fisher que el fin del capitalismo de plataformas" (Espluga).

of the genre have mostly narrated this turn by reference to the three most canonical modern dystopias and their paradigm-shifting influence—Yevgeny Zamyatin's *We*, Aldous Huxley's *Brave New World* and George Orwell's *Nineteen-Eighty-Four*. Besides, more contemporary-oriented studies have narrated the turn by reference to the proliferation of dystopian narratives across media and throughout popular culture generally.[16] So perhaps there is more than one dystopian turn—or perhaps, like capitalist modernity, the dystopian turn has arrived in succeeding waves, until the waters of hopelessness eventually submerged the whole beach.[17] When and where utopianism persisted or revived—as in the case of certain Soviet SF or certain American SF of the 1970s—it is now virtually gone, or at least overshadowed by the hegemony of dystopian narratives and imaginaries across media and cultures.[18]

16 For reference studies of dystopian literature, see Stock's *Modern Dystopian Fiction and Political Thought* (2018); Baccolini and Moylan's *Dark Horizons* (2003); Moylan's *Scraps of the Untainted Sky* (2000); or Booker's *The Dystopian Impulse in Modern Literature* (1994). Beside these, for a more transmedia-oriented study of contemporary dystopias, with sections for literature, cinema and theater, see also Vieira's *Dystopia(n) Matters* (2013). Predating these, Elliott's *The Shape of Utopia* (1970), already devoted a chapter to the growing "fear of utopia" during the Cold War (84–101) and, in that same decade, Chad Walsh's *From Utopia to Nightmare* (1972) already placed the turn at the very title of his study.

17 Baccolini and Moylan do suggest this idea in passing, noting that "the contemporary historical moment is interrogated by critical positions that necessarily work within a dystopian structure of feeling (and perhaps that "moment" has recurred, as has the dystopian genre, in one form or another since the onset of twentieth-century capitalism—beginning in its monopoly and imperialist phase, taking another form in the 1940s and 1950s, and yet another in the 1980s and 1990s)" (Baccolini and Moylan 4). This observation could be read in parallel to Jameson's insights about waves of modernization: speaking of an "existential uneven development," he calls modernism "a culture of incomplete modernisation" while postmodernism would be a culture of the time when "the premodern [definitively] vanishes" ("The End of Temporality" 699). It is with Jameson's schemas in mind that I am suggesting the existence of two main waves of dystopianism: a modernist and a postmodernist one, although it is beyond the scope of this work to probe into the validity of this speculation.

18 Certain media—especially visual media (cinema, television or videogames) that are subject to commercial pressures more intensely than literature under the

Thus seen, Moylan's notion of a "dystopian structure of feeling" emerges as a way to theorize the broader atmosphere entailed by the so-called dystopian turn in fiction, thus historicizing the turn and suggesting the use of "dystopia(n)" as a valid concept for cultural-materialist theorization.[19] Of course, there is something potentially tautological in taking this hypothesis too mechanically: we have historically witnessed a rise of dystopian fiction because history itself has become dystopian—so problem solved! But clearly, the present narrowing of the imagination to its most hopeless, cynical and pessimistic—or the "slow cancellation of the future," in Franco Berardi's phrase—is not so simple a phenomenon.[20] After all, a

---

publishing industry—seem to have been even more irremediably dystopian than literature (still the object of most studies). As Simon Spiegel has recently argued, in fiction films, utopias "seem to be non-existent" because "a classic positive utopia lacks some of the basic elements required for a narrative film" and he suggests that if we want to find film utopias, "we turn to non-fiction films" such as Peter Joseph's *Zeitgeist: Addendum* (2008). But clearly, these are still a minority that is clearly drowned by the outflow of blockbuster dystopian films.

With regard to the American exceptions, one should refer to the critical utopias of Joanna Russ, Ursula K. Le Guin, Marge Piercy and Samuel R. Delany, studied by Moylan's *Demand the Impossible* (1986, edited and re-published in 2014). Besides, for a reflection of the dialectical relationship that can be theorized between First-World and Second-World utopias, see Jameson's "Progress Versus Utopia"; as well as, for more detailed studies of Soviet utopias, his *Archaeologies*.

19 Predating and perhaps influencing Moylan's "The Necessity of Hope," Gregory Claeys's *Dystopia* (2017) is one of the first monographs to have used centrally and consistently the notion of "dystopia" within a context that is not primarily cultural or fictional, but mostly political and historical. Another recent example with a more sociological than cultural use of "dystopia" can be found in Eva Paus's *Confronting Dystopia* (2018), although the term is then scarcely and vaguely employed, as it is used just twice throughout the book (5, 18) and then twice again, in the volume's and another chapter's titles (115).

20 This is a term that could be located mid-way between Brown's use of left melancholy and Fisher's use of capitalist realism, as it narrates the slow decline of "the psychological perception, which emerged in the cultural situation of progressive modernity, the cultural expectations that were fabricated during the long period of modern civilization, reaching a peak in the years after the Second World War. Those expectations were shaped in the conceptual frameworks of an ever progressing development, albeit through different methodologies: the Hegelo-Marxist mythology of *Aufhebung* and instauration of the new totality of Communism;

structure of feeling is, in Raymond Williams's definition, a complex set of "meanings and values as they are actively lived and felt [...] over a range from formal assent with private dissent to the more nuanced interaction between selected and interpreted beliefs and acted and justified experiences." And, methodologically speaking, a structure of feeling is "a cultural hypothesis, actually derived from attempts to understand such elements and their connections in a generation or period, and needing always to be returned, interactively, to such evidence" (R. Williams, *Marxism and Literature* 132–3).[21]

Having thus defined structure of feeling, it nonetheless remains necessary to define the other element of Moylan's formula: the dystopia(n). Although this concept is further explored in Chapter 3 (as an audio-visual genre), it is already necessary to make a distinction between *anti-utopia* and *dystopia*, as the two terms (along with others like cacotopia) have been often used interchangeably as the simple opposite of utopia—and when they are differentiated, there is not a clear consensus on the difference (see McAlear; as well as Blaim). For present purposes, however, it seems much more productive and clarifying to propose that *dystopia* would be an ambivalent *narrative genre* within which contrasting *ideological impulses, the utopian and the anti-utopian,* are put into dialog, resulting in a complex interplay of hopefulness and cynicism. In other words, dystopia would be a genre in which a critical and/or satirical attitude towards an undesirably

---

the bourgeois mythology of a linear development of welfare and democracy; the technocratic mythology of the all-encompassing power of scientific knowledge, and so on" (*After the Future* 18–19). This idea is in fact cited by Fisher in the introduction to his later book (*Ghosts of My Life*).

21 In his 2020 novel *The Ministry for the Future*, SF writer Kim Stanley Robinson expands upon this definition, very didactically, with the present moment in mind: "how you feel about your time is partly or even largely a result of that time's structure of feeling. When time passes and that structure changes, how you feel will also change—both in your body and in how you understand it as a meaning. Say the order of your time feels unjust and unsustainable, but also falling apart before your eyes. [...] it feels that way to us. But a little contemplation of history will reveal that this feeling too will not last for long. Unless of course the feeling of things falling apart is itself massively entrenched, to the point of being the eternal or eternally recurrent individual human's reaction to history" (124).

oppressive society would never fully overshadow the possibility of transforming the world for the better and it may, therefore, be seen as a synthesis of anything that is more one-sidedly utopian or anti-utopian. Contrary to the concept of *anti*-utopia, which names a radical opposition to the utopian—both as imagined place and as ideological impulse—dystopia would thus name a bad place in which utopian possibilities may linger. This is the schema that Moylan appears to follow when he proposes that

> Dystopias negotiate the social terrain of Utopia and Anti-Utopia in a less stable and more contentious fashion than many of their eutopian and anti-utopian counterparts. As a literary form that works between these historical antinomies and draws on the textual qualities of both subgenres to do so, the typical dystopian text is an exercise in a politically charged form of hybrid textuality, or what Raffaella Baccolini calls 'genre blurring.' Although all dystopian texts offer a detailed and pessimistic presentation of the very worst of social alternatives, some affiliate with a utopian tendency as they maintain a horizon of hope (or at least invite readings that do), while others only appear to be dystopian allies of Utopia as they retain an anti-utopian disposition that forecloses all transformative possibility, and yet others negotiate a more strategically ambiguous position somewhere along the antinomic continuum. (*Scraps of the Untainted Sky* 147)

In these ways, dystopia is not a simple negation of what Jameson (following Bloch) calls the "Utopian impulse"—that is, a universal human wish for a better state of things, which may be found "governing everything future-oriented in life and culture; and encompassing everything from games to patent medicines, from myths to mass entertainment, from iconography to technology, from architecture to eros, from tourism to jokes and the unconscious" (*Archaeologies* 2). Thus, one would assume that even within a dystopian structure of feeling such as is theorized by Moylan, utopian desire and dreaming is not simply negated. The utopian impulse is, more specifically, repressed, submerged, or co-opted—but it nonetheless remains alive. This is no trivial qualification, insofar as Moylan, in speaking of a dystopian structure of feeling, is not confronting us with an unchangeably negative (anti-utopian) totality—such as the picture painted by Fisher's "capitalist realism"—; he is ultimately advocating for a negation of negativity, for an anti-anti-utopianism that would let us rekindle the utopian impulse within and against the present's hopelessness.[22] Just as within the dystopian genre, within a dystopian structure of feeling there can still be hope.

In Moylan's life-long work, the notion of a "dystopian structure of feeling" seems to have organically evolved from a more text-oriented concept towards a more holistic hypothesis.[23] In fact, Moylan's latest monograph, *Becoming Utopian: The Culture and Politics of Radical Transformation* (2021), begins by counterposing his well-established theorization of (critical) dystopias *as a narrative genre* to his newer understanding of dystopia *as a structure of feeling*. Moylan helpfully clarifies that "As opposed to the recognized capacity of dystopian narrative not only to warn but also to stimulate transformative political action, this neoliberal dystopian structure of feeling functions as an ethical and political inoculation that normalizes a passive indulgence in our terrifying reality, thereby paralyzing radical challenges to its terms and conditions" (*Becoming Utopian* 2). In that volume, however, the concept is scarcely used (understandably, given its focus on utopianism), and it was Moylan's 2020 essay "The Necessity of Hope in Dystopian Times" that primarily prompted my interest in the term, insofar as it is, self-consciously and centrally, "the first part of a project addressing the current dystopian structure of feeling and the possibilities for a refunctioned utopianism" ("The Necessity of Hope in Dystopian Times" 190).

---

22 In the introduction to his 2005 *Archaeologies* collection, Fredric Jameson already made a call for anti-anti-utopianism (using that term precisely), proposing that "we may now have recourse to that ingenious political slogan Sartre invented to find his way between a flawed communism and an even more unacceptable anti-communism. Perhaps something similar can be proposed to fellow-travelers of Utopia itself: indeed, for those only too wary of the motives of its critics, yet no less conscious of Utopia's structural ambiguities, those mindful of the very real political function of the idea and the program of Utopia in our time, the slogan of anti-anti-Utopianism might well offer the best working strategy" (*Archaeologies* xvi).
23 The concept was employed twice in *Dark Horizons* (2003), although with a meaning that is evidently more restricted than the one Moylan would later give the term, as it seems to denote a structure of feeling that is more directly emanating from dystopian fiction (see Baccolini and Moylan 4, 150).

Moylan's article opens by historicizing the present's dystopian structure of feeling in the following way, as a markedly anti-utopian moment that sets great challenges on any attempt at reviving utopianism:

> The current global order threatens humanity and all of nature. Harm abounds everywhere. Economically, the worldwide incursion of neoliberal capitalism produces alienation and exploitation in all aspects of everyday life. Politically, the overdetermined array of corporate power, superpower aggression, and the failure of democratic politics to uphold the utopian potential of justice and peace increases the privileges of the rich and powerful and unevenly subjects people around the world to lives of intensifying vulnerability and immiseration. Culturally and existentially, accelerated by these social depredations, virulent hatred feeds a spreading wave of xenophobia (attacking on grounds of race, ethnicity, gender, sexuality, age, or any other mode of perceived difference that appears to threaten an already vulnerable populace). And environmentally, with the downward spiral of climate catastrophe, planetary life is facing total destruction. In the face of these dire conditions, for those of us (in our diverse intersectional situations) who aim to transform this current reality in the spirit of a just, equal, and healthy existence for all of humanity and nature, it is clearly time for the political exercise of the hopeful, transformative utopian impulse. Yet, even as we engage the utopian problematic and praxis, we need to recognize the ways in which capitalism's retrieval mechanism "subsumes and consumes" the radical potential of utopianism. ("The Necessity of Hope in Dystopian Times" 165–6)

Thus seen, utopian impulses are not dead today—and can never be—but they clearly swim upstream against the strong, overflowing currents of left melancholy, capitalist realism and a more general hopelessness in the face of mounting catastrophes. Our dystopian structure of feeling is, in a sense, today's (capitalist) realism and, even if utopianism is not dead within it, Moylan's apocalyptic picture is far from an exaggeration. One could go through something like the IPCC's reports to weigh (and to be weighed down by) the overwhelming amount of scientific evidence that suggests a global collapse soon, but for my present purposes it would be pointless to, in a positivistic way, list all the events that feed into to this structure of feeling.[24] What is clear is that what makes this a dystopian

---

24 The latest report by the Intergovernmental Panel on Climate Change, *Climate Change 2022: Impacts, Adaptation and Vulnerability (Working Group II Report)*, indeed attests to the unsustainability and the irreversibility of the multiple and multidimensional harms that await human and natural ecologies. If one were to survey

structure of feeling is the might of anti-utopian tendencies, as expressed in a dominant mood of hopelessness *vis-à-vis* historical events, which goes hand in hand with the daunting difficulties faced by any utopian impulses, which remain but struggle.

Having defined this mood, however, we cannot dismiss one crucial question yet, still only partially answered: how did we get to this "dystopian structure of feeling" in which reality seems to behave like (and, to an extent, outmanoeuvre) dystopian fiction? Much remains to be said about the larger dynamics that led here and we should continue to unpack the structural contradictions of *the epoch as a whole*, the broader conditions that made possible this hegemonic sense of hopelessness. In this sense, besides conceptualizing dystopian ways of thinking and feeling in the abstract, there is the need to periodize properly, to define historical specificities. As Kim Stanley Robinson explains, "periodization makes it easier to remember that no matter how massively entrenched the order of things seems in your time, there is no chance that they are going to be the same as they are now after a century has passed, or even ten years" (121). And what do we periodize with? To understand contemporary culture, one finds the term *postmodernism* and, to understand contemporary political economy, there is the concept of *neoliberalism*. These two are, without a doubt, indispensable to grasp the present epoch. Accordingly, in the next section, I survey the two phenomena, emphasizing their dialectical inseparability and their semi-autonomy within the epoch's whole. Clearly, one should not forget, as it often happens, that in talking about neoliberalism and postmodernism, one is still inscribed within the *longue-durée* history of capitalist modernity. These are, merely, the latest "-isms" to describe the latest period of the globally dominant social formation.[25]

---

its findings, predictions and suggestions, the impression of living in dystopian times would not dissipate—on the contrary, it would be like falling considerably deeper into a rabbit hole of pessimism. And for good reasons.

25 Here I am using "social formation" as opposed to the more strictly economic concept of "mode of production," but it should be clear that my use of "social formation" is intended to encompass both the cultural and the economic dimensions of capitalism, which are, after all, not fully separable, even though capitalist self-perception would tend to make us think so. Furthermore, when I specify that capitalism is the

1.2. Periodizing with Two Late Capitalist-isms

Giving us a clear toolkit for the task of periodization, the Marxist theorist Bertell Ollman helpfully sketches the seven "levels of generality" that are implied in historical-materialist analysis (86–99), which can indeed be used in literary and cultural theory, as Barbara Foley suggests. As she summarizes them, the seven levels are:

> (1) the immediate circumstances surrounding unique individuals; (2) the particular epoch in capitalism informing the moment under examination, a period of some 20-50 years; (3) the era in which capitalism has been the dominant mode of production, some 300-500 years; (4) the still longer timespan constituted by class society, some 5000-8000 years, depending on location; and (5) the timespan common to all humans since their evolution into *Homo sapiens*. The two remaining levels of generality can take us beyond history to ontology [...]: (6) denotes the features that all forms of human and animal life have in common; while (7) comprises the material qualities that humans share with all other existing matter, organic and inorganic. (Foley 31–2)

Ollman himself clarifies that even though "each of these levels brings into focus a different time period, [...] they are not to be thought of as 'slices of time,' since the whole of history is implicated in each level, including the most specific" (Ollman 89). In this sense, one should be especially wary of explaining anything by exclusive reference either to the specific situation of individuals (level 1) or to a timeless human nature (level 5). Clearly, such a move would amount to reinforcing the status quo's naturalizing mechanisms—and more importantly, it would intensify our hopelessness in the face of history, insofar as cultural, social, political or economic phenomena would appear as the result of an individual's or a species' fate.[26]

"dominant" social formation, the implication is not that there are no others, but rather that there is a conflictual co-existence with "residual" and "emergent" social formations. This conceptual triad (dominant, residual and emergent) is borrowed from Williams (see *Marxism and Literature*).

26 In this regard, I would stand with Barbara Foley's observation that such a theoretical move would problematically allow "to deny, or at least minimize, the types of causality operative on levels two through four—that is, the levels where class analysis, especially of capitalism, figures prominently. [...] [Instead,] causality comes to

Therefore, in order to avoid a naturalizing reduction to levels 1 and 5, while speaking of postmodernism and neoliberalism I overemphasize levels 2 and 3 of Ollman's schema, regarding these as two semi-autonomous, epochal phenomena that are, in turn, inscribed within the longer era of capitalist modernity. In so doing, the main difficulty lies in that their dynamics are not self-evident, especially because their hegemony is sustained by the capitalist-realist fantasy that our historical predicament is just "natural" or "post-historical"—and this gives us all the more reason to periodize properly. What is here examined, therefore, is, on the one hand, the underlying logics of postmodernism and neoliberalism and the ways whereby they have naturalized their own dynamics (level 2)—and, on the other hand, I also examine how these two phenomena have continued (and naturalized) certain dynamics set off by the longer capitalist era (level 3).[27] In

---

    be construed either as, on the one hand, the exercise of distinct individuality or, on the other, the fatalistic pressure of an unchanging human condition. [...] some of the most influential schools [of literary criticism] have proven prone to bypassing historically based causal analysis and positing abstract notions of human nature and language, often premised upon the belief that the most general statements about what it means to be human are for that reason the most valuable and profound (31).

27 It is beyond my scope to delve into the nature—and even less the history—of capitalism. Nonetheless, I should acknowledge that my understanding is profoundly indebted to Ellen Meiksins Wood's definition of it as a social formation characterized by the population's generalized *market dependence*. Commodification *per se* predates capitalism, as commerce existed since antiquity and capitalism emerges only *after the majority becomes market dependent*—first and foremost, *to eat*, as Wood's analysis of early-modern English agrarian capitalism shows. In her words, "capitalism was born when market imperatives seized hold of food production, the provision of life's most irreducible necessity" (81)—so it is only after basic subsistence was commodified that a system oriented towards profit-maximization (or surplus extraction) could emerge. Thus, capitalism is a system in which more and more would be commodified: natural resources, manufactured goods of all kinds and, of course, human bodies—in the generalization of waged labor, but most brutally in the case of the trans-Atlantic slave trade. As Marx himself put it, "the veiled slavery of the wage-labourers in Europe needed the unqualified slavery of the New World as its pedestal" (*Capital Volume I* 925). Now, with the inestimable aid of digital technologies, commodification continues its seemingly endless, ever-expanding subsumption of increasing aspects of life: most notably, culture and sociability.

these ways, my schematization of both postmodernism and neoliberalism is mediated by the phenomenon of *commodification*, which—as Marx's *Capital* demonstrates in its very first chapter (*Capital Volume I* 125–77)—is a cornerstone to understanding capitalist societies.[28] Postmodern cultures and neoliberal economics are no exception and, notwithstanding their semi-autonomous specificities, one can observe (and one should emphasize) that there is a clear continuity: both can be explained primarily by reference to commodification's intensification and expansion into increasing spheres of life. In other words, this epoch is to be approached as a step further in the dominance of exchange-value over use-values, in the primacy of abstract, homogenizing quantification over the heterogeneous qualities of subjects and objects.[29] The on-going process of capitalist commodification leaves

---

28 The very first line of *Capital* tells us: "The wealth of societies in which the capitalist mode of production prevails appears as an 'immense collection of commodities'; the individual commodity appears as its elementary form" (K. Marx, *Capital Volume I* 125). The commodity or, perhaps more importantly, *the process of commodification* is thus what lies at the structural basis of the capitalist mode of production.

29 For a deeper approach to the dialectical nature of the commodity, it is worth revisiting one of Marx's most suggestive passages:

> A commodity appears at first sight an extremely obvious, trivial thing. But its analysis brings out that it is a very strange thing, abounding in metaphysical subtleties and theological niceties. So far as it is a use-value, there is nothing mysterious about it, whether we consider it from the point of view that by its properties it satisfies human needs, or that it first takes on these properties as the product of human labour. It is absolutely clear that [people change] the forms of the materials of nature in such a way as to make them useful [...]. The form of wood, for instance, is altered if a table is made out of it. Nevertheless the table continues to be wood, an ordinary, sensuous thing. But as soon as it emerges as a commodity, it changes into a thing which transcends sensuousness. It not only stands with its feet on the ground, but, in relation to all other commodities, it stands on its head, and evolves out of its wooden brain grotesque ideas, far more wonderful than if it were to begin dancing of its own free will. (*Capital Volume I* 163–4)

Beyond Marx's evocative-provocative language, the key here is that, as he elaborates in succeeding pages, a commodity is a thing—anything, be that a wooden table, the latest smartphone, or any work of art—that acquires a kind of supra-sensuous second nature: it acquires an abstract value that does not have any relation to that thing's objective properties, a value that is based on the commodity's capacity to be exchanged and, thus, a value based on a simple question: how much of something else (not necessarily money) can I obtain through this thing? In short, anything

nothing untouched and postmodernism and neoliberalism both shed light upon different aspects of this.

1.2.1. Postmodernism

Postmodernism is now an irremediably worn off, vaguely catch-all term, not only because of its nuanced and variegated uses in academia, but also because of its more recent popularization as a slur. Indeed, a considerable number of TV personalities and popular thinkers of the right (as well as certain fringe communities of the left) frequently refer to postmodernism as something like an intellectual plague—even, a presumed "neomarxist" takeover of universities and/or Hollywood, thus treating postmodernism almost as a conspiracy theory.[30] Evidently, this reactionary, paranoid usage is not what interests me here—although it is worth keeping it in mind, as it speaks of the epoch's (dystopian and quixotic) propensity for imagining systemic trends as secret conspiracies (see Dean, *Aliens in America*; Bratich; Gulyas; Costantini). What interests me here is the use of postmodernism as a periodizing label, one that has been used in an endless number of disciplines. "Postmodernism" may, indeed, be used to refer to certain aesthetics, philosophies, or politics.[31]

---

that is commodified is treated as though its principal value is not in itself but in the market and its value, in the eyes of its owner, becomes a matter of exchange-value. The qualitative uniqueness of any given commodity is thus dissolved, or turned on its head, by an alchemy of abstract equivalence. Commodification makes everything the same in the eyes of capital.

30 Treating postmodernism as a cabal-like conspiracy is the ludicrous position of Canadian psychiatrist Jordan Peterson, who has gone as far as to post online "a list of writers he considers 'Postmodern NeoMarxists,' which ran as follows: 'Ibram X Kendi, Ta-Nahesi-Coates, Robin DiAngelo, Kimberle Crenshaw, bell hooks, Andrea Dworkin, Michel Foucault, Naomi Klein, Catherine McKinnon, Judith Butler, Jacques Derrida and, perhaps above all, Michel Foucault'" (qtd. in Savage). It is in this sense that is now possible to argue that postmodernism has started to function as an alt-right conspiracy theory (see Nevado Encinas), which does not *per se* undermine its conceptual validity but it does certainly compromise it.

31 In this regard, there is an endless number of essays, monographs and introductions to postmodernism available, ranging from early theorizations in the 1970s, academic

However—although I later return to elements of postmodern aesthetics in Chapter 2 (primarily, reflexivity)—my emphasis here lies on the more abstract, historicizing uses: on postmodernism understood as an epistemology and a cultural hegemony.[32]

Postmodernism is generally assumed to be a Western phenomenon that emerged in the decades after World War II, but it would not become hegemonic until approximately the 1970s. By the early twenty-first century, however, a range of thinkers, including some of its earliest theorizers, have proclaimed it dead (e.g. Hassan, "Beyond Postmodernism"). And after its presumed demise, there seems to be a growing host of proposed successors: "digimodernism" (Kirby), "metamodernism" (Vermeulen and van den Akker), or even "post-postmodernism" (Nealon).[33] But are we ready to abandon the term? I cannot aspire to provide an answer to these terminological conundrums here and my assumption is that at least two of the essential characteristics of the postmodern still retain their explanatory potential within the present situation: the distrust of master narratives and the commodification of culture.

The single most popular account is Jean-François Lyotard's *The Postmodern Condition*, originally published in 1979. According to this book, the distrust towards and/or rejection of "grand" or "master" narratives—those totalizing narratives that provide coherence to our otherwise

---

monographs and introductions produced between the 1980s and the early 2000s and even polemics published as recently as 2021 (see Hassan, "POSTmodernISM: A Paracritical Bibliography"; Hutcheon, *A Poetics of Postmodernism*; Hutcheon, *The Politics of Postmodernism*; McRobbie; Bertens; C. Butler; McHale, *Postmodernist Fiction*; Connor; Jeffries; Anderson).

32 It would have been possible here to observe a difference, namely that "The word *postmodernism* generally refers to a form of contemporary culture, whereas the term *postmodernity* alludes to a specific historical period." Nonetheless, as Terry Eagleton does, I have here "tended to stick to the more familiar term 'postmodernism' to cover both of these things, since they are clearly closely related." This is because, like Eagleton himself, I am more interested in the broader "culture or milieu or even sensibility of postmodernism as a whole" rather than with "the more recherché formulations of postmodern philosophy" (Eagleton vii–viii).

33 For a recent survey that engages with these three and a number of other "post-postmodern" alternatives, see Bolaño Quintero.

fragmented positive knowledge of the world—would be a defining feature of postmodernity, if not its key epistemological characteristic. Lyotard pays considerable attention to the state of the sciences and, in this regard, he argues that "The decline of narrative can be seen as an effect of the blossoming of techniques and technologies since the Second World War, which has shifted emphasis from the ends of actions to its means" (Lyotard 37). Thus, postmodern epistemology favors a focus on technique rather than on telos, which is to say that it overvalues specific, specialist truths while distrusting any overarching, totalizing purpose of knowledge, which is a significant hindrance to the construction of any kind of collective, politicizing narratives. Therefore, the most politically relevant implication of Lyotard's proposition is that postmodernism entails a deep distrust towards any teleological vision of history—a generalized skepticism towards visions that would assume that History is (or can be) guided by some form of progress, or that it advances (or may consciously be oriented) towards any kind of utopian horizon. Thus, postmodern epistemology favors a depoliticizing climate in which only the fragmented, diverse truths of individual experiences can be significant, whereas attempts to provide unifying political narratives would be met with distrust—if not outright rejection.

In these ways, the whole intellectual and affective panorama seems overdetermined by a generalized *fear of progress*—or a *fear of utopia*, one might say, both political and technological—due to (among other things, but centrally within the Western imagination) the traumas of the Second World War, which tragically illustrated Walter Benjamin's maxim that civilization is inseparable from barbarism. Indeed, as Terry Eagleton slyly notes, certain postmodern intellectuals seem to overhastily indulge in "the idea [...] that the Enlightenment led inevitably to the concentration camps" (46)—and ironically, in so doing, postmodernism proposes its own reversed teleology: the idea that totalizing attempts to "move history forward" ultimately lead to catastrophe.[34] Thus, in postmodern epistemology

---

34 In this manner, it would seem as though this catastrophist teleology is based upon a radical simplification of Adorno and Horkheimer's *Dialectic of Enlightenment*, reducing their dialectical theorization to its most negative side. As opposed to this, perhaps the best formulation wherefrom one can dialectically think history is still Walter Benjamin's maxim that "There is no document of civilization which is not at

one finds the pre-history of some of the same anti-utopian logics already considered, in the sense that alternatives to the status quo seemed less and less imaginable already *before* the post-Cold-War emergence of left melancholy and capitalist realism.

Do these attitudes endure? If, as argued above, the present's structure of feeling is hopelessly trapped in a seemingly eternal present, it would appear that this older distrust towards master narratives is not gone, but rather more naturalized. Lyotard's postmodern condition, of course, may not necessarily manifest as skepticism per se: it might as well manifest itself as cynicism, melancholy, anxiety, or hopelessness—but the void left by the eviction of grand narratives remains. And now, not only do we seem to have abandoned (or forgotten) about imagining a more utopian alternative to the present mode of production; we also seem to have stopped believing in capitalism's own teleology of progress, especially after seeing how capitalist "progress" is literally leading to catastrophe. In this way, the safest assumption may be that our dystopian structure of feeling is an intensified postmodern climate—a climate in which *climate* itself has validated the postmodern fear of progress. Today, the most believable destiny of history is wholesale planetary collapse, but because we are still postmodern, we cannot (yet) put our faith in any radically alternative vision of the future.[35]

Of course, none of this is to say that the postmodern epoch does not allow for subversive or oppositional practices: in fact, these practices flourish, but they often remain on the level of a defense of differences, identities and particularities—especially of those disfavored by the status quo—and such practices tend to fall short of constructing an alternative hegemony, because that would involve a "grand narrative" of collective

---

the same time a document of barbarism. And just as such a document is not free of barbarism, barbarism taints also the manner in which it was transmitted from one owner to another" ("Thesis on the Philosophy of History" 256).

35 All in all, perhaps Lyotard's main claim needs to be qualified and, as Jameson suggests in his preface to *The Postmodern Condition*, we should take "a further step that Lyotard seems unwilling to do in the present text, namely to posit, not the disappearance of the great master-narratives, but their passage underground as it were, their continuing but now unconscious effectivity as a way of 'thinking about' and acting in our current situation" ("Foreword" xii).

solidarity and the plotting of an alternative, utopian course of history. Thus, the key in this case is that, if subversive and oppositional politics partake of postmodern epistemology, then any anti-establishment movement "could only ever be a strategic skirmish or fleeting subversion, a rapid guerrilla raid on the fortress of Reason, since for it to become systemic would be for it to fall victim to the very logic it threw into question" (Eagleton 7). Furthermore, it even seems that

> There are those radical thinkers who genuinely believe that a belief in totality is just a mesmerizing hindrance to real political change, as with the kind of mentally blocked student who feels unable to say anything unless he or she has grasped everything. Anti-totality may here be more of a strategic than a theoretical point: there may well be some sort of total system, but since our political actions cannot dent it as a whole we would be better advised to trim our sails and stick to more modest but more viable projects. (Eagleton 11)

Indeed, the main critique raised against so-called identity politics—another abused term, often caricatured as postmodernism's political expression—is precisely this rejection of utopian, collective aims that would transcend particular interests, however legitimate those may be. In other words, the problem would be that postmodern politics, as Nancy Fraser argues about some liberal branches of feminism, seems to be "aimed more at valorizing cultural difference than at promoting economic equality" (Fraser, *Fortunes of Feminism* 4), even though much feminism has been, can be and still often is about more than "simply culture."

In these regards, the shift undergone by feminist movements, as criticized by Nancy Fraser, can be seen as a clear example of how such postmodern tendencies may affect a specific political movement:

> Unable to transform the deep gender structures of the capitalist economy, [feminists] preferred to target harms rooted in androcentric patterns of cultural value or status hierarchies. The result was a major shift in the feminist imaginary: whereas the previous generation had sought to remake political economy, this one focused more on transforming culture. The results were decidedly mixed. On the one hand, the new feminist struggles for recognition continued the earlier project of expanding the political agenda beyond the confines of class redistribution; in principle they served to broaden, and to radicalize, the concept of justice. On the other hand, however, the figure of the struggle for recognition so thoroughly captured the feminist

imagination that it served more to displace than to deepen the socialist imaginary. The effect was to subordinate social struggles to cultural struggles, the politics of redistribution to the politics of recognition. (*Fortunes of Feminism* 4)

Of course, as Fraser acknowledges, all of this "was not, to be sure, the original intention" (*Fortunes of Feminism* 4) and her comments are not meant to discredit the movement to which she belongs: this is rather a cautionary diagnosis of dominant tendencies within the broader climate of postmodernism and neoliberalism. And besides, certain of the critical concepts developed during this era—such as "intersectionality" (coined by Crenshaw)—clearly have the potential to forge an alternative hegemony in a way that acknowledges the heterogeneous complexity of interlocking axes of oppression (gender, race, sexuality, class, etc.), while at the same time allowing for the construction of a counter-hegemonic force that may give a common political purpose to diverse identity-positions.[36] To put it more simply: talk of intersectional oppression allows talk of intersectional solidarity and, in this way, the concept of intersectionality—hastily dismissed as a divisive "trap of diversity" by some critics (Bernabé)— shows one possibility for plotting a utopian, counter-hegemonic "grand narrative" of progress that is also conscious of diversity.[37] Thus seen, the

---

[36] One attempt at theorizing an intersectional counter-hegemony is provided by Nancy Fraser's herself, in her most recent work ("Climates of Capital"), where she constructs a critique of capitalism in the age of climate change that accounts for and synthesizes the insights of ecocriticism, feminism and anti-colonialism within a critique of the system's inherent tendency to be parasitical upon divisions of gender, race, class and nature-economy.

[37] As one of the earliest proponents of the concept of intersectionality (see her *Black Feminist Thought*), Patricia Hill Collins took a decisive step towards an emphasis on what one could call "intersectional solidarity," emphasizing the potential of intersectionality as a totalizing concept that may allow for the construction of an alternative hegemony. In Collins's words,

> intersectionality is far broader than what most people, including many of its practitioners, imagine it to be. We have yet to fully understand the potential of the constellation of ideas that fall under the umbrella term intersectionality as a tool for social change. As a discourse, intersectionality bundles together ideas from disparate places, times, and perspectives, enabling people to share points of view that formerly were forbidden, outlawed, or simply obscured. [...] Intersectionality is well on its way to becoming a critical social theory that can address con temporary social problems

anti-utopian trap of postmodern epistemology seem to be based on a falsification, since recognition and redistribution, diversity and equality were never opposites: on the contrary, they dialectically inform one another, just like the concepts of individual and totality, or identity and universality.[38] In this regard, the anti-totalizing, fragmenting bias of postmodern thinking is far from unchallenged—and as Fraser puts it, more utopianly, "the young feminists of this generation seem poised to conjure up a new synthesis of radical democracy and social justice," a synthesis of "redistribution [and] recognition" (*Fortunes of Feminism* 16).

Considering the hegemony of this radically anti-utopian epistemology, one might legitimately ask *how* it came to be. In this regard, another key factor behind the emergence of postmodern culture that may help us account for the endurance of this de-politicizing, anti-totalizing distrust of grand narratives is *the commodification of culture*, a phenomenon that has been the object of multiple Marxist studies. In the post-war context of the emergence and consolidation of a (hegemonically Anglo-American) capitalist culture industry structured around cinema and television (and other "newer" media later), the dynamics of expanded cultural commodification show crucial parallels—and in many ways explain—the fragmenting and the leveling of forms of knowledge that is so characteristic of the epoch. However, this realization is not to be turned into a one-sided denunciation of postmodern culture as a "degraded" or "totally capitalistic" culture. Instead, the expansion of cultural commodification in the postmodern epoch must be examined dialectically, as a phenomenon composed of contradictory tendencies, utopian and anti-utopian. As Fredric Jameson's

---

and the social changes needed to solve them. But it can do so only if its practitioners simultaneously understand and cultivate intersectionality as a *critical* social theory. (*Intersectionality as Critical Social Theory* 2)

38 On this matter, one could refer to Nancy Fraser's two-dimensional theory of justice as an attempt to break with these false oppositions within feminist politics ("Feminist Politics in the Age of Recognition") and it is also worth consulting Judith Butler, Ernesto Laclau and Slavoj Žižek's collective reflection on the challenges and possibilities for (re)constructing an alternative hegemony and a sense of universality, in a way that incorporates *and* transcends the postmodern sensibility towards difference and contingency (see Butler *et al.*)

Postmodernism tells us, "In place of the temptation either to denounce the complacencies of postmodernism as some final symptom of decadence [...], it seems more appropriate to assess the new cultural production within the working hypothesis of a general modification of culture itself with the social restructuring of late capitalism as a system" (*Postmodernism* 61). Following Ernest Mandel's periodization of capitalist technological developments, Jameson proposes to think of nineteenth-century realism, early-twentieth-century modernism and late-twentieth-century postmodernism, as cultural reflexes of

> three fundamental moments in capitalism, each one marking a dialectical expansion over the previous stage. These are market capitalism [Mandel's age of "steam-driven motors"], the monopoly stage or the stage of imperialism [Mandel's age of "electric and combustion motors"], and our own, wrongly called postindustrial, but what might better be termed multinational capital [Mandel's age of "electronic and nuclear-powered apparatuses"]. [...] [L]ate or multinational or consumer capitalism, far from being inconsistent with Marx's great nineteenth-century analysis, constitutes, on the contrary, *the purest form of capital yet to have emerged, a prodigious expansion of capital into hitherto uncommodified areas*. This purer capitalism of our own time thus eliminates the enclaves of precapitalist organization it had hitherto tolerated and exploited in a tributary way. One is tempted to speak in this connection of a new and historically original penetration and colonization of Nature and the Unconscious: that is, the destruction of precapitalist Third World agriculture by the Green Revolution, and the rise of the media and the advertising industry. (*Postmodernism* 35–6, my emphasis)

Thus seen, postmodernism emerges in an epoch marked by "a prodigious expansion of capital into hitherto uncommodified areas," including, most crucially for this book's purposes, culture, art and communication.

Although, of course, culture, art and communication were never fully free from market pressures throughout the capitalist era, "aesthetic production today has become integrated into commodity production generally: the frantic economic urgency of producing fresh waves of ever more novel-seeming goods (from clothing to airplanes), at ever greater rates of turnover, now assigns an increasingly essential structural function and position to aesthetic innovation and experimentation" (*Postmodernism* 4). Thus seen, one can hypothesize that this structurally determined incentive to innovation and productivity has very likely exerted an influence upon postmodernism's valuation of differences, particularities and identities, insofar as that tendency is analogous to any advertiser's overvaluing of their product's pseudo-uniqueness—although that does not in itself discard the (occasional) emergence of genuine difference and novelty. Structurally speaking, then, the post-war emergence and consolidation of a *culture industry*—a term that I here favor over "mass culture" or "popular culture" in order to emphasize culture's status as a commodity—is also the most likely cause of another commonly observed characteristic of the postmodern epoch.[39] Specifically, I refer to the "effacement of the older distinction on which modernism depended for its specificity, [...] the securing of a realm of authentic experience over against the surrounding environment of middle- and low-brow commercial culture" (*Postmodernism* 63).[40]

39 In this regard, I am following Theodor Adorno's own observation in "Culture Industry Reconsidered" that, in his and Horkheimer's earlier *Dialectic of Enlightenment*, they first "spoke of 'mass culture' [but then] replaced that expression with 'culture industry' in order to exclude from the outset the interpretation agreeable to its advocates: that it is a matter of something like a culture that arises spontaneously from the masses themselves" ("Culture Industry Reconsidered" 12). Besides, regarding the use "popular culture," I would agree with Jameson's related proposition that it is "essential to distinguish between the emergent forms of a new commercial culture—beginning with advertisements and spreading on to formal packaging of all kinds, from products to buildings, and not excluding artistic commodities such as televisions shows (the 'logo') and best-sellers and films—from the older kinds of folk and genuinely 'popular' culture when the older social classes of a peasantry and an urban artisanat still existed and which, from the mid-nineteenth century on, has gradually been colonized and extinguished by commodification and the market system" (*Postmodernism* 63). Even if there is now a greater degree of consumer feedback and semi-autonomous participation in the culture industry, as scholars like Henry Jenkins have shown, this does not change the fact that it is still a culture mediated by an industry's productions or platforms. It is, however, beyond my scope to engage in the polemics surrounding popular culture studies, now an established field and it is absolutely not my intention to imply that all scholars in the field are insensitive to the commodifying forces of contemporary culture (see Storey, for instance).

40 Of course, this is not to say that there was a total opposition between modernist "high" culture and commercial "low" culture; rather, theirs was more like a dialectical relationship, one with bi-directional influences. Thinking about classical Hollywood, for instance, one should entertain the hypothesis that the culture

Commodification thus significantly explains both the proliferation of cultural differences and the levelling of cultural hierarchies.

But what does commodification entail beyond this heterogeneity and de-hierarchization? Reviewing Adorno and Horkheimer's landmark critique of the culture industry, Jameson helpfully schematizes the broader effects of commodification as follows:

> In a world in which everything, including labor power, has become a commodity, ends remain no less undifferentiated than in the production schema—they are all rigorously quantified, and have become abstractly comparable through the medium of money, their respective price or wage—yet we can now phrase their instrumentalization, their reorganization along the means/ends split, in a new way by saying that by its transformation into a commodity a thing, of whatever type, has been reduced to a means for its own consumption. [Thus] the various forms of activity lose their immanent intrinsic satisfactions as activity and become means to an end. ("Reification and Utopia in Mass Culture" 131)

In this sense, it seems at the very least ironic that in an age where, as Lyotard put it, emphasis shifts from ends to means, commodification makes everything oriented towards a single end, a teleology that remains unsaid because of its universality: market valorization, the realization of exchange-value over and above any use-value. Along this line of thought, Jameson then focuses his attention on commodified art and culture:

> The force of the Adorno-Horkheimer analysis of the culture industry [...] lies in its demonstration of the unexpected and imperceptible introduction of commodity structure into the very form and content of the work of art itself. Yet this is something like the ultimate squaring of the circle, the triumph of instrumentalization over that "finality without an end" which is art itself, the steady conquest and colonization of the ultimate realm of non-practicality, of sheer play and anti-use, by the logic of the world of means and ends. ("Reification and Utopia in Mass Culture" 132)

The consequences of this process are thus squarely anti-utopian: it would seem that, under commodifying pressures, culture is always a means to an end—its own circulation as a commodity. In this sense, culture is

---

industry's productions perhaps were not the "vulgar" antagonist of modernism, but rather a kind of "vernacular modernism" (see Hansen).

necessarily semi-autonomous with regard to capital. Even if the cultural object in question were an artwork (a novel or a film or a videogame, say) with strong subversive connotations, postmodern culture cannot pretend to be autonomous like the high modernisms once did—or rather, like theorists such as Adorno prescribed (see *Aesthetic Theory*). In fact, so-called high-culture, where it remains today, has been definitively "rebranded" as a luxury commodity, as a piece of "cultural capital" to be exploited by corporations (see Wu).

Nevertheless, the culture industry's seemingly endless expansion *does not necessarily subordinate* postmodern culture to the commodity's logic: above all it makes it *always semi-autonomous*, dialectically inseparable from market compulsions. Commodified culture retains the potential of functioning differently, in parallel or in excess of dominant logics. In this sense, it is not only postmodern epistemology and politics that can be self-defeating, the capitalist culture industry can also be self-defeating. As anti-capitalist documentary filmmaker Michael Moore puts it in an interview for the documentary *The Corporation* (2003),

> You know I've always thought it's very ironic that I'm able to do all this and yet what am I on? I'm on networks. I'm distributed by studios that are owned by large corporate entities. Now why would they put me out there when I am opposed to everything that they stand for? And I spend my time on their dime opposing what they believe in, okay? Well, it's because they don't believe in anything.
>
> They put me on there because they know that there's millions of people that want to see my film or watch the TV show, and so they're going to make money. And I've been able to get my stuff out there because I'm driving my truck through this incredible flaw in capitalism: the greed flaw. The thing that says the rich man will sell you the rope to hang himself with if he thinks he can make a buck off it? Well, I'm the rope. I hope. I'm part of the rope.
>
> And [the rich] also believe that when people watch my stuff, or maybe watch this film, or whatever, they think that [...] [people]'ll watch this and they won't do anything because we've done such a good job of numbing their minds and dumbing them down [...] People aren't going to leave the couch and go and do something political. They're convinced of that.

I'm convinced of the opposite. I'm convinced that a few people are going to leave this movie theatre or get up off the couch and go and do something, anything, to get this world back in our hands. (Achbar and Abbot 2h20'22"-21'44")

Cases of overtly anti-capitalist culture notwithstanding, it still seems that, generally, within a postmodern world of commodified culture, depoliticization and fragmentation are built-in tendencies, as even subversive and oppositional cultures can be thrown into the furnaces of commodification. But this is perhaps a dangerously anti-utopian conclusion, just like Mark Fisher's hypothesis of capitalist realism, which can lead one into fatalism or cynicism when interpreted non-dialectically.

On the whole, therefore, understood as part of a dystopian structure of feeling, postmodernism should not be defined as a monolithic movement or moment, but rather as a cultural climate that is rife with contradictions between anti-utopian and utopian impulses. Of these, I have highlighted two main dialectical contradictions: an unresolved tension between the negation of grand narratives and their underground persistence and another unresolved tension between the expanse of commodifying sameness and a flourishing of cultural differences. Thus, whether or not one is comfortable with the term, this epoch is still postmodern for at least two reasons: because (1) it is haunted by the void left by the grand narratives of the past, which still need to find an (as of yet) hard-to-imagine alternative, and because (2) its culture still struggles with the commodifying pressures exerted by an ever-mightier culture industry—now not just an industry, but an all-encompassing society of the spectacle that could even be an entirely new mode of production, as McKenzie Wark argues.[41] Of course, none of these tendencies make sense in isolation, as postmodernism emerges within

---

41   Debord's "society of the spectacle" is a step forward in conceptualizing the more pervasive reach of the culture industry after the invention of television, given that Adorno and Horkheimer mostly aimed at classical Hollywood, but "society of the spectacle" may itself need updating for the digital age, as recent theorists acknowledge (see Briziarelli and Armano). Nonetheless, this is not to say that neither of the concepts have lost validity and their proponents offered revisions (Adorno, "Culture Industry Reconsidered"; Debord, *Comments on the Society of the Spectacle*). The idea that this expansion may amount to a qualitatively new mode of production, Wark's hypothesis, is explored at the end of this chapter.

a larger, dynamic totality, so we now turn to another periodizing concept, postmodernism's necessary sibling in political economy: neoliberalism.

1.2.2. Neoliberalism

Following a roughly parallel timeline to that of postmodernism, neoliberalism begins to emerge as an intellectual doctrine in the post-war years, but it does not become hegemonic until the 1980s, beginning with Ronald Reagan's US presidency and Margaret Thatcher's UK premiership—although one should not forget that, before arriving to liberal democracies, neoliberal policies were first "tested" by Augusto Pinochet's criminal Chilean dictatorship (see Harvey, *A Brief History of Neoliberalism*; as well as Klein). Although most often associated with the beliefs of economists like Friedrich Hayek and Milton Friedman, neoliberalism is, by one definition, the political philosophy of a global, interdisciplinary group of thinkers who were loosely organized around the Mont Pèlerin Society, one private think-tank founded in 1947 in Switzerland, which is still active today. The Society's statement of aims reads as follows:

> The central values of civilization are in danger... The group holds that these developments have been fostered by the growth of a view of history which denies all absolute moral standards and by the growth of theories which question the desirability of the rule of law. It holds further that they have been fostered by a decline of belief in private property and the competitive market; for without the diffused power and initiative associated with these institutions it is difficult to imagine a society in which freedom may be effectively preserved. (Hartwell 41–2)

Beyond the Cold-War-apocalyptic and anti-communist undertones of this declaration, one can easily discern the ideological coordinates of this group. Plainly, this is a staunch defense of the capitalist "free" market, presenting it (utopianly) as a decentralized (with "diffused power") and dynamic (with "initiative") system that safeguards "freedom"—and in this sense, it is no surprise that neoliberalism has been called the epoch of "capital resurgent" (see Duménil and Lévy).

Neoliberalism's main tenets, as synthesized by Philip Mirowski based on the Mont Pèlerin Society's history, are

- (a) that "'the market' is an information processor more powerful than any human brain," a kind of efficient super-computer that "always surpasses the state's ability to process information;"
- (b) that "market society must be treated as a 'natural' and inexorable state of humankind," an idea often conveyed by pseudo-scientific evolutionary and genetic metaphors;
- (c) that one must "redefine the shape and functions of the state," thus favoring "formats of techno-managerial governance that protect ideal market from what they perceive as unwarranted political interference" and, in turn, also "treating politics as if it were a market;"
- (d) that "freedom" must be seen "as trumping all other virtues," but crucially, this is exclusively understood as "negative" freedom;[42]
- (e) that "capital has a natural right to flow freely across national boundaries," while "the free flow of labor enjoys no similar right;"
- (f) that "pronounced inequality" is not "an unfortunate by-product of capitalism," but rather a "necessary functional characteristic of [the] ideal market system;"
- (g) that "[c]orporations can do no wrong, or at least they are not to be blamed if they do," even in the case of monopolistic concentrations of power (like Big Tech's), which are (contra classical liberalism) not to be demonized nor prosecuted;
- (h) that "[t]he market (suitably reengineered and promoted) can always provide solutions to problems seemingly caused by the market in the first place," precisely because it is deemed the most efficient information processor (Mirowski 434–40).

---

42   As defined in "Two Concepts of Liberty," positive freedom would be that kind of *freedom that is enabled by* rights or resources to which one has access, while negative freedom would be primarily *freedom from* interference by other actors (see Berlin).

In these tenets, we can see that neoliberalism as an ideology revolves around utopian conceptions of the free market that deem it the most efficient social mechanism—simultaneously envisioning the market as an artificially created, complex computing system, while also naturalizing it as a biologically determined formation. Following these ideas, neoliberalism in practice entails a series of policies by now well known to most populations globally: market deregulation (meaning less restrictions to the global financial flows of capital, at the expense of local labor rights), the privatization of public services (meaning the de-nationalization of once publicly owned companies) and a reduced and less progressive income taxation (meaning less taxes, but especially and disproportionately for corporations and for the most affluent).

These policies are often challenged, but they still largely set most political agendas and their consequences are also well known to most populations globally. Primarily, neoliberal policy has caused a widening income gap between (both global and local) rich and poor and—in countries with something like a welfare state—it has also caused a decline in the quantity and the quality of public benefits and services due to so-called austerity measures (a neoliberal euphemism for budget cuts, privatization and/or outsourcing of services).[43] Thus, in this epoch what is being commodified *en masse* is not only culture, but also a growing number of public services that were once considered to be (at least on paper) *human rights*. As Marx once said of commodification, "[n]othing is immune from this alchemy, the bones of the saints cannot withstand it, let alone more delicate *res sacrosanctae, extra commercium hominum*" (*Capital Volume I* 229). Indeed, for neoliberalism, nothing is sacred enough as to be exempt from commodification.

One question arises automatically: how is it conceivable that suchlike policies, which plainly only benefit a miniscule elite, have become the by-default playbook for politicians across the spectrum? How is it possible that neoliberal politics are still, by and large, "the new way of the world"

---

43   For a comprehensive, *longue-durée* and statistically documented analysis of the inequalities entailed by neoliberal policies, see Thomas Piketty's bestselling *Capital in the Twenty-First Century*.

(see Dardot and Laval), even though (ironically) neoliberalism has been proclaimed dead in numberless crises (see Plehwe et al.), most notably during the 2010s Great Recession?[44] One answer to this question is that neoliberal policies have often been imposed technocratically—as "structural adjustment programmes" by institutions like the IMF, the WTO or the ECB—and by military force in the case of Western-backed "regime changes" across the Global South—as in the above-mentioned case of Chile, or in the case of US-backed Iraqi regimes. It is thus clear that neoliberalism, in theory and in practice, is nothing less than a project aimed for the global "restoration of class power" (Harvey, "Neoliberalism as Creative Destruction" 29), which is stealthily undermining democratic institutions (see W. Brown, *Undoing the Demos*; *In the Ruins of Neoliberalism*) and resulting in the collapse of redistributive, egalitarian policies on both sides of the old Cold War, "gradually in the West" and "[e]xplosively in the East" (Kaldor 26). Of course, in the 2010s, grassroots movements such as the Spanish 15-M movement, or Occupy Wall Street in the US—as well as certain "left-wing populisms" later in the decade—have contributed to popularizing crucial criticisms against neoliberal policies and there is, moreover, a whole "world literature" of resistance against the neoliberal order (see Deckard and Shapiro), but, by and large, such policies are still being implemented around the globe.[45]

---

44 During this crisis, even the British magazine *The Economist*, a worldwide reference for (neo)liberal thinking since the nineteenth century, took a moderately critical stand against neoliberal policies, as observed in Alexander Zevin's history of the magazine. Although previous crises such as the dotcom bubble and IMF interventions in the global south were dismissed as "small bumps on the road to globalized capitalism" (345), after 2008 "the Economist—hurricanes, cliffs, ruins, free-falling globes on the cover—suddenly declared it 'time to put dogma and politics to one side and concentrate on pragmatic answer.' There was no such thing as laissez-faire in a foxhole, for 'when global finance stops only governments can start it again'" (360).

45 On the matter of populist opposition to neoliberalism, one could mention the rise of "left populist" parties in Southern Europe such as Podemos or Syriza, as well as the rise in power and popularity of leftist leaders such as Jeremy Corbyn in the UK or Bernie Sanders in the US, among others (see Mouffe; Damiani; Tamames).

To better grasp this situation, one must examine neoliberalism not only as a political-economic praxis of a small elite, but also as a covertly totalizing philosophy, one that has become, in many regards, *a common sense* that feeds into our dystopian structure of feeling.[46] Some of the above-listed tenets of neoliberalism have implications beyond the realm of policy, suggesting a grander worldview that naturalizes (and idealizes) the workings of capitalism and, in this sense, Fisher's "capitalist realism" may be seen as a conceptual supplement to neoliberal hegemony, as he himself acknowledged (see Fisher and Gilbert). So how does this common sense operate? Given the discredit of grand narratives, neoliberalism seems to operate in a symbiosis with the broader climate of anti-utopian hopelessness and depoliticization. Based on Friedrich Hayek's radical epistemology, which considers the whole of society unknowable (except, of course, for the market) and thus renders all individual perspectives equal (and equally impotent), neoliberalism can easily appeal both to radical individualism and to anti-totalizing sentiments. Therefore,

> neoliberalism masquerades as a radically populist philosophy, which begins with a set of philosophical theses about knowledge and its relationship to society. It seems to be a radical leveling philosophy, denigrating expertise and elite pretensions to hard-won knowledge, instead praising the "wisdom of crowds." It appeals to the vanity of every self-absorbed narcissist, who would be glad to ridicule intellectuals as "professional secondhand dealers in ideas." In Hayekian language, it elevates a "cosmos"—a supposed spontaneous order that no one has intentionally designed or structured—over a "taxis"—rationally constructed orders designed to achieve intentional ends. But the second, and linked lesson, is that neoliberals are simultaneously elitists: they do not in fact practice what they preach. When it comes to actually organizing something, almost anything, from a Wiki to the Mont Pèlerin Society, suddenly the cosmos collapses to a taxis. (Mirowski 425-6)

---

46 Of course, there could be many other ways to approach neoliberalism: "as an aggregation of ideas, a discursive formation, an over-arching ideology, a governmental programme, the manifestation of a set of interests, a hegemonic project, an assemblage of techniques and technologies, and what Deleuze and Guattari call an 'abstract machine'" (Gilbert, "What Kind of Thing Is 'Neoliberalism'?" 8)

In this manner, the first thing to be avoided when examining neoliberalism's logic would be to take at face value its appeals to "individualism" and "freedom." Instead, one should remember that the neoliberal's clear goal is, ironically, to *construct* free markets—no longer conceiving of the market as a space of spontaneous relations between free actors (as Adam Smith's liberalism), but rather as something to be actively engineered, promoted and expanded. As Michel Foucault observed long ago, "Neoliberalism should not therefore be identified with laissez-faire, but rather with permanent vigilance, activity, and intervention" (Foucault 132). And in fact, one can go as far as to say, like Mark Fisher, that neoliberalism has brought a kind of "market Stalinism," given the blooming and bloating of bureaucracies—not just the states' but also the corporations', or a Kafkaesque mix of both (*Capitalist Realism* 39). Once again, then, in a rather Freudian twist, we find that the disavowal of grand narratives paves the way for a tragic return of the repressed.

Thus, neoliberalism has one grand narrative of progress that consists in the relentless expansion of the so-called free market. But what is its implicit conception of the totality and the individual? Wendy Brown proposes the concept of "neoliberal rationality" as a way of thinking about the spread of commodifying logics beyond the market as such.[47] What this implies is that, in parallel to the expanse of commodification *per se*, non-commodified spheres of life are also conceived according to market logics—thus installing what Mark Fisher calls a "business ontology" (*Capitalist Realism* 17). In Brown's words,

> neoliberalism transmogrifies every human domain and endeavor, along with humans themselves, according to a specific image of the economic. All conduct is economic conduct; all spheres of existence are framed and measured by economic terms and metrics, even when those spheres are not directly monetized. In neoliberal reason and in domains governed by it, we are only and everywhere *homo oeconomicus*, which itself has a historically specific form. Far from Adam Smith's creature propelled by the natural urge to "truck, barter, and exchange," today's *homo oeconomicus* is an

---

47 Brown's approach follows and expands upon Foucault's earlier analysis of neoliberalism as a common-sense and many others have taken similar approaches, in particular when conceptualizing the neoliberal refashioning of individual subjectivity as a *homo oeconomicus* (see Read; Layton; Fleming).

> intensely constructed and governed bit of human capital tasked with improving and leveraging its competitive positioning and with enhancing its (monetary and nonmonetary) portfolio value across all of its endeavors and venues. These are also the mandates, and hence the orientations, contouring the projects of neoliberalized states, large corporations, small businesses, nonprofits, schools, consultancies, museums, countries, scholars, performers, public agencies, students, websites, athletes, sports teams, graduate programs, health providers, banks, and global legal and financial institutions. (*Undoing the Demos* 10)

Here, Brown's core idea is that neoliberalism is not only remaking economies: it is also remaking "city and soul" in the image of the economy. Her two leading examples are, on the one hand, academia's prioritizing of quantifiable metrics, which remakes higher education into a competition for the production of so-called cognitive or human capital; and on the other hand, the state's prioritizing of economic growth, which re-frames non-commodified public services and justice as incentives to consumption and investment (*Undoing the Demos* 22–7). Thus, "neoliberal rationality disseminates the model of the market to all domains and activities, even where money is not at issue," because, very importantly, "economization may not always involve monetization" (*Undoing the Demos* 31)—something that is crucial in order to understand digital media's relationship with capital as well.

Nevertheless, it would be a mistake to assume that the subsumption of all spheres of life by neoliberal rationality was ever fully realized—that is, that the neoliberal's "utopia" was taken seriously and at face value by the majorities in all cases—or to assume that this hegemony was built merely upon mere conviction and/or deception. Writing at the end of the 2010s—the decade of the Great Recession—Annie McClanahan offers a corrective and a warning against wrongly imagining that these are "shifts driven primarily by a change in discourse." Instead, McClanahan argues that neoliberal rationality is primarily fueled by "the introduction of economic exigencies into the lives of people once shielded from them" (118). Given the rising poverty and spreading precarity of this epoch, which reached the so-called middle classes,

> Capitalism resolved, temporarily, the crisis in the reproduction of the working class via the provision of credit, offering us just enough debt—and, for those eligible

> for mortgages, just enough asset equity—to compensate for decades of wage stagnation. The maintenance of a population willing to take on increasing amounts of debt necessitated an ideology of investment and a conception of the subject as canny speculator. The decimation of the social safety net that attended a crisis of capitalist profitability, in turn, required an exculpatory discourse of personal responsibility as its political alibi. [...] Yet [these discourses] are not the cause of [neoliberal] economic processes. Nor are they as universal or as effective as critics claim. The vast majority of people living under capitalism struggle to keep their heads above water, and while the belief in the entrepreneurial self may briefly salve the pain of putting the cost of groceries on one's almost-maxed-out credit card, the urgent need for the food in the cart is probably more decisive. For these reasons, then, [...] we ought not to rest so easy on terms like human capital and entrepreneur. Better, I think, might be terms like *precarious, dispossessed, surplus, and wageless*. (McClanahan 123)

Thus, in light of this more materialist, class-based analysis, McClanahan concludes that "contrary to Gramscian accounts of 'common sense,' exclusion is still managed via coercive material violence more than ideology and mystification, which means that 'common sense' today may look something more like 'All cops are bastards' or 'Fuck debt' than like a deluded homo economicus" (McClanahan 124). The hegemony of neoliberalism is also to be defined by its possible and constant *negation*—by the possibility of resistance to its violent, neo-imperialist logics seeking to dispossess the majorities around the world (see Harvey, "The 'New' Imperialism: Accummulation by Dispossession"). As McClanahan argues, with collective political mobilization, it would only take a simple logical step to realize that "what unites us today is not the 'neoliberal' fantasy of entrepreneurial ambition and self-appreciation but the ever more common knowledge of that fantasy's historical end" (McClanahan 127).

At least for the purpose of analyzing contemporary culture, therefore, it is undoubtedly best to conceive of neoliberal hegemony dialectically: as much defined by its totalizing rationality as by resistance against it; as much by its economic euphemisms as by the people's mockery of them; as much by its discourse of efficiency as by its realities of exclusion, exploitation and extraction; as much by its praise of individual freedom as by its spread of precarity; as much by the discourses of pioneering entrepreneurship as by the proliferation of "bullshit jobs" (see Graeber). Moreover, however complex neoliberal discourse may seem, which to a great extent it is, one also needs to keep in mind that public and private institutions today, with their technocratic conception of governance, have often excused their abuses by overemphasizing the complexities of an ever abstracter financial market, as in 2008. In these cases, the neoliberal "appeal to complexity displaces accountability" (Dean, "Complexity as Capture" 148)—that is, because reality as a whole is unknowable in Hayekian epistemology and only the market may approach total knowledge, there are no individuals or institutions to be held accountable. In this sense, one should add one final dialectic of neoliberalism: that it is as much defined by its real complexity as by its false complexity; as much by its pretense of sophistication as by the shameless simplicity of its apologies.

Overall, then, just like postmodernism—or like any other cultural hegemony and social formation—the neoliberal order too contains the seeds of its own undoing. Like Marx and Engels once said of capitalism itself, the neoliberal order is in many ways "like the sorcerer who is no longer able to control the powers of the nether world whom he has called up by his spells." Thus, if we are to truly grasp these phenomena as part of an undoubtedly bleak, *but still ambivalent* dystopian structure of feeling, it is necessary to grasp their dynamics dialectically. That is, one must understand the contrasts established between the epoch's anti-utopian imposition of increasing commodification by all means possible and the epoch's utopian valuation of individual freedom and difference—as well as the contrasts between anti-utopian denials of any alternatives to capitalism and the remaining utopian longings for their realization. Of course, this is not to say that the "ideological" side of these contradictions is a mere lie to be "unveiled," but rather to propose that both neoliberalism and postmodernism are not only "conceptual abstractions" but above all "real abstractions" (see Soren-Rethel 160–7)—that is, they are both disembodied phantoms, haunted by contradictory impulses, *but they have palpable material consequences*. None of these are inconsequential "lies," they are "fantasies structuring reality," as Žižek would put it: they are embedded and entwined within the system's dynamics, so "lifting the veil of ideology" is never enough. Besides, as I have been suggesting, neoliberalism and postmodernism are primarily mediated by their belonging to an epoch of expanded commodification and it is this distinctively capitalist phenomenon that in the last instance explains their interrelated contradictions—but their contradictions, as I have also suggested, are also becoming the target of growing resistance and opposition, even if for the time being we remain in a global neoliberal order.[48]

Or maybe not. Maybe the global neoliberal order is already morphing into something else. Maybe this dominant social formation is being subsumed (or has already been subsumed) by an emergent order—by something worse, as McKenzie Wark suggests. Perhaps, the neoliberal understanding of the market as a computer network is now more than just a metaphor and is literally true. And maybe, both postmodern epistemology and neoliberal ideology have only paved the way for the much more radical individualism that looms over digital culture. For an answer, my attention turns now to new media technologies, considering the extent to which they correlate with the dynamics of both postmodernism and neoliberalism—as well as more broadly, with the dynamics of commodification. Do these technologies make our dystopian structure of feeling even more dystopian? That is the question now.

1.3. Understanding New Media: The Extensions of Capital

> Hiding greyly behind that sexy rock star, technology, is a much more sinister and powerful figure. It is the entire social system that surrounds us; hence the sense of

---

[48] Besides the evident existential risk posed by the climate crisis, it is also likely that capitalism may collapse by its own internal contradictions. This has been the argument of a group of leading historians and economists: asking whether or not capitalism has a future, Immanuel Wallerstein, Randall Collins, Michael Mann, Georgi Derluguian and Craig Calhoun together wrote in 2013 that "something big looms on the horizon: a structural crisis much bigger than the recent Great Recession, which might in retrospect seem only a prologue to a period of deeper troubles and transformations" (1–2). Furthermore, along similar lines, the economist Wolfgang Streeck gives capitalism "a diagnosis of multi-morbidity in which different disorders coexist and, more often than not, reinforce each other" (*How Will Capitalism End?* 13) and, more specifically, he names five major systemic disorders that threaten its future: "stagnation, oligarchic redistribution, the plundering of the public domain, corruption and global anarchy" (*How Will Capitalism End?* 28).

> being at the mercy of an all-encompassing, autonomous process which we cannot control. If you add the monster's location in time (during and after the Industrial Revolution) I think you can see what is being discussed when most people say 'technology.' They are politically mystifying a much bigger monster: Capitalism in its advanced, industrial phase. (Russ 256)

Neoliberal capitalism and postmodern culture cannot be fully understood without also grappling with the media technologies that both enabled and were enabled by their dynamics. And, relatedly, one cannot fully understand the expansion of commodification that characterizes this epoch without also grappling with the media technologies that enabled and were enabled by such expansion. David Harvey—following Karl Marx's observation of "the annihilation of space by time" (*Grundrisse* 524)—has repeatedly emphasized the role of new technologies in enabling the "time-space compression" that has enabled and driven the emergence of a global market (*A Brief History of Neoliberalism* 4), observing how these decades' developments have contributed to an "accelerating turnover time in production [that] entails parallel accelerations in exchange and consumption" (*The Condition of Postmodernity* 285). This commodified acceleration of both cultural and economic life, however, does not entail an acceleration of any kind of historical "progress," especially not in this epoch in which the only utopian horizon imaginable is the neoliberal expansion of markets, with their nefarious social and environmental consequences. On the contrary, the time-space compression enabled by media technologies should be seen as another crucial contribution to what Fredric Jameson described as "the reduction to the present in postmodernity" ("The End of Temporality" 709) and Guy Debord as the "eternal present" of the "integrated spectacle" (*Comments on the Society of the Spectacle* 9–12).

Furthermore, the spread of media technologies is also crucial to understanding the very shift *from ends to means* that was described by Jean-François Lyotard (37), which may be now better understood as a shift from political deliberation to technical expertise—as well as, in many places, as a gradual, stealthy shift from social democracy to neoliberal technocracy. Besides, in contributing to such an epochal shift, it has been proven again and again that new media technologies have generally contributed to disguise and to deepen pre-existing injustices and inequalities.[49] Nonetheless, even though new media clearly contribute to reifying postmodern and neoliberal dynamics, one should avoid "the sense of being the mercy of an all-encompassing, autonomous process which we cannot control," as Joanna Russ warns us. Thus, I here rewrite Marshall McLuhan's famous motto of considering networked media as "extensions of man"—that is, as somewhat neutrally supplementing "human nature" by extending "our central nervous system itself in a global embrace, abolishing time and space as far as our planet is concerned" ("Introduction to the First Edition" n.p.). Instead, the goal in this section is to consider new media as extensions *of capital*.[50] Of course, they are *never only that*: but at the same time, they are *always that*: computational tools of control and commodification.

49 In this regard, there is a growing literature that critically examines contemporary technologies (so-called new media and, particularly, algorithms) as tools of intersectional exploitation and oppression (see Vaidhyanathan; Crary, *24/7: Late Capitalism and the Ends of Sleep*; Fuchs and Mosco; Browne; O'Neil; Eubanks; Apprich et al.), as tools of intensified resource extraction (see Parikka, *A Geology of Media*; Moore; Taffel; Crary, *Scorched Earth*) and as tools that undermine rights, most notably free speech (see Suzor; York).

50 Using the mercilessly polemical style that is so characteristic of him, the theorist of the spectacle Guy Debord once denounced the naïveté of MacLuhan's formulations, calling him

> the spectacle's first apologist, who had seemed to be the most convinced imbecile of the century, changed his mind when he finally discovered in 1976 that 'the pressure of the mass media leads to irrationality,' and that it was becoming urgent to modify their usage. The sage of Toronto had formerly spent several decades marvelling at the numerous freedoms created by a 'global village' instantly and effortlessly accessible to all. Villages, unlike towns, have always been ruled by conformism, isolation, petty surveillance, boredom and repetitive malicious gossip about the same families. Which is a precise enough description of the global spectacle's present vulgarity, in which it has become impossible to distinguish the Grimaldi-Monaco or Bourbon-Franco dynasties from those who succeeded the Stuarts. However, MacLuhan's ungrateful modern disciples are now trying to make people forget him, hoping to establish their own careers in media celebration of all these new freedoms to 'choose' at random from ephemera. And no doubt they will retract their claims even faster than the man who inspired them. (*Comments on the Society of the Spectacle* 33–4)

1.3.1. The Concepts of Technology and New Media

First, we must ask: how exactly it is that the concept of technology is (or can easily be), in Russ's words, "politically mystifying a much bigger monster"? In order to be careful with the notion of "new media," it is first necessary to unpack the ambivalences of the broader, umbrella term of technology. In this regard, the cultural historian Leo Marx provides a historical and ideological overview of the relatively recent (in a timespan of centuries) term "technology," a word that only began acquiring its contemporary meaning around the turn of the nineteenth-to-twentieth centuries and "did not gain truly wide currency until after World War I, and perhaps not until the Great Depression" ("The Idea of 'Technology'" 248).[51] In the time of the Enlightenment and the early industrial revolution, what was then known as the "mechanic arts" were commonly seen as a practice *subordinated* to scientific and political progress, as well as (perhaps shockingly to us now) subordinated to the fine arts—a hierarchy of values that is nonetheless easy to grasp insofar as it mirrors the ideological overvaluation of intellectual over manual labor. The mechanic arts of that time, inherently associated with discrete tools and machines, thus had a "belittling" connotation when "compared to the tacit uniqueness and unity" and "the more abstract, cerebral [and] neutral" qualities of the word technology as we understand it today (L. Marx, "The Idea of 'Technology'" 242).

Gradually, with the arrival of inventions that were not strictly mechanic (electrical and chemical, for instance) and the construction of large-scale systems such as the railroad, the telegraph, the electrical lines, or the Taylorist factories, the more abstract, systemic and totalizing conception of technology that is dominant today could and would begin to replace older ideas and imageries.[52] Delving into this shift, Leo Marx explains that

---

51   Of course, the term has a pre-history before acquiring its contemporary meaning: it "had been available since the seventeenth century" but "it had referred specifically and almost exclusively to technical discourses or treatises" and "it was seldom used before 1880" (L. Marx, "The Idea of 'Technology'" 247)

52   The gradual nature of this terminological and ideological change can be seen in the fact that, despite being clearly concerned with "technological matters," Karl Marx never used the term. In this regard, Leo Marx observes that "though he described

> the crucial difference is that the concept of "technology," with its wider scope of reference, is less closely identified with—or defined by—its material or artifactual aspect than was "the mechanic arts." This fact comports with the material reality of the large and complex new technological systems, in which the boundary between the intricately interlinked artifactual and other components—conceptual, institutional, human—is blurred and often invisible. [...] By virtue of its abstractness and inclusiveness, and its capacity to evoke the inextricable interpenetration of (for example) the powers of the computer with the bureaucratic practices of large modern institutions, "technology" (with no specifying adjective) invites endless reification. The concept refers to no specifiable institution, nor does it evoke any distinct associations of place or of persons belonging to any particular nation, ethnic group, race, class, or gender. A common tendency of contemporary discourse, accordingly, is to invest "technology" with a host of metaphysical properties and potencies, thereby making it seem to be a determinate entity, a disembodied autonomous causal agent of social change—of history. Hence the illusion that technology drives history. ("The Idea of 'Technology'" 249)

In this manner, a tendency towards technological determinism is inevitably embedded in the very notion of technology, which is mystifying for its abstractedness and thus "invites endless reification."[53] This is not a mere conceptual clarification, as it has broader implications for a time in which technology and media are virtually everywhere.[54] Nowadays, it even seems that ideologies of technology function as a contemporary pseudo-religion—and more specifically, as a US-nationalist "American theology" (see Dinerstein) with its own prophets (see Aschoff, *The New Prophets of Capital*). In any case, the concept of technology is both sign and symptom of a grander, gradual series of changes in dominant ideologies:

> industrial machinery as embedded in the social relations and the economic organization of an economy dominated by the flow of capital, he still relied, as late as the first (1867) edition of *Capital*, on 'machinery,' 'factory mechanism,' and other relics of the old mechanistic lexicon" ("The Idea of 'Technology'" 244)

53   In a broader sense, Timothy Bewes's work argues that the anxieties triggered by reification "have become virtually universal in advanced capitalist societies" (xii).

54   Indeed, in the present epoch, "many remain attached to the fallacious image of the internet as a free-standing technological assemblage [...], and the prevalence of hand-held devices amplifies this illusion" (Crary, *Scorched Earth* 5).

> the advent of the concept of technology, and of the organization of complex technological systems, coincided with, and no doubt contributed to, a subtle revision of the ideology of progress. [...] the simple [Enlightened] republican formula for generating progress by directing improved technical means to societal ends was imperceptibly transformed into a quite different technocratic commitment to improving "technology" as the basis and the measure of—as all but constituting—the progress of society. This technocratic idea may be seen as an ultimate, culminating expression of the optimistic, universalist aspirations of Enlightenment rationalism. But it tacitly replaced political aspirations with technical innovation as a primary agent of change, thereby preparing the way for an increasingly pessimistic sense of the technological determination of history. ("The Idea of 'Technology'" 250–1)

Thus, in parallel to the postmodern discrediting of utopian master narratives of progress, the contemporary conceptualization of technology also reinforced contemporary hopelessness, further displacing the political in favor of the technical and fostering an imaginary in which there seems to be no room for agency in the face of technology.[55] This reified understanding of technology, together with historical traumas with specific inventions such as the nuclear bomb and other military "wonders," thus fostered what Leo Marx calls "postmodern technological pessimism," which is "a fatalistic pessimism, an ambivalent tribute to the determinative power of technology" as opposed to an "inevitably diminished sense of human agency" ("The Idea of 'Technology'" 257).

This was Leo Marx's diagnosis in 1994 and his work clearly synthesized the role of technology in postmodern epistemology as well as, indirectly, in the neoliberal re-imagination of the market as the most powerful networked technology. Today, a strikingly similar diagnosis could be made and the migration of corporate and state power from politics to technology partly explains the resilience of neoliberalism's global hegemony, despite

---

55 As Herbert Marcuse denounced in the 1960s, "technology [...] provides the great rationalization of the unfreedom of man and demonstrates the 'technical' impossibility of being autonomous, of determining one's own life. For this unfreedom appears neither as irrational nor as political, but rather as submission to the technical apparatus which enlarges the comforts of life and increases the productivity of labor" (*One-Dimensional Man* 164).

mounting challenges.[56] Nonetheless, the story is, again, not so simple, for in between the early 1990s of Marx's essay and the late 2010s of the so-called "techlash" (the backlash against tech), there existed something else called cyber-utopianism. In this sense, the arrival of new technologies has been accompanied by their own, semi-autonomous cultural dynamics—what Colin Milburn aptly calls "technogenic culture," which is not entirely explicable through postmodern or neoliberal frameworks. But before these issues, there is another more pressing question: what are new media and how can one define them?

There are, evidently, several similarities with the concept of technology. "New media" is just another real abstraction, a conceptual shorthand for a complex system that is inseparably intertwined with the broader social order wherefrom it emerges and, as such, it is another term that invites endless reification and mystification. Just like technology, talk of new media is significantly flexible, especially as the "new" element of the phrase is profoundly relative and potentially misleading. For the purposes of this book, I am generally equating new media with *networked, digital devices* such as the smartphone, thus drawing a line that would exclude any "new medium" before them.[57] However, new media cannot be exemplified by one device, which might have led to attempts at, instead of defining, listing

56   What I here call "the migration of power from politics to technology" may just be another aspect of the transition from "disciplinary societies" to "control societies" observed by Gilles Deleuze in the 1990s, enabled by technologies like computer networks that allow "ultrarapid forms of free-floating control that replaced the old disciplines operating in the time frame of a close system" (4). In a way that anticipates recent talk of algorithms, Deleuze claims that power operates by "modulation, like a self-deforming cast that will continuously change from one moment to the other" (4). For more elaborate explorations of the logics of contemporary "control," see Galloway's *Protocol*, Chun's *Control and Freedom*, or Franklin's *Digitality*.

57   Other "older" media often listed as pivotal to the emergence of what we now understand as new media include the telegraph, the radio and perhaps the most important of them: the television (see S. C. Murphy). More recently, other examples of new media obviously include videogame consoles, virtual- or augmented-reality technologies, social media platforms and digital media more generally, with the internet or "the digital" thus standing as the underlying infrastructure of all of them (see Creeber and Martin; Flew and Smith).

new media exhaustively (Creeber and Martin 170–8). Thus, for reasons of my focus on dystopias that offer a totalizing view of societies with diverse science-fictional devices, I here conceptualize new media not through any specific technology or list of technologies, but as *the ever-changing totality of networked, digital devices*. Of course, writing in the early 2020s it seems that, of all media, this is now "the smartphone society" (see Aschoff, *The Smartphone Society*), but this situation may not last, as even Big Tech and *The Economist* begin to recognize ("After the Smartphone: Silicon Valley's Search for the next Big Tech Platform"). Tying our theorization to a specific, fleeting device would tend to obscure the structural and epochal dynamics that underlie it and, therefore, smartphones (or any other specific devices) are but the paradigmatic example of a larger complex of digital devices that Jonathan Crary theorizes as "the internet complex" of "24/7 capitalism" (see *24/7*; *Scorched Earth*) or Benjamin Bratton as "the stack." It is thus not trivial to remember that "New media are always changing. They are, by their very nature, fluid in ways that traditional media—tied to a technological form—are not. As such, new media are difficult to define if we confine our view to the physical tools that produce them" (Flew and Smith 270). But define them we must.

Benjamin Bratton's model of a "planetary-scale infrastructure" (xvii) is profoundly clarifying in this regard, insofar as it offers a view of the totality of new media in their global interconnectedness, inseparable from the physical infrastructures that sustain them and the digital platforms that unite them. In Bratton's words, this "model does not put technology 'inside' a 'society,' but sees a technological totality as the armature of the social itself." Thus, Bratton proposes to think of "an accidental megastructure called The Stack," a concept that "is informed by the multilayered structure of software protocol stacks in which network technologies operate within a modular and interdependent vertical order" (xviii). From this perspective, Bratton theorizes six layers for this (emergent and fractured) global stack, which are synthesized elsewhere by McKenzie Wark (*Sensoria* 175–92):

(a) The *earth layer*, which refers to the mass resource extraction and energy consumption required for the whole. As the model's science-fictional language puts it, "the stack is a hungry machine" and it "terraforms the earth [...] according to a seemingly logical but haphazard geodesign" that, as per Wark's sources, makes it "the fifth largest energy suck on the planet" and rising higher up the ranking (188–9).

(b) The *cloud layer*, which is the geopolitical or "governing nexus" of any stack—whether primarily corporate (i.e. Google) or statal (i.e. China). The cloud is thus what "produces and polices" the flows of information and thus operates by "extracting rent or profit" on the basis of "asymmetries of information" (185–7).

(c) The *city layer*, which is "the old-fashioned topography" of the polis, but now "absorbed into the stack" and turned into "a platform for sorting users in transit." As Wark aptly puts it, it is the layer where "cement meets computation" and "architecture becomes interface design" (184).

(d) The *address layer*, which is the layer where information of any kind is stored, coded and interconnected as abstract, quantifiable data and, thus, this is also the place for "endless metadata: about objects, then metadata about the metadata about those objects, and so on" (183).

(e) The *interface layer*, which "mediates between users and the technical layers" just sketched. "The interface connects and disconnects, telescopes, compresses, or expands layers, routing used actions through columns that burrow up and down through the stack," as is it the layer that "turns tech into images and images into tech" (181).

(f) The *user layer*, finally, which "is not where the rest of layers are mastered by some sovereign consciousness, it is merely where their effects are coherently personified" in a "stylized persona" that is not even necessarily human (179).

Of course, Bratton's multi-layered model of the stack is self-consciously "speculative and projective as well as analytical" and it even refers to itself as "science fiction" (Bratton xvii–xix). Thus, if we take his suggestion seriously, Bratton's *The Stack* can be seen as a theoretical new media dystopia: a speculative, estranged representation of the present's media-technological structures.[58] And, of course, I do not say this to disqualify the model. On the contrary, Bratton gives us a versatile theory in which ecology, economy, society and psychology are all inseparably intertwined by the mediation of new media; a model of the present (and of present perceptions of the future) in which media are not imagined as mere neutral tools, but rather as part of an emergent technological order that is inseparable from global history and geography.[59] This model, evidently, has implications well beyond the scope of this book and it shows the limits of my engagement with new media, as I am mostly concerned with the layers that are most visible in my corpus of new media dystopias—the interface and user layers, primarily. However, it is still helpful to take Bratton's model as a reminder of the potential profundities of any study of new media and, most importantly, the stack is essential to my understanding of *new media as the historical counterpart of our sub-genre's nova*.

But what does it mean in SF theory to talk about the *novum*? In Darko Suvin's life-long theorization of the genre, beginning with *Metamorphoses of Science Fiction* (1979), "the minimal generic difference of SF [is] the presence of a narrative *novum* (the dramatis personae and/or their context) significantly different from what is the norm in 'naturalistic' or empiricist fiction" (*Metamorphoses* 3). Thus, in other words, "SF is distinguished by the narrative dominance or hegemony of a fictional 'novum' (novelty,

58 I am not the first to entertain the possibility of analyzing works of theory as works of SF beyond certain authors' flirtation with SF concepts and one of the first to have done so seriously was Istvan Csicsery-Ronay Jr's "The SF of Theory: Baudrillard and Haraway," published in a 1991 special issue of *Science Fiction Studies* on the interrelations of SF and postmodernism.

59 In this sense, Bratton warns us that it can be misleading to equalize stack platforms with analogous social formations like market or state, as they

> possess an institutional logic that is not reducible to those of states or markets or machines, as we normally think of them. They are a different but possibly equally powerful and important form. [...] Part of their alterity to normal public and private operations is the apparently paradoxical way that they standardize and consolidate the terms of transaction through decentralized and undetermined interactions. Platforms can be based on the global distribution of Interfaces and Users, and in this, platforms resemble markets. At the same time, their programmed coordination of that distribution reinforces their governance of the interactions that are exchanged and capitalized through them, and for this, platforms resemble states. (41–2)

innovation) validated by cognitive logic" (*Metamorphoses* 63). One key to grasp Suvin's understanding of the *novum*, which diverges from Ernst Bloch's earlier theorization, is the much-debated notion of *cognition*.[60] In this regard, one should clarify that Suvin's use of "cognition"—at least in my working understanding of it—is not meant to refer (exclusively) to scientific, non-ideological forms of knowledge, but rather to *the semblance of cognitive logic*.[61] That is, Suvin's cognition refers to a common-sense version of "the logical" that is *historically produced* and therefore partially ideological.[62] Suvin himself insists upon historicity as an essential feature of the SF *novum*, which is more specifically defined as

60 In a triad with the notions of *Front* and *Ultimum* (see *The Principle of Hope, Volume One* 195–205), Bloch defined the *novum* as "the real possibility of the Not-Yet-Conscious, Not-Yet-Become" (*The Principle of Hope, Volume Three* 1371); in other words, the *novum* would be the emerging novelty, generated by a vanguard of change in the already-existing (the front), which is, in turn, leading towards the utopian horizon of the ultimum. Transcending Bloch's rigid Marxist-Leninist conception of historical movement, however, "In Suvin's refunctioned sense—informed by the likes of Antonio Gramsci and Raymond Williams—the ineffective metaphor of the Front gives way to a meaning closer to Williams's notion of a structure of feeling, which allows for the naming of a variety of historically specific sites and instances (often contradictory but nevertheless oppositional) in which radical *novums* are to be found." Therefore, "Suvin's novum is not the reified 'novelty' produced by capitalism, or indeed the vanguard privileged by orthodox Marxism; instead, it is the dialectical force that mediates the material, historical possibilities and the subjective awareness and action engaged with those possibilities" (Moylan, "'Look into the Dark': On Dystopia and the Novum" 58).

61 Here I have in mind, though not exactly follow, Carl Freedman's notion of the "cognition effect," which slightly modifies Suvin's notion of SF cognition. In Freedman's view, "What is rather at stake is what we might term (following a familiar Barthesian precedent) the cognition effect" (18). In Chapter 3, I comment upon China Miéville critique of both notions (Suvin's cognition and Freedman's cognition effect).

62 In a later work, Suvin himself would make this argument again with greater clarity and conciseness: "Born in history and judged in history, the novum has an ineluctably historical character. So has the correlative fictional reality or possible world which, for all its displacements and disguises, always corresponds to the wish-dreams and nightmares of a specific sociocultural class of implied addressees" (*Positions and Presuppositions in Science Fiction* 76).

a mediating category whose explicative potency springs from its rare bridging of literary and extraliterary, fictional and empirical, formal and ideological domains, in brief from its unalienable historicity. [...] it is possible to distinguish various dimensions of the novum. Quantitatively, the postulated innovation can be of quite different degrees of magnitude, running from the minimum of one discrete new "invention" (gadget, technique. phenomenon, relationship) to the maximum of a setting (spatiotemporal locus), agent (main character or characters), and/or relations basically new and unknown in the author's environment. [However,] this environment is always identifiable from the text's historical semantics, always bound to a particular time, place, and sociolinguistic norm, so that what would have been utopian or technological SF in a given epoch is not necessarily such in another—except when read as a produce of earlier history; in other words, the novum can help us understand just how SF is a *historical* genre. (*Metamorphoses* 64)

It is from this theoretical perspective that the contemporary moment is—at least as imagined by new media dystopias—profoundly marked by the hegemony of a *novum* that reaches into all spheres of life with an unprecedented depth and scale: the network of new media technologies that serve as the infrastructure of today's global capitalism—that is, Bratton's stack. Thus, the *novum* in this sense is not to be mistaken for the commodified "newness" of a device in isolation—the "novelty" of the latest iPhone model, for example—since, as Wendy Chun aptly puts it, such devices are in effect constantly updating to remain the same.[63] Instead, my argument is that *new media are now re-imagined as a science-fictional* novum *when they are understood as a totality and a totalizing force that seems to be taking history in a dystopian direction*.[64] In this sense, just

63   Chun's argument goes beyond her provocative title formula, as she interestingly proposes that new media are not only by design reliant on constant updates (of software and hardware) to be competitive in a market of accelerated obsolescence, but they are also in effect constantly disturbing and revolutionizing our habits so long as they remain a habitual, seemingly essential part of our lives. Thus, new media foster a climate of "enduring ephemerality" and "obsolescent ubiquity" (*Updating to Remain the Same* 15). This, clearly, may be seen as yet another factor reinforcing the sense of inhabiting a perpetual present of the spectacle, as Guy Debord once put it.
64   In this sense, I am here using *novum* in its strongest sense, as opposed to what Suvin calls the *pseudo-novum*: the inconsequential and superficial novelty produced by marketing. Thus, Suvin counterposes "the yearly pseudo-novum of "new and improved" (when not "revolutionary") car models or clothing fashions to a really

like most *nova* in speculative narratives, new media are here understood as an essential part of system-wide dynamics that have impinged upon every aspect of—provocatively speaking—"the SF world that we inhabit," from our reality's "setting" and "characters," all the way to broader social relations.⁶⁵ In other words, it now appears (in the collective imagination at least) as though new media technologies are the hegemonic force that is driving history, which explains their centrality in fictional and non-fictional accounts of the present. The open question here is whether new media—in a sense, "the SF *novum* of our times"—are felt as a utopian or an anti-utopian force within our already hopeless structure of feeling. New media, as we shall now see, have functioned, dialectically, in both ways—though they are far from neutral.

1.3.2. Dialectics of the Digital

There are probably as many names for the present epoch as there are brands of smartphones, beginning with, obviously, "the smartphone age," as well as the more vaguely inclusive "the digital age." But besides these, one could endlessly add modifiers like "network," "information,"

---

radical novelty such as a social revolution and change of scientific paradigm, making, say, for life-enhancing transport or dressing." And further, he argues that "a novum is fake unless it in some way participates in and partakes of what Bloch called the 'front-line of historical process'—which for him (and for me) as a Marxist means a process intimately concerned with strivings for a disalienation of people and their social life. Capricious contingencies, consequent upon market competition and tied to copyright or patent law, have a built-in limit and taboo defined precisely by the untouchable sanctity of competition" (*Defined by a Hollow* 87). Elsewhere, Tom Moylan succinctly summarizes Suvin's distinction as "the open, political organ of the New and the economically or politically reified product" ("'Look into the Dark': On Dystopia and the Novum" 60).

65 Providing a more detailed examination of the degrees of magnitude of the *novum*, Suvin recently elaborated a graphic schematization of the degrees of modification that are entailed by a *novum*, which range from the mere semblance of novelty of the commodity all the way to singularity-level events ("On Communism, Science Fiction, and Utopia" 147).

"cognitive," "internet," or "postindustrial" to the nouns "age," "society," or "capitalism"—to name but a few.[66] For reasons of scope and to avoid this mystifying alphabet soup, here I am most reliant on those theorizations that centrally acknowledge the enduring dominance of the capitalist mode of production: primarily, on Shoshanna Zuboff's "surveillance capitalism" and certain critiques of it and, more secondarily, on Nick Srnicek's "platform capitalism"—although I also use the much widely accepted "digital capitalism" as a more neutral, umbrella term.[67] Thus, to understand the so-called digital age, I now examine how the spread and implementation of new media technologies—the emergence of a global stack—has deepened the dialectics of postmodernism and neoliberalism, to a great extent cohering with both their utopian and their anti-utopian undercurrents.[68] "For all its historical novelty, the internet complex is a magnification and consolidation of arrangements that have been operative or partially realized for many years," as it is "a patchwork of elements from different eras" that is "traceable back to the configurations for financializing flows of electricity devised in the 1880s" (Crary, *Scorched Earth* 6). Because of this, here I am not periodizing *per se*; that is, I am not implying that "the digital" is a new age that comes after (or because of)

[66] There is an large amount of literature on the subject, but a few landmark studies illustrate the centrality of these concepts: Beniger's *The Control Revolution*, Bauman's *Liquid Modernity*, Castells's *The Rise of the Network Society*; Moulier Boutang's *Cognitive Capitalism*, or Schwab's *The Fourth Industrial Revolution*. Echoing these and other models, Seb Franklin begins his own study of the period by critically noting that "The desire to account for the present socioeconomic moment has led to what can only be described as a frenzy of periodization" (xiii).

[67] Although there are many others, two paradigmatic studies of digital capitalism would be Dan Schiller and Christian Fuchs ("Capitalism or Information Society"), which Jonathan Pace critiques, complements and synthesizes elsewhere.

[68] One of the first monographic studies of digital capitalism (Schiller) indeed focused on how neoliberal reforms went hand in hand with the deployment of new media technologies and computer networks. As Pace synthesizes Schiller's use of the term, "digital capitalism alternately signifies a historical period, in which digital technology makes possible transnational production chains; a property regime, in which digital infrastructure is privately owned; and a management style, in which digital media permeates major capitalist enterprises" (3).

the postmodern and the neoliberal, since it is probably safer to assume that they developed symbiotically, for reasons already outlined. What I am proposing is to explore an aspect of the same epoch that is as much overdetermined by the expansion of commodification as postmodernism and neoliberalism—or perhaps even more so.

The many inventions that enabled the creation of a global network of media technologies have transnational roots, but digital capitalism was undoubtedly born in the United States of America during its (still ongoing) neoliberal epoch.[69] Even more specifically, one can safely say that digital capitalism is a Californian product of the late 1980s and 1990s, since, still today, "globalized" digital capitalism remains heavily anchored in California. Indeed, the US corporations popularly known as Big Tech—primarily, Apple, Alphabet, Microsoft, Amazon and Meta—are amongst the biggest corporations worldwide by market capitalization and most of them have roots in and around San Francisco's Silicon Valley, a place that is now metonymic of global technological power.[70] Therefore, to understand digital capitalism, one must understand what Richard Barbrook and Andy Cameron called "the Californian ideology," which is a profoundly cyber-utopian way of imagining the role to be played by new media in the twenty-first century. The emergence of this ideology thus counterbalances Leo Marx's earlier

69 Although the political origins of digital capitalism lie in US neoliberalism, the technical origins of the technologies that form today's global stack can also be found "within the utopian megastructures of 1960s experimental architecture, counterculture cybernetics, Soviet planning schemes, and many other systems of sociotechnical governance, both realized and imagined" (Bratton 46).
70 At the time of writing this note (mid-2022), Apple, Google (Alphabet from 2015), Microsoft, Facebook (Meta from 2021) and Amazon—often referred as the Big Five of Big Tech—are among the minute group of corporations to have exceeded a market capitalization of $1 trillion and the first of those three have even risen above $2 trillion (figures in US dollars). However, this is not to say that digital capitalism is an exclusively American phenomenon, as Chinese companies like Tencent and Alibaba, as well as the Taiwanese manufacturer TSMC have all figured among the top 10 most valuable corporations worldwide by market capitalization. If anything, digital capitalism is thus the most valued business model nowadays and its corporations (mostly American but not only) plague the global rankings of market capitalization, which attests to the centrality of the digital for contemporary capital.

theorization of "postmodern technological pessimism," because—at least in the Californian milieu that nurtured digital capitalism—pessimism seemed to dissipate for a while (or perhaps for a few), although it would later return with a vengeance. As Wendy Chun puts it, "the image of the Internet has shifted radically from the mid to late 1990s, when it was seen as 'cyberspace,' an anonymous and empowering space of freedom in which no one knew if you were a dog, to the mid to late 2010s, when the Internet was commonly conceived of as a space of total surveillance or as a privatized space of social media" (*Updating to Remain the Same* ix).

Writing in 1996, Barbrook and Cameron theorized "the Californian ideology" as a "new faith has emerged from a bizarre fusion of the cultural bohemianism of San Francisco with the hi-tech industries of Silicon Valley," an "amalgamation of opposites" that is "achieved through a profound faith in the emancipatory potential of the new information technologies" (44–5). But this is not simply a technophile creed: the Californian ideologues are also "passionate advocates of what appears to be an impeccably libertarian form of politics—they want information technologies to be used to create a new 'Jeffersonian democracy' where all individuals will be able to express themselves freely within cyberspace" (45). In this manner, the Californian ideology taps into the postmodernist longing for a flourishing of diversity and into the neoliberal anti-government rhetoric of radical individualism, combining their most utopian energies and projecting them into cyberspace. "Crucially, influenced by the theories of Marshall McLuhan, these technophiliacs thought that the convergence of media, computing and telecommunications would inevitably create the electronic agora—a virtual place where everyone would be able to express their opinions without fear of censorship" (48). Thus, the Californian ideology effects a radical reversal of the dystopian connotations of cyberspace,[71] a term that predates digital capitalism and was first coined in William Gibson's 1980s cyberpunk literature, where cyberspace was imagined as an invasively corporatized

---

71 Mark Zuckerberg's more recent attempt at reversing the connotations of the term "metaverse" could be seen in parallel to this, as another example of a dystopian notion—one originally coined in Neal Stephenson's novel *Snow Crash* (1992)—which is re-imagined as a corporate utopia. I return to this concept in Chapter 2, where I propose recuperating it for the study of new media reflexivity.

space, a space of violence, exclusion and exploitation that nonetheless also functioned (utopianly) as a compensatory escape from corporeal reality.⁷²

Quite tellingly, the same year of Barbrook and Cameron's essay also saw the publication of John Perry Barlow's manifesto, *A Declaration of Independence of Cyberspace* (1996), which—together with similar documents—stands as a testimony of the ideology of the digital age's Founding Fathers.⁷³ Barlow's text passionately expresses that "We must declare our virtual selves immune to your sovereignty, even as we continue to consent to your rule over our bodies. We will spread ourselves across the Planet so that no one can arrest our thoughts. We will create a civilization of the Mind in Cyberspace. May it be more humane and fair than the world your governments have made before" (Barlow n.p.). Barlow's libertarian cyber-utopia, however, betrays itself, insofar as it exemplifies a fetishization of the digital world and self—in particular, of the interface and user layers, which are falsely imagined as separate from the global reality

---

72 The term "cyberspace" first appeared in Gibson's 1982 short story "Burning Chrome," although it would later become most popular by association with his 1984 novel *Neuromancer*. Thorough studies of Gibson's oeuvre can be found in most of the academic literature devoted to the cyberpunk sub-genre, where Gibson is regarded as canonical (see Vint, "Afterword"; McFarlane et al., *The Routledge Companion to Cyberpunk Culture*). Besides, it is interesting to note how Gibson, after the advent of the digital age proper (post-1990s) began to shift the setting of his novels away from cyberpunk futures and much closer to contemporary reality, though he has maintained his critical-dystopian approach to technological power (see Nilges). In Chapter 2, I return to this phenomenon, proposing that reflexivity has significantly displaced speculation within the fabric of SF narratives.

73 A similar text in both form and content, published in 1994, would be "Cyberspace and the American Dream: A Magna Carta for the Knowledge Age" (Dyson et al.), which also conflates cyber-utopian and neoliberal discourses while giving them a marked US-nationalist flavor.

Besides, if I do not use gender-neutral language in "the digital age's Founding Fathers," it is not only because of the historic reference, but also to point at the fact that digital-capitalist elites are overwhelmingly masculine, to such extent that Silicon Valley is called a "brotopia" (see Chang). But furthermore, digital culture as a whole—like the whole of Western society but in some ways more intensely—is dominated by patriarchal dynamics, as a number of studies have proven and criticized (see Salter and Blodgett; S. Scott).

of extraction, expropriation and exploitation that enables the stack's existence. The digital dream of ubiquity and disembodiment is thus nothing but a high-tech version of the older Cartesian binary—a hierarchy where the mind comes before and above corporeal reality. Moreover, the utopian libertarianism of Barlow is only partial, for even though it openly rejects state dependence, it seems to naturalize market dependence—a textbook neoliberal gesture often used for undermining local state power in order to subordinate it to global corporate power.[74] In these ways, more generally, Barlow's manifesto illustrates how the Californian ideology is a "contradictory mix of technological determinism and libertarian individualism" (Barbrook and Cameron 49), which expects liberation by subordinating individual and collective agency to the network.

Nevertheless, to understand these cyber-utopian ideologies, it is not enough to notice their discursive fetishes and disavowals, one must also comprehend how digital individualism has been *materialized* in the stack's design. Cyber-libertarianism is not just an ideology, it is another real abstraction, or, one might say, a technologized abstraction. As Bratton's model makes clear, the stack generates *an implied user*. So, who is this implied individual who interacts with the digital interface? Most studies on digital subjectivity and selfhood seem to coincide on the fact that a kind of radical individualism is the default, that a new kind of *homo economicus*—now a "quantified self" in a profounder sense—is favored by the system's design

---

74   Nonetheless, as we saw upon considerations of neoliberalism, anti-government rhetoric does not entail anti-government policy: neoliberalism has not consisted of replacing or eliminating the state, but of refunctioning and subordinating it to the market. And besides, not all states have been weakened equally from the rise of transnational corporations. As Evgeny Morozov argues about the rising power of US and Chinese Big Tech,

This [debilitation of states] may be the case for weaker European or Latin American countries, all but colonized by American firms in recent years. But can the same be said for the United States itself? What of the longstanding links between Silicon Valley and Washington, with Google's former CEO, Eric Schmidt, leading the Defense Innovation Board, an advisory body to the Pentagon itself? What about Palantir, the company co-founded by Thiel which provides essential links between the us surveillance state and American tech? Or Zuckerberg's argument—apparently effective so far—that breaking up Facebook would embolden the Chinese technology giants and weaken America's standing in the world? ("Critique of Techno-Feudal Reason" 121–2)

(see Arnold; Cheney-Lippold; Bernard; Della Ratta et al.). Thus, although this is not only a product of technology, digital capitalism has nonetheless further solidified the ironic truth that *individualism is now the dominant mode of conformity* (see Kelly), generating a "reputation economy" that is driven by quantifiable metrics of personal worth and recognition (see W. Davies).[75] As Eli Pariser famous phrase puts it, algorithmically personalized platforms tend to enclose individuals in a self-replicating, self-referential "filter bubble" that, despite the Californians, does not then enable an "electronic agora," but rather splinters social cohesion by reinforcing biases and prejudice along intersectional axes. Therefore, some have observed that the internet complex functions as an anger-venting "twittering machine" (Seymour), while others criticize that—in so-called cyberspace—"a sociality outside of individual self-interest becomes inexorably depleted, and the interhuman basis of public space is made irrelevant to one's fantasmatic digital insularity" (Crary, *24/7* 89).[76] Although for now it suffices to observe the renewed dominance of individualism in the digital sphere, in Chapter 4 I return to these ideas, arguing the digital age seems to have turned users into *new media quixotes*, metaphorically (if not literally) deluded by their (our) immersion in the digital interface, as certain new media dystopias suggest.

75   Focusing on the intersections of new technologies and neoliberalism, Byung-Chul Han's *Psychopolitics* also explores how the individual(ist) self is intensely impinged by both.
76   Jonathan Crary's claim here should be seen in the context of his 2013 critique of "24/7 capitalism," where he denounces that

> if and when [new media] devices are introduced (and no doubt labeled as revolutionary), they will simply be facilitating the perpetuation of the same banal exercise of non-stop consumption, social isolation, and political powerlessness [...]. And they will too occupy only a brief interval of currency before their inevitable replacement and transit to the global waste piles of techno-trash. The only consistent factor connecting the otherwise desultory succession of consumer products and services is the intensifying integration of one's time and activity into the parameters of electronic exchange. Billions of dollars are spent every year researching how to reduce decision-making time, how to eliminate the useless time of reflection and contemplation. This is the form of contemporary progress—the relentless capture and control of time and experience. (*24/7* 40)

Of course, none of this is meant to imply that digital networks have entirely disabled the possibility of political mobilization, since digital individualism—just like neoliberal rationality—is the technologically predisposed and culturally hegemonic tendency, but *it is still a tendency*. As an example of the enduring possibility of collective solidarity, the 2010s are full of examples of so-called cyber-activism, although, arguably, many of those cases show that mass mobilization effectively begins after leaving the "electronic agora" and moving into the public square.[77] Furthermore, the 2010s have also been the decade of the so-called "techlash," as there has been an outpour of scholarly studies and critical essays directly targeting the problems entailed by the digital age, as exemplified by the majority of the works that I cite in this section as well as an unmanageable host of other publications.[78]

77 For studies of "hacktivist" movements such as Anonymous or WikiLeaks, the works of Gabriella Coleman provide a multi-layered, cultural and anthropological account that holistically considers these movements' digital and corporeal lives (*Coding Freedom: The Ehtics and Aesthetics of Hacking*; *Hacker, Hoaxer, Whistleblower, Spy: The Many Faces of Anonymous*).
With regard to the move from virtual to physical mobilization, one can observe how anti-austerity movements such as the Spanish 15-M or Occupy Wall Street, for instance, heavily relied on social media platforms as mobilizing tools, but their most visible and effective actions were those effected on public spaces. Theorizing the embodied nature of mobilization in the wake of such movements, Judith Butler (a public supporter of Occupy) theorizes along these lines in her *Notes Toward a Perfomative Theory of Assembly*; which expands upon previous work like "Rethinking Vulnerability and Resistance." Relatedly, the so-called Arab Spring, often taken as paradigmatic of a "social media revolution," is perhaps best seen as only supported by new media and reliant on transcending the online sphere (see Soengas; Eaton).

78 Some of the first techlash works that I read while I was working on my MPhil thesis were two books with titles that clearly capture the zeitgeist: *Radical Technologies: The Design of Everyday Life* (Greenfield) and *New Dark Age: Technology and the End of the Future* (Bridle). But besides these, "For almost every year since 2013, a defining feature forecast or declared in retrospect by at least one major publication—*Economist*, *Guardian*, OED, FT—has been the 'techlash.' If we were to locate an origin-point for this discourse, it would probably be Edward Snowden's 2013 revelations, but the tech giants really became a matter for establishment concern with the political upsets of 2016" (Lucas 132).

Nonetheless, despite these challenges, one should bear in mind that cyber-utopianism today remains heavily influential and perhaps hegemonic, at least in certain elite circles. One of its most visible manifestations today is what Sherryl Vint and others call "the futures industry," or what J. Jesse Ramírez calls "business SF."[79] With these terms, said authors refer to the future projections of corporations, which generally keep trumpeting utopian scenarios of full automation and/or complete digitalization regardless of their feasibility or desirability.[80] One only needs to think of mainstream banks' promises of automated investment or digital attention—while they close in-person offices and implement worker lay-offs—or, alternatively, of governments' promises of a "fair and green digitalization," as though the currently existing global stack was not by default unfair and environmentally destructive.[81] In the end, then, all such cyber-utopian mythologies

---

79 On this matter, see the special issue of the journal *Paradoxa*, entitled "The Futures Industry," with an introduction by Sherryl Vint, who expertly explains the recuperation of SF tropes, narratives and symbols by capitalist corporations—something enabled by the fact that SF "has always been bound up with ideologies of progress through technology and industry" ("Introduction to 'The Futures Industry'" 8)

80 Such corporate utopianism could also be linked to the frequently foretold "technological singularity"—that is, the presumed arrival (within a safely distant number of years) of AI systems with superhuman intelligence. Vernor Vinge's 1993 prediction that "within thirty years" we will have access to such technologies and thus "the human era will be ended" (11) can be seen as yet another cyber-utopian manifesto of the 1990s and an early example of a prediction that has been repeated *ad nauseam*. As opposed to these "apolitical" and technophilic discourses of some unimaginable AI system, I would here side with Steven Shaviro's sly suggestion that "the flows of Capital have now become autonomous—and strictly speaking unimaginable. They have liberated themselves from any merely human dimensions, and from whatever feeble limits Fordism and Keynesianism might previously have placed upon the single-minded pursuit of capital accumulation. In that sense, the Singularity is already here" ("The Singularity Is Here" 115–16). Similarly disproving such discourses but from a macro-economic perspective, no singularity seems to be near, since even the relatively more modest project of productive automation has stagnated in the majority of economic sectors globally (see Benanav).

81 Although he is not alone in making this argument, Jonathan Crary's works go along these lines and his stands as the most maximalist critique of the digital age:

are, as Ramírez puts it, "boringly unimaginative" (85), as they fetishize technological *pseudo-nova* while disavowing any systemic, truly utopian (or, at least, significant) *novum*. Thus seen, the digital age not only confines users within a "personalized" cyberspace of individualist illusions, but it also further entraps the epoch's collective imagination within an end-of-history, hopeless mood of capitalist realism.[82]

Although more could be said of the subjective and ideological dimensions of the digital age, one must now move onto another question: what about digital capitalism *as capitalism*? Having sketched its cultural dynamics, its commodifying dynamics now call for clarification. The single most influential account of the phenomenon is Shoshanna Zuboff's *The Age of Surveillance Capitalism* (2019), both a critical theorization and a historical overview of the digital economy as it developed since the turn of the millennium. Her account, though mostly analytical, is also marked by a disenchanted, dystopian tone—almost left melancholic—as she herself frames her narrative as "the darkening of the digital dream and its rapid

---

Ever since the late 1990s we've heard repeatedly that the dominant digital technologies are "here to stay." The master narrative that world civilization has entered "the digital age" promotes the illusion of a historical epoch whose material determinations are beyond any possible intervention or alteration. One result has been the apparent naturalization of the internet which many now assume to be something immutably installed onto the planet. The numerous mystifications of information technologies all conceal their inseparability from the flailing stratagems of a global system in terminal crisis." (Crary, *Scorched Earth* 7)

82   In his latest critical essay on the digital age, Jonathan Crary makes a similar argument, with much more depth, clarity and conciseness:

The initial claims of the internet's permanence and inevitability coincided with various "end of history" celebrations, in which free market global capitalism was declared triumphant, without rivals, dominant in perpetuity. Even though, in geopolitical terms, this fiction quickly exploded in the early 2000s, the internet seemed to validate the post-history mirage. It appeared to introduce a uniform, default reality defined by consumption, unhinged from a physical world and its mounting social conflicts and environmental disasters. The advent of social media, with all its apparent opportunities for self-expression, briefly suggested a debased fulfillment of Hegel's horizon of autonomy and recognition for everyone. But now, as a constitutive component of twenty-first-century capitalism, the internet's key functions include the disabling of memory and the absorption of lived temporalities, not ending history but rendering it unreal and incomprehensible. (Crary, *Scorched Earth* 8)

mutation into a voracious and utterly novel commercial project that I call surveillance capitalism" (chapter 1, n.p.).[83] So what is surveillance capitalism? At the very basis of Zuboff's theory lies the concept of "behavioural surplus," which refers to how corporations exploit user data—not only by selling micro-targeted attention to advertisers, but also by manufacturing large amounts of "raw" stored data into behavioral predictions through the employment of diverse computing mechanisms.[84] In turn, such predictions can be sold to external parties (corporate and statal) in "behavioral future markets," or they can also be used within the corporation's platform "to nudge, coax, tune, and herd behavior toward profitable outcomes." Zuboff's maximalist position is that "automated machine processes not only know our behavior but also shape our behavior at scale. With this reorientation from knowledge to power, it is no longer enough to automate information flows about us; the goal now is to automate us" (chapter 1, n.p.). Therefore, corporations such as Google (for Zuboff, the pioneer surveillance capitalist), Meta (the old Facebook) and Microsoft "are now locked into the continuous intensification of the means of behavioural modification" (chapter 1, n.p.).

In all these ways, Zuboff's model paints a world in which profoundly anti-democratic, illiberal practices are both facilitated and normalized by the instrumentalization of digital technologies—in short, a world in which

---

83 In a critical review of Zuboff's monograph, Rob Lucas gives a biographical flavor to Zuboff's disenchantment, posing that "If *Support Economy* [Zuboff's 2002 book] was a management consultant's utopia, *Surveillance Capitalism* is the dystopia that emerges when prophecy fails" (135). See also Evgeny Morozov's review of Zuboff's monograph in relation to her previous works ("Capitalism's New Clothes").

84 Zuboff herself wisely recommends vagueness about the specific mechanisms employed:

> Surveillance capitalism employs many technologies, but it cannot be equated with any technology. Its operations may employ platforms, but these operations are not the same as platforms. It employs machine intelligence, but it cannot be reduced to those machines. It produces and relies on algorithms, but it is not the same as algorithms. Surveillance capitalism's unique economic imperatives are the puppet masters that hide behind the curtain orienting the machines and summoning them to action. (chapter 1, n.p.)

mass surveillance and manipulation is just business as usual.[85] However, notwithstanding Zuboff's enlightening portrayal of the nefarious consequences for users' privacy and autonomy, this mode of critique—at an extreme that is often echoed by new media dystopias—verges on a paranoid conspiracy theory of "a mind control ray out of a 1950s comic book, wielded by mad scientists whose supercomputers guarantee them perpetual and total world domination" (Doctorow, *How to Destroy Surveillance Capitalism* n.p.). Zuboff's model of a "parasitic" and "rogue mutation of capitalism"—a system that has built a "global architecture of behavioural modification" and "seeks to impose a new collective order based on total certainty" (Zuboff "The Definition," n.p.)—is perhaps conceding too much to the system's self-proclaimed powers of manipulation and prediction—and Zuboff's claims do give too much credit to Big Tech's patents and marketing literature, as Doctorow observes. In this sense, Zuboff's dystopia comes to feel overwhelmingly anti-utopian, leaving little room for resistance after "turning us into a behavioural psychologist's lab rats" (Lucas 132).

Compensating for this, Cory Doctorow's own critique of surveillance capitalism corrects and expands Zuboff's perspective: "If our concern is how corporations are foreclosing on our ability to make up our own minds and determine our own futures, the impact of dominance far exceeds the impact of manipulation" (*How to Destroy Surveillance Capitalism* n.p.).[86]

85   If one is reminded of Adorno and Horkheimer's denunciation of the mid-twentieth-century culture industry as an instrument of "mass deception," then surveillance capitalism would appear as a confirmation of the Frankfurt School's worst fears in a scale unimaginable to them. Indeed, a number of studies have attempted to update the culture industry model for the digital age (see González De Ávila, "La teoría crítica ante la cultura visual"; Fuchs, *Critical Theory of Communication*). But one need not go back to critical theory to realize how surveillance capitalism is commodifying practices once thought-of as "totalitarian": it can suffice to look at the recent example given by the Pegasus scandal, whereby a private company was shown to have aided hundreds of governments worldwide (notably Spain) to conduct espionage against political targets (see Farrow).

86   More specifically, Doctorow criticizes Zuboff's uncritical attitude towards certain sources, arguing that "the surveillance capitalism critique makes an exception for the claims Big Tech makes in its sales literature—the breathless hype in the pitches to potential advertisers online and in ad-tech seminars about the efficacy of its products: It assumes that Big Tech is as good at influencing us as they claim they are

That is to say, the bigger problem is Big Tech's monopoly power, which was allowed to grow out of all proportion with the connivance of succeeding US governments—which is only logical given their dogmatic acceptance of neoliberal doctrine and their "strategic" need for allies in developing the technologies needed for post-9/11 surveillance.[87] Such concentration of wealth and power is, to Doctorow, the most crucial factor, since "monopolies can capture their regulators, crush their competitors, insert themselves into their customers' lives, and corral people into 'choosing' their services regardless of whether they want them—it's fine to be terrible when there is no alternative" (Doctorow, *How to Destroy Surveillance Capitalism* n.p.).[88] Thus seen, the dystopia is not only surveillance, it's also an extreme concentration of power in a few hands.

An expanded conception of surveillance capitalism—one that incorporates both Zuboff's and her critics' insights—sheds light on some of the most readily graspable consequences of this system, in the sense that it clearly captures the prejudicial consequences for users' rights and freedoms.[89] However, as Bratton's stack model makes clear, the user is just the tip

---

when they're selling influencing products to credulous customers" (*How to Destroy Surveillance Capitalism* n.p.)

87   In his review of Zuboff, Rob Lucas summarizes this strategic alliance with great clarity: "The political climate after 9/11 led to a 'surveillance exceptionalism' that facilitated Google's metamorphosis, as it discovered its elective affinities with the CIA; for their part, US security apparatuses were happy to avoid constitutional checks by handing off the task of data collection to a weakly regulated private sector" (Lucas 136). For a study of the ways in which technological innovations were driven by "national security" interests, see Linda Weiss's *America Inc.?*

88   In a way that coheres with Doctorow's observations, Srnicek's own theorization of "platform capitalism" makes clear that "a tendency towards monopolization is built into the DNA of platforms: the more numerous the users who interact on a platform, the more valuable the entire platform becomes for each one of them. Network effects, moreover, tend to mean that early advantages become solidified as permanent positions of industry leadership" (56).

89   In an account of the state of free speech in the age of surveillance capitalism, Jillian C. York describes today's internet as a space "in which groups already marginalized by society are further victimized by unaccountable platforms, and the already powerful are free to spread misinformation or hate with impunity"—to which she adds: "Welcome to dystopia" (15).

of the iceberg. Indeed, despite Zuboff's "Marxish" undertone (Lucas 132), "for user-ism, the problem with 'surveillance capitalism' is the surveillance of user-consumers, not capitalism as such" (Morozov, "Critique of Techno-Feudal Reason" 112). Thus, as a supplement, there is the idea of "platform capitalism," Nick Srnicek's alternative concept. Above all, Srnicek's insistence on the centrality of the "platform" highlights that digital capitalism "is something broader than just the tech sector defined according to standard classifications"; it is a system in which corporations "across traditional sectors—including manufacturing, services, transportation, mining, and telecommunications" are all caught in the same data-driven dynamics.[90] Essentially, the platform is a space—but against cyber-utopianism, it is a commodified space, a corporate colony of sorts.[91] Srnicek's concept thus provides an account that goes beyond user-centric surveillance, emphasizing instead the role of all kinds of data extraction:

> the platform has become an increasingly dominant way of organising businesses so as to monopolise these data, then extract, analyse, use, and sell them. The old business models of the Fordist era had only a rudimentary capacity to extract data from the production process or from customer usage. [...] The platform, on the other hand, has data extraction built into its DNA, as a model that enables other services and goods and technologies to be built on top of it, as a model that demands more users in order to gain network effects, and as a digitally based medium that makes recording and storage simple. [...] For companies like Google and Facebook, data are, primarily, a resource that can be used to lure in advertisers and other interested parties. For firms like Rolls Royce and Uber, data are at the heart of beating the competition: they enable such firms to offer better products and services, control workers, and optimise their algorithms for a more competitive business. [...] In every case, collecting massive amounts of data is central to the business model and the platform provides the ideal extractive apparatus. [...] Far from being mere owners of information, these companies are becoming owners of the infrastructures of society. (Srnicek 48–50)

---

90 Again, Bratton's stack model—itself fashioned after the platform model but significantly expanding it—should remind us of the depth and reach of the digital beyond the digital sector *per se*.

91 This not merely a metaphor and there are, in fact, a considerable number media theorists who are explicitly thinking the digital economy through the terms of colonialism (see Couldry and Mejias) and imperialism (see Jin).

Nonetheless, concentration of power is never total since, paradoxically, "the tendency of major platforms to grow to immense size thanks to network effects, combined with the tendency to converge towards a similar form, as market pressures dictate, leads them to use enclosure [of digital platforms] as a key means of competing against their rivals." Thus, at the same time as there is a growing monopolization, "capitalist competition is driving the internet to fragment" (Srnicek 64).

In all these ways, the global stack of digital platforms and surveillance is, indeed, one mighty apparatus, well beyond the dreams of past corporations and the nightmares of past critical theorists. In this epoch, mass commodification operates symbiotically with mass computation, as both are quantifying machines that "magically transform the local, contingent and individual into the general, universal and global" (Joque 13).[92] And besides, through the quasi-omnipresent spread of audio-visual interfaces, digital capitalism also instrumentalizes cinematic language to the point of functioning as a "cinematic mode of production" (see Beller), which mediates not just our ideological-affective sense of reality, but also our pre-conscious sensory perception (and thus our aesthetic enjoyment)—an aspect of digital power to be explored in subsequent chapters.[93] Computational code and digital image are thus pivotal to the ongoing expanse of commodification.

Nonetheless, the digital age is also haunted by the unresolved (and probably rising) tension between lingering dreams of individual self-determination and cyber-utopianism on the one hand and the ever more concentrated, quasi-panoptic power of a small cluster of corporations on the other. Furthermore, the power of digital capitalism is built upon

---

92 For meditations of the symbiotic functioning of computation, control and commodification, see Cathy O'Neil's *Weapons of Math Destruction*, or Justin Joque's *Revolutionary Mathematics*. For a longer history (or prehistory) of digital logics, see also Seb Franklin's *Control: Digitality as Cultural Logic* and, for a thorough report of the increasing interrelationships between Big Tech and Big Finance, see Fernandez et al.

93 In a work that could be considered an early antecedent of the techlash, Beller's *The Cinematic Mode of Production* (2006)—following Guy Debord—insisted on the affinities between the abstracting logics of commodification and the abstracting logics of the cinema, suggesting that audio-visual spectacle may now be more determining than commodification.

abstract speculations and calculations, which makes it even more prone to bursting like a bubble relative to capitalisms of the past. Indeed, digital capitalism "has created an economy where statistics and algorithms are *more efficient at creating new realities* (e.g. the virtual world of derivatives trading, the platforms of social media and contract labor, and the private social world of filter bubbles) *than they are at representing a world*" (Joque 7 emphasis added). Therefore, as shown in Adam McKay's 2021 apocalyptic satire *Don't Look Up*, this is a system that might very well continue single-mindedly speculating and calculating the potential surplus value to be extracted from a meteor about to destroy the planet—up until Earth is literally destroyed. And at least so far, this does not sound entirely unrealistic, as digital capitalism keeps fully focused on its drive towards data and capital accumulation all the way through a climate catastrophe that it itself is fueling. It would be entirely unrealistic conclude with a "power to the user" here, since individual agency is clearly outmanoeuvred by the stack's scale, but what should be clear is that the hegemony of capitalism is politically enabled—and it may soon be politically (or environmentally) disabled.

All in all, borrowing a powerful phrase from Gregory Claeys, this historical epoch may be considered as "the dystopia which dwarfs all others" (Claeys, "Foreword: A Utopian/Dystopian Spectrum" xxi). Fictional new media dystopias be humbled. However, one should not simply dismiss technology as bad: any dystopia is ambivalent and the stack, as such, is a cursed blessing: "Ours is an era in which startlingly powerful forces of production are ripping the planet to pieces at a faster rate than ever before, but the very same technology driving the disaster is also the basis of sophisticated ways of knowing the extent of the damage. This is Cassandra with augmented reality, and it leads to all sorts of ugly feelings" (Wark, *Capital Is Dead* 123). Whether we are turned into Cassandras or Don Quixotes—or a bit of both—would be a matter of debate, but it is nonetheless clear that the stack is a cursed blessing in the sense that it is both what enables the endurance (or the worsening) of already existing inequalities and injustices and, also, what potentially helps us to develop a profoundly nuanced, critical view of the totality. Indeed, this book would be nothing without the internet, but not thanks to its commodified circuits—not thanks to corporate social media or of for-profit publishing platforms, but thanks to its capacities for fostering transnational communication and for democratizing access to information.[94]

1.3.3. New Media Capitalism, or Worse?

The basic intuition that everything seems bad and probably worsening was at the very basis of this epoch's structure of feeling and I have tried to sketch the cultural, politico-economic and technological dynamics that seem to be generating it, with an emphasis on how and why new media are imagined as the hegemonic *novum* of these "science-fictional times." Under the complex historical matrix of left melancholy, capitalist realism, postmodernism, neoliberalism and digital capitalism, we have come to perceive our times as dystopian and our future as, most likely, more dystopian—in other words, we have come to inhabit a dystopian structure of feeling. Within this structure of feeling, there are lingering utopian impulses—not to be dismissed, as they are the seeds of resistance, opposition and even an emerging alternative hegemony[95]—but the

---

94 Indeed, notwithstanding the predominantly anti-utopian tendencies of the internet complex as it functions under the present mode of production, cyberspace is still the place where one can find incredibly valuable channels of divulgation that are relatively independent of the systemic pressures of digital capitalism. Four crucial sources of inspiration for me during my years of research for this book were Paris Marx's podcast *Tech Won't Save Us* (2020–), which regularly interviews contemporary critical thinkers on technology; Paul Walker-Emig's podcast *Utopian Horizons* (2017–), whose guests are utopian-studies academics who explore utopian and dystopian fictions; Carlos Fernández Liria's YouTube channel *La filosofía en canal* (2020), which offers expert critical surveys of key philosophical figures from Plato to Marx; and David Harvey's podcast *Anti-Capitalist Chronicles* (2018–), which introduces key concepts of Marx's theory in relation to contemporary issues.

95 Of course, one should resist the temptation of idealizing any alternative hegemony as an inherent good, as it is perfectly possible that the end of neoliberal capitalism is brought about not by the emergence of some democratic, intersectional eco-socialism (Fraser, "Climates of Capital"), but by a reactionary, anti-democratic and authoritarian regression (see Stiegler; Mair; Streeck, *Buying Time*; W. Brown, *In the Ruins of Neoliberalism*). Indeed, this reaction is already underway (and in power) in many places, given the growing host of alt-right nationalisms such as

dominant dynamics are still markedly anti-utopian: still today (or *even more* today), Walter Benjamin's angel of history keeps seeing "one single catastrophe which keeps piling wreckage upon wreckage" ("Thesis on the Philosophy of History" 257). In this context, it seems that even works of critical theory that seek to challenge this structure of feeling—including this book—to an extent also contribute to this mood, even if only by acknowledging its dominance, as well as perhaps by unconsciously reproducing it. This seems to be the case with several theorists who are making the "this is bad and getting worse" argument on a systemic scale, proposing that this is not capitalism anymore, but something worse, as McKenzie Wark and others propose.[96]

This tendency can be first illustrated by a growing literature on "techno-feudalism," "neo-feudalism" or "re-feudalization" (see Supiot; Durand, *Techno-Féodalisme*; Dean, "Neofeudalism").[97] Very schematically, such accounts—of a more or less Marxist tenor—tend to rely on an implicit distinction between (feudal) expropriation and (capitalist) exploitation—with

---

Trump's, Bolsonaro's, Modi's, Orbán's and Putin's—not to mention the authoritarian digital capitalism of China. Thus, the possibility that the alternative is worse is precisely what McKenzie Wark proposes in her work, analyzed just below, which interestingly (or perhaps, worryingly) suggests that we are already living in something worse than capitalism. Wark's argument is of a different kind—focused on the dominant mode of production rather than on political systems—but it clearly supplements those better-known, well-founded fears of rising authoritarianism.

96 Before the techno-feudal theories and Wark's own model, David Graeber made a similar, prescient suggestion in 2007, when he argued that "capitalism as an engine of infinite expansion and accumulation cannot, by definition, continue in a finite world. Now that India and China are buying in as full players, it seems reasonable to assume that within forty years at most, the system will hit its physical limits. Whatever we end up with at that point, it will not be a system of infinite expansion. It will not be capitalism; it will be something else. However, there is no guarantee that this something will be better. It might be considerably worse" ("qtd. in Crary, *Scorched Earth* 53).

97 These accounts, in turn, may be seen in parallel to another growing body of literature that emphasizes the importance of rents within the digital economy, which similarly suggests a non-capitalist logic (see Moreno Zacarés).

the former relying on rents, while the latter relies on productivity.[98] And in a crucial sense, both surveillance and platform models seem to prove techno-feudal theories right, insofar as they emphasize control over spaces and subjects—a form of domination that seems closer to "direct" feudal subjection than to "indirect" market dependence.[99] These theories speak of an uncanny intuition that the present system is qualitatively worse than capitalism as generally imagined, that somehow its control is more "total." Analytically, however, speaking of techno-feudalism is perhaps

98 David Harvey's account of neoliberalism—although not engaging directly with feudal notions—does emphasize the centrality of "accumulation by dispossession" (that is, violent, politically enabled extraction and enclosure) over and above productivity-oriented exploitation (see "The 'New' Imperialism: Accummulation by Dispossession"; "Neoliberalism as Creative Destruction"). Speaking of the techno-feudalist debate, Morozov notes that "Harvey muddied the waters some more, making 'accumulation by dispossession' the main driver of neoliberalism, which he defined as a political project, redistributive rather than generative in outlook, that aimed to transfer wealth and income from the rest of the population to the upper classes within nations or from the poor countries to richer ones internationally" ("Critique of Techno-Feudal Reason" 103)

99 Evgeny Morozov suggests this explicitly: "Reading Zuboff's vivid descriptions of the symbolic and emotional violence, deception and expropriation that propel the Google-driven digital economy, one might wonder why she dubs it 'surveillance capitalism,' rather than 'surveillance feudalism'" ("Critique of Techno-Feudal Reason" 109).

In turn, these polemics clearly echo the distinction between political/state dependence and economic/market dependence proposed by Marxist historians like Robert Brenner and Ellen Wood, essential to their understanding of the transition from feudalism to capitalism. In Wood's account, "market dependence gives the market an unprecedented role in capitalist societies, as not only a simple mechanism of exchange or distribution but the principal determinant and regulator of social reproduction." Further clarifying the specificity of capitalism, she continues:

This unique system of market dependence has specific systemic requirements and compulsions shared by no other mode of production: the imperatives of competition, accumulation, and profit-maximization, and hence a constant systemic need to develop the productive forces. These imperatives, in turn, mean that capitalism can and must constantly expand in ways and degrees unlike any other social form. It can and must constantly accumulate, constantly search out new markets, constantly impose its imperatives on new territories and new spheres of life, on all human beings and the natural environment. (97)

counter-productive to a good understanding of the present, at least according to Evgeny Morozov's critique. In his words,

> the great outstanding question is whether Google and its peers are like that non-capitalist owner of the waterfall who 'need not lift a finger' in order to share in the surplus value generated somewhere else. [...] if so—if the tech giants really are lazy rentiers who are ripping everyone off by exploiting intellectual-property rights and network effects—why do they invest so much money in what can only be described as production of some kind? What kind of rentiers do that? Alphabet's R&D spending in 2017, 2018, 2019 and 2020 was $16.6 billion, $21.4 billion, $26 billion and $27.5 billion respectively. Does that not count as 'lifting a finger'? [...]
>
> If these are lazy waterfall-owning rentiers, they are peculiarly masochistic ones: why not just rest on their laurels, fire everyone and stop spending? And who, looking at these numbers, could really believe [...] that capitalists are now external to production? What then are they spending all this R&D money on? More telling still, a close analysis of the balance sheets of Google, Amazon and Facebook shows that they have fewer intangible assets than other big corporations—in fact, today they own relatively fewer intangibles than they did ten to fifteen years ago. It is easy to see why: all this data requires extensive physical networks and vast data centres—but such trends create a big hole in arguments that overemphasize the intangible assets. ("Critique of Techno-Feudal Reason" 118)

Thus seen, perhaps the present is only "feudal" if one overemphasizes a corporate-colonized cyberspace—if one looks through the "virtual window" (Friedberg) into an online space fully controlled by a Big Tech overlord—but not if one realizes the competitive market dynamics that call for the constant development and maintenance of the stack's physical infrastructure. The techno-feudal imaginary seems to say: if this seems worse than capitalism, could this be a reactionary return to capitalism's premodern other? Especially now that capitalism's modern other—the once-utopian ghost of communism—is vanished, why not revive the anti-utopian ghost of feudalism? It is easy to see how such a derogatory conception of the present's power structures channels frustration and anger with increasingly almighty, undeniably parasitical elites—and their growing reliance on monopolistic rent-extraction is an undoubtedly fair critique posed by these theories. However, to think that, rather than techno-capitalism, we live in techno-feudalism does not offer any consolation and, "by vainly invoking the latter, we risk whitewashing the former's reputation" (Morozov, "Critique of Techno-Feudal Reason"). In the end, then, perhaps the two social formations are not mutually exclusive and, even if one is dominant, there is no reason to think that they cannot co-exist within a "multi-layered dystopia"—something that both proponents and critics of the techno-feudal model seem to acknowledge despite their polemics.[100] Although it is beyond my scope and expertise

100 Evgeny Morozov ends his critique of techno-feudal theories by debunking the false oppositions that supposedly underlie these models and proposing that

> Marxists would do well to acknowledge that dispossession and expropriation have been constitutive of accumulation throughout history. Perhaps the luxury of employing only the economic means of value extraction in the 'properly' capitalist core was always due to the extensive use of extra-economic means of value extraction on the non-capitalist periphery. Once we make that analytical leap, we no longer need to bother with invocations of feudalism. Capitalism is moving in the same direction it always has been, leveraging whatever resources it can mobilize—the cheaper, the better. In this sense, Braudel's one-time description of capitalism as 'infinitely adaptable' is not the worst perspective to adopt. But it does not adapt continuously and, when it does, it's not a given that the upward-redistributive tendencies win out over the productive ones. (Morozov, "Critique of Techno-Feudal Reason" 126)

However, m in a direct response to Morozov's critique, Jodi Dean seems to agree there can be no simple return to feudalism and (implicitly) that perhaps there should be a third term (for which McKenzie Wark's theory, examined here, could be useful):

> Dependent on the market for access to our means of subsistence, we become dependent on the platform for access to the market. If we are to work, the platform gets its cut. If we are to consume, the platform gets its cut as well.

> As it produces new social-property relations, new intermediaries and new laws of motion, the ongoing process of separation is not a 'going back' to historical feudalism, as Morozov would have it, but a reflexization, such that capitalist processes long directed outward—through colonialism and imperialism—turn in upon themselves. With advances in production seemingly at a dead end, capital is hoarded and wielded as weapon of destruction—its wielders new lords, the rest of us dependent, proletarianized servants and serfs. If feudalism was characterized by relations of personal dependence, then neofeudalism is characterized by abstract, algorithmic dependence on the platforms that mediate our lives. ("Same as It Ever Was?" n.p.)

At the time of writing this and presumably long after, this debate still goes on and further responses to Morozov's polemics will probably continue to appear in the pages of *New Left Review* and elsewhere; a more recent example is Ström.

Contemporary Capitalism as a New Media Dystopia 105

to settle any such dispute, the very term "neo-feudalism" perhaps betrays itself in suggesting that, even if things are worse, they are at least familiar, a high-tech version of "good old," premodern oppression. However, even if there is, indeed, a return of certain pseudo-feudal dynamics, couldn't we do with a better term to name the specificities and complexities of the digital dystopia?

In this context, McKenzie Wark's *Capital is Dead: Is this Something Worse?* (2019) stands as one of the boldest speculative theorizations on the possibility of the end of capitalism as the dominant social formation—and crucially, although there are affinities, Wark hypothesizes this scenario without relying on any binary opposition of feudalism and capitalism. In the pages that follow, I examine Wark's model as a paradigmatic new media dystopia in the realm of critical theory, as a work whose speculations revolve around the hegemony of one *novum*: Bratton's global stack of new media technologies.[101] Wark's theory is an ambivalent emblem of the times, insofar as it is *both* a radical rebellion against *and* a proud product of our dystopian structure of feeling. But why proud? In pursuing her speculation, Wark self-consciously embraces a dystopian imagination and she interestingly defends it as an antidote against hopelessness: "So the bad news is: this is not capitalism anymore, it's something worse. And the good news is: Capital is not eternal, and even if this mode of production is worse, it is not forever. There could be others. That's the struggle today. OK, so that's not particularly good news. But there is also this: an end to left-melancholia, that eternal sadness about eternal capitalism." And to this, she adds: "To think that we live in an illusory world of capitalist realism still might concede too much reality to the belief in eternal Capital" (*Capital Is Dead* 29). Thus, Wark's speculation seems to self-consciously assume the task of SF itself—critical estrangement—as well as the task of the critical dystopia—reviving hope in dark contexts. What if ... this is

---

101 Wark explicitly references and often thinks through Bratton's stack model, although she prefers to call this infrastructure "the vector of information." Nonetheless, she seems to acknowledge that they are roughly equivalent, twice saying "what Benjamin Bratton calls the stack, [or] what I call the vector" (*Capital Is Dead* 113–18).

worse than capitalism? How would that dystopia play out in theory? And where could utopian impulses emerge in that context?

Wark begins with a critique that may be very well read as a caution against the kind of capital-centric schematization that I have attempted throughout this chapter—but most importantly, this is a critique that applies not only to leftist thinking, but also to hegemonic perceptions of the social totality:

> One thing that the left and right now seem to agree on is that the society on which we live is called capitalism. And strangely enough, both now seem to agree that it is eternal. Even the left seems to think that there is an eternal essence to Capital and that only its appearances change. The parade of changing appearances yields a series of modifiers: this could be necro capitalism, communicative capitalism, cognitive capitalism, platform capitalism, neoliberal capitalism, or computational capitalism. But short of an increasingly allegorical or messianic leap into something other, it is as if this self-same thing just went on forever. [...]
>
> This capitalism that we have all agreed to live in, has it not become too familiar, too cozy, too roomy an idea? Why are we so *devoted* to its name? The reality the term tried to describe is, of course, far from comfortable. Capitalism is a world of exploitation, domination, and oppression. Capitalism, if this is what this still is, appears to be like a steam-hammer smashing not only the social but also the natural conditions of its existence to pieces. But then maybe this is the thing to ask about. Why have we become so comfortable with a way of describing an uncomfortable reality? Do we want a certainty in language that can't be had anywhere else? [...] Capitalism atomizes and alienates. It renders everything precarious—except its own hold on the imagination. (*Capital Is Dead* 21–2)

Among other things, here Wark is unwittingly teaching a lesson about the functioning of the critical dystopia: that speculating with the worst-case scenario can be, in the end, profoundly liberating—at least for the imagination. So, what is the worse social formation that is emerging? The core hypothesis of *Capital is Dead* is that

> There's a whole political economy that runs on asymmetries of information as a form of control. It may even amount to a new kind of class relation. Sure, there is still a landlord class that owns the land under our feet and a capitalist class that owns the factories, but maybe now there's another kind of ruling class as well—one that owns

neither of those things but instead owns the vector along which information is gathered and used. (*Capital Is Dead* 3)

In this manner, Wark does not rely on any binary opposition of political economies, but instead proposes a sort of layered co-existence: the idea that "there are new forms of exploitation, inequality, and asymmetry as a layer on top of the old ones we're more used to" (*Capital Is Dead* 9). In her model, neither capitalists nor landlords—that is, neither the "capitalism" nor the "feudalism" of the neo-feudal models—are the dominant ruling class, even though neither of them have disappeared (that is, they are not literally dead, as the title could suggest). Instead, both have been accidentally displaced by a new kind of ruling class, which Wark calls the "vectoralist" class, which commands a "vectoralist" mode of production.[102] In a three-fold matrix of class antagonisms, both land-based and labor-based relations of domination—the landlord-farmer relation and the capitalist-worker relation—have been subsumed by a new global structure that not only commodifies land and labor, but also commodifies information, creating a third kind of class antagonism, between "vectoralist" and "hacker" classes. Thus, Wark's highly heterodox account nonetheless continues to assume the centrality of commodification—just like Marx's *Capital* in this regard, but in a new, more abstract form.[103]

---

102 Wark explains the emergence of this new social formation as an accident, a dynamic originating in capitalism but spiralling out of it: "what at first appeared to assist capital to defeat labor in the overdeveloped world was also a defeat for capital. The novel forces of production that enabled this outflanking of labor became themselves the new dominant forces of production. Power over the value chain moves from the ownership and control of the means of production to ownership and control of the vectors of information. Whole new industries arose, as did whole new corporations-the so-called tech sector. But actually all corporations become increasingly organized around the ownership and control of information" (*Capital Is Dead* 57)

103 Wark herself suggests that her account of co-existing social relations is based on an orthodox reading of Marx: "As is much clearer from Marx's political writings than from *Capital*, there are always may subordinate classes, just as here can be more than one ruling class. Modes of production are multiple and overlapping" (*Capital Is Dead: Is This Something Worse?* 14)

So how does her theory's main *novum*—the global stack, or the vector of information, as Wark calls it—shape this new social order? The key is that digital "technologies made information very, very cheap and very, very abundant. They gave rise to a strange kind of political economy, one based not only on a scarcity of things but also on an excess of information" (Wark, *Capital Is Dead* 5). Crucially, "Making information a force of production produces something of a conundrum within the commodity form. Information wants to be free but is everywhere in chains. Information is no longer scarce, it is infinitely replicable, cheap to store, cheap to transmit, and yet the whole premise of the commodity is its scarcity" (*Capital Is Dead* 42). Therefore, because of the challenge posed to commodification by information, a new property regime is necessary in order to perpetuate power and wealth asymmetries in a context of abundance:

> Like the enclosures or the joint-stock company before it, intellectual property law becomes the form of a new kind of relation of production, more abstract than its predecessors, and one that makes not land or physical plant, but rather information itself, a form of private property. Like those preceding forms of private property, this one crystalizes into a class relation. As an absolute form of private property, it creates classes of owners and nonowners of the means of realizing its value. Land as private property gave rise to the two great classes of farmer and landlord. Capital as private property gave rise to the two great classes of worker and capitalist. Is there a new class relation that emerges out of the commodification of information?
>
> For this thought experiment, let's say it does. I call those classes the hacker class and the vectoralist class. The hacker class produces new information. But what is "new" information? It is whatever intellectual property law recognizes as new. It's a strange kind of production. Where the farmer grows crops through a seasonal cycle and the worker stamps out repetitive units of commodities, the hacker has to use their time in a different way, to turn the same old information into new. Getting this done is not like the seasonal repetitions of farming or the clocking-on of the worker. It happens when it happens, including time spent napping or pulling all-nighters. The workplace nightmare of the worker is having to make the same thing, over and over, against the pressure of the clock; the workplace nightmare of the hacker [including us academics] is to produce different things, over and over, against the pressure of the clock. (*Capital Is Dead* 42–3)

In this sense, the age's ironic pressure to conform by being unique—with roots in postmodern epistemology, neoliberal rhetoric and digital individualism—can be explained by the nature of "hacker work," which is under constant pressure to produce qualitatively distinct new information. The hacker's alienation would therefore derive not from the meaninglessness of routine and repetition, but from the pressure to produce "difference" and "novelty" for their own sake—or rather, for the sake of the vectoral class's project of endless data accumulation. In this manner, even the semblance of difference and novelty is valuable as commodifiable information—and so the internet is flooded with all kinds of noise and nonsense, from fake news and disinformation all the way to hate speech and conspiracy theories. Because that's the data economy, folks! So, above all,

> One thing that is distinctive about an information political economy is the way it instrumentalizes difference rather than sameness. The farmer and worker produce units of commodities that are equivalent within their kind. What I call the hacker class has to produce difference out of sameness. It has to make information that has enough novelty to be recognizable as intellectual property, a problem that landed property or commercial property does not have.

> By hacker class I mean everyone who produces new information out of old information, and not just people who code for a living. Part of the struggle of our time is to see a common class interest in all kinds of information making, whether in the sciences, technology, media, culture, or art. What we all have in common is producing new information but not owning the means to realize its value. And yet the way we go about this is not quite the same thing as labor, just as being a worker is not the same thing as being a farmer. (*Capital Is Dead* 13–14)

In these ways, Wark is taking a theoretical step that again echoes SF. Borrowing the hacker, the often-oppositional protagonist of cyberpunk and post-cyberpunk fiction, this model broadens and re-politicizes its meaning. Continuing her previous work (*A Hacker Manifesto*), Wark re-imagines hackers as the subordinate class of the new "vectoral" mode of production, thus encompassing anyone who produces information— be that for a wage, as in research institutions, the media or the tech industry, or "for free," as in the case of users, consumers and spectators. And again, within this new class relation, "Forms not only of class but also of gendered and racialized discrimination have migrated from relations of property, authority and expertise and have been encoded as technical (or algorithmic) forms of power" (*Capital Is Dead* 89), which amounts to saying that the hacker class remains caught within a matrix of intersectional oppression. The old dystopias live on through the new. Nonetheless, despite the anti-utopian advance of ever-abstracter commodification and of new forms of domination, in this dystopian model of a post-capitalist world there is also a new potential agent of utopian transformations: the hacker class.[104]

Finally, although much more could be said of *Capital is Dead*, one should note that Wark's model also offers a possible socio-historical explanation of the widespread reflexivity of new media culture, which is precisely the issue to be explored in the next chapter. Because of their data-driven abstraction, new media technologies and the kind of commodification that they enable tend towards self-referentiality as an easy means of producing more "new" and "different" information in the absence of truly new and different things. As Wark puts it, "Information technology is a sort of meta-technology, designed to observe, measure, record, control, and predict what things, people, or indeed other information can or will or should do" (*Capital Is Dead* 5). Thus, as ever more abstract metadata flourish, commodification seems free to flee physical reality, functioning as a purely self-referential reality—that is, as pure self-valorizing value, as Karl Marx once defined capital itself.[105] Thus seen, one can still doubt if this

104 Wark, of course, is not the first to imagine hackers as revolutionaries, as there are examples from the 1980s (Steven Levy's *Hackers: Heroes of the Computer Revolution*) and more contemporary examples (Colin Milburn's *Respawn. Gamers, Hackers, and Technogenic Life*)—not to mention the host of cyberpunk narratives that feature hacker heroes, beginning with Gibson's *Neuromancer*.

105 Marx uses the expressions "self-valorization" and "self-valorizing value" on a few occasions throughout volume 1 of *Capital* (roughly twenty times in my English edition), but the concept is crucially used as a synthetic synonym for the functioning of capitalism. In fact, Marx once refers to self-valorization as a phenomenon "at the very roots of the capitalist mode of production" (*Capital Volume I* 612). In this sense, if the capitalist economy is profoundly self-referential, it would be a mistake to attribute the spread of reflexivity exclusively to the rise of Wark's vectoralist mode of production, as its seeds seem to have been planted before the present epoch. In fact, Adorno and Horkheimer's *Dialectic of Enlightenment* already denounced the assimilation of culture by the logics of advertisement,

whole system is a new and worse mode of production, or if it is just "the purest form of capital yet to have emerged" (Jameson, *Postmodernism* 36), or even "capitalism in its terminal, scorched earth phase" (Crary, *Scorched Earth* 34). In any case, self-referentiality seems to be the norm, insofar as the abstract, quantifying functioning of commodification now also targets information, itself an abstract, quantifying thing. Digital capitalism—or rather, the "vectoral" mode of production—thus creates a new world where commodification can continue on its own, without physical and planetary limits—although obviously, this disembodied limitlessness is just an illusion, but still an illusion with potentially disastrous consequences. It is along this line of thought that Wark provocatively answers her central question:

> how is this worse than capitalism? The vectoral infrastructure throws all of the world into the engine of commodification, meanwhile modifying the commodity form itself. There is nothing that can't be tagged and captured through information about it and considered a variable in the simulations that drive resource extraction and processing. Quite simply, we have run out of world to commodify. And now commodification can only cannibalize its own means of existence, both natural and social. It's like that Marx Brothers film where the train runs out of firewood, so the carriages themselves have to be hacked to pieces and fed to the fire to keep it moving, until nothing but the bare bogies are left. (*Capital Is Dead* 48)

Thus, the destructive and self-destructive tendency of ever more self-referential commodification is probably the most anti-utopian tendency of this epoch's structural dynamics—and, against this, what is the remaining utopian force of the hacker class? It is perhaps best to conclude here with one of Wark's most hopeful and self-conscious passages:

> I opted to call us the hacker class. Twenty years ago, that was perhaps too romantic a term, on the border of legality, outside the logic of commodification. Now it has exclusively criminal associations. If anything, it's an index of how much the vectoralist class has succeeded. It is all but inconceivable now that there could be an open-ended,

---

profoundly self-referential. Wark herself acknowledges a continuity and a debt with the critique of the culture industry, as she suggests that the vectoralist mode of production "descends from what was formerly the culture industry. But it is no longer an industry apart, commodified leisure. It's now integrated into the whole of production and consumption" (*Capital Is Dead* 56).

playful, experimental approach to making the new appear out of the old in techniques of information that would be entirely contained with the commodification and control of the information vector.

But just as the industrial working class retained a utopian feeling about what labor should be like from craft labor, so too it is possible to hold onto a feeling about what it's like to make elegance appear that wasn't there before with a technique for transforming information, and to do it on one's own time, with one's own goals and objectives. This is what it might mean to hack. (*Capital Is Dead* 51)

Thus understood, hacking in Wark's broad sense, which encompasses intellectual labor, artistic production, or even user interaction through watching, gaming, or browsing, still allows for uncommodified, semi-autonomous experimentation and play and, perhaps, for counter-hegemonic, utopian world-building. But this is, of course, overemphasizing hacking's utopian potential and presupposing collective class solidarity, because "the hacker"—if imagined as a lone hero or part of a vanguard elite, as in certain new media dystopias—is clearly nothing in *vis-à-vis* the global stack, perhaps just a ridiculous Quixote absurdly tilting at the stack.[106] And, besides, "Class consciousness is always a rare and difficult thing. Unlike other identities, it has to be argued contrary to appearances" (*Capital Is Dead* 50). Therefore, even if Wark's notion of "the hacker class" does name a potential collective agent of utopian transformation, this means nothing without the existence of a renewed, multi-dimensional, intersectional class consciousness. Without that, dystopia goes on.

---

106 Indeed, it is one thing to speak of the hacker class and an entirely different thing to speak of "the myth of the lone hacker," which—as Jonathan Crary notes—"perpetuates the fantasy that the asymmetrical relation of individual to network can be creatively played to the former's advantage" (*24/7* 46). And elsewhere, Crary specifically denounces that "Edward Snowden's spurious claim that network technology is 'the great equalizer' perpetuates an elitist hacker fantasy that has little relevance to most people's lives or to the building of mass movements and new communities" (*Scorched Earth* 23–4). However, I would tend to think that Wark's collective conceptualization of the hacker class compensates for at least a part of what Crary denounces, although his critique does point at the need for broader forms of solidarity between the multiple ruled classes.

1.4. Defining the New Media Dystopia, Real and Fictional

Throughout this chapter, I have surveyed the historical dialectics that underpin the present epoch—specifically theorizing it as a dystopian structure of feeling in which hegemonic hopelessness seems to emerge and thrive in a symbiosis with the dynamics of new media technologies (understood as the totality of Bratton's stack, or as Wark's vector). In approaching the present's structure of feeling, I have attempted to provide a totalizing survey, sketching epochal dynamics that cut through spheres as distinct as culture, ideology, policy, economics, or technology. Of course, I am aware that "the construction of a historical totality necessarily involves the isolation and the privileging of one of the elements within that totality [...] such that the element in question becomes a master code or 'inner essence' capable of explicating the other elements or features of the 'whole' in question" (Jameson, *The Political Unconscious* 12) and, in this sense, this totalizing theorization—like any other—is inevitably a partial totality, shaped by the interpretative hegemony of new media. Thus, I must insist that my guiding presupposition has been that new media technologies play a hegemonic role in this dystopian structure of feeling and this is a non-verifiable hypothesis (at least in any empirical or quantifiable manner), but it is my hope that a solid case has been made for its plausibility, its reasons and its dynamics.

And how could we synthesize the multiple dialectics of this dystopian structure of feeling? What are the main utopian and anti-utopian forces at play within this structure? Notwithstanding many of the above-examined nuances, my main observation is that, on the utopian side, this epoch has witnessed a flourishing of individualistic heterogeneity and intersectional diversity, as well as a valuation of autonomous self-determination, all of which are visible across postmodern epistemology, neoliberal rationality and digital cyber-utopianism. At the same time, on the anti-utopian side of the story, this epoch has witnessed an advance of commodification through political, economic and technological means, which has entailed the subordination of increasing spheres of life to a global machine of power—one that feeds off pre-existing injustices and inequalities as well as creating new ones.

This abstraction-producing machine—itself a very real (or technologized) abstraction, epitomized by Bratton's stack but not reducible to it—is (probably) still predominantly capitalist, but (if we trust Wark's account) it is plausibly morphing into a something else that is maybe worse. Furthermore, what looms in the not-so-distant horizon—global eco-social crises triggered by climate change—is, indeed, the biggest dystopia of all, perhaps the political unconscious of all culture today (see Bould, *The Anthropocene Unconscious*). Thus, it remains true that it is easier to imagine the end of the world than the end of capitalism—but perhaps that is changing by sheer force of necessity. Perhaps such a profoundly dystopian reality does not necessarily lead in a hopeless, anti-utopian direction; on the contrary, perhaps this is the challenge that re-kindles the utopian impulse worldwide. Or perhaps not, of course.

So far, however, we still seem to dwell in a global new media dystopia.

Fictional new media dystopias, which are the focus of the remainder of this book, are therefore narratives that are *not only formally reflexive* regarding their medium of distribution and consumption (mostly video-on-demand platforms), as the next chapter examines, but also share *profound ideological parallelisms* with an epochal structure that is deeply haunted by new media and its associated dynamics, as this chapter has established. These new media dystopias—as products and critiques of the epoch's technoculture, consumed through digital interfaces but often satirical towards them and their users, dystopian in an age in which such genre is less and less unrealistic (if it ever was)—are thus, above all, *ambivalent* in how they relate to the real new media dystopia. Reality may be stranger (and worse) than fiction, but the latter may still provide tools of "cognitive mapping" for us to understand the former.

Of course, it is evidently difficult for character-centric narratives to provide a totalizing view and the new media dystopias here analyzed generally focus on the user and interface layers, thus overemphasizing an individual's (and generally, a hacker-class) experience of new media technologies—not to mention that, as Anglo-American productions, they only show a local, relatively privileged view of the whole. But still, rewriting Adorno (*Minima Moralia* 50), one might say that the whole is the dystopia, but a tiny crack in your screen is the best magnifying glass. Even in their partiality and their ambivalence, new media dystopias are still valuable as culture of the epoch—and despite dominant tendencies, such value must be defined through something other than quantification. Even if these are some of the top-rated SF series of the past decade, let us say: online ratings be damned, for they belong to the data dystopia.

CHAPTER 2

New Media Reflexivity: Self-Referentiality and Self-Consciousness in the Audio-Visual SF of Digital Platforms

[S]cience fiction [is] the most cinematic of all film genres. This is not only because, for the best effect, science fiction films must be seen and heard in cinema auditoria; but also because the technology of cinematic illusion displays the state of its own art in science fiction films. Since the films themselves are often about new or imagined future technologies, this must be a perfect example of the medium fitting, if not exactly being, the message.

—Annette Kuhn, *Alien Zone: Cultural Theory and Contemporary Science Fiction Cinema* (1990, 6–7)

[In a] möbius-like relationship [...] SF is the cinema's own genre, a media-specific showcase as much or more than a mechanism for adapting SF writing into film.

—Brooks Landon, *The Aesthetics of Ambivalence: Rethinking Science Fiction Film in the Age of Electronic (Re)production* (1992, 89)

The infrastructure of life in our properly post-cinematic era has been subject to radical transformations at this level of molecular space-time of prepersonal affect. [...] something of the nature and the stakes of these changes can be glimpsed in our contemporary moving-image media, including by means of formal transformations of images and their production, editing, and distributions, which changes are themselves not infrequently taken up by post-cinematic productions in self-reflexive allegorizations of the new media environment and its novel situations of image-viewing.

—Shane Denson, *Discorrelated Images* (2020, 25)

Reflexivity seems to flow through the veins of audio-visual SF—and oftentimes it clogs them. According to Kuhn, Landon, Denson and other theorists, more and more SF narratives seem inevitably and inherently about their own medium. That is, more and more SF narratives seem to be becoming reflexive and even more reflexive when, like new media dystopias, they are shaped by the narrative hegemony of a medial *novum*—that is, an SF *novum* that, more literally or more allegorically, stands for the device(s) where SF circulates and is consumed. However, audio-visual SF is no exception: the whole circulatory system of postmodern and digital culture also seems to throb with a reflexive pulse, given phenomena like the mainstreaming of the "meta," which Werner Wolf calls "the meta-referential turn," and the endlessly re-mediating logics of new, "post-cinematic" media, which some even call meta-media.[1] Therefore, in the context of an increasingly self-referential mode of production, increasingly self-referential culture and increasingly self-referential digital interfaces, new media dystopias appear as a symptom of contemporary capitalism's self-referential tendencies. However, perhaps they are not just any symptom and my contention is that new media dystopias offer a peculiarly representative condensation—and, to an extent, a self-conscious critique—of those trends that both allow and call for the theorization of *new media reflexivity*, a concept with potential resonance beyond SF and the dystopian sub-genre.

Speaking of reflexivity, however, immediately summons a whole host of terminological ghosts, many of which are haunted by a lack of conceptual clarity. Here one finds another alphabet soup: reflexivity, metafiction, meta-referentiality, self-consciousness, self-referentiality, meta-literature, meta-cinema, meta-media and even meta-modernism—a metaverse of meta-terms, one might say, some as mystifyingly abstract as the first of them: metaphysics itself.[2] Looking for a solution to these conceptual

---

1   For the most influential theorization of remediation, see Bolter and Grusin (cf. also Chun, *Updating to Remain the Same*); for an exploration of the contemporary spread of the "meta" across media, cultures and even in dominant modes of ideology and subjectivity, see, respectively, Wolf (*Metareference across Media*; *The Metareferential Turn in Contemporary Arts and Media*) and Archer (*The Reflexive Imperative in Late Modernity*); for a contextualized use of the concepts of meta-media and meta-technologies, see Wark (*Capital Is Dead*; *Sensoria*).

2   Section 2.2 in this chapter returns to some of the most text-oriented of these terms, subsuming them and/or replacing them with Pedro Javier Pardo's theoretical model of *reflexivity*. With regard to "meta-modernism," this term used in some theorizations of a post-postmodern cultural climate, one supposedly "oscillating between

complications, this chapter begins by establishing the potential relevance of a formally rigorous study of reflexivity within contemporary debates in SF studies. Although such debates often go beyond—or do not strictly follow—a formalist understanding of reflexivity, they still provide the sociohistorical background of a phenomenon that can then be more rigorously understood with Pedro Javier Pardo's transmedia model of reflexivity. In this way, after surveying both the former debates and the latter model, Pardo's formal concepts are applied and partly rethought within the context of digital platforms, which is where the production, distribution and consumption of audio-visual narratives is migrating in this epoch—if it is not already the dominant medium of cultural consumption. With this purpose, this chapter offers two case studies that formally illustrate and contextually nuance the theorization: Amazon's serialized adaptation of Philip K. Dick's *The Man in the High Castle* (2015–19, created by Frank Spotnitz) and *Black Mirror*'s interactive film *Bandersnatch* (2018, directed by David Slade; written by Charlie Brooker).

While *The Man in the High Castle*—not a new media dystopia, but an adaptation of a postmodern SF novel—is taken as a cautionary illustration of the possibilities and the problematics of projecting the notions of literary reflexivity onto moving-image media; *Bandersnatch*—a new media dystopia *sensu stricto*—stands as an emblem of the formal peculiarities and the ideological ambivalences of reflexivity within the context of a video-on-demand platform (Netflix, in that case). Finally, after both theorization and analysis, this chapter concludes by defining the specificities of *new media reflexivity* in narratological terms and meditating upon its contextual ambivalences within and towards the present's dystopian structure of feeling. All throughout, both my theorization and my analyses are methodologically dialectical, based on the assumption that the omnipresence of reflexivity—even if to a great extent a by-product of socio-cultural and media-technological dynamics—need not necessarily cancel out the critical and utopian potentials of art and culture. In other words, new media reflexivity is here regarded *both* as a symptom of digital capitalism's dominant

---

a modern enthusiasm and a postmodern irony" (Vermeulen and van den Akker 1; see also Andersen; Rowson and Pascal).

dynamics, which predispose a degree of commodified self-referentiality *and also* as a potential mode of estrangement that can be allied with SF's own estrangement—and directed against the system from within.

2.1. The "Meta Question" in SF Studies

In previous passages, I have suggested that new media dystopias, more than speculating with future scenarios or building alternative realities, seem to be primarily concerned with *reflexively examining their own medium of consumption and distribution and, therefore, in so doing, also reflecting upon their media-dominated moment*. But is this somehow a non-speculative form of speculative fiction? I would not go as far as to proclaim that this reflexive turn marks "the end of speculation," which would make this book just another absurd declaration of "the death of SF" (see Luckhurst for a critique of this tendency). Nevertheless, what I do think worth exploring is the extent to which *some contemporary SF seems to be gravitating away from a speculative pole without fully abandoning it, at the same time as it draws closer to a reflexive pole without fully becoming metafiction*.[3] In this sense, my idea is that new media dystopias do not signal

---

3   In theorizing these two poles of the speculative and the reflexive, I am taking inspiration from—though not strictly following—Robert Scholes, a pioneering theorist of both SF and metafiction, who often seemed to imagine the two as related but distinct literary forms that, in their own ways, challenged the presumed divide established between realism and fantasy. Of all his works, this dialectic of the speculative and the reflexive is evoked, in a somewhat different language, by the very title of his *Fabulation and Metafiction* and it is also explored within his *Structural Fabulation*, one of the first scholarly vindications of the value of SF. Scholes, even if probably the first, is not the only theorist to note the affinity of metafictional and SF forms. Indeed, as Robert Briggs observes in his essay on "meta-science-fiction," Scholes is accompanied, in this regard, at least by Larry McCaffery and Brian Attebery. These "three writers differ in how they posit the relations between SF and metafiction, [...] but each affirms in his own way a spiritual affinity between the two forms" (689).

the "end of speculation" in any absolute sense; rather, my assumption is that new media dystopias continue the SF function of estrangement via a *reflexive mode* that sometimes contrasts and sometimes complements SF's *speculative mode*. By "becoming meta," the new media dystopia offers *a formal and narrative solution* to a series of *ideological and contextual questions* that have haunted SF studies for a while: how does science-fictional estrangement adapt to the fact that reality in general and new media in particular seem increasingly science-fictional? Although often without following a rigorous, formalist definition of reflexivity, there seems to be a consensus in SF studies that there is something like a "reflexive turn" within the genre and, particularly, within (post-)cyberpunk—the best-known SF sub-genre about digital technologies.

2.1.1. Historicizing (Post-)Cyberpunk's Reflexive Turn

One might say that new media dystopias are *necessarily reflexive on a formal level* if they are to realize, more broadly, the same *ideological function* that Fredric Jameson attributed to a closely akin SF subgenre, cyberpunk: that of "cognitive mapping," or offering a "privileged representational shorthand for grasping a network of power and control even more difficult for our minds and imaginations to grasp: the whole new decentered global network of the third stage of capital itself" (Jameson, *Postmodernism* 36–7). The function remains, but the forms have necessarily changed since the 1980s. The most obvious reason for this change is that the infrastructure of what we now call digital capitalism (or vectoralist mode of production) is evidently more complex and "more developed" on a technical level. However, in a sense ironically, today's global "network of power and control" may be easier to grasp than the technologies that Jameson had in mind. Indeed, can it be so difficult to have at least a working understanding of the logics of digital capitalism when we literally carry its products in our pockets and use them for work, sociability and leisure? In this sense, the risk today is *not so much not being able to understand a radically new reality, but rather naturalizing a ubiquitous new media reality,* which poses a challenge for any narrative of estrangement. No longer shocking, cyberpunk has "become so ubiquitous as to be invisible" in the sense that we now "inhabit a cyberpunk future" (Vint, "Afterword: The World Gibson Made" 228).[4] In this regard, new media dystopias can be seen as a part of what some have called "post-cyberpunk," at least insofar as these are cyberpunk-inflected audio-visual narratives that cohere with cyberpunk's thematic concerns *but* do not speculate with a "cyberspace" or a "metaverse" in an imagined somewhere or somewhen else.[5] Instead, the distinctive feature of the new media dystopia is that it examines the real "cyberspace" or "metaverse" of actually-existing digital capitalism and, for this reason, our sub-genre tends to be formally reflexive with regard to currently existing media—the same media that are used to distribute and consume them.

The unintentionally ironic reappropriation of cyberpunk concepts by digital-capitalist elites is one of the most significant and readily visible signs of the radical ideological shift undergone by SF imaginaries—and this is, to my mind, the foremost contextual explanation for the genre's reflexive turn. While William Gibson first coined "cyberspace" to refer to the hyper-capitalist cyber-dystopia of an even more dystopian offline world (see "Burning Chrome"; and also *Neuromancer*), John Perry Barlow's

---

4   Since the 1980s, the time of the publication of *Mirrorshades: A Cyberpunk Anthology* (edited by Bruce Sterling, first published in 1986), cyberpunk has mutated from an SF sub-genre into a whole culture, with manifestations across media, arts and even in critical theory (see Murphy and Vint, *Beyond Cyberpunk*; McFarlane et al., *The Routledge Companion to Cyberpunk Culture*; McFarlane et al., *Fifty Key Figures in Cyberpunk Culture*).

5   The notion of post-cyberpunk has been suggested in *Rewired: The Post-Cyberpunk Anthology* (2007), where it is defined as a continuation of cyberpunk's "adversarial relationship to consensus reality" in a context in which "reality itself is everywhere mediated, and what comes between the characters and reality must constantly be interrogated" (Kelly and Kessel xii). Nevertheless, despite its conceptual value in opening the way to new conceptualizations (like my "new media dystopia"), Graham J. Murphy notes that "differentiating between 'cyberpunk' and 'post-cyberpunk' seems akin to splitting hairs, especially considering the cyberpunk label is unwilling to give up the ghost" (532) and I would concur with him in that (a) it seems premature to proclaim cyberpunk's death and (b) post-cyberpunk remains vaguely undefined.

Declaration of Independence of Cyberspace soon rewrote it as the radically libertarian utopia of an electronic agora (see Section 1.3.2 of Chapter 1). And similarly, while Neal Stephenson first coined "metaverse" to refer to another cyber-dystopian VR run by Mafiosi corporations (see *Snow Crash*), Mark Zuckerberg's 2021 rebranding of his Facebook corporation as "Meta" has re-appropriated the term to promise an augmented-reality version of social media that shall presumably be better for everything: productivity, communication, entertainment, etc.[6] Even the Wachoswki sisters' iconic "matrix"—the digital dystopia from the eponymous franchise (*The Matrix*; *The Matrix Reloaded*; *The Matrix Revolutions*)—seems to have become acutely aware of its present-day status as a corporate commodity, as evinced by the overtly self-conscious irony of its 2021 reboot (Lana Wachowski's *The Matrix Resurrections*).[7] In such a context of corporate re-appropriation of SF—the historical moment of what Vint and others call "the futures industry" and Ramírez calls "business SF"—even William Gibson, widely regarded as the founding figure of literary cyberpunk, has gravitated away

---

6   Zuckerberg is neither unaccompanied nor unaided in making this radical rewriting of Stephenson's term and one could also note the role of Matthew Ball's 2020 essay "The Metaverse." In such essay, this technophile thinker, popular amongst Californian circles, heralded the imminent arrival of the metaverse as a fulfillment of long-awaited techno-utopian promises. And quite tellingly, one of the benefits that are most emphasized by Ball is the metaverse's status as a "fully functioning digital economy" (n.p.). With a probably unintentional honesty, Ball thus reminds us how new media are, as I put it in Section 1.3, extensions of capital.

7   Within the diegetic world of *The Matrix Resurrections*, the three previous instalments of the film franchise are re-imagined as an overexploited franchise of videogames, designed by their actual protagonist (Keanu Reeves) and produced by their actual producer (Warner). Thus, the new film has its cake and eats it, insofar as it makes a critical caricature of itself, its producers and its fandom and at the same time it gets to nostalgically replay the same old narrative formulas without the speculative and philosophical *gravitas* of the three previous films. Nonetheless, this intensified reflexivity is probably not to be dismissed from a nostalgic attachment to the original and it is interesting as a symptom (and to some extent an immanent critique) of the broader epochal shift from the speculative to the reflexive.

from speculation and towards a formally reflexive concern with the limits of the genre within a context that challenges its estranging capabilities.⁸

Observing this tendency in Gibson's work since his 1990s Bridge trilogy, which is set in a relatively less remote future than his "proper" cyberpunk of earlier years, Robert Briggs notes that "SF's predictive potential has not been overcome so much as displaced" (673) and that "prediction, popularly accepted as a marker of SF's generic identity, is increasingly displaced from the narrative form itself and onto particular objects and characters appearing within the novels' diegetic worlds," which dramatize the impasse of any speculative efforts in the present context (675). In this regard, Briggs argues that Gibson's oeuvre "starts to take on a strange kind of metafictional quality, activating the idea of prediction not simply as a contested description of SF's *raison d'être*, but moreover as the very object of science fictional speculation" (675)—and, thus, this meta-generic kind of reflexivity leads Briggs to speak of Gibson's recent works as examples of "meta-SF," a term with a long but contradictory history of conceptual uses that on the whole attest to the genre's increasing affinity with the "meta" after postmodernity more generally.⁹ In the specific case of Briggs's

8   In a way that emphasizes the "presentism" of the epoch's (and SF's) imagination, a 2006 editorial of *SFS* already noted that "We find ourselves between, on the one hand, a posthumanity few believe in, entranced by the prospect of a technological transcendence that will make the future mute and inaccessible; and, on the other, a future that has collapsed so completely into the present that our most influential SF artist, William Gibson, has excised it entirely from his latest, most artistically ambitious novel" ("Editorial Introduction" 388).
     Of course, even if I am taking him here as a representative case, Gibson is neither absolutely paradigmatic nor entirely alone in such a status, as the founding figures of cyberpunk are a broad collective that is not restricted to SF writers, with figures such as J. G. Ballard, Jean Baudrillard, Charlie Brooker, William Gibson, Donna Haraway, the Wachowskis or Janelle Monáe (see McFarlane et al., *Fifty Key Figures in Cyberpunk Culture*). Thus, one should bear in mind that, as Graham J. Murphy observes in an overview of the sub-genre, "A significant problem for early cyberpunk […] was Gibson's success: the popularity of his narrative vision eclipsed the diversity of cyberpunk's early practitioners" (521).

9   Briggs is not the first to use this term, as it has been in circulation since at least the 1970s, when Carlo Pagetti's essay "Dick and Meta-SF" was translated for the second volume of *Science Fiction Studies* (see Pagetti et al.). Subsequently, in two

interpretation, he observes that speculation with the future no longer provides the formal structure of the genre, but rather becomes its object—that is, SF becomes speculation about speculation.

In a similar vein but focusing more on Gibson's later *Pattern Recognition* (2003), the first of his novels with a contemporary setting, Mathias Nilges has spoken of a "realism of speculation." Making an argument that nicely supplements Briggs' more formalist reading from a more socio-historical perspective, Nilges meditates upon "the dialectic of speculation that binds

---

essays published in 1980, Teresa Ebert and Carl Malmgren analyzed the SF of Samuel R. Delaney and Philip K. Dick, respectively, with an eye on the presence of postmodern reflexive forms (see Ebert; Malmgren, "Philip Dick's Man in the High Castle and the Nature of SF Worlds"). Years later, again Malmgren would propose using the term "meta-SF" to categorize a range of reflexive SF by Dick, Ursula K. Le Guin and Joanna Russ (see "Meta-SF: The Examples of Dick, LeGuin, and Russ"). However, as Amanda Dillon would note in her thesis on metafiction and science fiction, Malmgren "stops short of identifying what makes these stories metafictional science fiction [...] rather than straightforward metafiction on a large scale, metaphorical level" (21)—a lack of formalist systematization that Dillon's thesis addresses. Other than these articles and two three-page-long sub-sections within surveys of the genre—one about "Metafictional SF" in Bould and Vint's *Concise History of Science Fiction* (see 106–8) and another about "Postmodernist Self-Reflexivity" by Veronica Hollinger in Seed's *A Companion to Science Fiction* (see 234–6)—the term "meta-SF" is rarely used and most often invoked rather anecdotally. The only exception, to my knowledge, is Dillon's PhD thesis, which very carefully examines the ontological affinities of SF and metafiction through a detailed analyses of a corpus of new wave SF novels and short stories. Throughout her thesis, Dillon often comes close to arguing that SF is always implicit metafiction insofar as the speculative genre, like metafiction, would systematically foreground poesis over mimesis, but she wisely cautions that this is just a *potential* affinity. A stronger and, perhaps, more debatable version of this argument is also made by Brian McHale's *Constructing Postmodernism*, where the author proposes that SF, by definition, "is self-consciously 'world-building' fiction, laying bare the process of fictional world-making itself" (*Postmodernist Fiction* 12). However, notwithstanding the potential value of "meta-SF" as a possible sub-phenomenon within postmodern/new-wave literary SF, in my view it is preferable *to keep distinguishing the reflexive and the speculative* and to focus on *the dialectic established between them*, considering them as two modes of cognitive estrangement, in theory clearly distinct though in practice often overlapping.

together the financial imagination," itself closely associated with the digital-technological imagination, "and the critical and political potential of speculative fiction in our time" (36–7). Following Fredric Jameson and Arjun Appadurai, Nilges argues that, with its "meta-SF" formal qualities, Gibson's novel "allows us to understand speculation as both the dominant logic of contemporary capitalism and as a guiding principle of the immanent critique of this form of capitalist thought via speculative fiction" (Nilges 38).[10] In other words, if SF is now often meta-SF, or speculation about speculation, that is because speculation itself has become essential to capitalist reality and, therefore, formal reflexivity becomes an essential tool for a more abstract kind of contextual reflection on the present. That is, if SF becomes a critique of the present from within dominant ideologies and imaginaries—if it becomes an immanent critique, that is—the implied opposition of SF and realism becomes at least partially blurred.[11]

Considering these theorizations, it appears that even literary SF such as Gibson's (but not only) would seem almost fated to become either some (arguably) "reflexive" form of "meta-SF," or a new kind of "realism" for these (provocatively speaking) "SF times"—or maybe a bit of both things at once. But is this historic-aesthetic tendency as contradictory towards "the

10   In an essay that reflects upon Gibson's turn, Jameson has similarly observed that "the representational apparatus of Science Fiction, here [in Gibson's *Pattern Recognition*] refined and transistorized in all kinds of new and productive ways, sends back more reliable information about the contemporary world than an exhausted realism (or an exhausted modernism either)" (*Archaeologies* 384), a position that clearly inspires Nilges's own arguments. But besides Jameson, Nilges also draws from Arjun Appadurai's understanding of speculation as "a form of immanent critique" that "does not ally itself with transcendental or utopian positions. It inhabits its object, and finds within it the limits of its own assumptions and reveals alternative normativities" (Appadurai 208; qtd. in Nilges 50), a specific understanding of speculation that makes it easier to imagine its affinity with reflexivity.
11   In this regard, Nilges draws from Ernst Bloch's conception of realism, understood "not as fidelity to truth, as in Lukács, but as a matter of immanent critique, as a relationship to the present that is at every point also bound up with speculation on that which is missing, which it turn traces in the existing the latent potential and those unfulfilled desires and repressed wishes that open up the present to the futurity of what Bloch famously calls the 'not yet'" (54).

essence of SF" as it seems? Should one really say that this is no longer SF? Against the dominance of "presentism" both in our dystopian structure of feeling and in SF generally, it seems necessary to return to a definition of SF that allows to grasp how this whole turn need not be the genre's negation but, perhaps, even be coherent with its presumed function under these changed historical circumstances. And the genre's definition begins with a simple question: was SF ever simply about the future? Was speculation ever reducible to prediction? If we are indeed confronted with a reflexive turn, as the aforementioned studies seem to suggest from varying theoretical backgrounds (some of which are contradictory with the framework to be employed later), then there is a need to rethink our definition of SF in order to then incorporate a clearer, rigorous understanding of what reflexivity is—formally speaking—and what it can—ideologically speaking—say about our dystopian, media-dominated times. To be sure, as can be gathered from these studies, reflexivity has gained importance *vis-à-vis* speculation at the same time as the present has become "science-fictional," but this should not lead us into simplistically associating reflexivity with the present and speculation with the future. Observing that we live in a "cyberpunk reality" that poses serious limits and challenges to most (post-) cyberpunk fiction—and to audio-visual narratives especially—may serve as a socio-historical explanation for this reflexive turn, but it is not valid as a rigorous definition of SF, nor of reflexivity. So we must begin defining both.

2.1.2. Speculation and Reflexivity as Modes of Estrangement

Although SF is popularly and by default associated with the future, "futurism" cannot be the defining criterion of the genre—and it never was, at least not since the emergence of SF studies as an academic field. Already in the 1970s, when SF theory and literature were flourishing together, Ursula K. Le Guin herself sentenced that "Prediction is the business of prophets, clairvoyants, and futurologists. It is not the business of novelists. A novelist's business is lying" (xix). As she puts it, "science fiction isn't about the future" (xxi), which is to say that SF "is not predictive; it is descriptive" (xviii) and, therefore, in its own way, about the present.¹² But what is SF's "own way" of speaking about the present? For an answer, one must turn to Darko Suvin's concept of "cognitive estrangement," the most influential definition of the genre, proposed during that same decade and systematized in his *Metamorphoses of Science Fiction* (1979).

In the previous chapter, I already touched upon Suvin's concept of *the novum* as the hegemonic force within an SF narrative: the novelty (or novelties) around which SF narration revolves in accordance with cognitive logic—or, more specifically, in accordance with a historically situated semblance of the logical. However, the *novum* is only a formal-thematic device—even if the hegemonic one—within the genre and, as such, it still needs to be understood as part of SF's structural functioning as "the literature of cognitive estrangement." In his most concise and most quoted passage, Suvin defines SF as

> a fictional tale determined by the hegemonic literary device of a *locus* and/or *dramatis personae* that (1) are *radically or at least significantly different from the empirical times, places and characters* of 'mimetic' or 'naturalist' fiction, but (2) are nonetheless—to the extent that SF differs from other 'fantastic' genres, that is, ensembles of fictional tales without empirical validation—simultaneously perceived as *not impossible* within the cognitive (cosmological and anthropological) norms of the author's epoch. Basically, SF is a developed oxymoron, a realistic irreality, with humanized

---

12 Elsewhere in the same 1973 introduction to *The Left Hand of Darkness*, Le Guin makes this point in the clearest of ways:

> All fiction is metaphor. Science fiction is metaphor. What sets it apart from older forms of fiction seems to be its use of new metaphors, drawn from certain great dominants of our contemporary life—science, all the sciences, and technology, and the relativistic and the historical outlook, among them. Space travel is one of these metaphors; so is an alternative society, an alternative biology; the future is another. The future, in fiction, is a metaphor. A metaphor for what? If I could have said it non-metaphorically, I would not have written all these words, this novel; and Genly Ai would never have sat down at my desk and used up my ink and typewriter ribbon in informing me, and you, rather solemnly, that the truth is a matter of the imagination. (Le Guin xxii–xxiii)

Furthermore, Le Guin's same novel seems to reflexively return to this polemic in one chapter—specifically, when one Handdara foreteller (an alien clairvoyant) explicitly tells the protagonist that their job is not to predict *per se*, but in so doing "to exhibit the perfect uselessness of knowing the answer to the wrong question" (74).

nonhumans, this-worldly Other Worlds, and so forth. Which means that it is—potentially—the space of a potent *estrangement*, validated by the pathos and prestige of the basic cognitive norms of our times. (*Metamorphoses* viii)

Ultimately, the presumed (and prescribed) function of SF is estrangement and offering a critical cognition of the present. As Suvin explains later,

> Even where SF suggests—sometimes strongly—a flight from this context, this is an optical illusion and an epistemological trick. The escape is, in all such significant SF, one to a better vantage point from which to comprehend the human relations around the author. It is [...] a device for historical estrangement, and an at least initial readiness for new norms of history, for the novum of dealienating human history. [...] the critic, in order to understand [the genre] properly, will have to integrate sociohistorical into formal knowledge, diachrony into synchrony. History has not ended with the 'post-industrial' society: as Bloch said, Judgement Day is also Genesis, and Genesis is every day. (*Metamorphoses* 84)

With such grandiose claims, Suvin is setting the bar high, proposing that SF's ideal function is nothing less than demystifying historical dynamics in order to allow us to imagine anew a utopian horizon for history. However, he himself acknowledges that "an opposed tendency toward mystifying escapism dominates in second-rate SF and shows even in the masters," since the genre is shaped "by the practical and cognitive limitations of fiction steeped in the alienation of class society" (*Metamorphoses* xi).[13]

For the time being, however, let us assume that SF today—and the new media dystopia in particular—is still the kind of fiction that can at least try to provide a critical, totalizing overview of the present as an ongoing (and thus open) part of history. Along Suvin's line of thought, Fredric Jameson similarly argues that "the most characteristic SF does not seriously attempt to imagine the 'real' future of our social system. Rather, its multiple mock futures serve the quite different function of transforming our own present into the determinate past of something yet to come." Thus, SF "enacts and enables a structurally unique 'method' for apprehending the present as

---

13 Speaking of SF's "masters," Suvin canonizes writers from all ages: Lucian of Samosata, Thomas More, Cyrano de Bergerac, Jonathan Swift, Mary Shelley, Jules Verne, H. G. Wells, or Karel Čapek, among others that he studies in the historical part of his *Metamorphoses*.

history, and this is so irrespective of the 'pessimism' or 'optimism' of the imaginary future world which is the pretext for that defamiliarization" ("Progress Versus Utopia" 152–3). From this perspective, then, SF does not operate through "pure" extrapolation and one could say that it could even function through some kind of "intrapolation," an exploration of its own conditions of possibility—whether these conditions are, I would add, ideological or medial. In other words, cognitive estrangement need not be built upon the imaginary strangeness of the new or the remote, it can also be built upon the often-unimagined strangeness of the here-and-now—and therefore, through the many reflexive devices to be surveyed later, it may also be built upon the strangeness of its own medium.

In dissociating SF from prediction and instead insisting upon estrangement, these definitions will allow us to develop a view of SF as a *potentially* reflexive genre, especially since reflexivity can also have an estranging force—and other authors have suggested this possibility even more explicitly than Suvin.[14] Besides Briggs's and others' conceptualizations of "meta-SF,"[15] several key figures have suggested that SF might need to become reflexive with regard to its habits and conventions, or even that it is inherently so. Stanisław Lem, who himself wrote some of the most notably reflexive SF of the past century,[16] once wrote about the need for a "metafuturology." Presumably appealing to both SF critics and creators, Lem proposed an ambivalently reflexive attitude towards futuristic speculation, especially in the face of the growing numbers of "petty prophets" who

---

14 Suvin's theory does not directly express this, although he does suggest the possibility of distinguishing between modes of cognitive estrangement, between "two main species or models, the extrapolative and the analogical" (*Metamorphoses* 27).
15 See again note 9 earlier in this section.
16 See, especially, Lem's *The Futurological Congress* (1974), which has been analyzed as a "metageneric text" in the tradition of Philip K. Dick's *Ubik* and H.G Well's *The Time Machine* (see Philmus, "'Futurological Congress' as Metageneric Text") and as a "postmodern game of ontology" (see Swirski), given how it imagines a future in which drug-induced hallucinations have replaced reality. Interestingly, Lem's novella was loosely adapted to the screen in 2013, in Ari Folman's *The Congress*, a film which reflexively and speculative meditates upon the culture industry's role as an institution plausibly oriented towards the construction of a fully-immersive hallucination.

"prepare self-fulfilling programs" fueled by "political [and economic] opportunism" (Lem and Csicsery-Ronay Jr 269). Thus, Lem's metafuturology would be "the complement of prediction, the study of its greatest possibilities and its most painful limits" (264)—a critical-reflexive attitude that would be assumed not only by SF studies but also by much postmodern SF, which would often become a meditation upon the genre's possibilities even before (post-)cyberpunk's own reflexive turn.[17]

But besides Lem's *proposed* reflexivity, Fredric Jameson interestingly contends that SF—or at least, postmodern SF—is inherently and inevitably meta-science-fictional, in a markedly allegorical interpretation of reflexivity that nonetheless offers an ideological explanation of the formal phenomenon. Specifically, Jameson suggests that SF should not be read as "representation" of the future, but as a genre whose "deepest vocation is over and over again to dramatize our incapacity to imagine the future" ("Progress Versus Utopia" 153). Thinking about postmodern SF in general and commenting upon Ursula K. Le Guin's *Lathe of Heaven* and the Strugatsky brothers' *Roadside Picnic* in particular, Jameson observes that

> the very thrust of literary modernism—with its *public introuvable* and the breakdown of traditional cultural institutions, in particular the social "contract" between writer and reader—has had as one significant structural consequence the transformation of the cultural text into an *auto-referential* discourse, whose content is a perpetual interrogation of its own conditions of possibility [... and] this is no less the case with the utopian [or dystopian] text. Indeed, [...] as the true vocation of the utopian [or dystopian] narrative begins to rise to the surface—to confront us with our incapacity to imagine Utopia—the center of gravity of such narratives shifts towards an auto-referentiality of a specific, but far more concrete type: such texts then explicitly or implicitly, and as it were against their own will, find their deepest "subjects" in the possibility of their own production, in the interrogation of the dilemmas involved in their own emergence as utopian [or dystopian] texts. ("Progress Versus Utopia" 156)

---

17 For a reference compilation of postmodern (and cyberpunk) SF, see Larry McCaffery's *Storming the Reality Studio*; for a reference study of postmodern SF, see Damien Broderick's *Reading by Starlight*; and, finally, for an examination of postmodern SF which expressly focuses upon its metafictional aspects, see Amanda Dillon's *Prism, Mirror, Lens*.

For Jameson, then, SF would be not only about speculation, but also about the very (im)possibility of speculation. Thus, if a degree of reflexivity is already inherent to SF, isn't there even more reason to expect an intensified reflexivity in this epoch? In an age that is seemingly devoid of the capacity to imagine alternatives and haunted by the corporate appropriation of SF imaginaries, SF no longer needs to look outward, otherward or future-ward; it can instead look inward—into itself and into the new media platforms through which it circulates.

Whatever one makes of all these meditations upon reflexivity in SF—as a more or less inherent characteristic of the genre, as a proposed project for SF criticism and creation and as a historical dominant in the digital epoch—what seems to have been proven is that *reflexivity and speculation may be seen as two dialectically interrelated modes of estrangement, often contradicting but still compatible with each other and with the genre's presumed function*. In fact, one of the new media dystopias to be repeatedly analyzed in subsequent chapters—Lisa Joy and Jonathan Nolan's *Westworld* (2016–22)—is, to my mind, a clear instance of how speculation and reflexivity may even be complementary and mutually reinforcing with regard to estrangement. As I have already argued elsewhere taking distinct but complementary approaches (see "All the Park's a Stage"; "Subverting or Reasserting?"; "Allegorising Surveillance Capitalism"), the series' combination of the reflexive and the speculative allows it to function as a peculiarly potent and nuanced critical allegory of intersectional domination under digital capitalism—though not without ambivalences, as is explored in the next chapter.

For now, having surveyed "the meta question" in contemporary SF and in order to clarify the characteristics of this "turn" formally speaking, it is time to turn our attention towards a rigorous theorization of reflexivity as such—a concept that is, quite confusingly, often invoked without any definition, or merely suggested by unimaginatively adding the meta- prefix to more and more words.

2.2. Reflecting upon Reflexivity: Modes, Levels and Devices[18]

The wide range of meta-terms—the metaverse of the meta—has a long history, traceable to the first use of the prefix in Aristotle's *Metaphysics*, where μετά- signified *after* or *beyond*. However, in contemporary usage, the meta- prefix denotes a certain (self-)reflexive quality, being perhaps closer to αὐτο- than to μετά-.[19] At least generally, today's usage is traceable to—and vaguely coherent with—Roland Barthes' use of "metalanguage" and Roman Jakobson's identification of a "metalinguistic function," which referred to language referring to itself. In the wake of these structuralist terms, "metafiction" is coined by William H. Gass in 1970 and is then theorized by several literary scholars in the following years, of whom the most renowned were Robert Scholes ("Metafiction"; *Fabulation and Metafiction*), Robert Alter (*Partial Magic: The Novel as Self-Conscious Genre*), Linda Hutcheon (*Narcissistic Narrative: The Metafictional Paradox*) and Patricia Waugh (*Metafiction: The Theory and Practice of Self-Conscious Fiction*).[20] Although these scholars generally define metafiction as "fictional writing which self-consciously and systematically draws attention to its status as an artefact in order to pose questions about the

---

18 This section would not stand as it stands were it not for a continued discussion and collaboration with Lucía Bausela Buccianti, who was finishing her doctoral thesis on metacomics, now completed, at the same time as I was writing this part of my book. I am truly grateful to her for openly and generously sharing some of her references, ideas and doubts regarding reflexivity across media and, also, for her comradeship in building new knowledge by creatively using the theoretical model of Pedro Javier Pardo García.

19 Perhaps partly for this reason, I find Pedro Javier Pardo's use of the prefix "auto-," which I here translate as "self-," preferable to the use of the greatly distorted and dangerously flexible meta-prefix, the one used most frequently in theorizations of reflexivity, as in Wolf's "metareferentiality" (see notes below).

20 Although the term is only used once in Gass's *Fiction and the Figures of Life*, the observation that "many of the so-called antinovels are really metafictions" (Gass 25) would be immortalized by theories of metafiction, beginning with Scholes, who uses it as an epigraph ("Metafiction" 100).

relationship between fiction and reality" (Waugh 2), this definition was gradually muddled and/or diluted by the (ab)use of this and other interrelated terms, such as the aforementioned "meta-SF."[21] Furthermore, in addition to the inevitable simplification entailed by a concept's (or, in this case, also a prefix's) popularization, there is also the added complication of conceptualizing metafiction beyond the novel—the main object of study of the above-mentioned theories—and that is a necessary step towards a transmedia theorization of the meta, one that no longer remains bound to the written medium.

Fortunately for this book, film reflexivity is the second-most theorized, medium-specific form of reflexivity (see Stam, *Reflexivity in Film and Literature*; Blüher; Ames; Fevry; Pérez Bowie).[22] Furthermore, film is also a

21 Of course, not all these early theorists coincide with Waugh's narrow definition of metafiction as systematic self-consciousness. The most divergent approach, in this regard, is perhaps that of Linda Hutcheon's, insofar as her differentiation of "overt" and "covert" metafiction allows for a considerable hermeneutical flexibility in categorizing works as metafiction. Besides, Robert Alter does not use "meta-terms," but his definition of "the self-conscious novel" is broadly coincident with Waugh's definition of metafiction as systematic self-consciousness (see Alter xi)—and interestingly, he employs another, broader concept ("self-reflexiveness") to refer to a more general kind of reflexivity, in many ways akin to Pedro Javier Pardo's notion of self-referentiality, explained below.

Besides, in these passages, I am singling out the three works that happen to be the most influential for Pedro Javier Pardo's model, but there are uncountable studies of metafiction and/or self-consciousness published roughly at the time or after (cf. Inger; McCaffery, *The Metafictional Muse*; Boyd; Imhof; Stonehill; Currie), as well as studies of more specific reflexive phenomena, such as the self-begetting novel, the mise en abyme, or the metalepsis (cf. Kellman; Dällenbach; Malina; Kukkonen and Klimek).

22 With a rather overcautious phrasing, Werner Wolf observes that "the notion of 'metafilm' or 'self-reflexivity' in film is by now not entirely unknown in film studies," citing the works of Robert Stam, Christopher Ames, Christian Metz and Slavoj Žižek (*Metareference across Media* 5). Wolf then proceeds to enumerate virtually all media besides literature (painting, architecture, comics and even music), showing "the meta" is even less theorized almost everywhere else. Relatedly, Pedro Javier Pardo's own transmedia theorization of reflexivity seems to illustrate this, insofar as his model seems to have grown, chronologically, from reflexivity in literature towards, first, reflexivity in film, and later, reflexivity in theater—although, crucially,

common and prominent example in more transversal and transmedia theories of reflexivity, such as Wolf's and Pardo's.[23] However, since my goal in this chapter is, specifically, to examine reflexivity within new media SF, my engagement with these theories is necessarily partial and instrumental—transmedia in theory but medium- and genre-specific in practice. My hope, nonetheless, is to establish some grounds for a deeper dialog between SF studies and theories of reflexivity, as well as to reformulate certain ideas within the context of digital platforms, since these platforms have

---

he applies the same formal framework with admirable clarity and coherence (cf. "La metaficcion de la literatura al cine"; "Hacia una teoría de la reflexividad fílmica"; "La reflexividad teatral del escenario a la pantalla"; "Del metateatro a la metaficción teatral en el cine").

23 Here I will be following Pedro Javier Pardo's model, explained below, but Wolf's concept of "metareferentiality" stands as an alternative, contemporaneous conceptualization of what Pardo calls "self-referentiality," within which Pardo's "self-consciousness" (which Wolf seems to term self-reference) would fit as a subcategory, rather than as a distinct mode. Wolf defends his terminological choice by saying that "'metareference' generally helps avoid the problem that would occur if in a transmedial approach one chose a term that implied references to individual media or macro-modes only (as, for instance, 'metafiction', 'metadescription' and so forth). As for the prefix 'meta-' (rather than 'self-'), it seems best to mark the logical nature of the phenomenon under discussion, which implies the difference between an object and a metalevel. Moreover, the term has been chosen to show that the phenomena in question are special cases of, but not co-extensive with, self-reference" (*Metareference across Media* 15). His definition, however, seems to run the risk of conflating a broader kind of self-referentiality with the self-consciousness of artworks who refer to themselves as such for a more markedly anti-illusionist and/or estranging effect. In Wolf's words,

metareference can thus be defined [as] a special, transmedial form of usually nonaccidental self-reference produced by signs or sign configurations which are (felt to be) located on a logically higher level, a 'metalevel', within an artefact or performance; this self-reference, which can extend from this artefact to the entire system of the media, forms or implies a statement about an object-level, namely on (aspects of) the medium/system referred to. Where metareference is properly understood, an at least minimal corresponding 'meta-awareness' is elicited in the recipient, who thus becomes conscious of both the medial (or 'fictional' in the sense of artificial and, sometimes in addition, 'invented') status of the work under discussion and the fact that media-related phenomena are at issue, rather than (hetero-)references to the world outside the media. (*Metareference across Media* 31)

specificities that require refining the terms of analysis. Just as one might think, with McKenzie Wark, that a new mode of production is emerging on top of capitalism, my proposition in this chapter is that new modes and levels of reflexivity are enabled by digital platforms, especially if one considers how interfaces act as a mediating, pseudo-diegetic layer standing between the user and the diegeses of those fictional "contents" on offer in the platform. However, to understand the new, one must first understand the old—that is, the functioning of reflexivity in general, something that is usefully schematized by Pardo's model.[24]

2.2.1. Self-Referentiality and Self-Consciousness

To explain reflexivity, I hope that I can be excused to pause and say:

Dear reader,

Aren't you bored of this monograph? I surely am bored at the time of writing, locked in a lugubrious college room with my half-broken laptop and a pile of handwritten notes. However, I hope that, for a change, I can have a little fun writing this shamelessly un-academic paragraph. I am caught in between the pressing need to keep on writing and the temptation of switching from this word-processing programme to any social media. Saturated with the density of theory, I'd rather be saturated with the spectacle of digital platforms, falling down the rabbit hole of my filter bubble. And I would be a hypocrite, wouldn't I? How can I have the nerve of writing more than a hundred and thirty pages (and counting) against our new media dystopia if I can't resist the urge of turning back to its platforms? Well, of course, if you've been paying attention, you'd realize that I have not spoken of hypocrisy, but rather of capitalism's structural contradictions. So I thought: why not disrupt this book's style and structure for a second and pause to reflect on it? Wouldn't that help explain what reflexivity is in an explicitly self-conscious and self-referential way?

---

24 Although I am focusing on his own formulations, Pardo's model emerges from his collaboration with academics like Pérez Bowie or Gil González, with whom he has co-authored, co-edited and collaborated in research groups concerned with reflexivity and transmedia theory (see especially Gil González and Pérez Bowie; Pardo García and Gil González).

Much broader than metafiction, reflexivity is, in Pardo's theoretical model, "the process or act of reflecting upon or about the medium" ("Hacia una teoría de la reflexividad fílmica" 47, my translation), which is what the paragraph above does: it comments upon its genre (the academic book as a codified written form) and its medium (the word-processing program and digital technologies in general as a writing tool).[25] Furthermore, Pardo's model begins with two kinds of reflexivity: (1) "self-referentiality" ("autoreferencialidad" in the original Spanish) and (2) "self-consciousness" ("autoconciencia").[26] Whereas self-referentiality is the most "basic" kind of reflexivity, as it designates any artwork's reference to its "medium" broadly understood, self-consciousness is "a kind of self-referentiality squared, as it designates any artwork that refers to itself as an artwork" ("Hacia una teoría de la reflexividad fílmica" 51).[27] Going back to the paragraph above, one could therefore distinguish between (1) the self-referentiality of referring to academic monographs generally

---

25 All translations from Spanish-language texts are my own unless otherwise indicated.

26 The second, self-consciousness, seems inspired by definitions of metafiction in literature such as Waugh's and, precisely for this reason, Pardo suggests limiting our use of "metafiction" and "metafictional" to those works with *primary self-consciousness*. Besides, as his model makes clear, this is not a binary distinction between two mutually exclusive things, but a porous distinction of two kinds of reflexivity that often overlap and can co-exist in a range of complex combinations, especially as soon as one introduces the distinction between *covert* and *overt* modes (borrowed from Hutcheon, *Narcissistic Narrative*).

27 Pardo's usage of "medium" is much broader than my own (mostly restricted to the technological apparatus and platform). As clarified elsewhere, Pardo follows an expansively synthetic definition of "medium" as "a physical support for creation, a language from a semiotic point of view, a tradition of texts and aesthetic practices, and a communication technology," all of which come together as a medium within "a cultural field and a system of institutionalized agents and social practices" (Gil González and Pérez Bowie 13; qtd. in Pardo García and Gil González 16). Thus, from this definition, genres may also be seen as part of an artwork's medium, since they provide a text with a codified language, a set of formal devices and a shared imaginary, and it is probably in this "metageneric" sense that one may most rigorously speak of "meta-SF" as a very specific form of self-referentiality. However, for reasons of its variegated and often conflicting uses, in this book I am avoiding "meta-SF" to instead speak of *reflexivity within SF*.

and/or to critical theories specifically and (2) the self-consciousness of referring to this book's own process of writing and/or to its structure and ideas. Of course, as my reflexive paragraph illustrates, there can be significant overlaps between the two modes, as they are only totally distinct in theory, but self-referentiality and self-consciousness nonetheless conceptualize a useful distinction that is often obscured by (ab)uses of the meta- prefix.

Making this distinction within the broad field of reflexive art and culture seems essential in order to separate generic self-referentiality from self-conscious artworks (and self-conscious devices) that produce "a deliberate anti-illusionist effect and a critical distancing in the reader [or the user-spectator]" and, in turn, have an effect ranging "from the ludic to the didactic, in [Robert] Stam's terms" (Pardo García, "Hacia una teoría de la reflexividad fílmica" 52; see also Stam, *Reflexivity in Film and Literature*).[28] As a double kind of reflexivity that may combine the powers of the ludic ("I hope that I can have a little fun") and the didactic ("Wouldn't that help explain what reflexivity is?"), self-consciousness offers an anti-illusionist, distancing device for estrangement. Nevertheless, although not necessarily and perhaps only partially, self-referentiality may also fulfill that estranging function, especially in cases in which it is a form of indirect self-consciousness—that is, an indirect reflection upon the artwork itself via a reflection upon the medium generally.[29] In this sense, one cannot hastily

28 In addition to Robert Stam's ludic-didactic modes, Pardo also mentions how reflexive works may also be thought of as having effects ranging "from the epistemological to the ethical, in [Manuel] González de Ávila's terms" (Pardo García, "Hacia una teoría de la reflexividad fílmica" 52; see also González De Ávila, "Metasemiosis"). In any case, both the ludic-didactic and epistemological-ethical binaries should be thought as two dialectical opposites, not necessarily opposed but often complementary, as it should be obvious that perspectival playfulness and/or epistemological questioning can reinforce didactic, ethical and, of course, political purposes. Stam himself clarified that the ludic and the didactic "are by no means mutually exclusive, nor can they be simplistically attached to a given period, artist, or even text" (*Reflexivity in Film and Literature* xii).

29 Pardo goes much further in detailing the possible overlaps and potential recombinations of the modes, which are multiple and complex as soon as one hypothesizes with the possibility of direct and indirect modes. Thus seen, "not only is self-consciousness a form of self-referentiality, but self-referentiality can also be

equate the self-conscious with the estranging and the subversive, because the self-referential can also be a vehicle for such effects—and above all, because neither of the two modes are necessary estranging or subversive *per se*. Therefore, what should be clear is that, like SF, reflexivity more generally is, in a way, another form of "entertaining escapism"—and precisely as such, at least potentially, it is also an "escapism" towards an epistemological vantage point wherefrom to better comprehend both fiction and reality. Or, to put it differently: neither the "escapism" of the speculative nor the "narcissism" of the reflexive need be seen as "bad" characteristics of a "truly popular literature" that is "fully engaged with reality and fully grasps reality" (Brecht 85). On the contrary, the speculative and the reflexive may often be (at their best) allied as subversive formal devices, especially within a historical situation that is as science-fictional and media-dominated as the present.

Of course, saying that both reflexivity and SF are (potentially) means towards estrangement should not obscure one key difference that is at the same time a dialectical contradiction: whereas SF generally attains estrangement by an illusionist *immersion* into the diegetic world, self-consciousness generally attains estrangement by an anti-illusionistic *extraction* from the diegetic world.[30] In this regard, in reflexive SF there emerges a tension that may be described as a new version of "the metafictional paradox" once theorized by Linda Hutcheon. For her, self-conscious (or, in her language, "narcissistic") narratives can be both intramural and extramural—that is, these narratives at the same time refer to their fictional interiority and to the world external to the diegesis. Thus,

---

       self-consciousness, though always in an indirect way." Besides, cases like Brechtian theater further complicate the possibilities, since his plays "are often self-conscious in an implicit manner, without self-reference, though they can at times be so explicitly by alluding to their status as theatre plays, as is the case at the end of *Die Dreigroschenoper*" ("Hacia una teoría de la reflexividad fílmica" 53–5)

30 In one conversation about reflexivity and SF with Pedro Javier Pardo and fellow doctoral students Lucía Bausela, Rodrigo Bacigalupe and Paula Cantero, Pardo made one observation that has significantly shaped my formulation in these passages and I believe worth quoting it. At least as I recall it, he observed that, even if both SF and metafiction aim for estrangement, perhaps one could say that metafiction causes *estrangement by extraction*, while SF causes *estrangement by immersion*.

while he [*sic*] reads, the reader lives in a world which he is forced to acknowledge as fictional. However, paradoxically the text also demands that he participate, that he engage himself intellectually, imaginatively, and affectively in its co-creation. This two-way pull is the paradox of the reader. The text's own paradox is that it is both narcissistically self-reflexive and yet focused outward, oriented toward the reader. (*Narcissistic Narrative* 7)

In other words, the paradox is that, despite its anti-illusionism, self-consciousness still requires the existence of an illusion (and a suspension of disbelief) that may (or may not) be broken by self-conscious devices. The literary metafiction studied by Hutcheon was not only a reaction against "realist" or "mimetic" fiction, but also necessarily dependent— and one could even say *parasitical*—upon the continued existence of the suspension of disbelief with regard to an illusion.[31]

So how does self-consciousness work within (and against) SF? Although both SF and self-conscious fiction are, by definition, contrasted with realist and/or naturalist fiction, one cannot forget that SF still provides the cognitively believable illusion of (another) reality and, thus, self-consciousness can still operate in a parasitical relationship with this "unrealistic" genre. Despite the generic difference, then, the seemingly contradictory relationship of SF and the reflexive is still profoundly akin to that described by the metafictional paradox. And in any case, this is only an apparent paradox, so it is perhaps better described as *the dialectic of reflexivity*. Despite the contradictory impulses of immersion and extraction, in the end this tension can operate symbiotically and, perhaps, even generate a redoubled kind of cognitive estrangement. Thus, again I should insist that the speculative and the reflexive need not be seen as mutually defeating opposites, but as the two sides of a mutually reinforcing dialog.

---

31   Patricia Waugh expresses this dialectic with great clarity, arguing that "the essential deconstructive method of metafiction" consists of "the construction of an illusion through the imperceptibility of the frame and the shattering of illusion through the constant exposure of the frame" (31). In this sense, the prerequisite of deconstruction is a construction, so anti-illusionism requires an illusion, just like a frame-brake requires a frame, or a fourth-wall break requires a fourth wall.

2.2.2. Reflexivity across Diegetic Levels

Having defined reflexivity's main modes and dialectics, one should now ask: how do self-consciousness and self-referentiality operate? Following Gérard Genette's narratology, Pardo's model of reflexivity demands that we distinguish between three main diegetic levels—the extradiegetic, the (intra)diegetic and the metadiegetic, all of which are (at least potentially) present in any narrative, reflexive or not, regardless of medium:

> (a) The extradiegetic, first and foremost, is "the level at which the narrating act producing this narrative is placed" (Genette, *Narrative Discourse* 228), the place of the "narrating instance." Of course, even when the extradiegetic functions as an analogue, an allegory, or a simulation of them, this level is not to be confused with the author's real circumstances. Rather, the extradiegetic level refers to the circumstances surrounding the narrating agent, whether that is a fictionalized author, a character-narrator, or even a non-human agent (i.e. a machine producing a VR).[32] When this narrating instance is made explicit, the extradiegetic level can become the structural locale for representing (and potentially reflecting upon) the circumstances of creation, narration and/or reception. Therefore, this is a level that is always implicit in the act of narration, but not necessarily made explicit (verbally or visually).[33] However, if it is made explicit, the extradiegetic is

---

32 In saying "narrating agent" I am departing slightly from Genette, who uses "narrating voice," an expression that is in my opinion too narrowly focused on narration as a verbal act. Thus, to allow room for narratives from other media, I prefer the expression of "narrating agent," an expression that I have nonetheless derived from reflecting upon Genette's own work, particularly thinking about his insistence on *narration as an act*—thus, better than narrating voice, narrating agent.

33 Still, as I conjecture by the end of this chapter, one could argue that the digital platform functions as though it were an omnipresent extradiegetic layer, one that provides an interactive visualization of what Genette calls "the narrating instance" and, thus, a layer that constantly reminds the user that he is about to consume fiction, which kind of fiction and what else might go (or should go) next.

a potentially powerful place for reflexive practices, as the level of the narrative (or of the digital interface) where narration itself unfolds.

(b) Secondly, the intradiegetic (or simply, diegetic) level is where "any event a narrative recounts" takes place (*Narrative Discourse* 228). The very etymological meaning of "intradiegetic"—that which is inside or within the narrative—makes this clear: the intradiegetic is the "content" of the narrative; it is the story given (or, in SF, the other world being constructed) by the narrating agent from the extradiegetic level. However, just as "we shall not confound extradiegetic with real historical existence," we should also avoid confounding "diegetic (or even metadiegetic) status with fiction" (*Narrative Discourse* 230). Even in genres other than "realism," the diegesis can obviously consist of "real events" to a greater or lesser extent—but the key is that these events are contained within a narrative as its main "content." In any case, on this level, there are many possibilities for narrative reflexivity, some more overt and literal—that is, those stories that are (depending on medium) about readers, writers, spectators, filmmakers, software designers, or digital users—and others more covert and allegorical—that is, those cases that Pardo categorizes as "metafictional allegories," a concept to which I return below.

(c) Thirdly—though not necessarily finally—there is the metadiegetic level, which would be (if it is present) a "narrative in the second degree," a story-within-the-story produced by a character from the (intra)diegetic level (*Narrative Discourse* 228, see also 231–4). Potentially, this is not the final level, as there can be a meta-metadiegetic level, followed by a meta-meta-metadiegetic level and so on—but the relation would be the same: an agent within a story engages in the act of storytelling. And what are the possibilities for reflexivity on the metadiegetic level? Genette argues that metadiegetic narratives can have three kinds of relationships with the main diegesis: they can be (1) explanatory about some event or character, (2) unrelated acts of narration happening for their own sake (for entertainment or obfuscation of events), or (3) thematic narratives allowing contrasts or analogies with the main diegesis (*Narrative Discourse* 232–4).[34] It is this last kind of thematic relationship that allows for reflexive functioning and interpretation, insofar as, either by contrast or by analogy, the metadiegetic level would have a specular relation with the main diegesis—a kind of mirroring that is conventionally called a *mise-en-abyme*.[35]

Genette's schema of diegetic levels allows to map the potential places of reflexivity within narrative structures,[36] but this does not exhaust the possibilities. To have a more dynamic picture of how self-consciousness and self-referentiality operate, it is also necessary to consider reflexive devices that operate *across* levels. Immediately after discussing the three diegetic levels, Genette himself introduces the term "metalepsis"—borrowed from rhetoric—to refer to "any intrusion by the extradiegetic narrator or narratee into the diegetic universe (or by diegetic characters into a metadiegetic universe, etc.), or the inverse": an intrusion of a character

---

34 With regard to (1), retrospective narratives (in literature) and flashbacks (in film) are perhaps the most obvious examples of an explanatory metadiegesis. However, the relation between diegetic and metadiegetic is not to be mistaken for a temporal relation, as it is above all a narrative relation.
    Regarding type (2), Genette's example of a metadiegetic narration for the sake of narration (obfuscation or entertainment) is *Arabian Nights*, in which the stories-within-the-story generally have no connection (thematic or explanatory) with the main diegesis; rather, they illustrate how narration within the narrative can be an act like any other act done by a character.

35 The *mise-en-abyme*—an expression coined by André Gide and used in its original French in many other languages—is a metaphor inspired by medieval heraldry, since in heraldry, *abyme* refers to the central part of a coat of arms, where a smaller shield-within-the-shield can be placed for emphasis. Thus, the *mise-en-abyme* has long been used to refer to those metadiegetic narratives (and other devices) that function as "the mirror of the text" (see Dällenbach).

36 On the basis of Genette's levels and borrowing from previous theorists, Pardo proposes a distinct terminology for the kind of self-consciousness that may emerge at each of them: in the extradiegetic, one would speak of *discursive* metafiction; in the (intra)diegetic, of *narrative* metafiction; and in the metadiegetic, of *specular* metafiction (see "La metaficcion de la literatura al cine" 154).

in the level where their story is narrated, or of a narrating agent into the story they are narrating. Thus seen, metalepses would be "always transgressive" of narrative levels and they would produce "an effect of strangeness"—a *reflexive estrangement*, one might say. Commenting upon Jorge Luis Borges's fictions, Genette contends that "[t]he most troubling thing about metalepsis indeed lies in this unacceptable and insistent hypothesis, that the extradiegetic is perhaps always diegetic, and that the narrator and his narratees—you and I—perhaps belong to some narrative" (*Narrative Discourse* 234–6).[37] And do we—as Genette suggests here in a markedly postmodern fashion—belong to a narrative? Or, perhaps, to a dystopian narrative? *Do any of the abstract phenomena described in this book jump out of the page and shed light on the world around you, dear reader?* Rhetoric aside, what should be clear is that metalepses are an *a priori* impossible jump across levels that, if it has a self-conscious effect, may contribute towards estrangement.[38]

37   Here I am borrowing on Genette's *Narrative Discourse*, but he would later devote a book-length essay to the metalepsis, which has been translated to Spanish but not to English (see Genette, *Metalepsis*). In English, besides, there is one monograph devoted to the role of metalepsis in fictional characterization and the construction subjectivity (see Malina) and another about on the spread of metalepsis in popular culture (see Kukkonen and Klimek).
38   The metalepsis may be almost by definition self-conscious, but not necessarily, as Pardo observes. *A priori*, "in short-circuiting ontological levels," the metalepsis entails "a confession of fictionality" and it would thus be a marker of self-consciousness ("Hacia una teoría de la reflexividad fílmica" 51). However, metalepses may be in some cases justified intradiegetically, as a character's flight of fancy or as a drug-induced hallucination (see "Hacia una teoría de la reflexividad fílmica" especially 60, 77), among other possibilities that are allowed by non-realist fiction.
     In this regard, the anti-illusionist effect of metalepses may be significantly reduced or ambiguated within the framework of the SF genre. Although not necessarily, in SF, metalepses can easily be given an intradiegetic explanation that justifies transgressing diegetic levels. Here, one can think of cases in which the metadiegetic level is not a conventional narrative, but rather a VR or a bubble universe from which it is difficult (but not impossible) to escape. Or similarly, one can think of SF narratives that hypothesize with the possibility of a multiverse, of jumping between dimensions, etc. In suchlike cases, then a metalepsis need not be such an estranging device, but rather cognitively plausible within the SF diegesis.

2.2.3. Other Reflexive Devices

If we go beyond the most literally and most overtly reflexive, perhaps the most important device to be considered is what Pardo calls the "metafictional allegory." Thinking in terms of literature and cinema but speaking in a way that easily echoes across media, Pardo defines the metafictional allegory as "a story in which there are neither film people (actors, directors, scriptwriters, etc.) nor authors, characters or readers, but whose action turns them into their equivalents, emblems of these figures, in a way in which the story becomes an allegorical meditation upon fiction and cinema" ("La metaficcion de la literatura al cine" 168).[39] In this regard, allegory may be built *not only within but also across diegetic levels*, perhaps encompassing a multiplicity of levels and narrative agents both within and above the main diegetic world—as in *Westworld*, a new media dystopia that reflexively allegorizes the culture industry of the digital age.[40] Nonetheless, as a more covert kind of reflexivity, the concept of

39 In a much more nuanced way, Pardo makes two suggestions with regard to the use of "metafiction" and "metafictional": on the one hand, he advices using it to describe primary or systemic self-consciousness regardless of medium; on the other hand, he suggests replacing metafiction with terms like meta-cinema, meta-theater, meta-literature, etc. to refer to medium-specific self-referentiality. Thus, if a "metafictional allegory" is his term for allegorical self-consciousness, then one can speak of, for example, a "metacinematic allegory" or a "metaliterary allegory" for medium-specific, self-referential allegories (cf. "La metaficcion de la literatura al cine"; "Hacia una teoría de la reflexividad fílmica"). In this section and at least until I turn towards the specific analyses and the specific considerations regarding new media reflexivity, I am choosing to focus on the less medium-specific terms and I am also underemphasizing certain of the potential overlaps between these theoretical phenomena—overlaps that are observed both by Pardo and Genette, but that are, for the sake of conceptual clarity, better explained and considered while analyzing specific cases.

40 Although I return to *Westworld* in Chapter 3, this book does not focus centrally upon the series' reflexive aspects, as I have studied them elsewhere, but some aspects deserve clarification. In previous works, beginning with my 2018 article, I have already argued that the series (in its first season especially) functions as a complex metafictional allegory that encompasses both the extradiegetic level of creators, writers, audiences, etc. and the intradiegetic level of fictional characters within the context of a theme park. And insofar as narrative creation is juxtaposed with

the metafictional allegory is very flexible in a potentially confusing way, since detecting an allegory demands a hermeneutic effort from audiences and critics. Aware of this potential problem, Pardo theorizes the concept alongside other reflexive devices that may serve as markers of this kind of allegory or—in non-allegorical cases—as markers of the structural centrality of self-consciousness within a given narrative.

When and how do we, as the audience or as critics, decide to classify a narrative as self-conscious, not incidentally but structurally speaking? One possibility, proposed by Robert Alter, would be to look for the systematic recurrence of formal, stylistic and thematic devices, but this would be a highly restrictive criterion that would rule out works that are not self-conscious thanks to reiteration or repetition, but rather thanks to the structural centrality of a *metafictional anagnorisis* and/or a *metafictional epiphany*.[41] Borrowing from Aristotle's terminology, Pardo suggests that, "whereas in tragedy [...] the anagnorisis is the crucial moment when, by a twist of fate, the tragic hero discovers one fundamental, world-changing truth about themselves or the others," in self-conscious narratives, the metafictional anagnorisis "would be the moment when the character discovers their fictional status," with similarly strong effects ("La metaficcion de la literatura al cine" 155). Hence, while the metafictional anagnorisis would consist of a character's awakening to their own condition, the metafictional epiphany would consist of the audience's own awakening, provoked by some anti-illusionist revelation of the narrative's own status as fiction. In this way, as Pardo himself clarifies, a metafictional anagnorisis entails a

---

humanoid creation, the series functions as a "metafictional Frankenstein" that builds up toward the creatures'/characters' awakening (their metafictional anagnorises) and their encounter and confrontation with their creators (see "All the Park's a Stage"; see also Winckler for a Shakespearean reading). Besides, the series amply proves how reflexivity can become extremely extramural, in the sense that this markedly metafictional allegory also functions as a critical allegory of patriarchy and surveillance capitalism (see my "Subverting or Reasserting?"; "Allegorising Surveillance Capitalism").

41   Alter argues that—to be able to speak of "[a] fully self-conscious novel"—self-conscious devices must appear "from beginning to end, through the style, the handling of narrative viewpoint, the names and words imposed on the characters, the patterning of the narration, the nature of the characters and what befalls them" (xi).

metafictional epiphany almost by definition, but the latter can emerge elsewhere in the narrative by means of other self-conscious devices. Of course, speaking of anagnorises and epiphanies requires a justification that will be specific to each case, but using these concepts is extremely useful insofar as it personifies reflexivity in characters and/or audiences. In my view, it is only by theorizing the strong affective impact of such self-conscious devices that we can truly grasp and feel the estranging and even subversive power of reflexivity in SF and in general.

Furthermore, metafictional anagnorises are often followed by what could be called (in an analogy with Pardo's terms) the "metafictional confrontation": that is, an encounter with a narrating agent or creator in a level above or below—as in Miguel de Unamuno's *Niebla*, in which the main character meets the (fictionalized) author and complains about his fate, or in Joy and Nolan's *Westworld*, in which humanoid creatures not only meet their creators, but also literally organize a violent revolution against them and try to overthrow the system/fiction that subjugates them. Other paradigmatic cases of the metafictional confrontation may be found in older literary SF—again, Philip K. Dick is the one to give us an example, in his *Time Out of Joint* (1958)—but also in older audio-visual SF—one can think about Peter Weir's *The Truman Show* (1998), which is modeled upon said novel, or about the Wachowski's *The Matrix* (1999). In these cases, but also in general, metafictional anagnorises and epiphanies have the potential of being translated and/or mapped onto narratives of resistance, rebellion and even revolution—and these, whether successful or not, are a constant (if not an essential ingredient) of dystopian narratives, which brings us back to our main concern.[42]

Building upon all this theorization and returning to our main object of study, new media dystopias may now be thought of as a sub-genre in which the speculative is closely conjoined with the reflexive. More specifically,

---

42   Rüdiger Imhof calls this kind of thematized metafiction "the character-revolt" and the crude but clear comparison that he uses to explain the preceding metafictional anagnorisis lays bare the potential political connotations of this self-conscious plot development. "All of a sudden, the main character became aware that he was a character in a fiction, and, comparable to a man who feels inhibited, even crushed, by a system of society and opts out, he feels oppressed by the system" (117–18).

we can define new media dystopias as *a kind of reflexive SF in which the usual dystopian narratives of resistance, rebellion and revolution against the status quo are mapped (literally or allegorically) onto narratives of realization (epiphanies), awakening (anagnorisis) and confrontation with the narratives (and narrating agents and technologies) that shape digital-capitalist reality*. If, as Slavoj Žižek puts it, what we commonly call ideology is "an (unconscious) fantasy structuring our social reality itself" (*The Sublime Object of Ideology* 30), then the new media dystopia can be (at its best) a peculiarly science-fictional way of returning to the Brechtian ideal of estrangement in two interrelated senses: (a) in the sense that the new media dystopia is—like dystopias generally—critical, aimed against the established order (and particularly, against the new media order) and (b) in the sense that it foregrounds and lays bare its own position within and towards that order (and particularly, within and towards new media). Of course, this does not need to be the case in all new media dystopias—and not even in all aspects of a single one of them—so it is essential to analyze *how, to what extent and to what effect* reflexive devices operate in each narrative in order to, in the end, try to determine whether each one is just self-referential in a general, not necessarily estranging way, or whether it is self-conscious for "a deliberate anti-illusionist effect and a critical distancing" (Pardo García, "Hacia una teoría de la reflexividad fílmica" 52). Both of Pardo's modes of reflexivity (self-referentiality and self-consciousness) may overlap and their detection is, ultimately, dependent on interpretation, so—just like with the presumed critical effects of dystopias—closer analyses are needed to gauge the extent to which reflexivity is (or is not) an ally of SF's cognitive estrangement in each case.

So far, of course, this chapter's theorization has been overemphasizing reflexivity's critical and subversive potentials—but one should also emphasize that this is just an ideal, to be used as a hermeneutic hypothesis. The second half of this chapter shall begin to unearth the unavoidable ambivalences that emerge from the specificities of each reflexive narrative within the new media environment. The two narratives to be analyzed—the series *The Man in the High Castle* and the interactive film *Black Mirror: Bandersnatch*—are privileged here because they both feature self-referential and self-conscious devices in a central and systemic manner.[43] With exceptions, most of the other dystopias to be analyzed in the rest of the book are reflexive in more secondary and/or more allegorical manners, so it is essential to first understand reflexivity in its most overt manifestations, beginning with a series that tries to translate literary reflexivity into filmic reflexivity and then turning towards an interactive film that allows us to rethink and to nuance our understanding of reflexivity within the digital milieu.

2.3. Reflexivity from the Page to the Small Screen: Amazon's Adaptation of P. K. Dick's *The Man in the High Castle*

Philip K. Dick almost needs no introduction, neither for fans and connoisseurs of the genre, nor for academics and students familiar with SF studies. For coetaneous writer Stanisław Lem, Dick was "a visionary among the charlatans" (see Lem and Abernathy); for Fredric Jameson he "was the Shakespeare of Science Fiction" and his work, "one of the most powerful expressions of the society of the spectacle" (*Archaeologies* 345, 347).[44] With the passing of time, his oeuvre has not lost any of its fame or cultural significance. In the past decade in particular, Dick has been heralded and reinterpreted as a "canonical writer of the digital age" (see

---

43 Here I am leaning on another conceptual distinction of Pedro Javier Pardo. As he explains in his graduate course on metafiction, it is possible to distinguish between systematic and systemic metafiction: while the systematic entails repetition and re-iteration of self-conscious devices throughout a narrative, the second entails the structural and symbolic centrality of self-consciousness. Thus, by saying that these are cases of *systemic* reflexivity, I mean that reflexivity has a central, structuring role in *The Man in the High Castle* and *Bandersnatch* (and in our interpretation of them).

44 Nevertheless, after this eulogistic comparison, Jameson adds that "The most ineffectual way to argue Dick's greatness, however, is to claim his books as high literature," since "A mass-cultural sub-genre like SF has different (and stricter) laws that high culture, and can sometimes express realities and dimensions that escape high literature" (*Archaeologies* 345).

Kucukalic), which is retrospectively obvious considering his whole work's consistent preoccupation with late-capitalist technologies and ideologies (see Suvin, "P. K. Dick's Opus" and the associated *SFS* issue; and see also Fitting; Rabkin; Durham). Nowadays, in fact, one can hear about Dick's "endless adaptability" (Barnett) because of the ever-growing list of film and television productions that are based on his novels and stories.[45] *The Man in the High Castle* (henceforth *MHC*) is just a newcomer to that long list of audio-visual adaptations, but it is of particular interest here insofar as Frank Spotnitz's series adapts a well-known example of reflexive SF into an audio-visual series produced by Amazon Studios from and for digital platforms.[46] In examining this series, my goal is double: on the one hand, to meditate upon reflexivity's on-screen manifestations *vis-à-vis* their literary equivalents and, on the other hand, to begin considering how dystopian SF generally is re-shaped within and against the backdrop of digital platforms.

MHC's story is set in 1962, in various places of the US mainland, but—as is well known—Dick's novel presupposes an alternate-history timeline

---

[45] Here one can name but a few of the most memorable: firstly, Ridley Scott's *Blade Runner* (1982) and its sequel, Denis Villeneuve's *Blade Runner 2049* (2017), which are a loose adaptation and expansion of Dick's novel *Do Androids Dream of Electric Sheep?* (1968); secondly, *Total Recall*, with a 1990 version by Paul Verhoeven and a 2012 remake by Len Wiseman, which is based on "We Can Remember It for You Wholesale" (1966); thirdly, Steven Spielberg's *Minority Report* (2002), which is based on "The Minority Report" (1956); fourthly *A Scanner Darkly* by Richard Linklater (2006), based on Dick's *A Scanner Darkly* (1977); and finally, Moore and Dinner's series *Philip K. Dick's Electric Dreams* (2017), an anthology of adaptations of short stories also produced for Amazon Prime Video.

[46] The majority of articles about Dick's *MHC* have focused on its structural reflexivity in one way or another, although with divergent terminologies (see Pagetti et al.; Malmgren, "Philip Dick's *Man in the High Castle*"; Hayles; Rieder; Carter; Rossi, "Fourfold Symmetry"; Canaan; Mountfort).

Besides, with regard to the series' production, one should note that, before greenlighting the whole series, in January 2015 Amazon released the pilot in its streaming platform so that users could rate it and then decide whether the series would continue production. After becoming "Amazon's most watched pilot ever" according to the studio (qtd. in H. Lewis), the rest of season one was given a go in February and released in November.

in which the Axis Powers defeated the Allies in World War II. In this scenario, the US—like Germany in historical reality—has been split by the two winning superpowers: Nazi Germany controls the Eastern two thirds of the US, whereas Japan controls the Pacific states, with a neutral zone in the Rocky Mountains. In this alternate Cold War between Germany and Japan, the Nazis are in a position of military superiority, especially because they gained the upper hand after developing nuclear weapons, which they used to bomb Washington DC in 1945. Besides, as befits such a Cold-War scenario, there are growing tensions between the two superpowers as well as infighting for leadership in the German side, all of which generates a climate of fear for another world war. At this level of detail, except for some minor differences, the diegetic worlds of both the novel and the series are based on the same premises, although one significant difference is that the series' focuses much more on an underground anti-fascist resistance that is absent (and apparently defeated) in Dick's novel.[47]

The main characters, too, are borrowed from the novel—Juliana, Joe, Frank, Childan, Tagomi and the titular Man in the High Castle all remain, with slight changes and/or expanded character arcs—but some important additions of the series are Chief Inspector Kido (actor Joel de la Fuente) and Obergruppenführer John Smith (Rufus Sewell), as well as the latter's all-American-but-proudly-Nazi suburban family.[48] Thus, while Dick's original

47   In the novel, there was also an ongoing Nazi colonization of Venus and Mars, which is absent in the series, presumably because it would not seem as plausible today, whereas in the 1960s it might have. Additionally, in the novel Hitler is already dead and Martin Bormann in power, though he dies by mid-novel, leading to a fight for power within Nazi factions; in the series, however, Hitler is still in power at first, but ill, which prompts conspiracies and, eventually (when he dies), a similar fight for power.
48   One example that illustrates how characters roughly remain as in the novel but with expanded arcs is the love triangle between Juliana, Joe and Frank. In Dick's novel, Juliana and Frank are already divorced, Frank remains in San Francisco and Juliana leaves for the neutral zone, having an affair with Joe, until she kills him after Joe, a secret Nazi agent, uses her to get to the Man in the High Castle. In the series, however, Juliana and Frank are still living together at first and viewers witness their gradual separation and the growing tension between Juliana and Joe, which culminates in a murder scene very similar to the novel's, not only in terms of Juliana's reasons but also in terms of how he is killed (sliced throat in a hotel room). All

characters served to depict this alternate reality mainly from the perspective of oppressed, ordinary and/or outsider characters, the most significant contribution of Spotnitz's show is that Nazi and Japanese worlds are also explored from the perspective of members of their own police-paramilitary forces. Nevertheless, it would be a mistake to call the series a rewriting because of these or any other differences, as Amazon's *MHC* is rather an *expansive adaptation* whose main differences can be explained by the change in format (a short novel stretched into a four-season series with a runtime of forty hours approximately) and the change in medium (from literary to audio-visual).[49] Of course, indirectly, changes in format and medium have thematic implications but, in this case, the latter are generally explainable by way of the former.

Much more could be said about the details of this alternate-historical world, or about the changes and additions in both characters and plot that are entailed by its expansion.[50] However, one must move beyond the (intra)

---

this, of course, is not to say there are not differences and a relevant one is Joe, Joe Cinnadella in the novel, Joe Blake in the show: whereas in the novel he is a proudly fascist Italian veteran, in the series he is a young man from Brooklyn who struggles to embrace fascism fully (especially when Juliana comes into the picture).

49 Spotnitz himself confirms that he "tried to build out the world of the novel in ways that [...] were consistent with the themes" (qtd. in St James), which also speaks to how the series expands but in a way that is (at least *a priori*) coherent with the original diegetic world and themes. This intended fidelity, however, is trickier than it may seem at first and in a sense ends up betraying itself.

50 Among other aspects, the series has more space to delve into certain themes that were mostly relegated to the background in the novel, such as racism and ableism. Of course, this is not to say that Dick was insensitive to these issues, since his characters repeatedly mention a continent-wide holocaust of Africa—"Wiped out to make a land of—what? Who knew? Maybe even the master architects in Berlin did not know. Bunch of automatons, building and toiling away" (*Man High Castle* 17)—and, in the second chapter for a proposed sequel, Dick even shows a Nazi who collects malformed foetuses in glass bottles, gifting them to a colleague as very valuable "*Wunderkind*" ("The Two Completed Chapters of a Proposed Sequel to *The Man in the High Castle*" 121). By contrast to Dick's revelatory details, the series can afford to devote entire seasons to, on the one hand, the emergence of a Black Communist Rebellion in the Pacific that seeks to establish a new, more egalitarian state independent of both Nazi-Japanese and pre-existing American racism. And, on the other hand, Nazi ableism is also brought to the foreground already in season

diegetic level to analyze what interests us here: *MHC*'s reflexivity, which is built upon an interplay of diegetic levels. One interpretive key—if not *the* key—of Dick's novel (and Spotnitz's series) is that, within this Axis-dominated scenario, someone known as "the Man in the High Castle" is behind the underground circulation of materials that show an Allied victory in World War II. In Dick's novel, this consists of a novel-within-the-novel by a man called Hawthorn Abendsen (the Man in the High Castle's name), titled *The Grasshopper Lies Heavy*, which is banned in Nazi territories but popular and easily acquirable elsewhere. In Spotnitz's series, by contrast, *GLH* is the code-name used to identify a variety of newsreel films, which are also banned by the Germans, but widely circulated, nonetheless. However, both *GLH*s are not portrayals of our own historical reality, even though they seem so at first glance; instead, as viewers and readers gradually discover, both are windows into yet another alternate history (or histories). Abendsen's *GLH* novel, on the one hand, depicts an Allied victory that leads to an ostensibly more utopian scenario than our own reality; the *GLH* newsreels, on the other hand, show a multiplicity of alternate histories—both Allied and Axis victories, both more utopian and more dystopian than our own history.

In both versions, therefore, what we have is a kind of *mise-en-abyme*, a specular structure of alternate histories (*GLH*) within an alternate history (*MHC*), which invites both a self-referential meditation upon this SF sub-genre—and implicitly, a self-conscious reflection upon Dick's own novel—as well as, more generally, a meditation upon real history, which is itself re-imagined as one narrative out of many. In the novel, for instance, excerpts of *The Grasshopper Lies Heavy* are read and discussed by diverse characters—both fascist and anti-fascist, who react differently and thus offer supplementary commentaries upon both diegetic and metadiegetic levels. These occasions can allow for intramural kinds of reflexivity—as

---

one, with the revelation that Obergruppenführer John Smith's son, Thomas, has a muscular dystrophy that will make him a "useless eater," eventually, and his family struggles to hide this, contrary to Nazi doctrine—although, tragically, it is Thomas himself who, upon finding out, eventually decides to report himself in an act of patriotism, leaving the family devastated for the rest of the series.

when characters discuss whether or not *GLH* is SF—but it also allows for reflexivity of an extramural kind, in occasions in which reflexivity is turned outwards (towards history).[51] One scene of the latter kind with a very estranging and subversive effect is when Joe, an avowedly fascist Italian, objects against Abendsen's alternate history. In particular, Joe is sceptical towards *GLH*'s depiction of a Cold War between the US and UK that leads to social and economic progress in the former colonies— "relief to the masses in India, Burma, Africa, the Middle East"—as well as the end of racial discrimination in the US—"Whites and Negroes lived and worked and ate shoulder by shoulder, even in the Deep South." As Joe complains, Abendsen has supposedly "taken the best about Nazism, the socialist part" and "given the credit to [...] the New Deal"; however, Joe rightly notes that the US and UK "are both plutocracies, ruled by the rich" and so, "If they had won, all they'd have thought about was making more money" and "there would be no social reform, no welfare public works plans" (*Man High Castle* 155–7). Thus, by commenting upon a more utopian world (*GLH*) from within a more dystopian world (*MHC*), the novel, via Joe, generates a sense of estrangement and ambivalence about our own historical path—specifically, suggesting that capitalism is not as markedly different from fascism as we may commonly imagine.

Many other passages could be mentioned as illustrations of the (counter-)historical comparisons fostered by Dick's *MHC*, but—as our focus here lies on the novel's adaption—it is best to turn to Umberto Rossi's clarifying map of the "four-fold symmetry" established between historical and narrative levels embedded in Dick's original work ("Fourfold Symmetry" 407; see also his *The Twisted Worlds of Philip K. Dick*). As Rossi and others' analyses have shown, the novel's strength is its combination of the speculative (alternate history) with the reflexive (its *mise-en-abyme*

---

51   In a less theoretically dense version of a polemic that was referenced earlier in this chapter, a Japanese couple discusses Abendsen's *GLH*, with Betty arguing that it is not SF because there is "No science in it" and it is "Not set in future" (*sic*) and Paul counterarguing that it is, insofar as "it deals with alternate present" (*Man High Castle* 109). In turn, this conversation (and many others) about *GLH*, which is self-referential regarding SF, can also be read as self-conscious, implicitly vindicating *MHC* as SF and pre-empting a possible objection raised against it.

structure), which lets it function as a complex set of mirrors that shed a critical light upon each other.[52] Overall, Dick's reflexive SF novel is a powerfully estranging narrative that fosters a multi-layered, critical re-reading of SF as a genre that is much more valuable and varied than what certain stereotypes would have, as well as a re-reading of history as an ongoing and disputed narrative.

These conclusions, of course, are drawn from Dick's novel, but does this peculiar reflexive structure function in the televisual series in the same way? Discussing the range of possibilities whereby reflexive literature can be adapted to the screen, Pedro Javier Pardo theorizes three main possibilities: (1) suppression, (2) remediation and (3) transmediation. The first, as is obvious, would involve eliminating all traces of reflexivity and thus "cleaning the work of anti-illusionist interferences."[53] The second, remediation, would involve relocating literary reflexivity within a filmic narration—that is, adapting *MHC* to the screen but keeping *GLH* as a metadiegetic novel. The third, transmediation, would involve "finding filmic equivalences to self-conscious literary strategies" and thus leading to the disappearance of reflexivity's "literary origins" (see "Hacia una teoría de la reflexividad fílmica" 70–3). Transmediation is indeed what happens from Dick's to Spotnitz's *MHC*, particularly as regards *GLH*'s transformation from a novel into a series of clandestine newsreel films. Speaking at Comic-Con, Spotnitz was asked why they made the change and he

> responded, "That was actually the first thing that popped in my mind when adapting it for television, which was that instead of a book, it should be a film—because it's a visual medium." But Spotnitz said that this does raise some questions, because anybody can have a printing press, but making films is harder. At the same time, the films are just a "McGuffin," said Spotnitz. (Anders n.p.)

---

52 See especially Rieder and again note 46 for other studies of the novel's reflexivity, from both formal and ideological perspectives.

53 Besides citing film adaptations of Cervantes's *Don Quixote* and Unamuno's *Niebla* that do away with the source texts' reflexivity altogether, Pardo (in "Hacia una teoría de la reflexividad fílmica" 71) also mentions one case of adapted SF that suppresses the novel's reflexivity: the film adaptation of Kurt Vonnegut's *Slaughterhouse-Five* (1969), directed by George Roy Hill (1972).

Elsewhere, the series creator also argues that he "tried to build out the world of the novel in ways that [...] were consistent with the themes" (qtd. in St James) and this is true in the general sense that Dick's alternate world and the novel's diegetic-metadiegetic structure both remain, with changes and additions that are not intended as rewriting or revision. However, if the goal is to be "consistent with the themes," is it reasonable to treat *GLH* as a mere "McGuffin"? As already noted, *MHC*'s reflexivity is structural and—at least in Dick's novel—*GLH* is anything but a McGuffin, so this should make one approach the series with a hermeneutics of suspicion.

Although the *GLH* newsreels are a recurrent presence in the series just as the novel-within-the-novel was in Dick's novel, the role they play within the series' diegesis is substantially different. Just like there were reading scenes in the original, spectatorship scenes—such as Juliana's first encounter with the newsreels—abound throughout the series' four seasons. Here, however, these reflexive moments are scarcely used for critical reflection and/or sustained discussion between characters, as was generally the case with the *GLH* novel. As opposed to that possibility, one thing that the series usually does is using the reels for (re-)awakening the characters' lingering hopes for an alternative world. In the aforementioned scene, for instance, Juliana and Frank's discussion of the *GLH* newsreels is reduced to a simple confrontation of her faith—"they look real because they are real"—and his incredulity—"but they can't be"—and, after watching, Frank himself quickly dismisses and cuts Juliana's speculations, saying that "whatever they are, Hitler ordered them all destroyed" and "possessing them is treason" (Semel 24'14"-36"), which shifts attention to the question of what to do with the films. Thus, rather than engaging in any kind of reflexive commentary upon the films themselves, the thematic emphasis of the scene lies upon Frank's fear and Juliana's hope. The newsreel images have a strong effect upon Juliana especially, in her case given the fact that her sister had just died after giving them to her, so the films provide a perfect motivation for her sudden change into a rebel as well as for much of the series' relentless action and intrigue.[54]

---

54 Juliana's relationship with the newsreels is deeply shaped by her relationship with her sister Trudy, who is killed by Japanese police shortly after giving the reels to

This scene of spectatorship is no exception, insofar as it seems that, generally, *GLH* reels are not there to trigger discussion or reflection based on their content; instead, the reels are above all *instrumentalized* within the diegesis—that is, they are objects to be mobilized in the underground resistance's struggle against Japanese and German forces. Instead of the multi-dimensional dialectics fostered by Dick's *GLH*, newsreels are here reduced to tools/weapons within a struggle for power that is nowhere to be found in the novel—primarily, because all organized resistance had been crushed in the original *MHC* and, also, because Dick's novel is plagued with moral greys and circumstantial constraints that nuance all discussions, even what the fascists say. As opposed to that, the series represents a struggle between two clearly demarcated sides, each led by their own man in the high castle: the anti-fascist-in-hiding and film distributor Hawthorn Abendsen and the German *führer* and newsreel collector Adolf Hitler. Therefore, ironically—although for opposite reasons, in a dangerously empty kind of symmetry—it seems that both sides are deep down doing the same: both are driven by obsessive efforts to hoard and monopolize the mysterious newsreels, which are now more relevant as plot-serving instruments (McGuffins indeed) than as estranging mirrors within the text that let us look anew at history.[55]

Nevertheless, *MHC*'s reflexivity is not solely observable in its *mise-en-abyme* structure, but also in a series of aspects that are markedly self-referential and, by the end of the book, also implicitly self-conscious. One running theme in the novel was commodification, especially since Abendsen's *GLH* is described (and decried) as a best-seller on more than one

---

Juliana. In so doing, Trudy asks her to take care of them and deliver them to the underground resistance with which she had been collaborating. Crucially, both Trudy and the Resistance are additions of the series, wholly absent in Dick's novel, and it would seem that they contribute to the overall shift away from the philosophy of the book and towards a more action- and intrigue-driven plot.

55   A similar argument could be made about another sub-plot that is common to both the novel and series: Frank and Childan's attempt to make and marketize forgeries of "traditional American art." Whereas in the novel this is an essential part of Dick's reflexive meditation upon authenticity and fakeness within the context of commodified art, in the series this sub-plot is mostly a justification for action, intrigue and conflict between the resistance and the Japanese.

occasion. When Juliana visits a bookstore in the neutral zone, for instance, the narrator draws readers' attention to *GLH*'s commodification: "there it was, a bright stack of copies in fact, with a display sign saying how popular and important it was, and of course that it was verboten in German-run regions" (*Man High Castle* 198). Elsewhere, explicitly thinking about *GLH* as commodified culture, a Nazi official once complains that people like Abendsen will "write anything if they know they'll get paid. Tell any bunch of lies, and then the public actually takes the smelly brew seriously when it's dished out" (*Man High Castle* 127). Furthermore, this implicitly self-conscious concern with authenticity under commercial constraints is not just a passing remark made by one unsympathetic character, but a recurring theme that is returned to in the very end, when Abendsen confesses that he *is* a fake indeed, in the sense he himself did not create *GLH*. Rather, it turns out that Abendsen systematically consulted the I Ching (an ancient Chinese oracle massively used in *MHC*'s Japanese-influenced regions) so as to decide what to write—and it is known that Philip K. Dick himself also used the I Ching for deciding how to advance the plot of his own best-seller (see interview with Cover).

The novel, eventually, concludes with Juliana's metafictional anagnorisis—that is, her realization that "Germany and Japan lost the war" after all and that her world is an illusion, a "revelation" that she has precisely "through [Abendsen's] book" (*Man High Castle* 247). Ironically, therefore, it is thanks to a lie-within-a-lie that Juliana arrives at the truth by the end of Dick's *MHC*—and, in turn, with Juliana's awakening, readers are led to think that Dick's novel, itself another lie written for money, is nonetheless valuable for its "Inner Truth," as Juliana herself tells Abendsen in the very end (*Man High Castle* 247). On the whole, then, in an indirectly self-conscious manner, Dick seems to be acknowledging that he is "a hack" and "a consummate liar," but that his writing should not be judged solely (and unfairly) by that. Like Abendsen's *GLH*, Dick's own novel really was an award-winning best-seller, which is, for many, the epitome of a deceitful commodity—yet, in so being, the book is also much more than that: it is also a potential tool for rethinking the historical twists and turns that led to our world.

Now, if one turns back towards Amazon's *MHC*, however, no metafictional anagnorisis (of Juliana) or epiphany (of the spectator) of the kind that closes Dick's *MHC* can be found, which is yet another reason for suspecting that the series' attempted reflexivity has not been properly translated to the screen—or, at least, not given an equivalent structural prominence. Only the finale of season one, which closes when Nobusuke Tagomi meditates himself into the alternative of the alternative reality—the San Francisco of our own 1960s—could be read as both a metafictional anagnorisis and an epiphany. At least in the novel, the scene that inspires the ending of season one's finale is clearly both—an anagnorisis and an epiphany—insofar as this is the moment when Tagomi realizes that he is "Out of my world, my space and time" (*Man High Castle* 224) and, subsequently, gets lost in musings about reality as a "scheme of illusion" and himself as "a mask, concealing the real" (Dick, *Man High Castle* 227)—all of which foreshadows Juliana's own awakening, mentioned above.

In the series, by contrast, Tagomi's dream-like experience of interdimensional travel is visually staged rather than verbally narrated and he is shown confounded and speechless in a crowded square of our 1960s San Francisco. This is, undoubtedly, a powerful cinematic realization of the novel's sense of estrangement, given how the series' alt-historical scenography is suddenly replaced by another, equally otherworldly and rich in detail—a change that makes viewers partake in Tagomi's disorientation and amazement. Nevertheless, whereas the novel left Tagomi's and Juliana's awakenings partly unexplained and thus lent itself to an anti-illusionist interpretation, the series—in subsequent seasons—normalizes interdimensional travel, giving an intradiegetic explanation for this otherwise estranging event.[56] Once traveling between worlds is rendered both

---

56 Later seasons adapt and expand based on an idea that was already imagined by Dick (see his "The Two Completed Chapters of a Proposed Sequel to *The Man in the High Castle*"); namely, the idea that alternate histories emerge from alternate realities, which can be accessed via interdimensional portals. Dick's additional chapter indeed imagines the Nazis constructing a portal, to be used for colonizing other worlds—and the series borrows this, adding the idea that there are "travellers": people who can mind-teleport to worlds where their counterpart is dead. Ultimately, these people explain the origin of the *GLH* newsreels, since they are

normal and possible for a great number of characters, both Nazi and Resistance, the estranging effects of such a potentially self-conscious device are diminished, if not lost. Thus seen, Tagomi's San Francisco scene—all its cinematic achievement notwithstanding—*could have but does not* fully function as a metafictional anagnorisis (let alone an epiphany). Instead, it seems to have been transformed into a textbook example of the end-of-season "cliff-hanger."

Furthermore and finally, beyond the ways whereby the novel's *mise-en-abyme* structure and its metafictional anagnorises and epiphanies have been adapted, there are still other reflexive aspects, original to the series, which are worth considering for their medium-specificity. *MHC*'s animated credit sequence, which frames and opens all episodes, is an admirable achievement in this regard, as an example of purely visual reflexivity. Upon the flickering sound of a film projector and, some seconds before the theme song begins to play, the first image of the opening sequence is the light of a projector, seen from the screen's side. Already this can be read as self-referential—that is, as a way of foregrounding the visual medium itself—or perhaps also implicitly self-conscious—that is, a way of foregrounding the fact that *MHC* is itself a television show. The reminder of the opening sequence, which introduces viewers to this alternate reality via maps and landmarks, seems to play with the idea that this whole alternative world is nothing but a visual narrative, which is elegantly evoked by the presence of light beams that seem to be projecting this whole reality onto a black background.[57] Nevertheless, is the mere reiteration of reflexive symbolism enough? Opening sequences are easily automatized, no longer estranging once viewers get accustomed and, besides, most streaming platforms today allow viewers to skip them with a simple click that cuts straight to the "content." Overall and perhaps

---

brought by these travelers from alternate realities and Hawthorn Abendsen is just the collector and curator.

57 Interestingly, the pilot episode redoubles this reflexivity, insofar as the first properly diegetic image is also the light of a projector and the scene that follows shows Joe watching Nazi propaganda in a movie theater. This very first spectatorship scene, however, also turns away quickly from its reflexive potentials, as viewers quickly find that Joe is there in a kind of undercover mission to retrieve some information. This scene, of course, is not alone in this dynamic, as already observed.

despite itself, Amazon's *MHC* thus shows how the repetition of reflexive devices does not assure estrangement, since what matters is the structural centrality of these devices—but here, that got lost in translation.

Spotnitz's series is surely an example with as many potentials as problematics—and probably more of the latter—but precisely because of its ambivalence the show illustrates how reflexivity may operate (or fail to operate) in a visual medium. One should again insist that a transmediation is in and of itself not enough for the purposes of estrangement and that the most important factor is the structural centrality of reflexivity within this or any other narrative. Other reflexive aspects of the series—such as its representation of Nazi-American television broadcasting—are worthy of praise and could merit further analysis, but this TV-specific self-referentiality is sadly too secondary, both in terms of its scarce thematic importance and the little runtime that it receives. Nonetheless, there are still certain scenes of spectatorship that give viewers a glimpse into a mid-century, Nazified US television, with examples such as quiz shows or detective series where each genre's logic seems to fit with Nazi ideology extremely eerily and easily, thus facilitating uncomfortable comparisons of capitalist and fascist cultures in a way that Dick's novel itself did not do. Furthermore, season four redoubles this self-referentiality in one interesting manner, when Hawthorn Abendsen himself is kidnapped and coerced by the Nazis into hosting a television show entitled *Tales from the High Castle*, in which he discusses (and debunks) the content of the increasingly popular *GLH* newsreels that he had been distributing. This, however, was relegated to the opening of an episode, despite there being a clear potential for rebuilding the series' reflexivity around it.

Thinking back upon the whole, one could say that *MHC*'s "original sin" was that of being too mechanical in adapting; first, by insisting on being "faithful" despite the sheer impossibility of that and, second, by insisting on a "straightforward" transmediation of the most important piece of the novel—*GLH*, the novel-within-the-novel. In the end, despite certain moments and details, Amazon's *MHC* seems to have turned an ideologically provocative and productive structure of mutually mirroring diegetic levels into a pseudo-heroic, action-driven story of newsreel smuggling—which may be an overly controversial way of phrasing it, but what is clear is that the series has tended to *instrumentalize* the metadiegetic films rather than treating them reflexively. Because of this, the series generally underemphasizes the multi-dimensional dialogs to be had about their content and instead overemphasizes the warfare and espionage plots involved in distributing them. And perhaps most importantly, the series' approach also overemphasizes the revolutionary role supposedly played by the newsreels once they reach a wide audience, whereas Dick's novel was arguably more "realistic"—or rather, more convincingly ambivalent about this. As opposed to the series' idealization of the newsreels' circulation and reception, the novel showed how even an openly subversive novel such as *GLH* can be commodified and turned into a morbid best-seller, while also showing that—both *because of and despite* its wide circulation as a commodity—Abendsen's work could become widely accessible to readers like Juliana who are willing to take it seriously, trying to change themselves and the world in the process of reading. In a sense, therefore, Dick's concerns with commodification are only present here *in an ironic way*, in the sense that his own novel, *MHC*, like the intradiegetic *GLH*, has fallen victim to the same cultural dynamics that he once denounced, having been turned into a relatively superficial adaptation.

Besides, are viewers expected to believe that bulky, flammable newsreels could circulate as easily as handy paperback books? That is not true today and neither was it true in the epoch in which *MHC* is set. If the series' creators did want to aim at a reflexive kind of cognitive estrangement such as is present in Dick's original, then their treatment of visual media ought to have been more clearly coherent with the "cognitive logics"—or at least the semblance of internal logic—of *MHC*'s alternate world. The main problem, in this regard, is that the series seems to presuppose that the *GLH* newsreels can circulate as easily as any commodity—and, in a sense, they seem to behave like the viral videos of today's online platforms. However, imagining that audio-visual materials can be massively circulated and consumed by anyone is only believable in our present context—and even now, this is only *partially* believable, given that digital capitalism generates inequalities in terms of each user's access and impact. In these ways, the original novel's self-consciousness regarding Dick's own position as a "producer" of commodified culture seems to have virtually vanished in

New Media Reflexivity 163

the series. Reflexive only in the abstract but apparently unaware of its own status as a commodity, the series falls short of its most radical potential: the potential of playfully breaking with the illusions of commodified visual culture from within. Fashioning *GLH* films—and implicitly itself—as unambiguously "subversive" products, the series thus tears one of its most radical potentials from its roots.

In the end, one can only wonder what could have been of this "what could have been" story. Had it somehow acknowledged the implicit influence of the digital context, or had it explicitly set *MHC* in something like a Nazified version of the digital age, in which a reflexive meditation upon visual culture would be all the more pertinent, maybe it would have gained both political relevance and narrative strength.[58] Maybe, if it had thus transformed the original, it would have ironically been more "faithful" because it would have retained much more of the subversive power of Dick's *MHC*. Bridging the gap between literary and visual reflexivity via an exclusively formal jump—in an almost mechanical transmediation, as is the case here—is always a possibility, of course, but what Amazon's *MHC* makes clear is that a critical-reflexive focus on visual media cannot be purely formal, but—because media themselves are historical—necessarily also historicized, at least if one is expecting the cognitive estrangement of SF in general or the critical impetus of dystopias in particular. Of course, all of this is like asking *MHC* to become something else entirely and, even if it is a reflexive dystopian series produced in the same epoch, it is clearly not a dystopia concerned with media in any central way. Thus, our attention

---

58   If one goes back to debates about the nature of the digital economy, perhaps one can wonder what the *MHC* series could have been if it had explicitly played with the idea that—precisely because of the concentration of power afforded by digital technology—we are abandoning both capitalism and liberal democracy, but not because we are headed towards a better system. The already-discussed work of McKenzie Wark does suggest (though only passingly and provocatively) that, rather than "neoliberal,"

> the present might just as well be described with the equally retro term alt-fascist. It is all about securing ruling class power through the manipulation of racial and ethnic prejudice and the use of surveillance and overt violence to suppress dissent. It is centrally about the prison-industrial complex, expanded now on a global scale, as Angela Davis reminds us. (*Capital Is Dead* 112)

must now finally turn towards new media dystopias as such, the kind of narratives that are reflexive not only strictly speaking, formally—with regards to their medium—but also, in a more abstract way, contextually—with regards to our media-dominated world.

2.4. New Media Reflexivity in *Black Mirror: Bandersnatch*[59]

Charlie Brooker's *Black Mirror* (Channel 4 2011–14, Netflix 2016–present) has become an icon of 2010s SF television and it is the most popular new media dystopia—or rather, as an anthology of narratively independent episodes, one should probably say that it is *a varied catalogue of new media dystopias*, in the plural.[60] Elsewhere, I have already argued that "despite its fragmentary and centrifugal narrative structure as an anthology show, [the whole] coheres by its focus on contemporary media technologies," consistently fostering "critical reflections about how human subjectivity (the character's and the viewer's) is restrained and reshaped by a 'new media' architecture" ("Don Quixote as Gamer?" 198). More suggestively, J. P. Telotte has described *Black Mirror* as a collection of "fractured frames,"

59 All quotations from *Bandersnatch* in this section do not include the runtime in a parenthetical citation, since that would be impossible, as the interactive film by design varies and the Netflix interface does not offer the usual time navigation, but rather a menu of choices.

60 A considerable number of fans have nonetheless theorized that Brooker's show is set in a single diegetic universe, something that the series itself seems to suggest via "Easter eggs," intertextual references to *Black Mirror* episodes made by other episodes in relatively anecdotal and hidden ways. Drawing from such fan theories, Gerry Canavan has conjectured that the series could be moving towards a "post-anthology" format in which some kind of "[*Star*] *Trek*-style series continuity" may gradually emerge ("Hope, with Teeth: On 'Black Museum'" 259). This interpretation, however, was made on the basis of an analysis of "Black Museum," the concluding episode of season four, and—after an additional fifth season was released—it remains a speculation, a possibility that has not yet been foreclosed by the series but remains unconfirmed.

New Media Reflexivity

a programme that advertises itself in just a fractured fashion, using images of multiply cracked television screens and broken shards of glass, distorting the images—bits of faces, scattered scenes—reflected on them; one that offers both hour-long and feature-length episodes, as if holding out the possibility for multi-platform, multi-frame viewing; and one that persists in depicting those multiply-broken media frames through which we see our world and ourselves. Moreover, it pursues these 'fractures' by drawing on a format that, fittingly, is itself composed of what we might think of as separate frames that could well trouble the sort of consistent or unitary view that 'series' television most commonly projects for its viewers. (1–2)

Black Mirror, which Telotte here specifically interprets as a self-referential meditation on televisual seriality, would, more generally, be a new media dystopia that

projects a creeping sense that we are fast becoming little more than featured players: cast members in an ongoing, formulaic and serial story from which there is no escape, in which there is never any contact with the 'real'—apart from its screened or mediated representations—and in which there is no genuine subjectivity, only a scripted 'character' whose emotions and connections to others are just those allowed by the long form's narrative trajectory. (Telotte 18)

Taking Telotte's observations further and in a slightly different direction, this book approaches *Black Mirror* as—especially in this chapter—a paradigmatic showcase of the possibilities of new media reflexivity, since most of its episodes are concerned with digital technologies, platforms and users—thus being self-referential almost as a rule—some of them are often interpretable as metafictional allegories and others are explicitly and structurally self-conscious—the case of *Bandersnatch*.[61]

---

61 Although I find his analysis of the series extremely valuable, Telotte makes certain remarks that I hope that this book as a whole can disprove—specifically, his assertion that *Black Mirror* offers "a fragmented vision that frustrates easy conclusions and that the Marxist fantasy of coherence always blames on the whipping boy of capitalism. But then *Black Mirror*'s real focus is hardly economic: it is the modern self under the stress of various new technologies that almost inevitably seem, as Canavan rightly observes, to be 'put to harmful ends' (["Hope, with Teeth: On 'Black Museum'"] 266)—by governments, by multinational corporations, and especially by aggrieved individuals" (Telotte 7). How or why Telotte would think that capitalism—and digital capitalism in particular—is an exclusively "economic"

Winner of two Emmy awards and not undeservedly described as "the most unique and creative episode of the *Black Mirror* series" (Lay and Johnson 199) and as "*Black Mirror*'s conceptual Rosetta stone" (Conley and Burroughs 3), the interactive film *Bandersnatch* (directed by David Slade and written by Charlie Brooker) is as much an outlier within the series as it is a condensation and culmination of its themes and forms.[62] Released in 2018, between the fourth and fifth seasons, and made exclusively to be consumed in the Netflix interface, *Bandersnatch* has already attracted considerable academic attention from a range of perspectives.[63] Nevertheless, the single most defining feature of the episode is its reflexivity, as most studies acknowledge—although with the usual divergence in "meta" terminologies.[64] *Bandersnatch*'s formal experimentation is such that

---

      phenomenon seems profoundly debatable, as Chapter 1 should have proven; and how or why governments, corporations or individuals seem to be treated here as autonomous with regard to capitalism, rather than as semi-autonomous, constitutive parts of it also escapes my comprehension, especially insofar as the system is—as Marx himself emphasized—a social relation—and this is not to mention that "multinational corporations" are, for Marxists and non-Marxists alike, an almost clichéd embodiment of capital.

62   This, together with the fact that *Bandersnatch* contains hidden intertextual references to other *Black Mirror* episodes, already makes Slade and Brooker's film profoundly self-referential (regarding the whole anthology series, that is).

      The two Emmy awards were for "Outstanding Television Movie" and for "Outstanding Achievement in Interactive Media Within a Scripted Program," both won in 2019. These two awards could be deemed as redundant in a way, or perhaps as symptomatic of the difficulty of clearly classifying the interactive film within conventional categories.

63   At the time of writing, there are studies that have paid attention to *Bandersnatch*'s formal-thematic approximation to trauma (see McSweeney and Joy), to user outcomes, perceptions and discussions on social media (see Nee) and to its critical-reflexive meditation upon the digital interface within which it is consumed (see Conley and Burroughs; D'Aloia).

64   Conley and Burroughs, for instance, argue that *Bandersnatch* "readies its audience to engage in critical meta-reflection on the structured conditions of digitized (im)possibility," specifically by drawing attention to how "users of digital technology are dangled promises of open choice only to discover themselves recursively folded into networks of algorithmic acquiescence" (3). Elsewhere, D'Aloia speaks of its

New Media Reflexivity   167

the most common question asked about it is *what it is*, since it is neither film nor videogame, but something in between—simply "a Black Mirror event" according to some promotional posters and, in any case, a strange product of digital platforms, intentionally made to disturb fans of both media and viewers-users in general.[65] In this sense, *Bandersnatch* is made to be estranging, alienated even from the possibility of clear categorization. Much could be said about its relation with the long-running-but-never-fully-established tradition of interactive narratives (see McSweeney and Joy; as well as Nee), but here I primarily focus upon its reflexivity, of which interactivity is but a part and which is specifically adapted for the context of streaming platforms like Netflix itself. Therefore, as was the case with *MHC*, this analysis must begin by examining *Bandersnatch*'s peculiar diegetic structure.

Essentially, *Bandersnatch* is a choose-your-own-adventure narrative about the making of a choose-your-own-adventure videogame in 1984, a game that is itself based on a choose-your-own-adventure novel—all of which are titled *Bandersnatch*.[66] Thus, *Black Mirror*'s interactive film has two metadiegetic doubles with the same name: the videogame that main character Stefan (played by Fionn Whitehead) is making for one

---

"meta-transmediality" (28) and of the way it generates tensions "between self-reflexivity and self-referentiality (or between self-awareness and self-citation)" (29).

65 Charlie Brooker, in his characteristically scathing tone, has openly mocked both kinds of fans in an interview: "There's also some people that are like 'I don't want to make decisions', 'I don't want to do any of it' ... well, fuck off, then. Do something else! And then there's some people who think 'oh, it's too simple as a game' or 'games have done this before'—well, this isn't on a gaming platform, it's on Netflix" (qtd. in McSweeney and Joy 281).

66 Both the date and the videogame's name are a reference to one ambitious, failed project of the British company Imagine Software, whose own *Bandersnatch* was never released after the company went bankrupt in 1984. The date in which the *Black Mirror* film begins is, in fact, the day in which said company was declared defunct (July 9, 1984). The contents and structure of Imagine Software's game, however, are not known, so the reference seems to have no other purpose than underscoring how the film's own *Bandersnatch* is also a doomed project, as the user and Stefan shall find out. Besides, one could also conjecture that the year, 1984, could be meant to evoke Orwell's eponymous novel, which is too often cited as a rhetorical, empty shorthand for dystopias in general.

Tuckersoft company and the videogame's invented hypotext, a novel by the Philip-K.-Dick-like writer Jerome F. Davis (henceforth JFD).[67] Using the Netflix interface to make a series of binary choices when prompted (as in Figure 3), users partly guide and partly watch Stefan through his everyday life and his efforts to design the videogame, which are more or less successful depending on the choices made by the user on Stefan's behalf. Therefore, at least *a priori*, the film is neatly structured around the three diegetic levels described by Genette: (1) the extradiegetic level, which would be the Netflix platform, the interface wherefrom users get to decide the paths taken by Stefan's story, (2) the diegetic level, which would consist of Stefan's story as such, his struggle with designing the game before Tuckersoft's deadline while also undergoing therapy to work through both past traumas and present mental illnesses and (3) the metadiegetic level, which would include several narratives-within-the-narrative. Here, although the first metadiegetic narratives that would come to mind would be Stefan's

67 In a review, Ryan Britt notes that "Bandersnatch is basically a giant tribute [to] Philip K. Dick" and celebrates that, even though "The Netflix interactive movie isn't technically an adaptation of any of Philip K. Dick's stories or novels [...], for all practical purposes, it might be the most successful PKD adaptation of all time" (Britt n.p.). The main reason is the profound likeness of JFD and PKD as characters, especially given both authors' turn towards conspiracy thinking in their late careers. In the real-life case of Dick, this turn can be seen in his famous *Exegesis* (see edition by Jackson and Lethem), where he recorded his experiences with paranoia and hallucinations while showing his obsession with the seemingly random cypher 2-3-74, but Dick's obsessions can also be seen in the many letters that he sent to the FBI, in which he complained about being under governmental surveillance (see Philmus, "The Two Faces of Philip K. Dick"). *Bandersnatch*'s JFD thus seems to both mirror and caricaturize PKD's character, showing via biographies how JFD developed similar paranoias, as well as an obsession with a forking glyph, all of which, eventually, leads him to decapitate his wife. The other main reference to PKD in the film is even more explicit, in the form of a direct citation, as a poster of Dick's novel *Ubik* is shown in the flat of videogame designer Colin Ritman, a colleague of the main character Stefan. Beyond these, one could further speculate with more covert references as, for instance, one possible outcome of *Bandersnatch* seems borrowed from Dick's *Time Out of Joint*, which ends with the revelation that the protagonist's life was a simulation built and maintained by the government, with the complicity of the character's relatives.

New Media Reflexivity

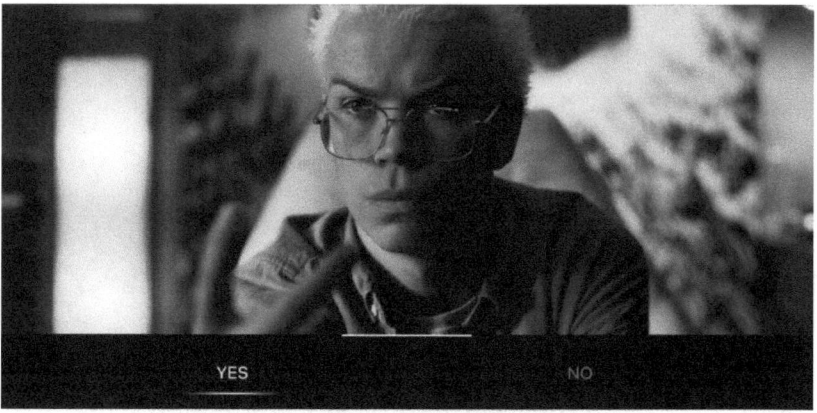

Figure 3. The Netflix interface's standard way of offering a binary choice to users: gradually, the lower margin of the screen widens and two answers appear for ten seconds, during which time users should click one—otherwise, the option on the left is automatically chosen. In this case, the question is whether Stefan wants to take LSD from his colleague Colin, who offers it as a way of overcoming his creative block and finding inspiration for coding again. Nevertheless, this is one example of a meaningless choice, since if the user refuses, Colin is seen dissolving the substance into Stefan's tea and only later, quite shamelessly, he tells Stefan (and implicitly us users) that "I chose for you."

game as well as JFD's novel (Figure 4), both are only present as invented intertextual references in a hypertextual relation between them—and at most, one could perhaps refer to them as "absent metadiegeses," as they are often shown and discussed, but never actually played or read. However, besides these two "metadiegetic Bandersnatches," Stefan also reads and watches two JFD biographies, an illustrated book and a VHS-recorded documentary, for inspiration, thus also allowing users to read and watch them—and to notice how closely they mirror and/or anticipate events in the main diegesis (Figure 5).

In these ways, one key to Netflix's *Bandersnatch* is that it is structured as a *mise-en-abyme* that, in and of itself, already allows for intensely reflexive kinds of (self-)commentary across these diegetic levels. However, besides that, another key to *Bandersnatch* is that the choices that it offers to users inevitably lead to transgressions between those same levels, in such a way that interactivity is subordinated to reflexivity. And how? One thing that

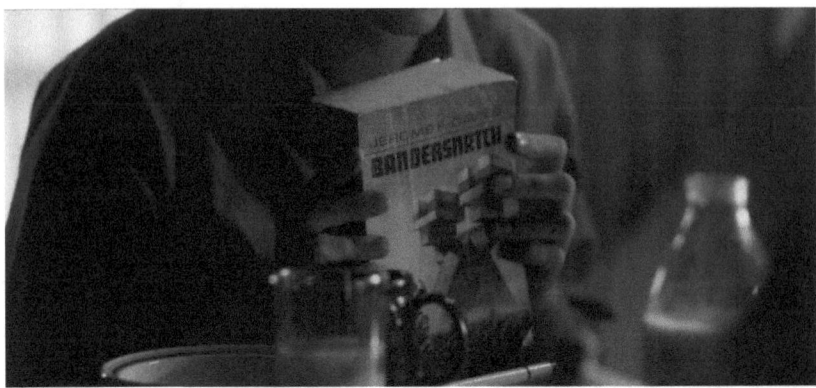

Figure 4. Stefan's copy of JFD's *Bandersnatch* book, in an old and worn-out copy that he inherited from his late mother. Here, Stefan is showing it to his father, who, unaware that it is a choose-your-own-adventure book, comments that JFD "can't be a good writer" since Stefan is "always flicking backwards and forwards in that"—something that Netflix users may very well end up doing too. In any case, his father's comments lead Stefan to explain that "you decide what your character does" just "like a game"—to which his father replies, in an unknowingly self-conscious manner, "how about you decide what you want for your breakfast?," which happens to be the very first choice that us, Netflix users, must make.

users may come to feel is that *Bandersnatch*'s interactivity is, ironically, a kind of "anti-interactivity." Only formally speaking, user choices are quite limited, not only because they are always binary choices between pre-established answers, but also because often—sooner or later, in one order or another—they lead through similar narrative pathways and eventually arrive at similar endings, most of them equally tragic for Stefan.[68] One Reddit user, reconstructed the whole film's flowchart of possible pathways, in an image that is, at the time of writing, still available online (see EngineeringMySadness) and, in one glimpse, one can notice how the

---

68 Most of the endings involve Stefan's death or his imprisonment for murdering his father and, in most of them, his game gets disappointing reviews—except in the narrative pathway in which Stefan decides to chop up his father's body, where it is hailed as "the perfect game." One is thus led to assume that the only way in which Stefan can "choose right" is by becoming the worst kind of psychopath.

New Media Reflexivity

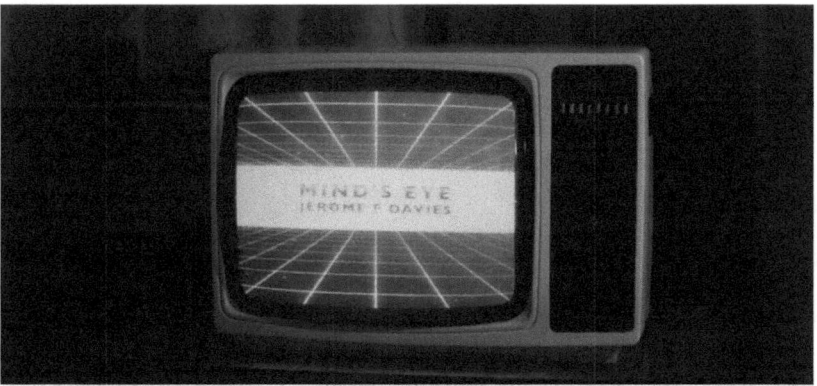

Figure 5. The documentary's opening credits, with its title: *Mind's Eye: Jerome F. Davies*. Stefan watches this documentary while coding his game, so in this scene users can hear the documentary's narrators and interviewees at the same time as they see Stefan's increasingly troubled and frustrated expressions. Seemingly blurring the borders between diegesis (Stefan's story) and metadiegesis (JFD's story), the documentary describes how JFD's "attempts to complete the complex, multiple narratives of *Bandersnatch* was to prove the final straw" and "the start of his complete mental collapse." Anticipating Stefan's possible metafictional anagnorisis (in certain narrative pathways), the documentary explains that "Davies became convinced he had no control over his fate" and that "whatever we do in this existence, there's another one out there in which we're doing quite opposite, which renders free will meaningless" and "nothing but an illusion." The documentary is one exemplary case of how *Bandersnatch*'s multi-level structure folds upon itself in a way in which the lower levels seem to self-consciously speak of the higher ones—the extradiegetic Netflix interface included.

whole's staggering complexity is generally designed for herding users back and forth within narrowly established channels, rather than for opening distinct, divergent pathways. Moreover, the issue is not just that choices are limited but that the film's interface itself coerces users into "choosing right," especially in those cases when a kind of "game over screen" appears, forcing users to return and reverse an apparently "wrong" choice in order to continue watching.[69] And last but not least, in a considerable number of

69 This is what happens in the very first choice that could change the narrative pathway, when Stefan is offered to make his game at Tuckersoft with the team. If he accepts, the game is a disappointment and users are forced to "try again" or else

occasions, the choices are absurd—"yes" or "fuck yeah" in one case that I comment below—or at least inconsequential, as in those cases where users must choose a product (i.e. a breakfast cereal, or a musical album) or cases where the outcome itself undoes the user's choice (see again Figure 3). In a sense, Stefan's helplessness in the face of tragedy pales in comparison to users' helplessness in the face of the interface.

All such limitations to interactivity therefore function—in combination—as metafictional epiphanies, especially insofar as they are constant reminders of the constraints placed upon the user's choices within the film's interface—and by extension, within digital platforms in general. A journalist wisely observed that "Netflix is a character in *Black Mirror: Bandersnatch*" (Romano) and, indeed, the interactive film can be said to be a dystopian double of the "freedom" offered by Netflix, which itself also operates by herding users within pre-established channels under the pretext of giving them "personalization," "autonomy" and "choice" while only offering the choice of what product to consume—as long as they keep consuming from their catalog (see Arnold; Alexander). Ironically, this is the same working premise of *Bandersnatch*, a choose-your-own-adventure narrative in which choice is sometimes meaningless and sometimes commodified (if not both) because, ultimately, what matters is that you keep watching, playing, trying and exploring—or, even, speculating and obsessing. Therefore, the film's whole (anti-)interactive design is one way in which the film is self-referential in a profoundly ambivalent way, since it both reproduces and demystifies the functioning of the platform where it circulates. As Conley and Burroughs have argued, it is because "we and Stefan both shape and are shaped by algorithmic acquiescence" that *Bandersnatch* seems to be "critiquing acquiescence while simultaneously legitimizing Netflix's usage of algorithms," with "the invisible hand of prior design granting the semblance of choice after-the-fact" (Conley and Burroughs 10). However, the film's reflexivity does not end in its self-referential relation to Netflix and suchlike digital platforms. Beyond

---

get caught in a loop that even the characters seem to vaguely remember; only if he rejects, then the narrative can continue and Stefan can make the game by working (and having mental breakdowns) alone at home.

Bandersnatch's (anti-)interactive design, which, strictly speaking, generates reflexivity from the extradiegetic level, there are also many self-referential and self-conscious devices within most narrative pathways—that is, in the diegetic level proper. Within that garden of forking paths, one can find several devices with an arguably stronger estranging effect: in particular, metafictional epiphanies, anagnorises and metalepses.

The first character who seems aware of his fictional condition is Stefan's colleague at Tuckersoft, Colin Ritman, a successful videogame designer whom Stefan admires (played by Will Poulter). If users go twice through an early narrative pathway—the very first return-loop that users may go through if they make one "wrong" choice—Colin anticipates some comments that Stefan had already made in the first iteration of their scenes together, something *a priori* impossible for an intradiegetic character—unless, of course, we interpret his words and actions as the springboard for the viewer-user's first metafictional epiphany. In another pathway—a relevant one, anticipated in *Bandersnatch*'s promotional trailer—Colin himself goes on a long rant that, although justified by his LSD use, seems to confirm his self-consciousness—or at least, his role as a mouthpiece for self-conscious commentary. Just as users witness Stefan's first experience with the drug in a quick-cut, VFX-heavy sequence that simulates his hallucinations, Colin is heard relentlessly and feverishly preaching:

> People think there's one reality, but there's loads of them, all snaking off, like roots. And what you do on one path affects what happens on other paths. Time is a construct. People think you can't go back and change things, but you can. [...] When you make a decision, you think it's you doing it, but it's not. It's the spirit out there that's connected to our world that decides what we do and we just have to go along for the ride.
>
> Mirrors let you move through time. The government monitors people, they pay people to pretend to be your relatives and they put drugs in your food and they film you.
>
> There's messages in every game. Like PAC-Man, do you know what PAC stands for? P. A. C. Programme and Control. He's Programme and Control Man. The whole thing's a metaphor. He thinks he's got free will, but really, he's trapped in a maze, in a system, all he can do is consume, he's pursued by demons that are probably just in his own head. And even if he does manage to escape by slipping out one side of the maze, what happens? He comes right back in the other side. People think it's a

happy game. It's not a happy game, it's a fucking nightmare world and the worst thing is it's real and we live in it. It's all code. If you listen closely, you can hear the numbers. There's a cosmic flowchart that dictates where you can and where you can't go.

I've given you the knowledge. I've set you free. Do you understand? [...]

We're on one path. Right now, me and you. And how one path ends is immaterial. It's how our decisions along that path affect the whole that matters. Do you believe me? [...] I'll prove it. One of us is going over. Over there [gesturing towards the balcony]. It wouldn't matter because there are other timelines. How many times have you seen PAC-Man die? Doesn't bother him. He just tries again. One of us is jumping [out, to commit suicide]. So who's it gonna be?

Immediately after, users are prompted to choose who will jump and both choices lead to narrative pathways that prove Colin right. If users choose Stefan, he jumps and dies, so a "game over" screen appears with the option of returning to a previous choice (including this one, which can be undone); if users choose Colin, he jumps and dies, to Stefan's horror and panic—but then Stefan immediately wakes up in his dad's car, back in the scene in which users chose to go with Colin rather than to therapy. In this iteration, however, therapy is the only choice and Stefan and Colin's trip is left behind as nothing but a bad dream. Whatever the outcome, therefore, Colin's description of a "nightmare world" with "a cosmic flowchart," where nothing matters "because there are other timelines," is immediately proven right by the diegesis' design—and besides, his speech offers literal descriptions of future choices and outcomes that shall keep proving him right, even in its most delirious details. With all the subtlety and the obviousness of Colin's PAC-Man allegory, this scene thus stands as a textbook example of a metafictional epiphany, one that causes the audience's estranging (re-)awakening to the interactive narrative's nature while also paving the way for the protagonist's subsequent awakening.

In later narrative pathways, often near some of the possible endings, it is Stefan who experiences metafictional anagnorises, although these awakenings are never the liberation that Colin (or Netflix) would proclaim, but rather the beginning of a complete mental breakdown. At first, users may gradually notice that Stefan seems bothered by some actions that he makes at their command and he explicitly tells his therapist that he does not feel "in control" because there is "someone else" or "an impulse" that guides even his tiniest decisions: "What I have for breakfast. What music I listen to. Whether I shout at dad, or …"—all of which are choices that have already been made by the user, that "spirit out there that's connected to our world," as Colin had put it. Immediately after Stefan's confession, in this same sequence users must choose whether the protagonist pulls his earlobe or bites his nails—but, in this case, Stefan surprisingly and painstakingly resists doing either of these things. This scene thus undermines both users' and Stefan's sense of control while also showing the character's growing self-awareness—a process that is less like an awakened ascent to a higher diegetic level and more like a despaired descent into madness. Soon after, *Bandersnatch*'s diegetic levels can be further blurred in a metalepsis that can happen—or not—at the user's whim. During a scene in which Stefan is alone in his room with his computer, incapable of working anymore, shouting that "[he] know[s] there's someone there" and asking for anyone to "give [him] a sign," users can make an appearance on Stefan's screen. Among other disturbing possibilities such as showing a glyph or revealing a government conspiracy, users are specifically given the choice of telling Stefan about Netflix (see Figure 6).[70] If they do so, he shouts: "What the fuck is Netflix? Seriously, what does that mean?"—and as users explain it, he eventually understands that he is "being controlled by someone from the future," as he tells his father. Interpreting this as both a panic attach and a sign of psychosis, Stefan understandably asks to be taken back to therapy.

---

70 The conspiracy, called PACS in line with Colin's PAC-Man allegory, consists in a Truman-Show-like (or Time-Out-Of-Joint-like) experiment done to Stefan by the government, with the collaboration of his parents and his therapist. In this scenario, which could be interpreted reflexively as a metafictional allegory, Stefan discovers that he has been under constant surveillance and that everything from his early life, including his mother's death, has been staged for the sake of the experiment.

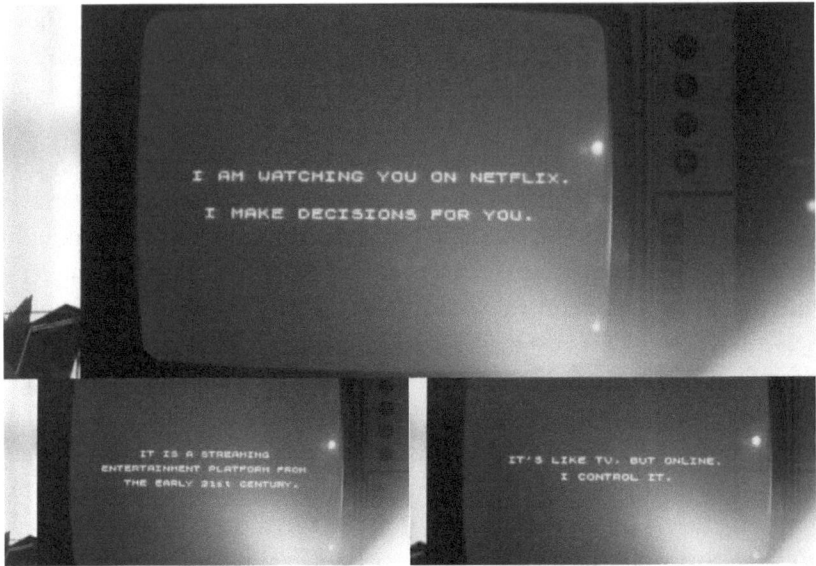

Figure 6. The user's intrusion into the diegesis—a descending metalepsis in Genette's terms—via Stefan's computer display. The explanations are continued in response to Stefan's questions but, eventually, interrupted when Stefan's father appears.

Once at therapy, Stefan seems convinced that this—the reality of Netflix—"is not a delusion," but his metafictional anagnorisis here continues to be more of a curse than a blessing. Dr Haynes, his therapist, mocks him, in fact, while also giving us another example of how reflexivity can be put to humorous and critical uses simultaneously. "What is Netflix? Is it a planet?"—she asks first—and then she goes further:

> So all of this is happening to entertain someone. Someone who's controlling you. So why aren't you in a more entertaining scenario? [...] look at you. You're in a small, ordinary room, in an ordinary part of the world, talking to an ordinary woman. If this was entertainment, surely you'd make it more interesting. Inject a little action, isn't that right? I mean, wouldn't you want a little more action if you're watching this now on telly?

In thus questioning Stefan and almost insulting him for his ordinariness, her questions stealthily shift their addressee and—once again—everything is blurred: the borders between the diegetic and the extradiegetic and the differences between Stefan and the user. This is made explicit by the fact that, just as Dr Haynes asks her last question, the interface demands another choice from users, those who are actually "watching this now on telly." And do users want more action, as she says? The only answers here are "yes" and "fuck yeah," so the joke is on viewers as much as it is on Stefan: like him, we too are being insulted for our presumed ordinariness, mocked for the very thirst for action with which *Bandersnatch* has been toying all along.

Ultimately, therefore, Stefan's gradual awakening is not only reinforcing his feeling of helplessness, it is also reinforcing *the users' feeling of helplessness* by offering the most absurd "non-choice" up to that point—a choice that sums up the film's "anti-interactive" form and philosophy and, in so doing, reinforces *Black Mirror*'s long-running thesis that we the viewers, like Stefan, "are fast becoming little more than featured players: cast members in an ongoing, formulaic and serial story from which there is no escape" (Telotte 18). And quite literally, there is no escape from this scene, which can lead to two dead ends that are also two endings of *Bandersnatch* as a whole: either (a), after choosing to fight Dr Haynes and his father, Stefan is dragged away, presumably to a psychiatric institution, or (b), after the user chooses to jump out of the window, the scene is cut, literally, in a revelation that this is being filmed. In this case, Stefan, now addressed as an actor called Mike, is told that he's "not scripted to jump out"—another metalepsis that he, who is still in-character, struggles to process. Either way, it appears that *Bandersnatch* does not imagine Stefan's metafictional anagnorisis as the preamble of any liberating rebellion or confrontation, but rather as a ridiculous and futile attempt to escape from an omnipresent and omnipotent new media dystopia—a reality of multi-layered, multimedia surveillance and control of which this interactive film is unashamedly part of. Under digital capitalism, the saying goes that if you don't see the product, it's because that's you; in *Bandersnatch*, similarly, if you don't get the joke, it's because it's on you.

Another possible ending of *Bandersnatch* redoubles and reinforces the feeling of being trapped within an endlessly recursive structure—specifically, by creating the illusion that the film itself is a self-begetting narrative. After going through the narrative pathway in which Stefan—in a morally hideous but egoistically "efficient" trade-off—murders, chops-up and JFD-style beheads his dad so as to get time to make the perfect game, *Bandersnatch*'s credits begin to roll on-screen, but they are inter-cut with an additional sequence that is set in the present day.[71] After a special news broadcast recalls Stefan's *Bandersnatch* and its tragic production history, the reporter goes on to announce that "in a move that's bound to cause controversy, a new coder wants to reboot the game for a new generation." This coder, who happens to be Colin Ritman's daughter Pearl Ritman (played by Laura Evelyn), declares that she is "developing this for streaming TV platforms," but,—in yet another humorously reflexive nod at users-viewers—she refuses to comment on the "rumour that [the] platform is Netflix." The broadcast then ends and Pearl Ritman is shown at work, where she is testing and watching her *Bandersnatch*, which seems to be exactly the one that users-viewers are about to finish. And in yet another turn of the screw, the film ends here by giving us one final and equally meaningless choice—producing another metalepsis that turns the presumably empowered author into another pawn within this all-encompassing, interactive platform (Figure 7).

In all these ways and more, the rabbit hole of reflexivity in the age of new media seems to run ever deeper and deeper and it is potentially endless, given the complexity of technical possibilities, the ever-growing multi-media diversity and the pervasiveness of interactive interfaces—but for what? In the end, as *Bandersnatch*'s Pearl Ritman shows, authors too are caught within "the game"—that is, within the ever-abstracter spirals of digital capitalism. In fact, discussing *Black Mirror*'s ongoing commitment with Netflix, even *Bandersnatch*'s real writer, Charlie Brooker, seems to think of himself as another helpless pawn of the system:

---

71 In this narrative pathway, Stefan gleefully shares his achievement with Dr Haynes in one final therapy session. Here, he explains how he made the perfect game in yet-another implicitly self-conscious confession that could have been uttered by Charlie Brooker himself: "I've been trying to give the player too much choice. So I just went back and stripped loads out. And now they've only got the illusion of free will, but really, I decide the ending."

New Media Reflexivity   179

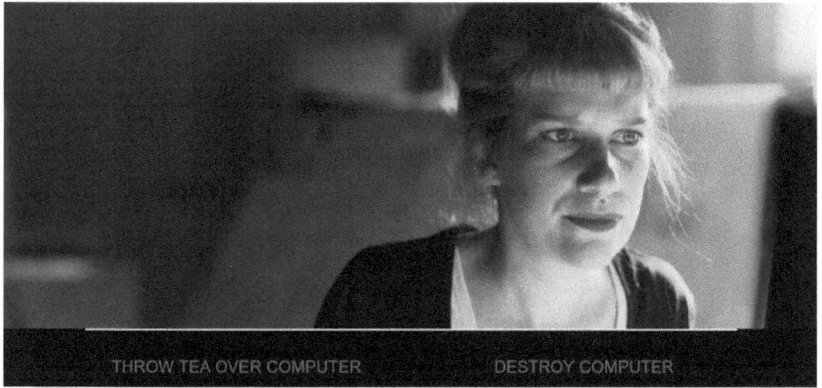

Figure 7. Pearl upon unwittingly becoming the user's avatar in one final metalepsis where the fictionalized creator becomes another character and pawn in the game.

> We can keep endlessly redefining what *Black Mirror* is. Which I suppose means we can never stop. We can never leave. We're trapped here forever. Like a ladybird glued to concrete. Help. Help us. For God's sake please help us.
>
> That's probably as good a way as any to end this book, isn't it?
>
> Now go away. (Brooker et al. 313)

In this passage, which ends a book about *Black Mirror* with another dose of the self-conscious cynicism that has long characterized not just the series but also its creator, Brooker is letting us know the crude reality behind *Bandersnatch*: that the creative minds behind digital platforms' most successful products are also caught—or perhaps, are most deeply caught—within their dystopian dynamics. Indeed, people like Brooker are acutely aware of the media's complex constraints—surely more than us theorists—and that awareness seems to be reflected and refracted through their productions.[72] An anthology series like *Black Mirror* that

---

72 Charlie Brooker's deeply reflexive speech and creative style in general could be traced back to the beginnings of his career and particularly to his *Screenwipe* show (BBC Four, 2006–8), a satirical programme that reviewed British television of the time.

has a kind of self-referentiality as its loose thematic thread—in the sense that it began focusing on new media technologies as "black mirrors"—is here turned into a fully self-conscious meditation upon itself and not just its medium—and, in so being, *Bandersnatch* seems to cynically conclude that it is as much critical as it is complicit. And yet, as this analysis has shown, it is precisely by playing by the rulebook of "platform entertainment" that *Bandersnatch* works so well and it is also precisely by being both ludic and didactic, both playful and serious about its subject matter, that the film offers a more potent kind of estrangement, one that is narratively smart and affectively memorable.

Ultimately, what lingers in the users' imagination is the feeling of helplessness—a helplessness that has been carefully constructed via an "anti-interactive" design and a tragic story that feed upon each other to convey the sense that Stefan's, Pearl's, Brooker's and the user's helplessness in the face of the interface are one and the same. In this way, *Bandersnatch* effectively resists one in-built tendency of both interactive narratives and new media productions, a tendency that may have worked against it. As Gabrielle Pedullà has argued, the potentially endless interactivity of new media goes against the presumed effects of tragedy—specifically, against the catharsis that ought to emerge from all epiphanies and anagnorises. This, in his view, is because new media (beginning with television) have given "us the illusion of not being prisoners: that is, of being able to interfere in the tragic chain of events without getting involved in the game" and, therefore, "The remote offers us shelter: it is the shield that makes our indifference possible, but also the instrument of our refusal to suffer with the imaginary beings who live and breathe in the images before us" (Pedullà 112–14). Pedullà's arguments here emerge from a genuine concern with a contemporary "crisis of empathy" (120), with which I sympathize—but this leads him to argue that what is needed is a return to the immersive, cathartic power of both theaters and movie theaters, especially since new media generate estrangement rather than empathy. However, I believe that *Bandersnatch* shows how even something that is a product of new media through and through can lead users towards empathy and identification—and it is perhaps no overstatement to say that, almost by necessity, because of how the film is designed, Stefan's tragic helplessness is also the user's, who is forced to feel like his avatar by way of so many reflexive devices. Thus, estrangement can also lead to empathy and, in this case, users may quit *Bandersnatch* with an uncomfortable but liberating feeling: the dreary awareness that we as individuals are insignificant *vis-à-vis* the global stack, but the hope that that situation may be changed once the feeling is shared.

Therefore, after viewing *Bandersnatch*, a series of deeply critical questions seem bound to eventually intrude into the users' thoughts: do we want to carry on accepting such degree of mediated manipulation? Do we want to keep on accepting a system of technologies that turns us into utterly helpless pawns like Stefan? The instinctive reaction is surely to turn off *Bandersnatch* once and for all, after getting fed up with its loops, but the nightmare world would still be all around us. Ultimately, the dystopia here is not so much that we the users manipulate Stefan, or that Brooker mocks us both, or even that Netflix plays with the whole lot of us (especially because other companies would gladly and promptly take its place)—instead, the problem is that new media as they currently exist under digital capitalism trap us within networks of manipulation by design, regardless of each user's intention. A critical reflexivity focused on new media, such as *Bandersnatch*'s, can be—potentially, of course—one way to become aware of this whole situation, with a political self-consciousness developing from narrative self-consciousness. Thus seen, there is still value, both knowledge and enjoyment, to be found by delving and descending into the high-tech hell.

2.5. The Ambivalences of New Media Reflexivity

This chapter has consisted of an examination of the phenomenon of reflexivity within the specific context of new media platforms and contemporary SF narratives, providing a necessary bridge, a conceptual basis and an interpretive language for subsequent chapters, insofar as reflexivity is an essential and inescapable formal feature of all the new media dystopias that are yet to be analyzed in this book. The chapter began, in a more theoretical vein, with (1) an attempt to offer a synthetic solution to ongoing debates on the matter within SF studies, specifically proposing to conceive of speculation and reflexivity as complementary modes of cognitive estrangement, especially a historical moment that seems to predispose a reflexive turn and it continued with (2) a survey of the modes, levels and devices of reflexivity, borrowing the main concepts from Pardo's theoretical model for the study of reflexivity across media, which offers a coherent interpretative language that saves us from the terminological conundrums and contradictions that emerge in many studies of reflexivity. Subsequently, the chapter continued, in a more analytic vein, with (3) a comparative study of both Philip K. Dick's and Frank Spotnitz's *The Man in the High Castle*, focusing on how the latter adapted the former's reflexivity for an audio-visual narrative, an attempt that should attest—by negative example—to how reflexivity is not a purely formal phenomenon, but also a historically and contextually rooted one. Finally, the chapter turned towards (4) a detailed reading of David Slade and Charlie Brooker's interactive film *Black Mirror: Bandersnatch*, which should have served both as a catalog of reflexive possibilities and as a specific example of *new media reflexivity*: a reflexivity that operates from and for contemporary digital platforms and that has—in general, potentially and, in *Bandersnatch*, effectively—a deeply estranging and critical-subversive function. This is also why, by my definition, I understand new media dystopias to be a reflexive kind of what Tom Moylan and others call the critical dystopia—that is, I am defining new media dystopias as estranging and potentially subversive SF narratives that stand in a profoundly reflexive relation with those technologies of digital capitalism that enable their production, circulation and consumption.

Formally speaking, then, the main specificity of new media reflexivity (when compared to reflexivity generally) is the interrelation of diegetic layers and the digital interface. If one wished to, for the sake of coherence, continue applying the conceptual apparatus of Gérard Genette, which Pardo's model also adopts and adapts, there could be at least two ways of conceptualizing this interface, depending on whether we regard it as a pseudo-diegetic level or as the locale of an intense transtextuality. One possibility, the one that was most employed for the interpretation of *Bandersnatch*, would be *to treat the user interface as an extradiegetic level*, considering that it functions as that which Genette calls "the narrating instance," insofar as the user (a relatively active narratee) chooses and controls the narration within the (limited) range of possibilities offered by the platform (a non-human narrating agent). Another possibility, again borrowing from Genette, would be *to conceptualize this layer as a digital paratext* that not only accompanies individual narratives but also (algorithmically) suggests possible transtextual relations between them, thus containing and correlating a range of commodified fictions. These two ways of narratively conceptualizing the interface seem both correct and compatible, but they each name a distinctive level of analysis that may have divergent degrees of importance within different reflexive narratives. Nevertheless, what is clear is that digital interfaces are in and of themselves a source of increased and deepened reflexivity—at the very least, of self-referentiality at the interface's level. Furthermore, if one wishes to go beyond the level of the individual interface, it might also make sense to re-appropriate Mark Zuckerberg's notion of the metaverse—or rather to re-re-appropriate it from Neal Stephenson, using it to conceptualize (and criticize) that extra-extradiegetic, macro-paratextual world of interfaces. In that way, the contemporary keyword "metaverse" could be used analytically to refer to that abstracter level that contains all the Netflixes and Amazons, to that digital multiverse where new forms of reflexivity are thriving under the eye and the control of contemporary capitalist corporations.

However, if the appearance of digital pseudo-diegetic levels is the main formal specificity of new media reflexivity, what remains to be pondered is the other term that I have often associated with reflexivity: ambivalence, a notion that brings us closer to contextual considerations. What are the ambivalences of new media reflexivity when thought not just narratively, but also historically? Here I hope that I am allowed to play with contrastive structures and to remind my readers to take the arguments that follow, not as the binary choices of digital code—or of *Bandersnatch*'s interface—but as dialectical pairs, where two opposing tendencies co-exist, interact and together result in a potential infinity of third terms. In so doing, my aim is to try to follow

> a method capable of doing justice to both the ideological and the Utopian or transcendent functions of mass culture simultaneously. Nothing less will do, as the

suppression of either of these terms may testify: [...] the older kind of ideological analysis, which, ignoring the Utopian components of mass culture, ends up with the empty denunciation of the latter's manipulative function and degraded status [...] [or] the complementary extreme—a method that would celebrate Utopian impulses in the absence of any conception or mention of the ideological vocation of mass culture. (Jameson, "Reification and Utopia in Mass Culture" 144–5)

In this case, when I began this chapter by observing the contemporary omnipresence of reflexivity, I acknowledged that this is, to a great extent, a by-product of dominant dynamics—but I was also careful to remind readers that this "mainstreaming of the meta" does not necessarily cancel out the critical and utopian potentials of art and culture. And there lies, I believe, the key dialectical tension, the deep, ideological ambivalence of this formal phenomenon.

On the one hand, as I suggested by the end of the previous chapter, self-referentiality is something that may be ultimately explained as a formal reflex of the logics of capital, which itself circulates for the purpose of self-valorization, moving as "self-valorizing value," in Marx's own phrase. In this sense, much of today's reflexivity may be derived in the last instance from the culture industry's tendency to advertise its productions from within its productions, or to showcase its platforms from within its platforms—and in this sense it is true that "Cultural entities typical of the culture industry are no longer *also* commodities, they are commodities through and through" (Adorno, "Culture Industry Reconsidered" 13). Thinking about SF culture specifically, several critics have argued that, nowadays, a considerable part of what I (following Pardo) have here termed self-referentiality is often the key mechanism of a "nostalgia industry" (Hassler-Forest, "'When You Get There, You Will Already Be There'").[73] Furthermore, especially in big

---

[73] It should be noted that, in suggesting this, Hassler-Forest is not being unambiguously condemnatory in speaking of a "nostalgia industry." The problem is not so much nostalgia, but the industry, and Hassler-Forest (following Boym) does make a "distinction between two types of nostalgic currents that have radically different political and ideological implications": restorative nostalgia, with a "conservative" and "politically regressive function," as opposed to reflective nostalgia, which critically "recuperates the sense of waning historicity" (Hassler-Forest, "'When You Get There, You Will Already Be There'" 183; cf. Boym).

transmedia franchises, self-referentiality is often put to the service of a quasi-religious grand narrative that holds audiences hostage while playfully rewarding them (cf. Canavan, "Hokey Religions"; Hassler-Forest, "Disney's Endgame"; Sebastián-Martín, "The Franchise Devouring Itself"). Although somewhat ironically, *Black Mirror* itself has begun to play this game, employing what could be called *commodified self-referentiality* not only in *Bandersnatch* but also elsewhere in the anthology series, where episodes frequently cite one another and even allow speculation about a shared universe (see Canavan, "Hope, with Teeth"). Thus, in a sense, even if self-referentiality wears a critical-dystopian dress, there is still no such thing as bad publicity.

More broadly, if one thinks back upon the epoch's dystopian structure of feeling, one can easily imagine a fitting function for reflexivity within the cultural climate of capitalist realism and left melancholy. The same Mark Fisher of *Capitalist Realism* invited us to think about the age's presumed "reflexive impotence"—the idea that we "know things are bad, but more than that, [we] know [we] can't do anything about it." To this idea, Fisher adds an important qualification: that "that 'knowledge,' that reflexivity, is not a passive observation of an already existing state of affairs. It is a self-fulfilling prophecy." Even though Fisher is not linking reflexive impotence with *narrative* reflexivity, he does consider this a "consequence of being hooked into the entertainment matrix," which would generate a state of "twitchy, agitated interpassivity," a kind of "depressive hedonia" (see *Capitalist Realism* 21–30). And, as was noted in the previous chapter, the algorithmic filter bubbles of digital capitalism do nothing but reinforce each user's tendencies—digging an ever-deeper and ever-more-self-referential rabbit hole for them.

In this context, what could be the by-default effect of narrative reflexivity if not a greater feeling of impotence? *Bandersnatch*, for instance, is explicitly designed to make users feel helpless, to drag them into a whirlpool of cynicism—and will users swim out of it, or will they drown all the way down? Whatever the individual user's reaction, what seems clear is that even *Bandersnatch*, the most overtly self-conscious new media dystopia, appears unable of turning the tide—and it may even reinforce the current, triggering a tricky undertow with its loops. In this way, speaking more generally and more literally, perhaps narrative self-consciousness, despite its oft-presumed estranging effects, can ultimately be as complicit with the status quo as the most commodified kinds of self-referentiality—or perhaps self-consciousness only makes everything worse, for what good does it do to think deeper and deeper about dystopian new media if we already know and feel their deleterious effects daily and directly?

On the other hand, of course, one should ask: is reflexivity necessarily a road to hopelessness and impotence? First of all, the heavy weight of the epoch's structure of feeling should not make one want to erase the essential difference between self-referentiality and self-consciousness, for—even when such a cultural climate seems to blunt the estranging edge of reflexivity altogether—the functioning of the two modes that Pardo theorizes is fundamentally different, especially insofar as self-conscious devices such as metalepses, epiphanies and anagnorises seem to have the most affectively poignant effects.[74] The two close analyses of this chapter have shown in detail the many possibilities whereby self-conscious devices can be turned critically against history (in *The Man in the High Castle*) or against new media (in *Bandersnatch*). Furthermore, if one returns to Moylan's definition of the critical dystopia, it cannot be forgotten that the negative-critical impetus of the dystopian (and the reflexive too, here) indirectly reawakens a utopian impulse, a desire for a better world that is sometimes rekindled vicariously, through rebellious characters such as those found in *The Man in the High Castle*, while other times it is directly reawakened in the users themselves—think of the frustration caused by *Bandersnatch*'s traps.

Besides, if self-consciousness does indeed have these critical-utopian effects, at least potentially, what of self-referentiality? Within this postmodern context of thoroughly commodified culture and media, a considerable part of self-referentiality seems to be but an echo of the commodity's logics. But a commodity, as Marx shows, always has a dual nature; it is never

---

74 Many theorists of "metafiction" (which should be, in Pardo's language, understood as a narrative with primary or structural self-consciousness) did make claims about the "subversive" and even "radical" qualities of it (see, respectively, Hutcheon, *A Poetics of Postmodernism* 3; Waugh 13). Nevertheless, these claims need to be nuanced and understood dialectically, against the possibility that the opposite may be also true to an extent.

only a commodity, so to propose that any commodified object is only defined by its exchange-value would be to fall prey to *commodity fetishism*—that illusion of the market whereby everything is made equal and each thing's unique qualities are lost in a sea of quantitative sameness. In other words, using a more contemporary language, reducing self-referentiality to pseudo-advertising would be to fall prey to neoliberal rationality, in this case by thinking economically about a cultural phenomenon. This is not to affirm that there is not commodified self-referentiality—there is, abundantly—but self-referentiality, too, can function under the logics of something other than market compulsions. Even when it is not explicitly estranging nor establishing a critical distance with the medium, a degree of self-referentiality is after all a necessary precondition for the new media dystopias that this book examines: for, if they did not at least reflect upon their medium, however abstractly or allegorically, how would a dystopian critique of digital capitalism from within its own products be possible?

All in all, the argument cannot as of yet be settled and I cannot promise that it will be settled whatsoever by the end of this book. So far, nonetheless, what seems indisputable is that very unsettledness: the fact that new media reflexivity is as much a symptom of digital capitalism's dominant dynamics as a potential mode of estrangement directed against the system from within. New media dystopias must therefore be described with contradictory phrases, as rebellious products, as commodified critiques, as discontent content, etc. In what follows, contradictions shall keep piling up as we delve deeper into these dystopias, for if their narrative reflexivity is already deeply ambivalent, their visual aesthetics are probably even more so.

CHAPTER 3

Between Critique and Mystification: The Aesthetic and Ideological Ambivalences of New Media Dystopias

> Ours is indeed an age of extremity. For we live under continual threat of two equally fearful, but seemingly opposed, destinies: unremitting banality and inconceivable terror. It is fantasy, served out in large rations by the popular arts, which allows most people to cope with these twin specters. For one job that fantasy can do is to lift us out of the unbearably humdrum and to distract us from terrors—real or anticipated—by an escape into exotic, dangerous situations which can have last-minute happy endings. But another of the things that fantasy can do is to normalize what is psychologically unbearable, thereby inuring us to it. In one case, fantasy beautifies the world. In the other, it neutralizes it.
>
> The fantasy in science fiction films does both jobs. The films reflect world-wide anxieties, and they serve to allay them.
>
> —Susan Sontag, "The Imagination of Disaster" (1965, 224–5)

> When viewed in cinemas, science-fiction films foreground spectacle at the levels of both image and [...] sound. Big budget science-fiction extravaganzas offer the total visual, auditory and kinetic experience of the *Gesamtkunstwerk*: the spectator is invited to succumb to complete sensory and bodily engulfment. Wherever cinema exhibits its own distinctive matters of expression—as it does with science fiction in displays of state-of-the-art special effects technologies—there is a considerable degree of self-reflexivity at work. Indeed, when such displays become a prominent attraction in their own right, they tend to eclipse narrative, plot and character. The story becomes the display; and the display becomes the story. Does it really matter, for example, that a film like *2001: A Space Odyssey* effectively lacks a plot? The enticement is not narrative involvement, nor even identification with characters, but rather the matters of expression of cinema itself, and this film's awe-inspiringly unfamiliar imagery. Spectators are invited to gape in wonder and abandon themselves to the totality of the audiovisual experience.
>
> —Annette Kuhn, *Alien Zone II: The Spaces of Science Fiction Cinema* (1999, 5)

Like the SF film tradition to which they belong and like all cinema regardless of genre, new media dystopias are not only a specific kind of narrative: they are also a specific kind of *spectacle*, closely akin to those described by Sontag and Kuhn. The conceptual apparatus in Chapter 2 has focused primarily upon the latter dimension, since new media reflexivity would be the most essential *narrative* feature of these dystopias, but it now becomes necessary to pay attention to the former dimension as well—their most spectacular dimension, their audio-visual aesthetics. Without considering new media dystopias as both narrative and spectacle, one's understanding of them would remain too partial and it would probably suffer from the biases that often haunt studies of non-literary media—an overvaluation of the verbal over the visual, which, in turn, entails several undesirable biases.[1] Trying to approach such dichotomy in a way that considers *the inherent ambivalences of an SF narrative as much as the inherent ambivalences of an SF spectacle*, this chapter is where I finish developing my definition of the new media dystopia.

Firstly and most theoretically, the chapter opens with a schematization of the sub-genre's aesthetic and ideological ambivalences, in a way that synthesizes (and re-problematizes) the historicizing and narratological propositions of previous chapters and then advances some hypotheses about the sub-genre's ambivalence *as specifically visual culture*. Throughout such theorization, my underlying assumption is that the new media dystopia is

---

1   Discussing frequent biases within studies of film adaptation, Robert Stam speaks of the twin phenomena of *iconophobia* and *logophilia*, two concepts that Javier Pardo has taught me to have in mind since the first day in his film course. Even in the absence of literature, consciously or unconsciously, this same prejudice may percolate through any study that (like this one) contrasts the narrative and spectacular dimensions of film or television, as the bias is deeply rooted in Western thought. Specifically, Stam warns us against the imagined

   superiority of literary art to film, an assumption derived from a number of superimposed prejudices: *seniority*, the assumption that older arts are necessarily better arts; *iconophobia*, the culturally rooted prejudice (traceable to the Judaic-Muslim-Protestant prohibitions on "graven images" and to the Platonic and Neoplatonic depreciation of the world of phenomenal appearance) that visual arts are necessarily inferior to the verbal arts; and *logophilia*, the converse valorization, characteristic of the "religions of the book," of the "sacred word" of holy texts. ("Beyond Fidelity" 58)

essentially ambivalent, both a form of critique and a form of mystification, both narratively and visually speaking. Besides briefly commenting and contrasting *Black Mirror*'s episode "Fifteen Million Merits" with Spielberg's film *Ready Player One* as two new media dystopias with a similar ambivalence but radically opposite ideological meanings, this chapter then analyzes two series that flesh out the sub-genre's ambivalences, Lisa Joy and Jonathan Nolan's four-season *Westworld* (2016–22) and Alex Garland's one-season *Devs* (2020). On the one hand, *Westworld* is re-examined as a complex metafictional allegory that allows a number of anti-capitalist interpretations, but also as a series in which narrative complexity itself seems to be as commodified as cinematic spectacle. *Devs*, on the other hand, is analyzed with an eye on how its narratively overt critique of digital capitalism goes hand in hand with a double-edged visual aesthetics that I have elsewhere conceptualized as *dystopian beautification*. To varying degrees, both series partake in both dimensions of the ambivalences, but together they show how there is no "good" or "bad" side in these dialectics, since both their narrative and spectacular dimensions may be critical and utopian in some respects, but mystifying and anti-utopian in others. Overall, then, the main thread of this chapter is the idea that new media dystopias both challenge and symptomatize the ideologies and aesthetics of digital capitalism—a historical system that is as dependent upon ways of thinking as upon *ways of seeing*, to use John Berger's famous phrase.

3.1. Cognitive, Critical and Complex? The Narrative Ambivalences of New Media Dystopias

Some classic definitions of SF and its dystopian sub-genre have already been surveyed in previous chapters and, in particular, Suvin's concept of "cognitive estrangement" and Moylan's of the "critical dystopia," respectively, have provided the basis for my understanding of genre and sub-genre. However, one potential problem with these concepts is that—at least from a superficial understanding, if not partly in the work of their original proponents—they gesture towards an ideal more than a reality; they are more prescriptive than they are descriptive. Of course, in my own analyses so far, I have tended to praise those aspects of certain new media dystopias that best approximate the ideal definitions of Suvin and Moylan, those aspects that best allow critical thinking within and against digital capitalism. In other words, I myself have been prescriptive and a degree of prescription seems necessary to orient one's aesthetic judgments, but prescription should still be compatible with a fair description of the ambiguous complexities of each case. Therefore, I believe that these narrative-oriented definitions of SF and dystopias should be nuanced within a more dialectical view of genre and sub-genre, which should, in turn, lead to a better understanding of our sub-genre, the new media dystopia. If taken too zealously, expecting that the ideal dynamics of SF and dystopian fiction *must be fulfilled* may very well lead one down a stale path of disappointments, especially once one realizes that most narratives "betray the ideal" in one way or another, becoming "failures" to a greater or lesser extent, an intuition that has haunted my own analyses in Chapter 2. But could we not explain apparent "failures" with an understanding of these narratives' inherent ambivalences and find their aesthetic value not so much in a determined ideological meaning, but in a very suggestive set of ambivalences?

3.1.1. *What Is "Cognitive" in the Estrangement?*

As was already explained (see Section 2.1), Suvin's definition of SF proposes that the genre "is—potentially—the space of a potent *estrangement*, validated by the pathos and prestige of the basic cognitive norms of our times" (*Metamorphoses* viii) and, here, one should not underemphasize that qualifying "potentially." For Suvin, cognitive estrangement *ideally* provides an "escape [...] to a better vantage point from which to comprehend the human relations around the author" (*Metamorphoses* 84), so its *ideal* function is nothing less than demystifying historical reality in order to imagine anew a utopian horizon of change, as he has suggested elsewhere. However, "even in the masters" that best fulfill Suvin's definition and thus entered his history of the genre, there is "an opposed tendency toward mystifying escapism," which derives from "the practical and cognitive limitations of fiction steeped in the alienation of class society" (*Metamorphoses* xi). In our case, those limitations would be attributable to at least three factors: the epoch's structure of feeling with its affective and ideological bias for anti-utopianism, the thoroughly commodified condition of postmodern culture generally and the circulation of new media dystopias specifically within the same media platforms that they reflexively represent. New media dystopias, therefore, can be said to "betray" Suvin's definition *at least* because of these structural limitations and they must necessarily be understood in dialog with them—a dialog that is, ambivalently, at times estranging and at times mystifying, as in *Bandersnatch*'s reproduction of Netflix's functioning.

Nevertheless, such ambivalence is not to be seen necessarily as a failure of the creative imagination or as a surrender to structural pressures, but to a great extent as an unavoidable consequence of the logics of cognitive estrangement itself. If one considers China Miéville's critique of Suvin's theory, the presumed "cognition" of SF should not be seen *only* as a "validation" of estrangement; perhaps "cognition" should *also* be seen as something partly mystifying and ideological. Carl Freedman, who reformulated Suvin's concept and in so doing inspired Miéville's critique, shed light on cognition's ambivalence by highlighting that

> cognition proper is *not*, in the strictest terms, exactly the quality that defines science fiction. What is rather at stake is what we might term [...] the *cognition effect*. The crucial issue for generic discrimination is not an epistemological judgement external to the text itself on the rationality or irrationality of the latter's imaginings but rather (as some of Suvin's language does, in fact, imply, but never makes entirely clear) the attitude *of the text itself* to the kind of estrangements being performed. (Freedman 18)[2]

2   Although his work is here taken as a landmark "post-Suvinian" SF theory, Carl Freedman is, of course, not alone in adopting and adapting the "cognitive estrangement" framework. On the contrary, a wide variety of SF scholars have engaged with Suvin's theory and particularly with its most contentious points, such as its strict distinction between SF and fantasy or its potentially confusing concept of cognition (see Parrinder; as well as Bould and Miéville, which contains Miéville's critique among others). As Mark Bould puts it with a fitting SF metaphor, "SF theory

As Miéville objects, however, any narrative "has no attitude to the kind of estrangements it performs, nor indeed to anything else" (235)—and yet, speaking of cognition as an effect (or, as I have done before, as a semblance or appearance) is a necessary step if we are to understand the dialectics of cognitive estrangement that Miéville sketches. Specifically, the SF writer and critic argues that

> the Freedman/Suvin theory is accurate in asserting that, for that folk-understanding of SF-not-fantasy, SF-ness is a function of the cognition effect [...]. However, any claim that the effect is a function of embedded cognitive rational rigour is untrue. To the extent that the cognition effect is about cognition, it is precisely *about* it, *about* a putatively logical way of thinking, not a function of it. And inasmuch as the experienced effect is in fact a function of authority, the 'cognition effect', in deriving supposed cognitive logic from external authority, is not only fundamentally a-rational but also intensely ideological. (Miéville 239)

In other words, SF plays with a kind of mediated cognition that is neither rational nor timeless, but rather related to, as Suvin's words partly conveyed, "the basic cognitive norms of our times" (*Metamorphoses* viii)— that is, the rational-looking authority of SF is historically situated and thus inseparable from its epoch's dominant ideology, on which it relies for legitimation *even when it aims at subverting or criticizing it*. This is what leads Miéville to claim, with brilliant clarity, that

> To the extent that SF claims to be based on 'science,' and indeed on what is deemed 'rationality,' it is based on capitalist modernity's ideologically projected self-justification: not some abstract/ideal 'science,' but capitalist science's bullshit about itself. This is not, of course, to argue in favour of some (perhaps lumpen-postmodernist) irrationalism, but that the 'rationalism' that capitalism has traditionally had on offer is highly partial and ideological—'could not', as Suvin himself has put it, 'but give reason a bad name'. (240–1)

In the context of new media dystopias, then, it is imperative to remember that their SF narratives' implicit appeals to "cognitive" logic will not be an appeal to an ahistorical rationality, but *an appeal to what seems logical*

---

and criticism have inhabited—not by any means always contentedly—the Suvin event horizon, or attempted to escape it" ("Introduction" 18).

under the hegemony of digital capitalism, which is without a doubt partly based upon scientific and objective knowledge, but also partly derived from the epoch's associated ideologies and structure of feeling.

3.1.2. The Perhaps-Not-So-Critical Dystopia

With regard to Moylan's definition of the "critical dystopia," there are potential problems that should be considered in order to avoid taking it as another timeless ideal that no narrative could ever attain. As was commented in Section 1.2.3, critical dystopias are not just "critical" in the sense of being pure negativity; they are ambivalent by definition, critical in a dialectical way. In critical dystopias, what Bloch and Jameson call the utopian impulse remains, *but it is ambiguated* by a critical attitude that does not go as far as to deny the impulse. In Moylan's words, the key is that

> Although all dystopian texts offer a detailed and pessimistic presentation of the very worst of social alternatives, some affiliate with a utopian tendency as they maintain a horizon of hope (or at least invite readings that do), while others only appear to be dystopian allies of Utopia as they retain an anti-utopian disposition that forecloses all transformative possibility, and yet others negotiate a more strategically ambiguous position somewhere along the antinomic continuum. (*Scraps of the Untainted Sky* 147)

In this way, the key to Moylan's conception is that critical dystopias position themselves *not as antagonists of the possibility of utopia*—since that would turn them into anti-utopias—*but as antagonists of the very worst of historical societies*. Ideally, dystopias would be the critical, negative "ally" of a constructive, positive utopian impulse, because their critical attitude stops short of being hopelessly deterministic, misanthropic or nihilistic (i.e. anti-utopian), thus allowing one to imagine transformations for the better. But can one separate the dystopian from the anti-utopian so easily when delving into textual and contextual detail?

Moylan himself notes that there may be some dystopias that "only appear to be [...] allies of Utopia" as well as others with a "strategically ambiguous position." Furthermore, even in those dystopias with "a horizon of hope," finding that horizon depends upon "readings" that consciously search for it. In these ways, the utopian in the dystopian is sometimes hidden, other times misleading, most frequently ambiguous and very often (if not always) dependent upon what could be called "a hermeneutics of hope." However, in the present context, can we expect a hopeful mode of reception and interpretation? Can we take for granted that the ambivalences of critical dystopias will be resolved in a utopian direction? As Chapter 1 already showed, we cannot: the epoch's structure of feeling is deeply shaped by various kinds of cynicisms and presentisms, which stand in the way of conceiving a better future—as well as by several technologic-economic determinisms and individualisms, which stand in the way of imagining any willed social transformation that breaks with dominant dynamics. In such a context, therefore, dystopian narratives confront significant challenges if they are to convey hope—but our task is to find if and how hope remains in dystopias.

In this context, if critical dystopias are to fulfill Moylan's ideal by being allies of utopia, my hypothesis is that they must be reflexive in another, more abstract and perhaps only provocative sense of the concept—not towards their medium, but towards their genre, which is by now *much more than a genre*, insofar as it shapes the epoch's structure of feeling. In other words, today's critical dystopias would have to be "meta-dystopian" in the sense that they would have to be reflexive with regards to dominant dystopian imaginaries, which they would both reproduce and criticize—however, in practice, what this means is that the best that new media dystopias can achieve is *an ambivalently critical and, perhaps, only temporary distance* from those dominant imaginaries. In this chapter's case studies and many other instances, then, if ambivalence is inherent to new media dystopias, a close reading is paramount so as to consider where and how the scales are tipped against (or in favor of) utopian hope and/or anti-utopian hopelessness.

Nevertheless, can one operate under the assumption that hope is always a utopian force? In this epoch, the problem is not only that hope is scarce, which it is, at least when thinking of certain realisms and melancholies, but also that there are certain kinds of hope that do not look towards a truly utopian horizon, but towards the fulfillment of promises within the established order. Such kinds of hope are profoundly akin to what Lauren Berlant usefully conceptualizes as "cruel optimism," which is to her an essential mechanism of the contemporary "political depression." In her words, cruel optimism "names a relation of attachment to compromised conditions of possibility" in which "the very vitalizing or animating potency of an object/scene of desire contributes to the attrition of the very thriving that is supposed to be made possible in the work of attachment in the first place" (21). In the context that concerns us here, this would entail considering the possibility that critical dystopias could be—to some extent or in some regard—investing their hope in some of the objects or scenes of what is an SF analogue of the worldly worst, rather than in an implicit utopian horizon or possibility. Thinking about new media dystopias specifically, one could thus ask: are these narratives playing with a kind of "cruel hope" that is attached to those same media technologies whose nefarious consequences they denounce? In the two series to be analyzed here, this ambivalence also seems to operate, since—even though both *Westworld* and *Devs* also demystify a number of illusions about technological "progress"—the hope that lingers in these narratives is to a great extent invested in those same technologies. Of course, in the abstract, one can be hopeful about "neutral technologies used differently."[3] But can one be hopeful about technologies that, far from being neutral, are ideologically and literally conceived as parts to be plugged the circuits of digital capitalism? One should be wary, therefore, of any hopes that are plugged into those circuits, for those hopes may not be utopian, but a crudely commodified hope.

3.1.3. Complex TV's Conundrums

Finally, one should not fail to consider the specific ambivalence of the new media dystopias selected in this book *as instances of serial "television,"* a narrative form of considerable prominence within the digital age's

---

[3] Perhaps no single technology should be thought of as neutral, not even potentially or abstractly, especially if one is reminded of Leo Marx's reflections upon the very concept of technology, which is mystifyingly abstract and, thus, conceals the fact that modern technology is defined by its deep embeddedness in social relations (see Section 1.3.1). Thinking through the other Marx's language, one might also say that what we now call "technology" is always part and parcel of capital's machinery; it is not like the tool of an artisanal laborer, made after that worker's needs, but rather a cog in a machine that implies an exploitative mode of production.

mediascape. Somewhat ironically, "television itself has expanded its scope across a number of screens and platforms, complicating notions of medium specificity at the very same time that television seems to have established a clearer sense of distinct narrative form" (Mittell 15). Nowadays, despite the ever-growing diversity of media and transmedia phenomena, the digitally distributed "TV" series has become established itself as a privileged narrative form, in terms of both popularity and prestige. To many commentators, the early twenty-first-century is indeed a—if not *the*— "Golden Age of Television," with some going as far as to argue that "TV is replacing movies as elite entertainment" (Thompson n.p.). But why? This process of legitimation—even canonization—is most attributable to the emergence and consolidation of what Jason Mittell's has termed "complex TV."[4] Considering a wide variety of series from the 1990s onwards—favoring David Simon's *The Wire* (2002–8), J. J. Abrams, Jeffrey Lieber and Damon Lindelof's *Lost* (2004–10) and Vince Gilligan's *Breaking Bad* (2008–13) in particular—Mittel speaks of a new dominant mode of televisual storytelling that is characterized by "narrative complexity." Contrary to the formulaic nature of past TV production (i.e. soap operas or sitcoms), the "new mode is not as uniform and convention driven as episodic or serial norms traditionally have been," to such an extent that "complex television's most defining characteristic might be its unconventionality" (18). But how did this come to be?

According to Mittell's account, complex TV is born in a peculiar historical situation, a time when the *narrative constraints* of broadcasted television continued to be expected and enforced—its strict impositions

---

4   Lest my paragraph invites any misinterpretations, it should be said that Mittel's work is intended as a "a model of contextualized evaluation that does not re-create universal aesthetic values but rather looks at how a series can define its own terms and parameters of evaluation and how television scholars might productively engage with questions of value." Furthermore, Mittel proposes that "we can enter into medium-specific debates over value without re-creating a canon or exclusionary critical practices, considering how complexity can function as an aesthetic asset in multiple ways" (14–15). Nevertheless, such intentions do not preclude that, both within and without academia, there is an emergent canon of serial television that is justified by reference to one form or other of the narrative complexity that Mittell has studied.

on the amount of screen time and the serial-episodic format that developed around those limitations. However, the *consumption constraints* of broadcasting were relaxed by the emergence of new media that enabled other kinds of consumer engagement. In other words, the constraints derived from the nature of broadcasting remain in place as a formal vestige of a past technological necessity and they "work to limit how stories can be told but also provide clear structures within which innovations can flourish, creatively challenging well-established norms" (33). However, first VHS, then DVD and later streaming platforms allowed a shift towards on-demand consumption, which, in turn, permitted the design of "complex narratives" made "for a discerning viewer [who can be expected] not only to pay close attention to once but to rewatch in order to notice the depth of references, to marvel at displays of craft and continuities, and to appreciate details that require the liberal use of pause and rewind" (38). Thus seen, the encounter of residual formal constraints and emergent consumer possibilities is what has enabled and fueled the development of complex TV, with narrative complexity emerging from a dialectic of structure and subversion.[5]

Furthermore, "complex television has become a mainstream trend" also because of "the broad availability of online fan sites to facilitate collective discussions and decoding practices among fans" and because of the existence of "an intertextual web that pushes textual boundaries outward, blurring the experiential borders between watching a program and engaging with its paratexts" (6–7). With this, Mittell refers to the growing number of ancillary materials—interviews, reviews, blog posts, podcasts, "inside the episode" clips, teasers, trailers and so on, all of which are made available on multiple media formats and digital platforms. Indeed, one key quality of digital interfaces as platforms of cultural consumption is that

---

5   What Mittell calls "complex TV" is, of course, only one *formal manifestation* that has emerged from the interplay of residual televisual conventions and emergent digital possibilities. Far from "experiencing a simple shift from 'broadcasting' to 'narrowcasting,' community to individual, or window to portal," the problem with *digital television* is that it "does not simply replace the window; rather, it repurposes, remediates, and constantly recalls and recirculates television's window-on-the-world positioning in the digital era" (Bennett and Strange 6).

they—as a kind of super-paratextual level—subsume and interrelate not just narratives but potentially all the content that circulates online, generally for the purpose of fostering more interaction—and often interaction of a greater intensity, like the kind expected and implied by complex TV. Thus, because one driving motivation of digital-capitalist production is the accumulation of user data via their interactions, corporations have tended to favor complexity, among other reasons, because complex productions provide "the basis for robust online fan cultures and active feedback for the television industry" (Mittell 35). Crucially, these are cultural communities who coalesce around their engagement with the production at hand and who often interact within the company's platforms (or within related digital platforms), providing an inexhaustible source of data about consumption habits, expectations and responses. Narrative complexity is, after all, as Mittell aptly puts it, a "planned confusion" (164), a designed intricacy that fuels the peculiar feedback loops of cultural production today. Thus it is that the digital age's "culture industry intentionally integrates its consumers from above" turning them into "an object of calculation" and "an appendage of the machinery" (Adorno, "Culture Industry Reconsidered" 12), as has been the norm since postmodernity's wholesale commodification of culture.

Potentially, however, if one returns to new media dystopias in particular, this complexity-friendly mediascape—both because of and despite its data-driven dynamics of commodification—does lay the ground for the flourishing of complex dystopian series that function as *critical* allegories, in the strong sense with which Fredric Jameson uses the concept.[6] Thanks to their extensive screen time, their structural enabling of experimentation and the greater engagement expected from audiences, the development of complex television is what has allowed the production of what

---

6   Jameson defines the allegory not simply as an analogy established between two levels (literal and allegorical), but as a four-level scheme where those two text-centered levels, in turn, invite extra-textual interpretations—first on a moral or subjective level and then on a political or collective level. In this context, then, by saying that new media dystopias function as *critical* allegories I am implying that they are not only science-fictional analogues of digital capitalism, but that they necessarily entail and invite both moral and political interpretations.

are, perhaps, some of the most narratively complex dystopias in a visual medium—a sophistication that makes them perhaps closer to the ideals of literary SF than any film or series before. Nonetheless, it is not the purpose of this book to engage in a legitimation of television through literary analogies, nor even to study them "as literature," but rather to examine the aesthetic ambivalences of this new narrative form.[7] Complexity, despite its aura of "literariness," should be taken neither as an inherent marker of quality nor (in dystopias) as a necessary reinforcement of their presumed critical-utopian function. The mainstreaming of complexity offers a fertile ground for narratives of cognitive estrangement, but it also leads to *a commodification of complexity*.

On one level, the most obvious, complexity has been used by channels and streaming platforms as part of—in the case of HBO especially, but not only—a "brand image of being more sophisticated than traditional television and thus worthy of a monthly premium (and generating future DVD sales)" (Mittell 34). The common phrase "Quality TV" is often used as part of an aesthetic judgment that praises narrative complexity, for good reasons, but it is also—and perhaps more commonly—a key phrase of a very successful marketing language that both favors the company's brand and flatters its audiences' sense of taste:

> Celebrated by enthusiastic audiences as complex texts that use the television medium to combine the production values and visual style of cinema with the narrative complexity of the novel, 'Quality TV' has in recent years bestowed a bourgeois sense of respectability upon a medium all too frequently maligned by highbrow audiences. (Hassler-Forest, "Game of Thrones: The Politics of World-Building and the Cultural Logic of Gentrification" 190)

Nevertheless, complexity is not only commodified *outside* of the narrative, in the realm of corporate marketing and consumer discourse; it is also commodified *within* the narrative itself. A recurring feature of complex TV is its implicitly reflexive "operational aesthetic," which is "akin

---

[7] *Television Series as Literature* is the literal title of a recent volume (Winckler and Huertas-Martín), which embraces this common comparison and takes it seriously both for the purposes of theorization and analysis, as in one chapter that sweeps through *Black Mirror* as a collection of fables (Bermúdez de Castro).

to [visual] special effects," but would consist of what Mittell calls "the *narrative special effect*" (43) In Mittell's own words, this "mode of attractions" happens

> when a program flexes its storytelling muscles to confound and amaze a viewer, as in the major temporal leaps forward seen on *Alias* ("The Telling"), the revelation of flash-forwards on *Lost* ("Through the Looking Glass"), or the incorporation of the backstory-retrofitted main character Dawn on *Buffy* [*the Vampire Slayer*]'s fifth season. These moments of spectacle push the operational aesthetic to the foreground, calling attention to the narration's construction and asking us to marvel at how the writers pulled it off; often these instances forgo strict realism in exchange for a formally aware baroque quality in which we watch the process of narrative as a machine rather than engaging in its diegesis. (43–4)

Furthermore, Mittell finds that "Individual episodes can trigger the operational aesthetic through narrative spectacle, but whole programs can also be predicated on such storytelling pyrotechnics, through either their larger arcs or their inherent structure" (47). This is indeed the case with new media dystopias such as *Westworld*, to be analyzed later, or *Black Mirror*, which is popularly remembered for episode endings that "screw your mind" with horrifying plot twists—a subversion of expectations that the series standardized to such an extent that a number of variations of "being black mirrored" or "doing a Black Mirror" are now registered in the popular *Urban Dictionary* (see "Black Mirror"). In any case, the consequence of complex TV's *standardization of subversion* is that now narrative spectacles "are used with such frequency and regularity as to become more acceptable narrative norms rather than exceptional outliers" (Mittell 48–9). In this sense, one is confronted with a mediascape in which complexity is created for its own sake—or rather, for no other purpose than the enjoyment that can be derived from engaging with it as a consumer-user-spectator. The aesthetics of complex TV are therefore best described with some irony, for their conventional procedure is to be unconventional and their structuring motif, subversion.

Thus, what about critical dystopias within this context? What about their implied antagonistic stance towards the worldly worst? Complexity may, indeed, provide the basis for a richly nuanced kind of dystopian storytelling, with potently estranging and critical-utopian effects, but that same narrative complexity could just as easily lead down a rather anti-utopian path, towards the feeling that the world is not only *too dystopian* but also *too complex* to even bother trying to transform it. Even if you feel like trying, you might fear that your expectations shall certainly be subverted—and, probably, as in so much "quality TV," the surprise shall not be a pleasant one. As not only *Black Mirror* but also HBO's flagship series *Game of Thrones* (Benioff and Weiss, 2011–19) have trained contemporary spectators into expecting, the plot twist at the end of it all shall not be utopian whatsoever, but horrible and heart-breaking. Seen in this light, the epoch's quasi-fetishist fascination with complexity might very well be a functional element of our dystopian structure of feeling—but the narrative complexity of certain series might also, with whatever ambivalence, give us a critical tool with which to challenge (or at least comprehend) the system's real complexity from within.

3.2. Beauty in Hell? The New Media Dystopia as Spectacle

Besides narrating our world's worst, new media dystopias also visualize it—and just like their narrative dimension, their visual dimension is riddled with ambiguities. Brooks Landon once defined SF film precisely through its "aesthetic of ambivalence" and my contention is that the sub-genre under consideration in this book does not only confirm this, but also condenses and intensifies SF film's inherent contradictions. Almost necessarily, new media dystopias have a double-edged attitude towards new media technologies, insofar as—in spite of, or in excess of their implied critical function—they also function as a display and a demonstration of such technologies' capacity for generating a sense of wonder—even constructing an experience of the beautiful and the sublime. From some perspectives, this ambivalence may be reproached or even rejected, as a sign that these dystopias are not critical, but hypocritical; however, I here concur with Landon in that ambivalence "can be seen as one of the genre's strengths" (25) and that, at their best, visual dystopias can function as a prism that reflects and refracts the ambivalences of technological progress in capitalist modernity. Elsewhere, I have begun conceptualizing this peculiar aesthetic ambivalence as "dystopian beauty," a phrase that synthesizes how the objects and the spaces of dystopian denunciation are also the objects and spaces of visual pleasure. Now, taking this concept of dystopian beauty as a window into the specificities of new media dystopias, the next section examines how our sub-genre implies a perspective that is both technophobe and technophile—a way of looking that sees both horror and beauty in media technologies, which I will call *a techno-ambivalent gaze*.

To grasp this ambivalence, however, one must go beyond these abstract observations and understand them as part of (1) the specificities of SF film and (2) the dominant aesthetic sensibility of digital capitalism. In other words, one must firstly understand how SF film has always been a genre of attractions and visual pleasures as much or more than a narrative genre, as well as, secondly, understand how the ideologies of digital capitalism have an aesthetic analogue. Only after surveying such phenomena, which both predate and predetermine the idiosyncrasies of new media dystopias, we will arrive at a working understanding of their ambivalence as a contemporary kind of SF spectacle.

3.2.1. *SF Film as Attraction and Visual Pleasure*

In Brooks Landon's words, "the science fiction film was born in ambivalence as an inherent structural tension pervaded even the very first SF movies when shorts such as *The Sausage Machine* showcased the modern technology of the cinema by mocking the modern technology of automation" (Landon 20). Beyond the purely anecdotal, Landon's early-cinema example here highlights the debt of SF film with what Tom Gunning termed the "cinema of attractions," a mode of conceiving the medium that predates the establishment of narrative cinema as the hegemonic mode of understanding film. Before becoming a storytelling medium in the eyes of virtually everyone, the early cinema of the late nineteenth and early twentieth centuries was dominated by a radically different logic, even though many still frame this period as a kind of "prehistory" in which a "primitive cinema" appears to be, from the present's perspective, "still" figuring out its own way of telling stories. Cautioning against this narrative-centric teleology, Gunning argues that the then-hegemonic conception

> sees cinema less as a way of telling stories than as a way of presenting a series of views to an audience, fascinating because of their illusory power (whether the realistic illusion of motion offered to the first audiences by Lumière, or the magical illusion concocted by Méliès), and exoticism. In other words, [...] the relation to the spectator set up by the films of both Lumière and Méliès (and many other filmmakers before 1906) had a common basis, and one that differs from the primary spectator relations set up after 1906. I will call this earlier conception of cinema, "the cinema of attractions." Although different from the fascination in storytelling exploited by the cinema from the time of Griffith, it is not necessarily opposed to it. In fact the cinema of attraction[s] does not disappear with the dominance of narrative, but rather goes underground, both into certain avant-garde practices and as a component of narrative films, more evident in some genres (e.g., the musical) than in others. (382)

In Gunning's view, early cinema was constructed not so much around telling but primarily around showing. In contrast with much narrative cinema, it was "an exhibitionist cinema" rather than a voyeuristic one and—perhaps most importantly—it was also a cinema where "the cinema itself was an attraction" in the sense that "audiences went to exhibitions to see machines demonstrated (the newest technological wonder ... [such] as X-rays or, earlier, the phonograph), rather than to view films" (382-3). In this sense, the cinema of attractions was (and is) not only about showing spectacles, but about showing itself, about showing what was then the latest mechanical wonder—or, more recently, the newest new media technology, be that hardware or software.

Besides Gunning's example of the musical, a genre in which the logics of the attraction have remained as important as the logics of narrative, one can obviously think of SF from a similar perspective. Even when dominated by narrative aspirations such as those described by Suvin, SF film is defined by its reliance on one form or another of *special effects* for effectively visualizing the *novum*. Indeed, as Landon observes, "special effects facilitate the depiction of SF stories by providing the necessary images of non-existent phenomena—futuristic cities, other planets, space ships, aliens, faster-than-light travel, rays, beams, mutation processes, and so on" (67).

Therefore, in SF film, the logics of cognitive estrangement are caught in a dialog with what I would call *the logics of spectacular estrangement*—the genre-specific logics of the attraction that inform the visualization of SF objects and environments. It is in this sense that the genre is *essentially* shaped by a dialogic tension between narrative and spectacle, or an "aesthetic of ambivalence," as Landon puts it.[8] Moreover, like the cinema of attractions generally, the attraction of an SF film would be double: the technological novelties shown on-screen as part of the SF diegesis and the media technologies that enable displaying such novelties in the first place. This is why Landon claims that SF "is the cinema's own genre [as] a media-specific showcase" (89), or Kuhn, that SF is "a perfect example of the medium fitting, if not exactly being, the message" (*Alien Zone* 7). Once again, ambivalence seems inseparable from a certain kind of reflexivity, although, in this case, the basic reflexivity of SF film would tend to be implicit or covert (unless elaborated through any of the narrative devices examined in Chapter 2).

The problem when considering the logics of spectacular estrangement is that the attractions of an SF film are as ambivalent as an SF narrative's "cognition." Potentially, of course, special effects are a means for visualizing the *novum*, as well as, also potentially, a means for visually reinforcing an explicitly reflexive narrative—but they are not only that. Special effects are a powerful way of centering viewers' attention upon a *novum* and, precisely by centering the viewers' gaze, they may also be *mystifying* everything around them. As Michael Stern argues,

> In SF film, the special effects which its consumers' way of seeing foregrounds as formal features—recognizes as 'special'—are ones that enact the possibilities, delights and terrors of glamorous new technologies: space flights, death rays, matter transmitters, cloning, living on the moon or at the bottom of the Pacific, socializing or fighting with aliens, being raped by a computer, and so on. A double effacement is at work in this way of seeing. The actual film maker's technology which makes these effects

8   It should be said that, as opposed to my theorization here, Landon does not explicitly employ Suvin's concepts, although he interestingly counterpoises "ideational spectacles (the big or new ideas) offered to us by the stories of SF film" and "the spectacles of the productions of those films," which are shaped by "the aesthetics of special effects" (66).

possible is lost to view, concealed, or ignored. And all of the other effects which make up the film are transformed from cultural artefacts into natural objects. (Stern 69)

In this sense, the spectacles of an SF film can be said to be, ironically, *an estranging form of mystification*; in and of themselves, they are estranging, startling, even disturbing, but we must ask: are they contributing to a larger exercise of cognitive estrangement? Or are they monopolizing attention and averting the viewers' gaze from the *novum*'s larger context? With special effects in SF, perhaps sometimes "more is less," as Greg Tuck succinctly argues about the genre's (ab)use of CGI (249).[9]

In the end, the *novum*'s function is not so much to call attention to itself: attracting and estranging viewers' attention is the prerequisite, but the (ideal) purpose of the *novum* is to serve as a bridge between the science-fictional and the historical, between the speculated and the already-existing. This, however, remains an ideal, as there is always an opposed, mystifying tendency in the technological spectacles of visual SF—a tendency that may redouble the mystification that is also inherent in common conceptions of technology, as Leo Marx showed (see Section 1.3.1). Indeed, one may come to feel, with Michael Stern, that

> SF films and TV shows help to construct and legitimize a world in which technology is an abstract category of effects without any specific social and political context, rather than a critical part of a whole way of life. SF foregrounds technology as a special effect—magical, socially ungrounded—while naturalizing the technologies of domination themselves. This is also the way news and advertising work [... and] also how advertising fetishizes commodities: it isolates them from the people and processes which produce them. [...] Like advertising, [...] SF makes technology into the source of magical objects which enter people's lives and transform them under the direction of higher, more powerful beings (whether aliens or ruling classes). (70)

9 Tuck's argument is a more recent mediation upon the ambivalences of special effects within SF cinema that follows Stern's line of thought. The main difference with the latter's arguments would be that Tuck's article is more interested with the use of CGI and other digital spectacles as a kind of "capitalist sublime"—an attempt at recreating the sublime that, in Tuck's opinion, fails insofar as it attempts to recreate the feeling of the unquantifiable with a focus on quantity of effect. My next section takes a different approach to the technological sublime, considering not as a failed effect but as an essential component of today's technological aesthetics.

Stern's words here describe an inherent tendency of much (if not all) SF, but the question remains as to *how* this happens not only on-screen, but in reception, insofar as mystification is above all a potential effect on the onlooker. To answer this, one must think beyond the genre's manipulation of attention (both towards and away from on-screen images via special effects); one should also consider the spectator's experience with those images: the *visual pleasure* constructed by the genre.

The experience of visual pleasure, as theorized by Laura Mulvey, speaks of the enjoyment that mainstream narrative cinema constructs for an implicit gaze that audiences should assume—and in much cinema, as in the Hitchcock films that she famously dissected, this is a patriarchal and heterosexual "male gaze." It is important to clarify, however, that the "male" in the "gaze" does not necessary refer to the gender identity or the sexual orientation of the specific onlooker, but rather to how cinema has generally constructed *a mode of seeing*—a gaze—in which "man" is positioned as the subject of the look and the agent of the narrative, whereas "woman" is positioned as the object of both the look and the narrative. In Mulvey's account, then, the pleasure of the male gaze derives from a sense of control, generated both by an identification with male characters and an objectification of the female body, which is reduced to an erotic spectacle for characters and spectators (both coded male). However, crucially, there is always an underlying ambivalence, for this kind of visual pleasure is accompanied by a fear that the object of the look (the female body) would look back, act on her own and thus unsettle the onlooker's illusion of control—a tension that Hitchcock's films self-consciously play with, in an ambivalently (self-)critical way, as Mulvey's analyses showed. Within this framework, erotic attraction becomes inseparable from misogynistic fear—something that parallels how technophobia and technophilia are inseparable in the gaze constructed by an SF film.

To be sure, much SF film has assumed and still assumes a male gaze in its on-screen visualization of women's bodies—but the key is that the visual pleasures that the genre promises are *not necessarily* premised on the eroticization of women (though they can be and still often are), but *primarily based on a similar eroticization of technology.*[10] In SF cinema, technology

10   In taking the logical step from thinking about gendered bodies on-screen to

Aesthetic and Ideological Ambivalences

is the spectacle and the attraction, which means it is also positioned as the main object of visual pleasure for its viewers. It is in this sense that the technological *novum* in an SF film could be said to be *feminized*, at least implicitly (in the reproduction of this gaze of eroticized control), if not also explicitly (in the representation of women cyborgs, gynoids and other feminine artificial creatures).[11] Although speaking in a different context, Joanna Russ once criticized SF's mystification of technology as "masculine" in a way that echoes Mulvey's framework, arguing that

> Both technophilia and technophobia are owner's attitudes. In the first case you think that you have either power or the ear of the powerful, and in the second case, although you may feel you have lost power, you at least feel entitled to it. Hence the scapegoating of modern industrial society, which ought to be controllable (by you) and knowable (ditto) and is neither. (257)

Just like the male gaze, what I call the "techno-ambivalent gaze" of SF film is both enjoying and fearing the object that is supposed to be controlled, but often threatens to resist or reverse that situation. Thus seen, such aesthetics are inseparable from a certain eroticism, which is far from exclusive to the genre.

---

gendered technologies, I am perhaps simply reproducing the core ideas of Donna Haraway's *Cyborg Manifesto*, which provocatively positioned the cyborg as a feminist subject for reasons that closely relate to the logical equation I am making here. A recent work of visual SF studies has also inspired my thinking here, Liz W. Faber's *The Computer Voice*, a monograph that I had the privilege of reviewing, which very interesting proposed to critically examine on-screen representations of AI without a mechanical body, in cases where all that is left is a voice hosted by a radically non-human—but still gendered—machine.

11 An SF film such as Alex Garland's *Ex Machina* (2014) illustrates this parallelism perfectly, in what could be described as a paradigmatic SF critique of the male gaze and the techno-ambivalent gaze, insofar as it narrates the creation of a gynoid that is thoroughly designed for her Frankensteinian creator's male gaze (see Kakoudaki; Oancea).

3.2.2. Technological Aesthetics of the Digital Age

Even if visual SF offers a privileged lens into these phenomena, the fact that there is an eroticization of technology—or at least a beautification— is something that both predates and transcends the genre. There is such a thing as an "erotic life of machines," as Steven Shaviro provocatively suggests ("The Erotic Life of Machines"), and what I conceptualized as SF's techno-ambivalent gaze is not restricted to SF. Since the industrial revolution, going through the various modernisms and leading up to the digital age, the present epoch has inherited and continued to develop a technological aesthetics. These aesthetics, paralleling Kant's own, would have their own versions of the beautiful and the sublime, though in such a way that the two aesthetic categories are tied to technology rather than to art, nature or the divine. This is, in a sense, a reversal of Kant's traditional paradigm, insofar as aesthetic pleasure is found in the artificial, in all of that which is predesigned and *a priori* controllable. Indeed, our culture senses the beautiful in a device's design and it senses the sublime in a system's sophistication. New media technologies are, indeed, made to be beautiful—just think of any product by Apple, the Big Tech company that most evidently designs desirable objects to be touched, held and owned.[12] And, relatedly, there is also a certain sublimity in the seeming omnipresence and omniscience of the stack—just think of the wonder (and the fear) that is generated by each new system-wide development, such as 5G recently.[13] Such an aesthetic is most crudely articulated in the advertising of digital-capitalist companies, who often seize SF imagery

---

12   In this regard, one can find serious discussions of aesthetics and Apple's designs in a place such as the *Journal of the Academy of Marketing Science*, with an article that argues that "rather than lagging behind the marketplace, research on these topics should also aid its future evolution" (Hagtvedt 428). Elsewhere, the company's aesthetics—particularly the iPhone's—have been examined as a Foucauldian mechanism for shaping an "Apple subject" (Gaughwin).

13   5G mobile networks became the object of widely popular conspiracy theories, especially during the COVID-19 pandemic, when certain celebrities echoed or even endorsed them. In these conspiracies, 5G networks and their associated technologies are above all feared, but they are feared in a way that almost deifies technology's presumed powers—thus feared in a way that is inseparable from mystified wonder.

Aesthetic and Ideological Ambivalences 211

and ideas and try to—though often fail to—purge them of their ambivalence.[14] However, there is a longer history to this phenomenon. Although (to my knowledge) the concept of "technological beauty" has not been theorized as such, the notion of a "technological sublime" has been present in a range of scholarship. In speaking of a technological aesthetics, therefore, I am only extrapolating from scholarship on the technological sublime and proposing to use the two as complementary terms within an aesthetics, associating "beauty" to the limited and concrete and "sublimity" to the apparently boundless.

How has the technological sublime been defined? Moving outwards from SF film into this larger aesthetic sensibility, Scott Bukatman establishes a basis for understanding how the genre's techno-ambivalent gaze relates to a deep, epochal anxiety. In his words,

> The presence of the sublime in the deeply American genre of science fiction implies that our fantasies of superiority emerge from our ambivalence regarding technological power, rather than nature's might. The might of technology, supposedly our own creation, is mastered through a powerful display that acknowledges anxiety but recontains it within the field of spectatorial power. [...]
>
> The sublime is, in these spectacles, an idealist response to significant and continuing alterations in lived experience. [...] Then and now, the language of consumption and the display of spectacle grounds the spectator/visitor and hides the awful truth: that an environment that we made has moved beyond our ability to control and cognize it. ("The Artificial Infinite: On Special Effects and the Sublime" 265–6)

Thus seen, the technological sublime is perhaps not so much a reversal of the Kantian, but a logical phenomenon within capitalist modernity, where technology assumes (or rather supplants) the role of nature. In this context, technology is no longer sensed as "our" object or "our" environment, but as a complex techno-ecology that escapes control and comprehension—a quasi-divine force that displaces and destroys the Earth's ecology both in fact and in the imagination. In this way, the

---

14 The most obvious example of this is, again, Mark Zuckerberg's attempted resignification of the "metaverse" as a utopian rather than dystopian concept, a marketing campaign that has failed to capture even the most ardent techno-utopians.

epoch's fear and fascination with the technological—both the beauty of devices and the sublimity of systems—is ultimately explained by the "radical eclipse of Nature itself," as Jameson once put it. "The *other* of our society is [...] no longer Nature at all, as it was in precapitalist societies, but something else" (*Postmodernism* 34–5).

The aesthetics of technology, of course, have a long history that can be traced further back, especially in the US, which is the cultural context where Leo Marx first coined the idea of a "technological sublime" (see *The Machine in the Garden*), paving the way for his student David E. Nye's monograph *American Technological Sublime*.[15] In this work, Nye introduces the phenomenon as "an essentially religious feeling" that "taps into fundamental hopes and fears" and, if experienced collectively, "can weld society together" around an "enthusiasm for technology" (xiii). In his words,

> For almost two centuries the American public has repeatedly paid homage to railways, bridges, skyscrapers, factories, dams, airplanes, and space vehicles. [...] The technological sublime is an integral part of contemporary consciousness, and its emergence and exfoliation into several distinct forms during the past two centuries is inscribed within public life. In a physical world that is increasingly desacralized, the sublime represents a way to reinvest the landscape and the works of men with transcendent significant. [...] Since the early nineteenth century the technological sublime has been one of America's central "idea about itself"—a defining ideal, helping to bind together a multicultural society. [...] Precisely because American society is so pluralistic, no single religion could perform that function. (xiii–xiv)

Nye's work goes on to offer a historical typology of technological sublimes, from the railroad's "dynamic," the city's "geometrical" and the factory's "industrial" sublimes, going through "electrical" and "atomic" sublimes and leading up to "the consumer's" sublime as the most abstract form that subsumes the previous. This list, offered by Nye in the 1990s, could be now completed with a "digital sublime" (see Mosco), referring to the specific fascinations (and fears) provoked by cyberspace's renewal of the promises of transcendence once offered by religion and by older

---

15   If one wanted to go even further back and speculate with the origins of this aesthetics, an obvious candidate would be Francis Bacon's *New Atlantis* (1626), the first technological (and technocratic) literary utopia.

technologies—a sense of sublimity that underpins many of the cyber-utopian ideologies surveyed before (in Section 1.3).

Digital interfaces such as Netflix's, Amazon's, Disney's, Apple TV's and others—the primary locale of consumption of our new media dystopias and most visual culture today—clearly cater to this aesthetic sensibility with their visual design. In this regard, Chapter 2's narrative-centric understanding of them as a super-paratext that allows finding—and algorithmically suggests—transtextual connections between the platform's contents should be complemented by an understanding of these platforms as a kind of spectacle. The old logic of the cinema of attractions whereby the cinematic apparatus itself was also the attraction remains at work here, but with the peculiarities of the digital milieu. With their geometrically harmonious, algorithmically dynamic design, which presents itself as "smart" and "user-friendly," such kinds of platforms could be described as a window into the digital sublime—a beautifully designed, virtual window of windows into the global stack's infinite library of text, images and data; a seemingly limitless world that almost simulates the wonder of Jorge Luis Borges's infinite "Library of Babel." Ultimately, as per Bolter and Grusin's double logic of remediation, the digital interface makes a spectacle out of its own sophisticated form of mediation at the same time as it—ironically—promises a "direct" gateway into a wholly different reality: the sublime reality of so-called cyberspace, which still today—techlash literature and (post-)cyberpunk dystopias notwithstanding—seems to offer a quasi-divine promise of transcendence from the offline world.[16] Thus, unless a frustratingly demystifying narrative such as *Bandersnatch* finds its way through our digital window, would we not secretly wish to surrender ourselves to the sublimity of the digital? However aware one may be of any platform's deceptive and addictive design, which is like a digital mall or online casino of sorts, the stack's allure is undeniable.

---

16   In a foundational study, one of Bolter and Grusin's central propositions was that digital culture is shaped by "the double logic of remediation," whereby new media cater both to the illusion of immediacy and to the experience of hypermediacy, in a contradictory drive to both disavow and elicit their mediation (and their remediation of older media).

As Nye argued, "the constant is not the technological object per se; it is the continual redeployment of the sublime itself," which "leaves observers too deeply moved to reflect on the historicity of their experience." Somewhat ironically, if one thinks of the inherent historicity, artificiality and reproducibility of everything technological, the technological sublime is therefore felt as "a unique and precious encounter with reality" that "is beyond words" (Nye xiv). Thus, extrapolating Nye's insights into digital capitalism's Americanized world, one can easily understand how technology in general and digital media in particular play a quasi-religious function still today. More than just an aesthetic sensibility with its own versions of beauty and sublimity, one can say—with Joel Dinerstein—that "technology is the American [and now global] theology" (569). All of this, of course, is not like an organized religion, but more like a pseudo-religion—an aesthetic sensibility with an underlying ideological bias that functions *as though it were religion*. Today's technological aesthetics would be, therefore, just one of the latest expressions of capitalism's functioning as—in Walter Benjamin's words—a "a pure religious cult, perhaps the most extreme there ever was. Within it everything only has meaning in direct relation to the cult: it knows no special dogma, no theology." Benjamin famously invited to "Compare the holy iconography [*Heiligenbildern*] of various religions on the one hand with the banknotes of various countries on the other" ("Capitalism as Religion" 260). Now, however, more than money, it seems that digital technologies are what function as capitalism's holy iconography—something that *Devs* explicitly explores, as shall be seen.

What I have been calling the technological aesthetics would be, overall, a highly mediated and historically construed way of perceiving the present world's apparatuses and networks—and it appears to be the *dominant* way of seeing them and hence another key component of our dystopian structure of feeling, something that explains our cruel and/or ironic attachment to the epoch's objects and structures. Visual SF generally and new media dystopias specifically, therefore, have to be understood as a reflexive representation of this dominant sensibility, as a genre that is peculiarly apt for either/both reproducing and/or subverting our culture's techno-ambivalent gaze. However, such subversion can only be partial: not only because subversion relies on the reproduction of at least part of that which is to be subverted,

Aesthetic and Ideological Ambivalences

but also because images—and visual culture generally—are especially prone to idealizing technology. Noting that the cinema has rarely filmed work and instead focused on "love or seduction," Jean-Louis Comolli makes an observation that seems crucial regarding film and television's role in the establishment of a technological aesthetic. In his words,

> The eroticism of machines is captured to perfection by the cinerotic machine [which achieves] the perfect regulation of a mechanical ballet. [...] The machine-tool is already an idealization of the work that perfects and improves it, rendering it more regular, prompter, cleaner, straighter. And since cinematography tends to redouble this idealization, the aspect of work most frequently filmed is unfailingly that which is most unreal [i.e., most mechanized]. [...] The cinema's eroticization of machines functions like the other, accessory side of work's mechanization of bodies. (20)

Thus, what underlies today's technological aesthetics is reducible to a simple dialectic. Maybe, our attraction for images of technology is a reflex of our epoch's attraction for the "efficient"—for all that which is "regular, prompter, cleaner, straighter" and gives everyone the illusion of control (while giving control only to a few). And even so, the ambivalence remains, for capitalist technologies do not only attract: they are also what make us fear that humanity—perhaps both the ruled and the ruling classes—has lost control over its creations. In this sense, our society fears that it has become "like the sorcerer, who is no longer able to control the powers of the nether world whom he has called up by his spells" (Marx and Engels 32)—yet we are still spellbound by the beauty and the sublimity of technology. Whether we see it as divine or demonic, we are nonetheless partaking in this pseudo-religious way of seeing technology, which is, by extension, a mystified way of seeing the structures that technology reifies and reinforces.

3.2.3. New Media Dystopias and Their Ambivalences

Writing in the mid-1960s and thinking back upon the so-called Golden Age of SF cinema, Susan Sontag famously wrote that SF is a spectacle of disaster. Even when evoking the looming threat of nuclear war, "the science fiction film [...] is concerned with the aesthetics of destruction, with the peculiar beauties to be found in wreaking havoc, making a mess" (213). Thinking about postmodern SF and writing in the 1990s, Scott Bukatman claimed, with a similar irony, that "Science fiction constructs a *space of accommodation* to an intensely technological existence [where] the shock of the new is aestheticized and examined" (*Terminal Identity* 10).[17] Throughout the genre's history, both its visual and its narrative dimensions have been defined by an "aesthetics of ambivalence" that has exceeded SF's boundaries to spread outward into digital culture, establishing the basis for an aesthetic sensibility that now seems to dominate and determine our ways of seeing. The ambiguities of both visual SF and its techno-ambivalent gaze, however, are further complicated in the dystopian sub-genre. Just as there is an obvious irony in the aesthetics of destruction, which finds beauty in disasters; there is an equally blatant irony in finding beauty—and even sublimity—in dystopian technologies and societies. In the sub-genre, technology and society are not only the objects of estrangement, but also the objects of critique—so how can a visual dystopia be critical within the framework of SF cinema's spectacles and digital culture's technological aesthetics? Clearly, the politics of these dystopias cannot be understood without their aesthetics and this requires considering how the politically horrifying can also be aesthetically pleasing.

In positing his theory of SF film's aesthetics of ambivalence, Brooks Landon takes note of "the phenomenon [...] of a film whose dystopic view of the future is seriously undermined by the seductive depictions of its special effects," a phenomenon that stretches as far back as SF cinema itself.

17 As opposed to Sontag, who wrote at a time when SF studies—let alone SF *film* studies—was not an established academic discipline, Bukatman is writing and making this claim in the context of an emergent scholarship on SF film, which was at the time in the process of distinguishing itself from literary SF studies. Other foundational works of SF film scholarship would be the monographs of Vivian Sobchack, especially her ground-breaking *Screening Space* (1987, re-published in 1997). And besides Brooks Landon's *The Aesthetics of Ambivalence*, the 1990s also saw the publication of two key essay collections, edited by Annette Kuhn, some of whose chapters have already been referenced (*Alien Zone*; *Alien Zone II*).

Aesthetic and Ideological Ambivalences

Discussing Fritz Lang's *Metropolis* (1927), William Cameron Menzies's *Things to Come* (1936) and other early films, Landon conjectures that "The notion that life could be so different, that the limits of the known could be so radically overstepped, must certainly have played a more significant affective role for its audience than could have the muddled and simplistic particulars of its story" (87). Thus, in visual dystopias we again find the possibility that, as in SF film generally, the visual spectacles of the genre may monopolize attention, take it away from the *novum*'s context and thus blunt the edge of estrangement. However, the specificity of the dystopian genre as a *critical* kind of narrative adds another possibility on top of that: the possibility that, as Landon's words suggest, some mystifying form of "seduction" like the ones here discussed may directly "undermine" the presumed dystopianism of the world and/or objects on-screen. This is a central contradiction in visual dystopias, but is it fair to refer to this aesthetics as a way of "undermining" the dystopian? The ambivalence of what I have elsewhere called the "beautified dystopia" need not be a self-defeating contradiction, at least not necessarily.

The first episode to be written of *Black Mirror*, "Fifteen Million Merits," for example, was apparently designed with this ambivalence in mind, as the episode's production design and cinematography demonstrate and as Charlie Brooker himself acknowledges.[18] In his words,

> "Fifteen Million Merits" was inspired by a lot of different things, but it mainly happened because my wife Konnie took the piss out of me. I was sitting on the sofa with an iPad and a laptop, and probably a phone, and a television, and she said something along the lines of "Literally, you'd be happy if you were in a box and the walls were

---

18   "Fifteen Million Merits" (directed by Euros Lyn) was released as the second episode of the anthology series' first season, in 2011, but it was the first script to be delivered to Channel 4 by Charlie Brooker and the one that paved the way for greenlighting the series (Brooker et al. 12). It should be said that here I am synthesizing my previous interpretations of the episode in the space of two contrastive paragraphs and my *Utopian Studies* and *Science Fiction Studies* articles may be consulted for a closer reading of both visual and narrative aspects. My analyses there can be then contrasted to another article (McKenna) that focuses more intently of the ideological—rather than aesthetic—double-edges of the episode's "Orwellian" mode of critique.

all screens." And I thought, "Yes, that's quite an arresting image." Also, I probably would. (Brooker et al. 32)

Regardless of the factuality of Brooker's humorous account, what this shows is that the episode, which constructs a society wallpapered with endless video screens, with no exteriors and no life other than the human, is structured around a paradigmatically techno-ambivalent gaze. Co-creator Annabel Jones acknowledges that while the episode protagonist's "room is a cell and it should feel like one, you want it to be a cell you would love to live in. The design is all about seduction and beauty" (Brooker et al. 36–7). In addition to being "an incredibly reductive piss-taking version of capitalism" in Brooker's own words (32), this dystopian world is also beautiful and even evocative of the sublime in certain shots that, with the aid of special effects, suggest a perfectly geometrical infinity of identically technologized spaces. This episode, therefore, illustrates how a seductive aesthetics need not contradict a new media dystopia's critical impetus, but make a crucial point about how ways of seeing, the characters' and the viewers', are an integral part of the whole world's oppressive functioning.

Nevertheless, the ambivalence of "Fifteen Million Merits"—or of any other new media dystopias that play with the epoch's technological aesthetics—need not necessarily be received as a contribution to its critical function. "Fifteen Million Merits," as I have argued elsewhere, does not assure but at least *facilitates* this interpretation because it is very clearly—in an implicitly self-conscious way—the story of *a user-spectator who is seduced but also discontent*, who throughout the episode struggles with his position within this society—and towards its technologies, a caricaturized double of digital capitalism's own. Thus, this episode not only reproduces the epoch's techno-ambivalent gaze, but also, reflexively, exposes and problematizes such an aesthetic sensibility, together with the structures that such a way of seeing helps sustain.[19] However, this is reliant on interpretation—and moreover, the episode's ending is deeply open-ended. As I already analyzed

---

19   In the terms of Todd McGowan, "Fifteen Million Merits" might be described as an example of what he calls "cinema of intersection," as a visual narrative that opens up to scrutiny the gaze that it constructs—in this case, the techno-ambivalent gaze of digital capitalism.

Aesthetic and Ideological Ambivalences

elsewhere, it is possible to arrive at both utopian and anti-utopian interpretations of the protagonist's ultimately failed rebellion, which leads to his re-seduction by and re-incorporation into the system. Overall, then, perhaps an ambivalence such as this episode's—or *Bandersnatch*'s, or *Devs*'s, or *Westworld*'s—is the most critical that a new media dystopia can become, insofar as they all are an SF mirror of what they denounce.

As opposed to the ambivalences of the new media dystopias that this book studies and favors, it can be enlightening to conclude this theorization by comparing and contrasting with what could be described as a paradigmatically *acritical* new media dystopia from the same epoch: Steven Spielberg's *Ready Player One* (2018), based on Ernest Cline's eponymous novel (2011). The exposition and *mise-en-scène* of the film does indeed bring viewers into an unambiguously dystopian future world, one that is—by all measures—dystopian because some form of digital capitalism still dictates the terms of everyday life. Here, the majority of offline spaces have become an overpopulated, insalubrious and barren junkyard and most people live in a sprawling megalopolis of trailer-homes that are piled upon each other in what can only be described as a chaotically *favela*-like equivalent of skyscrapers. The protagonist, a young working-class man, lives in one such trailer and—like the majority—spends most of his life connected to a virtual simulation called the OASIS, both for fun and for necessity. Indeed, since the OASIS's virtual currency seems to have replaced real-world currencies, everyone's work and leisure is directly or indirectly mediated by that digital platform. Thus, having brought viewers into such an undesirable and unequal world, Spielberg's film then narrates our working-class hero's efforts to win a contest in the OASIS that shall turn whoever wins into the platform's new owner, as per the OASIS's founder dying wishes—and, of course, he wins and he lives happily ever after as a benevolent digital capitalist. The mystification effected by Spielberg's narrative almost needs no explanation: simply, what is *a priori* dystopian is then redeemed by an all-American hero who, with the elite's consent, magically turns everything into his "utopia" and is hailed as savior.[20]

---

20   This is, of course, an utterly unimaginative and absurdly reformist "utopia," since the only change that the hero achieves is having the OASIS closed twice a week so that people enjoy "life offline," or at least whatever is left of it. However, because the

On top on this narrative, which so clearly disavows the critical implications of its initial premises while reducing its utopian impulses to a commodified happy ending, *Ready Player One* also constructs a mystifying visual aesthetics that undoubtedly helps in smoothing over the initial dystopian worldbuilding. In a way that completely casts asides the possibility of problematizing the epoch's quasi-religious way of seeing technology, Spielberg's film opts for an unambiguously *technophile gaze*, one that erases any fear or suspicion of technology and thus overemphasizes its beauty and sublimity. Although the film, like "Fifteen Million Merits," has a user-viewer as protagonist; there is neither self-consciousness nor ambivalence in his gaze, but rather an utter fascination for the OASIS's digital sublime—as well as, tellingly, an obsessive devotion towards the OASIS's creator, who is a sort of messiah. Inviting spectators to share the character's technophile gaze, most of *Ready Player One* is, accordingly, an ostentatious display of the possibilities offered by CGI and current animation techniques—seemingly as infinite and sublime as the possibilities offered to the OASIS's users, which promises a "limitless" VR experience of any imaginable world and of becoming any imaginable person. Thus, the promise of transcendence offered by what was once called cyberspace is reasserted here, both by the OASIS (to the characters) and by the film itself (to the spectators). In this sense, the film's promotional poster encapsulates the whole production's spirit: whereas the trailer-city dystopia is confined to a blurry portion of the background, everything else is about the characters—who live "an adventure too big for the real world"—within an ethereally bluish, geometrically harmonious and almost all-encompassing VR. In the end, then, though maybe in spite of itself, Spielberg's film is valuable as a symptom of the dominant technological aesthetics that other new media dystopias play with in much more nuanced ways, with a techno-ambivalent gaze rather than a one-sidedly technophile one.

To sum up these theoretical meditations, the aesthetic and ideological ambivalences of new media dystopias are, in all these ways, necessarily

---

film has left behind much of the offline world's miseries to focus upon the digital world, Spielberg seems to expect that viewers would have forgotten about everything undesirable in such a world.

Aesthetic and Ideological Ambivalences

explained by way of both their narrative and their visual dimensions and—as the contrast between "Fifteen Million Merits" and *Ready Player One* illustrates—the many ambivalences that I have been sketching throughout these past sections are only a range of possibilities that may (or may not) be present and pertinent in specific texts. By definition, the sub-genre may be ambivalent and each text may take those ambivalences in radically different directions, which is why it is worth remembering them all while analyzing. On the one hand, the inherent ambivalence of the "cognitive" in SF, together with the double-edged nature of the "critical" in the dystopia and of "narrative complexity" in contemporary audio-visual series must be kept in mind. On the other hand, one must also keep in mind the ambivalences of SF film's visual *nova* and of the epoch's technological aesthetics, as well the as blatant ironies of constructing beauty and sublimity out of dystopian horror. With these dialectics in mind, our mode of analysis remains on some level as speculative as the visual narratives that it examines, if only because spectators' reactions are not generally predictable and always idiosyncratic. However,—like good SF—what a good critical analysis should do is not predicting but estranging each visual narrative in order to arrive at a vantage point wherefrom to better grasp it within its context. New media dystopias are, from this perspective, a privileged tool for cognitive mapping within the present epoch insofar as they both expose and symptomatize its multi-dimensional dialectical contradictions, allowing us to turn something as overwhelmingly complex as this historical context's dystopian structure of feeling into something as strikingly clear as a narrative arc or an image. From this book's perspective, then, the question is not only that new media dystopias are narratively speaking, reflexive, but that they must also be read as a condensed, complex representation of the age's aesthetics and ideologies, in a mode of analysis that may open more questions than it answers but that in so doing paves the way for further questioning—or rather, hopefully, for a ruthless criticism of all that exists within the new media dystopia that is digital capitalism.

3.3. The Dialectics of Complexity in *Westworld*[21]

Out of all the new media dystopias studied here, Lisa Joy and Jonathan Nolan's *Westworld* (2016–22) is probably the most complex—for better and for worse.[22] Supposedly meant to take the baton of *Game of Thrones* as HBO's flagship series, *Westworld*'s first season gained critical and audience acclaim for the quality of its production and the sophistication of its themes, but after three more seasons, the series was prematurely canceled in 2022 and, even though the creators had hoped for one or two more, its fourth season became the final one.[23] According to *The Hollywood Reporter*, this was "an unexpected fate for a series that was once considered one of HBO's biggest tentpoles—an acclaimed mystery-box drama that racked up 54 Emmy nominations" (Hibberd). However, this cancellation was not as unexpected as the headlines would have it, but a death foretold, especially in light of production costs and a gradual decline in both viewership and ratings. Beyond the producers' economic reasoning, here I would argue that the main reason for the series' demise was its astounding complexity, which is, ironically, the very same thing

---

21 Although there will be some close analyses of certain of the series' details, this section primarily consists of a relatively abstract commentary of *Westworld*—a commentary that, above all, surveys the four seasons' general trajectory and most notable elements, synthesizes the findings of previous studies and puts them in dialog with this book's framework. Given the series' lengthy runtime and the diversity of critical concepts employed, an exhaustive close commentary of the whole would have been almost impossible.

22 Nolan and Joy's *Westworld*, particularly its first season, is an expansive adaptation of Michael Crichton eponymous film from 1973, which significantly rewrites and revises the original by bringing it closer to those versions of the Frankenstein myth (Mary Shelley included) that significantly humanize and empathize with the creatures, as I explored elsewhere (see "All the Park's a Stage").

23 Initially, it is reported that "Joy and Nolan—and even HBO—had plotted a six-season journey" (Goldberg) although, a month before its cancellation, co-creator Jonathan Nolan was saying that they "always planned for a fifth and final season" (Rice). Retrospectively, it would seem that the series' decline brought the number of seasons down from six to five, until it was canceled at four.

Aesthetic and Ideological Ambivalences 223

that first made it successful. *Westworld* would be, therefore, a showcase of the ambivalence of complexity—an instance of complex TV whose rise and fall is primarily explainable by that nature, although this should not be taken to imply that series declined in a perfectly linear way. Pausing to examine each season's semi-autonomous logics and then theorizing upon the whole, the series' constant complexity is taken as a paradigmatic case of the dialectics sketched in this chapter.

Overall, the concept that best sums *Westworld*'s narrative structure is Pardo's notion of the *metafictional allegory* (see again Section 2.2.3), especially in its first two seasons, which are set in the series' namesake: a mid-twenty-first-century theme park called Westworld. Owned and run by the Delos corporation, Westworld is a fully immersive theme park that recreates the late-nineteenth century "American West" of the popular genre. The park is populated by fully sentient, totally human-passing androids who—as embodied NPCs (non-player characters) of a material videogame—play every conceivable role within a scenario that is—as per the Western's conventions—centered around the white, frontier settlements, with outlaws, Native Americans and Mexicans mainly found in the park's more dangerous fringes.[24] Assigned to programmed loops within interlocking, interactive narratives, these android "hosts" serve as lifelike companions, antagonists or victims of the human "guests," who are offered access to a world where they can partake in any narrative and behave whichever way they desire—just like the feigned promotional website discoverwestworld.com promises. As paying customers of a luxury experience, guests are thus given a chance to "live without limits"—but also the assurance that hosts are programmed not to hurt a fly, since they are only capable of simulated violence against living beings. Besides, for further safety, hosts have their memories erased after every loop—that is, every time they die or get physically hurt, which occurs daily—and, in this way, they cannot remember

---

24   In this regard, the series has been defined as a "post-Western" (González), although within our framework one might wish to describe it as a meta-Western, thus emphasizing its genre-specific reflexivity, which is more defining than the spatiotemporal displacement of conventions that is only vaguely evoked by the post-prefix. Elsewhere, the series' self-referential relation with the Western genre has also been studied through the lens of nostalgia theory (Schubert and Ravizza).

(at first) their ceaseless suffering at human hands. In short, hosts are kept hostages of a fiction catered to customers.

In a way that epitomizes the park's brutal standards of violence, much of the first two seasons are spent following William's whole life—with Jimmi Simpson and Ed Harris playing the young and old selves of a Delos shareholder who has spent his whole life in an obsessive quest for the park's secret meaning, committing all kinds of atrocities to hosts along the way.[25] Nonetheless, the park is primarily explored from the perspective of two gynoids who become the series-long protagonists: a rancher's daughter, Dolores (Evan Rachel Wood) and a brothel's keeper, Maeve (Thandiwe Newton). Besides the park itself, *Westworld* also shows the park's "backstage," its allegorically extradiegetic level—that is, the hidden facilities where Delos's staff creates and repairs the hosts, designs their identities and narratives and supervises its functioning under the leadership of Dr Ford (Anthony Hopkins), Westworld's founder, and his assistant, Bernard (Jeffrey Wright), who is—unbeknownst to him—an android based on Ford's original business partner, dead for decades.

With such *mise-en-scène*, Joy and Nolan's series is from the outset a fine synthesis of the reflexive and the speculative, insofar as it speaks simultaneously of two kinds of creation: the narrative creation of fiction and

---

25 The revelation that Ed Harris and Jimmi Simpson were playing the young and old selves of the same character remained unrevealed until the end of the first season and it was the object of numerous fan theories. This kind of revelation shall become a repeated formula of the series in subsequent seasons, using the narrative strategy of never mentioning a character's real name—neither in dialog nor in the credits—so as to later generate a shock and some sort of retroactive interpretation of previous on-screen events. In the case of Harris and Simpson's character, the strategy seems to have a characterological justification, insofar as it is meant to highlight William's gradual descent into cynicism as he spent more and more time in the park, which changed him from the self-styled noble employee and adventurer of his first arrival into the ruthless shareholder and gunslinger of his later years. Thus it is that William turned into "the man in black," as the series' credited Ed Harris. Depending on our interpretive perspective, one can choose to see this character's arc as a gradual corruption of his morality, as a revelation of his truer, darker self, or as William's gradual internalization of the park's implied male gaze and of the expected ruthlessness of a man with his position in Delos's board.

the Frankensteinian creation of life. Employing its futuristic technologies to construct not just androids, but a self-enclosed, immersive world with a human-passing population, the theme park literalizes the Shakespearean "all the world's a stage." Indeed, this is an SF kind of metafictional allegory with equivalences to all the usual roles: the audiences/users (human guests), the actors/characters (android hosts), the writers (Dr Ford and Delos's workers) and the producers (the Delos corporation).[26] Besides, as the series gradually reveals, Westworld is only one of many Delos parks that are made re-using the same narrative formulas and technologies, though changing the scenery: Samurai-era Japan, Colonial India, a Game-of-Thrones-like fantasy world and presumably more. Accordingly, much of the series can be read as a reflexive meditation upon not only the Western genre, but also upon HBO's violence- and sex-explicit brand of "quality TV," that the park emulates.[27] Furthermore, more generally, the whole Delos park venture can also be read as a reflection upon commodified cultural production in the digital age. In this metafictional allegory as in reality, a façade of increasingly interactive, varied contents hides a culture industry that is monopolized by a handful of corporations that are, like Delos, in between a Hollywood major and a Big Tech giant.

Through the tensions between Dr Ford—the original creative mind— and some other "creative workers" hired by Delos, the backstage scenes repeatedly counterpoise two antagonistic views of culture that indirectly impinge upon the series' status as commodified "content." With a reflexivity that generally remains only implicitly self-conscious, *Westworld* gives voice to, respectively, a more "artistic" view that conceives of the park as

---

[26] This reference to the Shakespearean concept is a citation that the series itself makes, with Dolores's father quoting King Lear's words in the very first episode. After malfunctioning and presumably awakening to the nature of his reality, the android says: "when we are born, we cry we are come to this great stage of fools" (Nolan 58'40"-52"). The Shakespearean intertextuality of the series, furthermore, is not restricted to this detail, but omnipresent, especially in its first season (see Winckler).

[27] Much has been said the series' relation with HBO's kind of quality TV, which is not only defined by narrative complexity, but also by "abundant gratuitous nudity, sex and violence" (Koller 178). Like HBO, Delos too is shown to advertise its park in a profoundly similar way.

a quasi-philosophical quest for a deeper, transformative insight about the nature of existence and a more "commercial" one that centers upon the most commodified pleasures offered by storytelling technologies, whereby androids (and gynoids especially) are reduced to mere objects of sex and violence, with their sentience unacknowledged. Since the commercial view exerts greater influence, the park—like the show itself, by extension—is partly made for a techno-ambivalent, male gaze, insofar as it is appealing to the pleasures—and allaying the fears—that inhere in dominant ways of seeing bodies and technologies.[28] However, both despite and because it reproduces such a kind of gaze via a metafictional allegory, the series also exposes the complex apparatus—literally, the park's backstage facilities— that enables those ways of seeing the android other. One key vehicle for this demystifying reflexivity is, on the one hand, the runtime given to Dr Ford's lamentations about the fate of his own creations, especially since Delos wants to retire him in order to fully control and exploit the parks— and he resents them. On the other hand, of even greater importance are Dolores's and Maeve's perspectives and experiences of the systemic violence that Delos's parks construct and commodify. In a sense, then, the initial season of *Westworld* can be said to offer both a conservative and a progressive critique of the culture industry: one that looks back with nostalgia to a pre-capitalist past of non-commodified creation and another that longs for a revolutionary transformation.

As the first season is focalized from these two gynoids'—and the android Bernard's—perspectives, the narrative pivots around their gradual coming-to-terms with their experiences as the exploited objects within the park's fictions. Framing the series, the first thing to be shown by *Westworld*'s pilot episode is, in fact, Dolores's usual narrative loop: waking up in her family's idyllic ranch, running errands in the settler town, returning on horseback before sunset—and, most likely, getting raped and/or murdered,

---

28   The fact that Westworld often implies a male gaze, however, should not lead us into dismissing the ambivalence of reproducing such gaze, for it is, first, constructed within a critical-reflexive dialog with HBO's quasi-pornographic (or at least morbid) style of depicting sex and violence—and secondly, because even its frequent use of on-screen nudity need not be seen as objectification, but as part of the gynoids' and androids' characterization (see Campion).

either by some human guests that accompanied her home, or by some android bandits that would allow any guests around the area to save her and play the heroes (or not). Then, the following day, a variation on the same happens, and so it goes—seemingly *ad aeternum*. The remainder of the season plays with this implicitly self-referential—that is, meta-televisual—seriality, either to underscore the hosts' Sisyphean suffering within their episode-like loops, or to underline some minor change in their consciousness—as in Dolores' subtly violent, unexpected gesture right before the same pilot ends.[29] In the park, as in complex television, a tightly structured loop provides the structure within which subversion is possible.

Subsequently, throughout the episodes, the hosts' newly acquired capacity for retaining memories and experiencing "reveries"—a capacity given to them by Dr Ford in a wilful sabotage of Delos's management—puts them in the path towards becoming self-conscious. In the special case of Bernard, the unwitting host who lived as a Delos worker, his anagnorisis triggers a series of conversations with his boss and creator Dr Ford about the nature of his reality, often of great value as expositions of the series' reflexive philosophy. In the case of Dolores and Maeve, by contrast, their more traumatic awakenings within the park's violent loops eventually turns them into the leaders of violent uprisings against Delos's staff. And for Dolores in particular, becoming aware also gives her a justification to kill Dr Ford—something that he himself expects and literally toasts to—and to go human-hunting for a long time, in a stereotypically anti-utopian representation of the revolutionary rebel as a blood-thirsty fanatic.[30] Nevertheless, in all these ways, in *Westworld* one finds a clear case of a reflexive dystopia in

---

29 In this ending, the lead gynoid character, once again going through her narrative loop, unexpectedly kills a fly that is bothering her—and it is there that the episode cuts to black. This simple gesture—proof that the hosts might become capable of hurting a fly after all—offers a foreboding of the rest of the season's main arc.

30 In a previous article, where I explored the first- and second-season arcs of Dolores and Maeve, I criticized that "the series' critical impetus and allegorical subtleties, both its feminist- and its Marxist-tending connotations, are eventually reduced to a clichéd kind of "totalitarian terror" in a way in which "the goal of revolutionaries like Dolores seems to be caricaturized as either/both 'eat the rich' and/or 'kill the men'" ("Subverting or Reasserting?" 133).

which metafictional anagnorises and confrontations are mapped onto the development of a revolutionary consciousness and a rebellion; indeed, in the case of hosts, awakening to the fictionality of their lives is synonymous with awakening to the structures that subjugate them.

For this reason, *Westworld*'s metafictional allegory is not solely intramural—an implicit meditation upon itself as thoroughly commodified culture—but also clearly extramural, turned outward from itself and towards the wider world that it—as a dystopian narrative—denounces. The series' first two seasons have been read as a "metaphor of patriarchy" (see Belton) for reasons that should now be evident—the park's commodification of gynoid bodies, especially—and it might similarly be read as a meditation on parallel axes of domination, especially given the colonial ideologies that underpin the Western genre and, in that case, intramural and extramural reflexivity would be probably inseparable[31] Thus, even though the first two seasons take place within the self-enclosed and self-referential setting of the theme park(s), this metafictional allegory is by no means a "narcissistic narrative." The character of Dr Ford—as the most authorial voice in the diegesis—once verbalizes the most basic idea behind the series' ideological use of its reflexivity, explaining that

> The self is a kind of fiction, for hosts and humans alike. It's a story we tell ourselves [...]. Humans fancy that there's something special about the way we perceive the world, and yet we live in loops as tight and as closed as the hosts do, seldom questioning our choices, content, for the most part, to be told what to do next. (S. Williams 35'12"–36'-24")

In this manner, the hosts' dystopia—their experience of being thoroughly coded and trapped in loops within a very sophisticated storytelling

---

31   A great number of interpretations of the series, especially of its first two seasons, have focused upon its problematization of gender norms, especially insofar as *Westworld* literalizes the idea that gender is first coded into us and then performed—and subsequently stages a revolution led by the two gynoids against such patriarchal order. In so doing, as Mullen puts it, the series "draws attention to the ways in which gender is consciously constructed and reinforced, both for the hosts and for humans" (Mullen 9; see also Belton; Koller; Sebastián-Martín, "Subverting or Reasserting?").

machine—is also, in a very conventional SF analogy, our own dystopian experience of reality—the experience of being mere cogs in the digital-capitalist machine, of feeling alienated within a sophisticated network of power and control. Although this is at first only an indirect implication, occasionally voiced by characters like the above-cited Dr Ford in conversation with an awakened Bernard, *Westworld*'s later seasons literalize the most extramural implications of the allegory, especially as soon as the human world beyond Delos's theme parks is explored and exposed as having a system of control that is eerily similar to the parks. In turning outward from these metafictional scenarios, the technological mechanisms that enabled the guests' "utopia" of "limitless enjoyment" are gradually shown to be the same mechanisms that enable a dystopian future of digital-capitalist domination over the whole of humanity.

Before actually leaving Delos's parks, however, the second season provides a logical bridge between the metafictional allegory created by that whole scenario and the more literal kind of dystopian narrative of later seasons. In this season, which is mostly a narration of the chaos that ensued after the hosts' uprising, subsequently known as "the Delos massacre" or, euphemistically, "the Westworld incident," the company's driving motivations are explored further. Here, one finds out that, as in digital capitalist reality, the core driver of business is not making profit by selling a cultural commodity—selling tickets to the parks, in Delos's case—but rather accumulating data on a mass scale—the user data extracted from surveillance of the guests' behavior within the parks. Indeed, even after the whole massacre, one finds out that the Delos "rescue team" main priority is not finding human survivors, but retrieving the vast stores of data that had been gathered while the park was still operational. Here, a conversation between Bernard and the late Dr Ford is again the place where the park's (and the series') deeper logics are explained:

> [DR FORD:] Have you ever wondered why the hosts' stories have barely changed in thirty years?
>
> [BERNARD:] I always assumed the loops were for the hosts. To keep them centred. But that isn't it at all, isn't it? [...] The park is an experiment. A testing chamber. The guests are the variables and the hosts are the controls. When guests come to the

park, they don't know they're being watched. We get to see their true selves. Their every choice reveals another part of their cognition. Their drives. So that Delos can understand them. So that Delos can copy them.

[DR FORD:] Every piece of information in the world has been copied. Backed up. Except the human mind, the last analog device in a digital world.

[BERNARD:] We weren't here to code the hosts. We were here to decode the guests. (Kassell 14'05"-16'45")

And, indeed, Delos had been storing all guests' profiles in a mass server facility called "the forge," which Dolores and Bernard access before anyone from Delos ever arrives.

In a visualization that is deeply evocative of the sublime, the forge is—physically—an underground facility with countless computers, flooded and sombre for cooling purposes, stretching for an undetermined space with an endlessly replicating distribution. Virtually, however, it is entirely different. Once Dolores and Bernard plug themselves into the server's VR interface, the forge's data center is visualized as an immense, beautifully lit, old-fashioned library that contains one book per every human who had ever visited the parks. Besides such data, the forge also stores a virtual copy of the whole theme park, called "the sublime," an idyllically human-less simulation where hosts could be on their own—and many hosts do choose this as their destination after the parks' closure, with only a few leaving with Dolores for the human world beyond. In a stark contrast with the overwhelming scale of the physical facility and its VR interface, which, in turn, suggest the unfathomable amount of data that the forge can store, it turns out that the "code" that defines the behavior and identity of every single human being can be stored in a rather slim, small booklet. As opposed to the hosts, *Westworld* thus seems to suggest that humans are rather basic and inferior beings, insignificant *vis-à-vis* the machine's sublime scale. However, as the series keeps emphasizing in multiple manners, in a particularly postmodern fashion, there is no such thing as a perfect copy in this world of simulacra. According to the series' own logic, in fact, copies of human minds are, for some unspecified reason, unable to adapt to android bodies and they necessarily deteriorate within them, however perfectly human passing these bodies may be, but this is never a problem, because the point (for Delos at least) is not to copy, but to control.

Expanding upon this idea, much of the second season is, overall, a meditation upon both the impossibility of copying and the struggle for control. In a flashback-driven sub-plot that illustrates this logic, this season also recounts how Delos's founder, James Delos, began funding the park in a hubristic attempt to live forever as an android—a project that failed, since, as Dr Ford once puts it, "they learned to copy a mind like a soft-headed boy humming a tune someone else composed" (Kassell 17'43"-55"). Nevertheless, Delos's failure in making a perfect copy of the human did not stand in the way of commodifying it, so the experiment, in a sense, succeeded by enabling an entire business model out of technologies that *simulate* the human experience, as well as by indirectly providing a new mechanism of controlling humanity. The character of William, who still roams the park fully enjoying the post-massacre violence, experiences this in what seems to be another metafictional anagnorisis. Prone to (quite quixotically) believing that everyone is an android and everything is a narrative or a secret plot, Ed Harris's character here goes as far as to kill his daughter, believing her to be a gynoid imitation of her, sent by the company to take him away (or out). Realizing the fatal mistake and falling down a rabbit hole of paranoia and regret, William then doubts his own humanity and cuts his own flesh in the hope of revealing an android's mechanisms. Here, however, his anagnorisis is not metafictional, but merely tragic, as he merely re-discovers that he is just himself, his human self, falling into the same illusions that he helped build, but no longer in charge of the situation at all. Indeed, by the end of this second season, control has totally changed hands: just as William is taken away to a psychiatric institution, in shock and seriously wounded, Dolores escapes unnoticed by transplanting herself to the synthetically copied body of a Delos executive whom she had killed (Tessa Thompson)—and crucially, she takes with her the only copy of the forge's entire data. Copying, as Dolores does know, is not an end in itself, but a means for taking control—and control is precisely what humans have now lost.

The third season further demonstrates how humanity's loss of control is more an established fact than a feared future. However, this is not the case because of the hosts' rebellion in Delos's parks, a mere "incident" to the outside world, but rather because of the Earth's digital-capitalist organization, which at this point clearly becomes the central object of the series' cognitive estrangement and dystopian denunciation. In between multiple and often overcomplicated sub-plots of corporate espionage, Dolores, some undercover copies of herself and other escaped hosts now guide viewers through this new scenario—and, in particular, through the human world's elites, which extend beyond Delos. Standing out from the crowd of companies, the Incite corporation in particular owns a quantum supercomputer with a complex AI called Rehoboam—the season's main technological *novum*.[32] And what does this computer do? Apparently, Rehoboam is capable of predicting everything, everywhere—at least if given enough data. Delos's files on Westworld's guests, which Dolores had stolen, are therefore highly coveted and, as soon as the gynoid raises suspicions, both Delos and Incite shall try to hunt her in order to feed her data to Rehoboam.

So far, operating with the data extracted from everyone's use of digital platforms, Rehoboam has already been reconstructing everyone's life-stories and extrapolating into their futures—all in order to sell those self-fulfilling prophecies to corporate actors, who act upon them as facts and thus contribute to confirming them. Having placed itself at the very center of a digital economy, this computer is the *de facto* ruler and regulator of global economy and society—and, indeed, the machine itself, with its globe shape, seems like an abstracted double of the world that it is designed to control (Figure 8). Establishing such a tight, system-wide feedback loop, Rehoboam has been stifling any form of social mobility that may threaten the system' survival, thus reinforcing and deepening inequalities—and now, if it is improved with the incorporation of Delos's data, Rehoboam's may become almost omniscient and omnipotent, or at least better able to predict *and predetermine* everyone's existence.[33] Thus, in another reversal of the first

---

32 The computer's name is the same as a Biblical King of Israel, the last of a line, presumably in a foreshadowing of its demise. A previous version of the same computer, in keeping with the reference, was called Salomon.

33 Rehoboam's God-like nature has even motivated theological readings (see Gittinger).

Aesthetic and Ideological Ambivalences   233

two seasons' dynamics, humans are now the ones that shall go through a process of awakening. Here, the new focal character is Caleb (Aaron Paul), a precariously underemployed construction worker who does on-demand criminal jobs for an Uber-like platform and has no prospects of a better life—at least not until he meets Dolores.

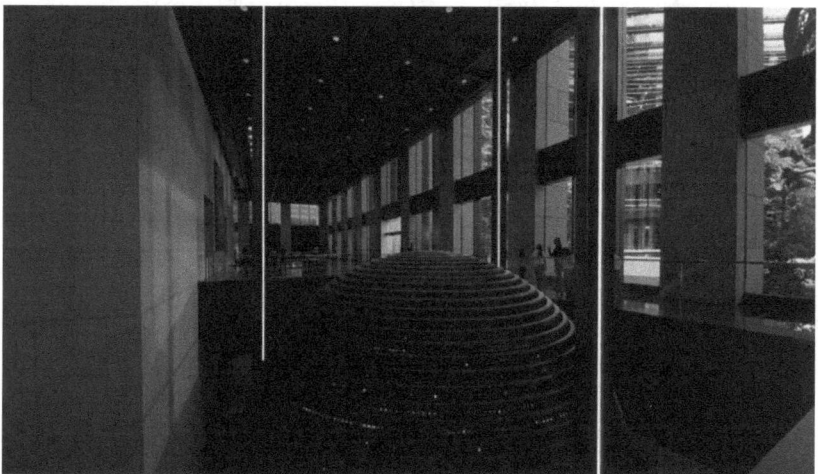

Figure 8. The Rehoboam computer within the Incite corporation headquarters. Its global shape and its undecipherable flicker of lights across horizontal lines, which could be said to simulate a global geography of data flows, again show how digital technologies' efforts at "copying" the world are but efforts towards controlling. Like most maps, Rehoboam's real power lies not only in its accuracy, but above all in its *simplifying* grasp of reality. Precisely because it simplifies the globe, it can rule over its otherwise uncontrollable complexity.

Just as she was once shown her own coding, this time it is Dolores who shows Caleb his "file"—Rehoboam's detailed extrapolation for his future, which is so fateful that even his suicide date is included. Thus, Caleb's swift metafictional anagnorisis understandably makes him follow her. At this point, having infiltrated this world's elites, Dolores deeply empathizes with the human majorities, keenly aware they are trapped in loops as tight as those of the parks' hosts. In this regard, the lines of struggle are clearly redrawn in this season to correspond less with a speculative human/non-human divide and more with the literal class inequalities that have become so characteristic of digital capitalism. In the world of *Westworld* beyond Westworld, a vast, diverse majority (non-human "hosts" included) stands subjected to a small elite, with companies like Delos and Incite monopolizing the vectors of information and employing them as a mechanism of control of unprecedented scale and scope—a mechanism that is here embodied in Rehoboam. Hoping to change this dystopian system, Dolores and Caleb soon leak Rehoboam's data for everyone to see the system's file on them, which triggers widespread indignation. However, this popular sentiment is soon appeased, in an anti-utopian twist that nonetheless seems sadly realistic, given the waning attention attracted by real-life scandals of the kind (e.g. the Snowden or WikiLeaks revelations). For the majority at least, it would thus seem that revelations need not lead to any revolution or even change, as the system is "resilient" even after its radical exposure. The system's mechanic emperor may be naked, but it's still the emperor.

Nevertheless, as the third season's down-spiral into violence demonstrates, this system is by no means perfect at predetermining through predictions and it—like capitalism itself—still depends on the use of repressive force, to be deployed against human "outliers" especially. As Dolores and Caleb discover, these are individuals whose behavior cannot be predicted or accommodated into Rehoboam's models, who are therefore imprisoned at Incite's behest and—only sometimes—released with a memory wipe, just like the parks' hosts. Just like the park failed at copying but succeeding at controlling, here Rehoboam fails at predicting but succeeds at predetermining—by force. Caleb himself, in fact, is one brainwashed outlier and, as he discovers, his on-demand criminal jobs consisted in hunting others like him—in yet another dystopian revelation that surprises himself and, presumably, the viewers, assuming they are not already inured to *Westworld*'s constant loop of "plot twists." The third season finale, in particular, seems like a perfect example of how even the most potently estranging events of past seasons can be reformulated in a loop: whereas the first season ended in the park's chaotic collapse, invoking an ambivalent hope of change for the better in spite of mass bloodshed, the third season tries to do exactly the same, though in the human world. And does it succeed?

After Dolores sacrifices herself for humanity and Rehoboam is destroyed, the system collapses and mass street violence ensues. As the future

Aesthetic and Ideological Ambivalences

city is left aflame, Maeve and Caleb are in thrall with the promise that, as she puts it, "this is the new world and, in this world, you can be whoever the fuck you want" (Getzinger 1h11'21"-29")—something that she, as the brothel's keeper in Westworld, used to say to newcomers about the "wild west." The irony of her statement *vis-à-vis* the park's reality (and the West's historical reality), however, is lost in this new context. What was previously shown to be a pre-scripted, commodified sentence—meant to appeal to the guests' taste for the "exotic" and the "adventurous"—is now re-uttered in an entirely serious way—apparently meant to be felt as utopian. Indeed, the scene's sublime solemnity is clearly reinforced by their awed expressions, the rising sound of Pink Floyd's "Brain Damage" as the extradiegetic music and the sublime sensation evoked by the whole scenario of destruction as witnessed from a drone-like perspective that slowly retreats and rises, backwards and upwards, towards transcendence. Just then, the episode cuts to black and credits begin to roll on-screen. However, only a few credits after this grand third season finale, another, rather mundane post-credit scene that—trailer-like—anticipates the next season's intrigues is introduced in a way that utterly spoils the sublime mood of the closing images. As per the series' ongoing logics, the loop of subversion continues and any hopes shall be further disappointed along the way. Here, if not earlier, the theme park's and Rehoboam's loops begin to pale in comparison to the series' own.

In another unintended irony, much of the season's (and the series') loop-like functioning is reflexively encapsulated in one part of Maeve's otherwise sketchy narrative arc.[34] Before she joins Dolores and Caleb in

---

34   As I have argued elsewhere in relation to the second season (see "Subverting or Reasserting?"), Dolores and Maeve's antagonism not only seems forced for the sake of convenience—the convenience of having an antagonism that propels the story forward—but it also seems to a great extent contrary to the series' initial impetus as an anti-patriarchal allegory (see Mullen; as well as Belton). Whereas the first season expounded the perspectives of two gynoids who had been forced into the roles of housekeeper and prostitute, angel in the house and fallen woman, thus giving them great reason to empathize in their parallel revolts against Delos; the second season significantly reversed their roles—with Dolores as the wicked woman and Maeve as the devout mother—in a way that continued to exploit their antagonism and— now rather unquestioningly—reproduced the reified images of the feminine that the park itself had constructed and commodified. The third season, in continuing

the above-described finale, Maeve is at first a host(age) in yet another park, one themed after Nazi-occupied Italy during World War II. Soon realizing that she has been revived and re-used after dying in the second season, Maeve goes through all the necessary steps to confront her creators/controllers once again. After committing suicide within the park's narratives to be taken to its backstage maintenance facilities, in a no longer estranging metaleptic jump, Maeve comes to realize that even this backstage is another stage—and what is worse, that she is trapped in a custom-made, VR prison. Formulaic metalepsis is thus followed by formulaic metalepsis—and for what? As it turns out, Maeve was being trained by Incite's Machiavellian owner, Engerraund Serac (Vincent Cassel), in order to be later sent after Dolores.[35] Therefore, her success in realizing that she was trapped in a theme park within a simulation is no longer part of a process of self-discovery, but rather part of a forced training in her most technical skills—her skills as a superhuman assassin. Despite its anecdotal significance to the season's larger arc, this sub-plot seems symptomatic of what *Westworld* has begun to do with itself: reformulating its own tropes in ways that do away with

---

their antagonism—further characterizing Dolores as driven by a fanatical hatred of the elites and Maeve as driven by a fanatical hatred of her counterpart—until miraculously solving it in the ending after Dolores's sacrifice, seems to offer no solution to this down-spiral in characterization of what had been two of the first seasons most complex subjects. Saying sketchy, then, is no overstatement, but a rather summarized description of a longer story that falls beyond my more abstract scope.

35 Notwithstanding the meritorious acting of Vincent Cassel, this character seems but a shadow of the earlier seasons' antagonists, the much more nuanced Dr Ford played by Anthony Hopkins and the William of Ed Harris—although the latter is, at this point, well on the way towards becoming a formulaic shadow of his past self. As for Engerraund Serac, his position as the Frankensteinian creator of Rehoboam is reduced to a fixation with saving humanity from itself, after having witnessed the destruction of his natal Paris with a nuclear bomb. As opposed to the layers of cynicism, tenderness and nostalgia that one can see in Dr Ford, or the complex quixotism of William, Serac seems but a stereotypical, one-dimensional villain with a savior complex. The most interesting detail of his character is perhaps what—in a generous interpretation—redeems his apparent one-dimensionality, since, before Rehoboam's destruction, it is revealed that Serac had been but the machine's puppet, obeying its every command at all times, with the AI's voice implanted in his ear.

their reflexive and critical potential and instead turn them into formulaic elements of a loop whereby expectations are endlessly subverted. Like Maeve, viewers are also being trained—trained to expect further manipulation, a higher level of control and, ultimately, an endless loop not just of *narrative* subversion, but also of the continuation of everything dystopian even in the face of the most outright kinds of confrontation. In a sense, what is subverted here is not "the system" or any structure, but the very meaning of subversion. As for Maeve, for viewers it may seem that each season finale's vague hopes are examples of a rather cruel optimism, since capitalism is proven capable of mutating endlessly, fleeing into ever-abstracter levels of control. Commodified complexity, in this case, is thus profoundly anti-utopian.

The fourth season, as the most fully-fledged synthesis of the most dystopian elements of all previous seasons, regrettably continues to illustrate the whole series' loop-like functioning. In this unexpectedly final season, viewers are once again taken into an *a priori* new SF scenario—but very soon, this comes to feel as a blend of the first two seasons' theme parks and the third season's digital-capitalist dystopia. Opening seven years after Rehoboam's collapse and taking viewers through a decades-long journey told from various timelines and perspectives, the season narrates how the surviving copy of Dolores who supplanted a Delos executive (played by Tessa Thompson) and an android imitation of William (Ed Harris) have together led a sophisticated plot against humanity. By first replacing the human elites with androids and then developing a technology for remote mind-controlling the entire population, by the late twenty-first century this evil Dolores has managed to create a world that radically reverses the first season's human-host hierarchy. As in a technophobic conspiracy theory, all humans are now controlled by a radiation-emitting tower—simply called "the tower"—and they are given pre-scripted identities, routines and jobs within a future version of New York, one superficially utopian (or "eco-utopian") for its lush, urban vegetation and its fully electrified transport. Here, while humans lead their lives unaware of any control, hosts-turned-guests are invited to visit—and tasked to hunt any humans who awaken to the deception. Furthermore, amidst the people and equally unaware of the system lives a new copy of Dolores called Christina (played by Evan Rachel

Wood), who has a fake job as a writer for NPCs in videogames—though her real job is to script every human life on the basis of her repressed-but-lingering memories of having herself lived in a "perfect" loop. Thus, the series again folds upon itself, re-copying characters and re-combining its scenarios in a complex, profoundly self-referential pastiche.

This fourth season, with its newly rebooted metafictional allegory, again follows some of its characters along their paths towards their anagnorises and confrontations. The once-again-innocent Dolores-double Christina gradually realizes that rather than giving everyone a worthy story in the videogames that she believes to be designing, she is in fact exercising control over every human life left on the planet, which is now confined to the city. Like Bernard was to Ford, Christina is merely an "empowered" puppet of her (and everyone else's) master, the "other Dolores" (Tessa Thompson). Here, however, as opposed to the first season, the literal and metaphorical dialogs between creature and creator—who are, in this case, two versions of the same person—are reduced to a clichéd confrontation of the former's naiveté with the latter's cynicism. Whereas Christina wholeheartedly believes that everyone should have a beautiful, dignified story, Dolores believes that the only way to give humans a relative utopia is by exerting absolute control. Ultimately, it seems as though the first season has been rebooted in a rather Manichean rewriting of its Frankensteinian musings upon creation and control within the contemporary culture industry, which are here reduced to a black-or-white confrontation between a hopeless romantic and a ruthless dictator. Indeed, whereas the series' theme park allegory accounted for the complex intersectional nature of domination in the West(ern), here the tables have turned not just literally in that hosts rule over guests now, but also in terms of the allegory's ideological depth. With so many layers and nuances removed, one is left with a shallowly technophobic portrayal of an android-supremacist technofascism, a dystopia which humorlessly sees itself as utopia. Some shades of the earlier allegorical layers do linger, but mostly as self-referential allusions or self-citations meant for the faithful viewer—and thus it is that, ironically, even though the series has ostensibly transcended its initial limits to look at new worlds beyond the parks, in so doing it has become mostly about itself, ultimately narcissistic despite its own potentials.

Aesthetic and Ideological Ambivalences 239

Another metafictional anagnorisis that structures the season is Caleb's, with his awakening functioning as a bridge between the two parallel timelines of the season. At first, the season switches between two seemingly unconnected narratives: Christina's life in her "new New York" loop and Caleb and Maeve's investigation of Dolores's evil plans after Rehoboam's demise.[36] As the viewer learns with the latter two, it appears that Dolores has been taking over most digital corporations' infrastructure with one clear mission. Specifically, Dolores plans to unleash her mind-control system through a fly-carried plague, which is to be tested with the human elites, whom she invites to yet another theme park's inauguration—the inauguration of a park set in the US 1920s. Dolores's new park is thus a glamorous lure for its bourgeois guests, though this time the trap is worse than Delos's old system of surveillance. While investigating the whole plot, Caleb and Maeve infiltrate this park and try to sabotage Dolores's plan by destroying the tower's prototype version. Along the way, however, Caleb is infected and—even though he miraculously resists mind control for a moment—he is captured and Maeve is *apparently* killed, buried under a pile of rubble. Immediately after this scene, just as Caleb is held captive and interrogated by Dolores, he learns that he is a host copy of himself, made by Dolores decades after he (really) died in that park. This resuscitation, as she explains, is an effort to learn why some individuals resist the tower's power, beginning with Caleb. However, when she learns nothing, Caleb is sent away with other copies of himself, who were as useless to her and,

---

36 These two narratives are, unbeknownst to viewers until Caleb's anagnorisis, not only set in different settings, but also different timelines, since Caleb and Maeve's story takes place more than two decades before the other events in the season. This mirrors the first season's structure, which also interspersed sequences set in the park's present with others set in its past without specifying the temporal leaps—that is, until the series reveals that actors Jimmi Simpson and Ed Harris had been playing the young and old versions of the same character, although the latter had been strategically unnamed on-screen and in the credits. The same happens in the fourth season with the character of Caleb's daughter, Frankie. Here, her child self is played by Celeste Clark and her adult self—who is for a long time not called by her name—by Aurora Perrineau. The revelation of her adult self's identity is made to coincide with Caleb's anagnorisis, since learning about his daughter's present age is a crucial component of his other realization.

for that reason, imprisoned and left to deteriorate and die—all of which, as viewers are expected to know, is what happens with all copies of human minds that are put into android bodies.

Now, the focal Caleb tries to escape before decaying and, on his way out of Dolores' prison, he finds clues left by past copies of himself—as well as corpses of his copies, who died trying to escape. This time, as opposed to his predecessors but thanks to them, Caleb makes it all the way out of the building and manages to send a voice recording to his daughter with a melodramatic apology for having abandoned her decades ago. Dolores, who irrupts in this scene unsurprised, had been expecting this escape and tolerating it with the hope of learning something about Caleb's capacity for resisting mind-control. Now, however, she is disappointed to learn about his "simple" and "primitive" reaction—thus, both Caleb's awakening and confrontation come to nothing. How can one interpret this latest anagnorisis? Caught in a dynamic of ceaselessly subverting expectations, it seems that the only (remotely) utopian hope that the series can summon after Caleb's awakening and attempted escape is the prospect a clichéd family reunion with a newly introduced daughter character—and even this scenario is openly mocked by one of the protagonists. As the ever-widening spiral of anagnorises, reduplications and pre-programmed confrontations keeps spinning out of the series' control, here one may ironically feel as disappointed as Dolores—though not disappointed with Caleb's all-too-human simplicity, but with the series' almost inhuman complexity, a complexity that can now only appeal to human hope in overly simplistic ways.

In an intense sequence of events that cannot be fully reviewed here, this final season's ending concatenates many of the series' classic tropes: (a) several character resurrections—Caleb's, by Dolores, and Maeve's, by Dolores's enemies—(b) another underground resistance—led by Caleb's daughter, Frankie (Aurora Perrineau)—and (c) another attempted uprising—led by Frankie, Bernard, Maeve and other "uncontrollable" humans and hosts from the resistance, which is followed by (d) another mass slaughter, triggered by the tower's collapse, until stopped by a suddenly repentant Dolores who, eventually, in another unconvincing reversal of her loyalties, sacrifices herself (again) for the people that she enslaved. Furthermore, finally, the whole spiral is closed off with (e) yet another pseudo-utopian promise. With the Earth almost barren and humanity almost extinct after endless war, exploitation and extraction, now the promise is that the almost-forgotten "sublime" of the second season might still provide a virtual space where hosts and humans might do things differently—whatever that means. With one final sequence that takes viewers into a new, VR Westworld park, a Christina who is as unbelievable naïve as in the beginning closes the season by promising that "Maybe this time, we'll set ourselves free" (R. J. Lewis 57' 40"-44")—but with the series canceled, that time never came.

And would it have come? Although one may be wrong in speculating, there is no reason to believe that the series would have broken out of its own spirals. Season after season, one dystopian scenario has followed another, often outmanoeuvring the previous one's evils and, although all seasons have invested utopian hopes in narratives of resistance and revolution, these hopes have been systematically disappointed in an ironically predictable kind of subversion. Indeed, in a cruel use of *Westworld*'s hallmark "plot twist," each season has shown that all revolutions have led to bloodshed, terror and/or totalitarianism and—worse—that revolutions only happen at the ruling classes' behest. For their part, the ruled classes are—from the series' outlook—not only extremely violent when uncontrolled, but also incapable of self-organizing, only capable of reacting chaotically, in ways that trigger catastrophic consequences. One might, for good reasons, regard this whole moral as a lesson in twentieth-century history and one might reject it too, but what is clear is that the series closes off in an unambiguously and irremediably anti-utopian manner.

If the first season's uprisings only happened because Dr Ford re-coded the hosts and—in a literally suicidal way—wrote the narrative of their rebellion, the later seasons have not only repeated this profoundly anti-utopian twist, but significantly worsened it by abandoning the series' initial attempts at focalizing the whole narrative from the ruled classes' perspectives. Whereas the first season narrated resistance and revolution primarily from the perspectives of Dolores and Maeve, who were, intersectionally, the objects of modern patriarchy, of colonial racialization, of capitalist commodification and of digital control, the subsequent seasons have gradually abstracted themselves from the daily loops of dominated people's existences. Although Caleb first and Frankie later—to an extent—incorporate new subaltern perspectives as oppressed outliers of Rehoboam's and Dolores's systems of digital control, their narratives are quickly subsumed by the series' grander narrative, which can only be described as the Miltonic epic of new media dystopias—an internecine struggle between host and human grandees, a clash between the godly forces of technology and capitalism. Against the story of an Eve-turned-Satan who seems as doomed to fail as the feminine and the demonic in Milton—and, from the series' outlook, perhaps *deservedly doomed*, in light of all the evils done in Dolores's name—one may ask: is there any room left for any kind of day-to-day, human hope from below? Just as the series' shifting dystopian scenarios seem to suggest that control is inescapable, forever becoming more abstract *and worse*, the series' increasingly divine (or satanic) narrative focalization gradually forecloses the possibility of hoping for anything other than a *deus ex machina*—a miracle arriving from above, either from the series' writers themselves, or from same apparatuses of power that the series once seemed to expose and denounce.

It is thus ironic—but also deeply (ideo)logical—that the series had to close by reasserting the epoch's decaying but undying promise of digital transcendence. Elsewhere, investing hopes in a sublime cyberspace—that heavenly afterlife of our pseudo-religious way of seeing technology—may already feel like the ultimate cliché, but the series' complexity, with all its twists and turns, seems to make a strong case for it—either by convincing, by overwhelming, or simply by tiring its viewers. In the end, one cannot forget that the series' appeal stems not solely from its narrative complexity, but from its visual sophistication as well. On the one hand, the series narrates many of the fears and anxieties generated by new media technologies, but not always critically, insofar as its dystopian speculation often seems dangerously close to the mystifying tropes of technophobic conspiracy theories, especially in season four, which seems to revel in showing viewers the ultimate high-tech hell. On the other hand, *Westworld* also constructs profoundly awe-inspiring images of its *nova* that seem dangerously close to the technophile's idealized imaginings—from the first two season's images of the park's backstage facilities, the forge and the sublime, going through the cyberpunk-styled devices and cityscapes of the third season and ending with Dolores's superficially "eco-utopian" new New York. The series' opening credits—slow-motion animated images of the automated processes involved in creating the hosts and other *nova*—are probably the clearest and most recurrent manifestation of the series' technological aesthetics. Every episode, whatever its narrative, is indeed framed by this sequence, which is above all an accomplished eroticization of on-screen technologies, caught in their fascinatingly regular, slow motion (Figure 9).[37] Overall, then, perhaps precisely because the series decided to play with the "business SF" scenario of a "technological singularity," *Westworld* from the beginning fell into the techno-ambivalent way of seeing that conceives such a scenario—a hypothetical scenario in which so-called "AI" is as much an object of fear as an object of wonder.[38]

Westworld's multi-dimensional complexity, in the end, is what lies at the crux of the matter—and, even though the series is ambivalent throughout, its critical-reflexive attitude seems to have vanished somewhere along a path paved by commodification. In my first article on Joy and Nolan's show, written shortly after its first season, I wondered whether *Westworld* would be "as doomed by its ambitions as its characters" ("All the Park's a Stage" 64)—and half a decade later, it brings me no pleasure to say that my fears have come true. The series' paradigmatic narrative complexity, which turns *Westworld* into a showcase of reflexive devices and plots-within-the-plot that invite endless viewer speculation, has provided the base for a potently estranging dystopian allegory of an ever-shifting digital-capitalist reality—but all such complexity has become commodified across seasons, with its surprises becoming predictable and its sophistication formulaic. Its careful visual aesthetics, for their part, in many instances function as a powerful

---

[37] The sequence, moreover, adjusts itself to display the hegemonic *novum* of each season (hosts, Rehoboam and the tower, respectively), while also focusing on the construction of a different artificial animal: a horse in the first season, a buffalo in the second, an eagle in the third and a fly in the fourth—all of which symbolically encapsulates the hosts' series-long journey from being utterly domesticated to wildly rebellious, then flying free and eventually becoming an unstoppable plague.

[38] The technological singularity is the science-fictional idea that strong AI is about to be developed by capitalist innovation and that such AI shall supersede human control and capabilities (see Vinge for the technophile view; as well as Shaviro, "The Singularity Is Here" for a Marxist critique of the concept).

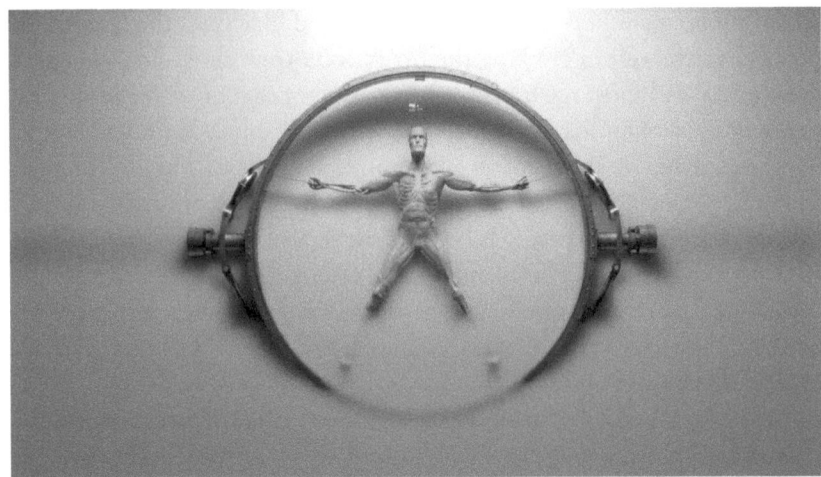

Figure 9. The opening sequence's last image before the series title: an android in the process of being built, in the Vitruvian Man's pose, sinks into a sea of white liquid.

supplement of the narrative's dystopian denunciation—acknowledging, with irony, the attraction exerted by new technologies. However, the series' seemingly self-conscious and critical reconstruction of a technological sublime lost all its irony by the end—and with Christina's final promise, *Westworld* seemed to fall for its own lure. Relatedly, the series' dystopian world building, which began as a metafictional rewriting of the Frankenstein myth within the context of digital capitalism, gradually became too self-referential in the most commodified way—and its systematic disappointment of hopes, gradually wore down any hopes that may have survived in the face of ever-worsening dystopian scenarios.

One can only wonder what could have happened if the series had approached the epoch's techno-ambivalent ways of seeing in a much more critical way—perhaps with as much critical distance as that which the series assumes *vis-à-vis* the male gaze, which is provocatively exposed in the first season, in the most narratively smart and aesthetically admirable part of the series. Perhaps, with more critical distance, more spaces for hope could have survived—but when all one can do is bear witness to a timelessly looping "epic" that narrates the conflicts between elites and their creations, the only attitudes that remain are hopeless and helpless: cynicism and/or devotion for a higher force—an impotent techno-ambivalent gaze. The simple anti-utopian idea behind our dystopian structure of feeling—the idea that there is nothing to be done about anything—in the end remains, perhaps with greater force after the full *Westworld* experience. Like Delos's guests, we too seem doomed to leave this series worse off than we arrived—but we may still choose to see, in spite of everything, the many critical potentials of new media dystopias. In the end, perhaps, one may denounce digital-capitalist reality precisely for being as absurdly abstract and as simply oppressive as *Westworld* and its worlds. And this, in a sense, turns this series into a powerful symbol of the times—potentially, a tool for thinking through high-tech hell, one circle after another.

3.4. The Digital and the Divine in *Devs*[39]

If *Westworld* was primarily defined by its endlessly spiralling narrative complexity, with reflexive and speculative layers piled upon each other, *Devs* (2020) is better defined by its *conciseness*. As a mini-series that was from the outset scheduled to have a single-season runtime, with only eight episodes in total, Alex Garland's new media dystopia gives us a simpler illustration of the narrative and visual ambivalences of the subgenre. However, contrary to the epochal bias that would equate quality and complexity, *Devs*'s simplicity—relative to a series like *Westworld*—is not to be taken as a marker of less quality, but perhaps of the contrary. With a significantly less convoluted narrative structure and a much more suggestive audio-visual aesthetics, the series offers a more condensed and

---

[39] This section builds upon two earlier analyses of *Devs*, which emerged in the framework of the Science Fiction Research Association's annual conference and journal (see "Review of *Devs*, Season 1"; "Silicon Valley as Cult? Mystifying and Demystifying Surveillance Capitalism in Alex Garland's *Devs* (2020)"). I am also indebted to the ideas of my friend and music BA Inés Bausela Buccianti, who took the time to analyze *Devs*'s musical score at my request, in ways that went much deeper than the terms of my analysis here.

compelling approach to what I have been calling the techno-ambivalent gaze. Insofar as it is premised upon the development of a God-like computer like *Westworld*'s Rehoboam but its story is otherwise "realistic" and "contemporary," *Devs* can be read as a more overt meditation upon the dominant ways of seeing technology *in the present age*.[40] With a careful combination of speculative and reflexive devices, Garland's series narratively and visually explores the divine qualities that are attributed to new technological developments, as well as the pseudo-religious practices that seem to emerge around such kinds of perceptions and preconceptions. Without recourse to a radical spatiotemporal displacement, *Devs*'s technological *novum* alone provides the basis for a potently estranging kind of reflexive dystopianism—although, of course, its relative simplicity does not do away with all the usual ambiguities.

On the most literal level of plot, *Devs* is a conventional spy thriller—an example of what some have called the "techno-thriller" or, more playfully, "spy-fi." The series is the story of a couple of computer engineers, Lily Chan (Sonoya Mizuno) and Sergei Pavlov (Karl Glusman), who both work for the Amaya corporation—a high-tech Leviathan of the likes of Alphabet, Meta or Apple, which is based in Silicon Valley, San Francisco. In the very first episode, Sergei is promoted to the most secret research-and-development sub-division of Amaya, called DEVS; however, in that same episode, as soon as he tries to leak information about DEVS, Sergei is assassinated by the corporation's hitman and head of security, Kenton (Zach Grenier), following the orders of the CEO and owner, Forest (Nick Offerman). Subsequently, most of the series is spent following Lily's grief, her growing suspicion about a cover-up, her disconcerting discoveries about Sergei— who was, unbeknownst to her, a Russian spy—and, above all, her efforts to infiltrate the DEVS project, where she seeks answers and revenge. All throughout, the series' switches between Lily's investigations and Forest's behind-the-scenes scheming in such a way that viewers are cognizant of the plots of both sides, but still caught in the suspense.

40   At the time of writing this, there is already a fascinating journal article that compares both series with an eye on their quasi-theological meditations upon free will and determinism, which have very universal, humanist echoes, beyond the present epoch's concern (see Gittinger).

Even though this dimension of *Devs*'s narrative is relatively conventional for the standards of thrillers and spy movies, in and of itself it already offers—potentially—the basis of a critical representation of digital capitalism's elites. Not only does the focus on conspiracies and espionage serve to epitomize these elites' abuses of power, but it also serves to partly expose the mechanisms that normalize such behavior. Here, although secondarily with regards to the main story, the collusion of Silicon Valley corporations and the US state is clearly exemplified in the ways whereby Amaya counts with the wilful support of police and politicians.[41] Furthermore, both despite and because of the Cold-War cliché of Russian espionage, *Devs* also illustrates the geostrategic importance of digital technology, which is at the center of new global struggles—as well as at the center of new class struggles, the struggles between "hacker" workers like Lily and Sergei and "vectoralist" overlords like Forest. Thus, clichés notwithstanding, Garland's spy plot places viewers squarely within the conflicts and controversies that characterize the present epoch, exploring them—class

---

41 The third episode features a scene that, on a first viewing, might seem to suggest that Amaya may face some degree of accountability and government oversight, since Forest faces pressure from a senator who visits the company's headquarters. In a private meeting, she threatens him with using the public's distrust of Big Tech:

> Do you know how easily I could crucify you in a public hearing? People have become scared of the tech companies, Forest. Really scared. AI is gonna create 60% unemployment. Instagram makes people feel like shit about their lives. Twitter makes them feel reviled. Facebook destroyed democracy. They use you. They need you. But they don't like you anymore.
>
> Now, there are other lines of questioning. Your company is an American success story, showing, again, how we lead the world in tech. While we understand and respect the competitive nature of your industry and the requirement for trade secrets, could you shed a little light on what you're working on in DEVS? ("Episode #1.3" 8'43"–9'35")

However, such illusion is quickly dispelled: in an almost Mafia-like gesture, the politician is reminded that she needs Amaya's technology and support to win re-election, as Forest simply asks if she would "continue to protect my company even if I stopped raising money for your campaign?" ("Episode #1.3" 25'04"–10"). Subsequently, this whole discussion and sub-plot fades away from the narrative (until the ending), which does nothing but confirm how Amaya is *de facto* above the law—and, thus, they can believe themselves above anything, like gods.

struggles especially—from within the entrails of Silicon Valley, explicitly historicizing the most speculative and spectacular elements of the series.

The DEVS project, facility and computer are the main objects of cognitive and spectacular estrangement—that is, the *nova* of *Devs*'s SF narrative and visual aesthetics. Beyond the spy-movie sub-plots, *Devs* revolves around Amaya's development of a quantum supercomputer. By first following Sergei and then witnessing the DEVS team's discussions, viewers learn that Amaya is building a machine that should be able of accurately extrapolating in all directions of time-space, thus achieving omniscience of all past, present and future events in the universe—hence the project's name, the Latin spelling for God.[42] The DEVS supercomputer, understandably, is kept in a secret facility—a square-shaped, cement building that is hidden in the clearing of a large forest that is fully owned by Amaya (Figure 10). If the exterior may already seem mysterious to a newcomer like Sergei (or the viewer), the interior of the facility is where the real wonders await. Within a giant, half-underground Faraday cage with a cubic shape, the DEVS computer is built into the center of a magnetically levitating cube-within-the-cube—a cube that contains not only the computer itself, but also multiple workspaces for Amaya's staff (Figure 11). Within the levitating cube, the computer itself stretches vertically through the facility's central axis, as though it were its mechanic skeleton—or a copper tree that seems to grow upwards towards the world, with its roots in the complex machinery. Around it, most walls are made of glass in such a way that the machine is (at least partly) visible from anywhere within the building—something that Alex Garland's characteristically contemplative cinematography exploits. In all these ways, the deeply dystopian scenario of an omniscient supercomputer is turned into the object of a paradigmatically techno-ambivalent gaze—that is, it is presented both as a feared corporate secret and as a fascinating technological wonder.

Although not a literal temple, this beautifully designed building, with a mechanic God at its altar, is in many ways *a sacred space*—at the very least,

---

42 The fact that this is a machine of extrapolation could be read as a sign of genre-specific self-referentiality—that is, as the basis for an implicit meditation upon SF. Nevertheless, this possibility remains implicit, as the most prominent kind of self-referentiality is with visual media, as shall be seen later.

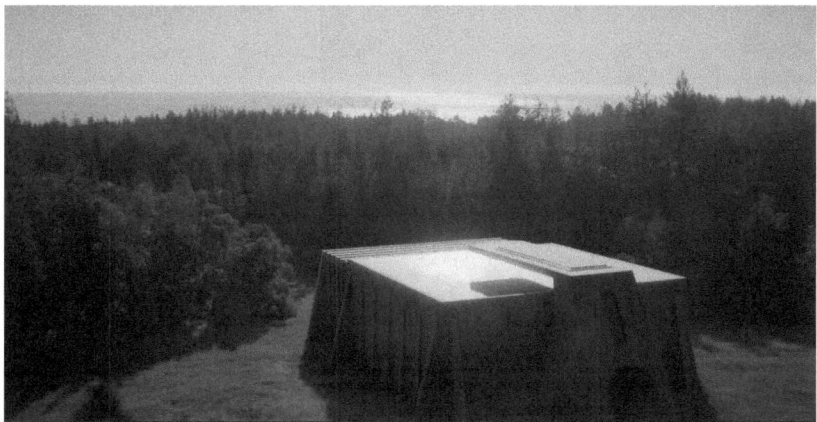

Figure 10. The DEVS facility from the rear side, as seen from an aerial perspective upon Forest and Sergei's arrival. Besides several outstanding side buttresses, the minimalist version of a cathedral's, a shallow water pool on the ceiling and a tower that seems to have some function in the facility's magnetism, the building is pure cement, austere and functional. Nonetheless, as the camera moves upwards and backwards to reveal the building, a ray of sunshine is reflected upon the facility for the whole take's duration, something that—together with so many details of production design, cinematography and sound—helps in evoking the sublime solemnity of the project. Subsequently, as seen from the front, the facility reveals a shape like a truncated pyramid—resembling a Mesoamerican or Egyptian temple—and no external features but a small, square door, two buttresses on either side and several Obelisk-like, golden posts guarding the door's surroundings.

in the etymological sense of being cut apart from mundane reality, like an image.[43] Indeed, the DEVS facility is cut from the exterior not only by a Faraday cage and a safety vacuum, but also by the staff's behavior, who are instructed and enforced—via non-disclosure agreements and the looming threat of being violently silenced—to keep the whole project an absolute secret. Besides, these workers are constantly supervised by Forest, who—as

43 For a philosophical reflection on the meaning of the sacred and on how it impinges on the perception and conceptualization of images (cinematic and others), see Jean-Luc Nancy. This could be read as, very implicitly, another self-referential dimension of the show, insofar as meditations on sacredness and religiosity are inherently related to meditations on visual images of all kinds.

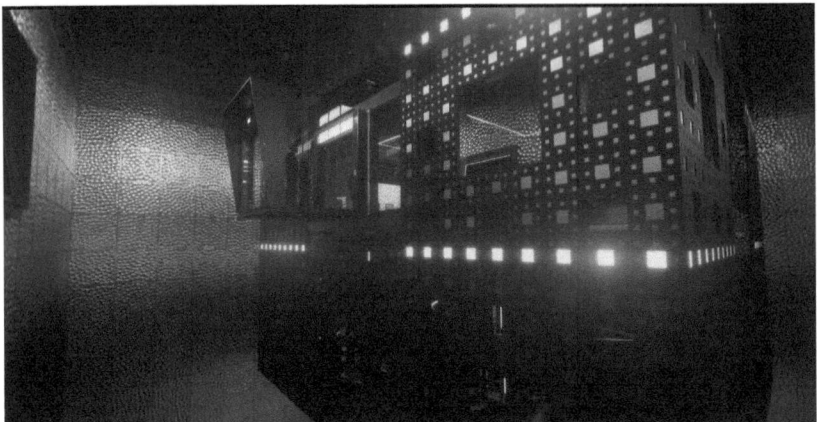

Figure 11. The cubic facility that magnetically levitates within the larger Faraday cage and is separated by a vacuum from it, with the only access being a levitating cubicle, in which Sergei and Forest can be seen arriving. In this take, which slowly pans to the right and slowly reveals the cube just as Sergei gazes around in astonishment, the facility's beauty and sacredness is emphasized by the musical score, which consists of Gregorian chants that rise in a crescendo at the same time as the frame widens slowly to reveal the whole facility.

Amaya's CEO and the most ardent devotee of DEVS—spends a significant amount of his time in the facility, either observing the project's progress or discussing with the staff. Forest's role as a cult leader—besides being suggested visually from the very opening image of the series, where he is seen hiding in the darkness of a forest—is further underscored by his almost fanatical proselytizing for the deterministic understanding of the universe that the machine's functioning suggests. If everything can indeed be predicted accurately by the computer, then everything in the universe would have to be predetermined, leaving absolutely no room for free will—and Forest is, for several reasons, predisposed to believe this. First, the main reason that drove him to promote the project in the first place was a mixture of nostalgia and regret: the unprocessed trauma of having witnessed his wife and daughter's death in a traffic accident that he wishes to have avoided. Thus, with Amaya, both his company and his daughter's name, he is building a monument to her memory, turning her into the corporate

Aesthetic and Ideological Ambivalences 251

image and, with DEVS, he is building a machine to meet her again—or, even, to resurrect her, at least virtually or on-screen. Furthermore, believing in a fully-predetermined universe is not only the perfect caveat for covering his guilt, but also a convenient alibi for engaging in all kinds of illegal and immoral practices—in the name of the company, for the sake of the project's secrecy, or to assure the fulfillment of the computer's predictions.

Nevertheless, in this digital-capitalist cult with a computer as god and an entrepreneur as prophet, there is no shortage of theological debates and an abundance of taboos and hypocrisy. As per Forest's commandments, enforced by Katie (Alison Pill), his right-hand physicist and the project's supervisor, it is, first, forbidden to use the machine to look into the future. All the research conducted to verify if the computer works must be, therefore, focused on the past and any transgressions of this commandment shall be punished. Second, it is also forbidden to even discuss anything about the many-worlds interpretation of quantum mechanics.[44] Since this interpretation would directly contradict Forest's belief in a single universe where everything is predetermined and pre-ordained, the staff is not allowed to take that theory into account while developing the computer's predictive algorithms and they are cautioned never to discuss it in front of him. These two commandments, however, are disrespected both from above and from below. Lyndon (Cailee Spaeny), the youngest worker at the project, eventually re-codes the DEVS software in accordance with the forbidden many-worlds theory—and after that tweak, the machine can finally offer perfectly accurate images of anything, anywhere, at any time,

---

44   This interpretation gives an elegant—but science-fictional—solution to the quandaries posed by Schrödinger's cat paradox, which—simply put—posits that, in the quantum realm, all measurements are simultaneously true until measured (i.e. the cat is both alive and dead in the famous hypothetic experiment, until observation confirms one or the other outcome). In the many-worlds interpretation of quantum mechanics, the main idea is that all quantum states are true *even after a measurement confirms one*—with the explanation being that they are true, but in different universes. Thus, according to this theory, every time a quantum measurement is made, the world "splits" into several worlds, into universes in which each possible measurement is true—and, thus, the universe is radically undetermined and open-ended, because it is always branching off into infinite universes that would be ever slightly different (see Vaidman's entry in the *Stanford Encyclopedia of Philosophy*).

as was intended. From then onwards, the computer works with Lyndon's "heretical" coding and Forest and Katie shall use it—as they have been secretly doing all the time—to examine both the past *and* the future. Lyndon's transgression, however, is punished in a scene that stands as a beautiful testament to the fatal truth of his discovery: a quick superimposed succession of several versions of the same jump off a dam, visualizing the many worlds' theory—and tragically demonstrating that the outcome is the same despite all quantum variation: death. As always, commandments and taboos are not made equal for everyone and this religion does not lack its own hypocritical hierarchy. In these ways, *Devs* is satirically representing Silicon Valley as a place where capitalism has mutated into a fanatical cult of technology.[45] However, at the same time, with its carefully crafted audio-visual aesthetics, the series also invites viewers to partake in this cult's devotion towards this technological sublime—as spectators. Indeed, in an implicitly self-conscious meditation, the practice that drives this cult is precisely spectatorship.

As befits a new media dystopia, *Devs* is not solely a dystopian representation of digital capitalism and a speculative narrative structured around a *novum*, it is also another paradigmatic case of new media reflexivity—a narrative that estranges the new media technologies where it is circulated

---

45   This was the central motif of my previous essay ("Silicon Valley as Cult?"), where the title itself suggested the idea, although it was interpreted with less detail, as befits a conference paper. In an interview of which I was unaware when writing my previous work, Alex Garland himself seems to confirm that his intentions went along a very satirical and critical line, even though he does not explicitly describe Silicon Valley as a cult. Specifically, when asked about Silicon Valley, Garland explains that it's like Wall Street in the 1980s. It's rabidly capitalistic, absolutely rabidly capitalistic and it's rabidly greedy, but, whereas in the 1980s the sense one had of Wall Street was that these people kind of knew they were sharks and, in a way, relished in being sharks and dressed in sharp suits and kind of lorded over other people and felt good about doing it, Silicon Valley has managed to hide its voracious Wall-Street-like capitalism behind hipster T-shirts and cool cafés in the place where they set up their... so that obfuscates what's really going on, and what's really going on is the absolute voracious pursuit of money and power. [However,] they believe themselves [because of that] veneer of virtue. (interviewed by Fridman 24'47"–26'00")

and consumed. In this case, the series' SF *novum*—the DEVS computer—is also the vehicle of the series' self-referentiality—and implicitly, the centerpiece of another metafictional allegory. Amaya's quantum computer does not only have a coding interface, which is repeatedly visible in DEVS staff's desktop screens; it also has an audio-visual interface, meant to be watched as spectators. Thus, besides playing with the logically fascinating possibility of achieving omniscience, the series also plays with the sensually fascinating possibility of seeing and hearing anything, anywhere, anytime. The only space in the DEVS facility with opaque walls is in fact an auditorium: a room with a wall-wide, cinematic screen and one austere pew where the projects' devotees—most frequently, Forest and Katie—can gaze in awe at the machine's predictions, here shown in the form of moving images. At first, before Lyndon's heretical tweak of the algorithm, the computer only rendered a black-and-white blur with barely recognizable views and muffled sounds—only recognizable for someone already familiar with them, as with images of Christ's crucifixion (Figure 12). However, after Lyndon's modification, the machine is capable of producing an audio-visual flow with a detailed resolution, full color and perfectly recognizable sound. This improvement is seen as the final confirmation of the divine powers of the machine and its new capabilities are demonstrated by going even further back, to humanity's and even the Earth's origins. The new mechanic god thus replaces the old and the characters-spectators are left in an ecstatic thrall *vis-à-vis* this new technological sublime—just as the real spectators of the series are caught in the spell of *Devs*'s visual and aural spectacles.

Through this implicitly self-conscious allegory of spectatorship, Garland's series reflexively encapsulates the pseudo-religious fascination that inheres in dominant ways of seeing new media technologies—in this case, in ways of seeing the quantum computer, which in a sense is but a video-on-demand streaming platform with omniscience. However, the illusion of control given to users by such a machine is precisely that: an illusion only. As in Jean-Louis Baudry's renowned critique of cinema (in "The Apparatus"), *Devs* is like another high-tech version of Plato's allegory of the cave, where an active engagement with reality is replaced by the passive consumption of images. Here, however, because of the machine's promise (and Forest's dogma) that everything is predetermined and pre-ordained,

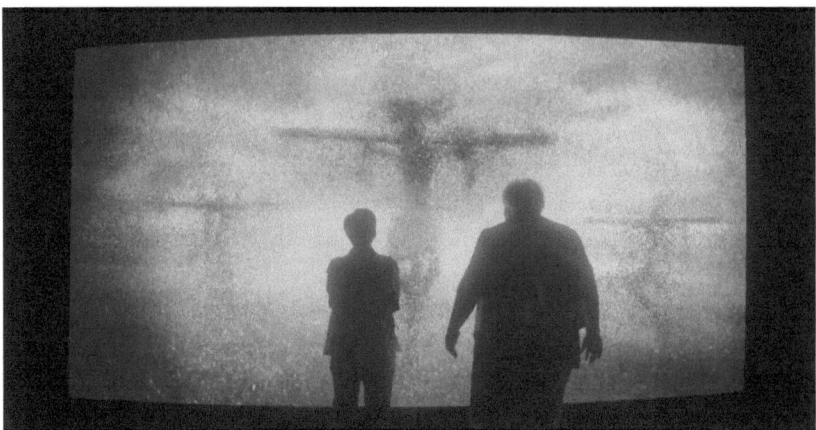

Figure 12. Lyndon and Stewart gaze at the computer's reconstructed images of Christ's crucifixion. One at a time, both stand up from their pew, driven by a kind of religious fervor that can be interpreted as a fervor both for the image itself and for the technology that generates it, since both are, in a sense, divine. The technological sublime is thus shown to be but a remediation of older religious sensibilities of the sublime, since both are, essentially, a confrontation with an incommensurable power, greater than oneself and larger than life.

there seems to be no escape. Unlike in Plato's own allegory, here there is no choice but to be a spectator of everything and everyone's life—including one's own life, since the illusion of free will has been entirely demystified. The staff experiences this very directly when—contradicting Forest's commandments—they try watching themselves one second into the future and, to their dismay, they discover that everything that they do is perfectly anticipated by the machine. In a profoundly alienating experience, it seems as though they themselves—rather than their image—are an imitation that echoes a pre-existing reality (Figure 13). This disturbing realization would be, therefore, another metafictional anagnorisis, if one understands this as an awakening to the fact that their future is as sealed as a finished story's—an awakening that utterly reverses their perception of what is real and what isn't. As one of them, Stewart (Stephen McKinley Henderson), says in awe: "a few hours ago, we were in reality and we were working on a sim. And now, we've pretty much traded. That's the reality.

Aesthetic and Ideological Ambivalences

Right there. It's not even a clone of reality. The box contains everything" ("Episode #1.7" 7'09"-7'39"). Another worker naively replies that at least it doesn't contain *them*—but, of course, the computer *does* contain them, just as it contains the whole of reality in the form of moving images that are, as in a streaming platform, available on demand.

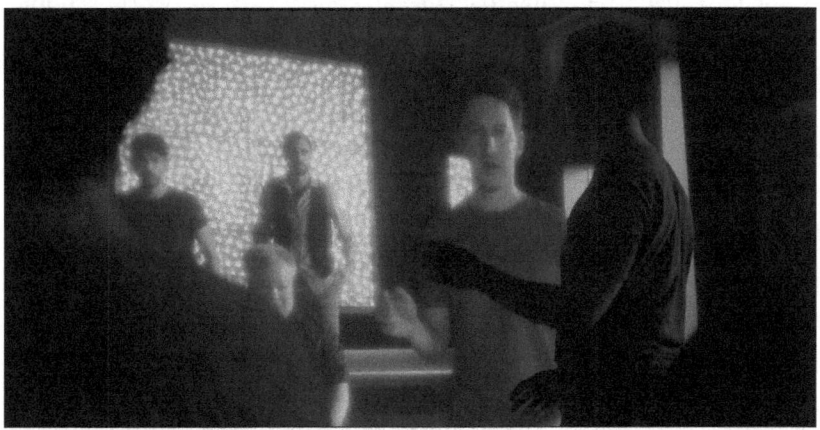

Figure 13. The DEVS staff watch themselves on-screen, in a prediction of the next second that is run by Stewart in order to demonstrate the computer's predictive capabilities to his most sceptical colleagues. In this scene, the impression is that of seeing themselves on a mirror that anticipates precisely what they are about to do, or starting to do, which leads to significant distress amongst them and an urgent desire to stop the machine's predictive engine in order to feel again in control. Here, therefore, the reaction to a metafictional anagnorisis is to reverse or repress the knowledge of one's own condition immediately.

As the cult and the corporation's leader, Forest of all people does nothing but accept future predictions and watch them confirmed—and he and Katie, contrary to all expectations and appearances, tolerate Lily's attempt to infiltrate the project because they have been watching it happen from the very beginning. As with *Westworld*'s loops of pre-programmed revolutions, with *Devs* it could also seem as though any rebellion against a data-driven dystopian order would necessarily be pre-scripted and pre-empted. Using Forest's own metaphor, one could say that any attempt at rebellion would be no rebellion at all, but simply another "tramline" towards an unavoidable destiny. Whether one fears or admires the supercomputer, whether one rebels against the cult or joins it, the fact is that the universe remains unchangeable regardless of anyone's position within, towards or against it. This interpretation, of course, rides on a train of thought that would bring us towards the most clichéd anti-utopian conclusion—that is, the idea that attempting to change oneself and/or the world is pointless and/or counterproductive. However, some details of *Devs*'s narrative development and resolution partly prevent and problematize that anti-utopianism. Besides, assuming that all people are *equally* helpless *vis-à-vis* the computer would be, in the end, an interpretation that would risk obscuring the responsibility of those with power and the agency of those without it—and Garland's series does make some class distinctions and, in so doing, offers some nuances that counter the mystifying abstractedness of its own (or rather, Forest's) deterministic discourse.

Even though Lily's rebellion was foretold from the beginning, how it happens deserves a closer analysis. First, one should consider that her mysterious death scene marks the point in the future after which the machine cannot predict anymore. Since this would prove that the DEVS computer is not truly omniscient, Forest and Katie turn this into another taboo of their cult, which maintains the mystery for viewers up until the series finale, which is when Lily finds out and experiences her own metafictional anagnorisis. Welcomed by an expectant Forest, Lily arrives at the DEVS auditorium demoralized and alienated, as Katie had already explained her the machine's functioning beforehand. Entering the room, she tells Forest: "I don't know what I am anymore. Something that makes no decisions, has no choices, follows a path I can't see. I'm not even choosing the words I speak now." To which he replies, slowly and solemnly but with an emotional glow in his eyes: "I've watched you speak these words before. Many times. And watched myself reply. As the words come, I don't feel as if I'm consciously repeating lines. They're just the things that, at this moment, I feel I want to say."

Here, his excitement in experiencing a prediction made by his own machine is not shared by Lily. Completely untouched by his egotistic ecstasy, she reminds him, with a contained but clear anger: "You've taken everything from me." Hearing this, Forest refers back to his deterministic philosophy with the self-assurance of a true fanatic, excusing himself by saying that "life is just something we watch unfold, like pictures on a screen" ("Episode #1.8" 4'26"-5'53".). Indifferent to her, Forest then delivers a long, inspired speech about the many potentials of the computer, especially of *owning* the computer, but Lily's anger keeps growing, especially after he laughs at her accusation that he is a "fanatic" who believes himself a "messiah." Thus, in this scene, it becomes clearer than ever that the DEVS cult's philosophy is a shamelessly convenient cover of their criminal and immoral deeds—and worse, that Forest wholeheartedly believes in his own delusions. If the deterministic discourse of the series has logical flaws, at least according to some reviewers, it is because it is not meant to be taken as a serious philosophy, but because it—as Forest's doctrine—is the hypocritical ideology of a corporate cult of technology. *Devs's* SF cognition is therefore, more than ever, "capitalist science bullshit about itself" (Miéville 240).

Following that scene, Lily and Forest then watch together what is about to happen to them up until the moment when Lily dies and the computer's predictions end. Here, Lily and Forest watch how her future self tries to kidnap him, then shoots him in the head and, eventually, dies of asphyxia in the facility's security vacuum. Being a spectator of her immediate future is the most emotionally intense moment of Lily's metafictional anagnorisis. However, in her case, watching is also what triggers her decision to not simply confront Forest, but also to contradict the predicted rebellion. Subsequently, even though she continues acting as anticipated for a while after they leave the auditorium, at one point Lily unexpectedly throws away her gun to avoid shooting Forest as she—and the viewers—had seen. Witnessing this, Forest and Katie react in absolute awe at her capacity to rebel against what they believed to be divine destiny. By Lily's own hand, free will suddenly exists again and, in a sense, her act seems to suggest—contra Forest and contra the dominant ideology of digital capitalism—that prediction and predetermination can never be total. Even if distorted and disempowered, a degree of free will and individual autonomy seems to remain even in the face of a God-like machine—but this would be taking our interpretation too far towards a naively utopian or cruelly optimistic extreme. Lily does rewrite destiny in a sense, but she and Forest still die, right then and there. The only change is *how* they die, which suggests the ultimate meaninglessness of her choice—especially since Lily ends up dying as in the predictions (Figure 14). Thus, even with a small but spectacular dose of free will, the outcome is the same. Lily's rebellion against her predicted rebellion is not enough—death was and is certain.

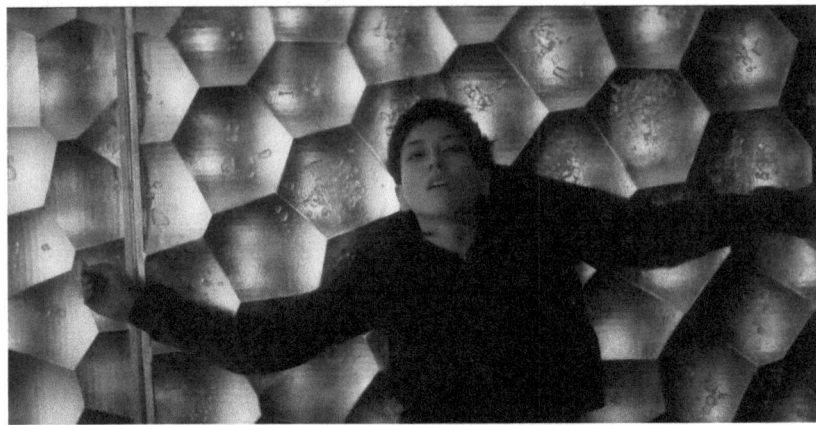

Figure 14. The last image of Lily's death, lying on the facility vacuum's floor in a Christ-like posture that is the exact same shown by the computer's prediction. The only difference is camera perspective: whereas the prediction used a long shot that cohered with Lily's estranged experience of viewing her future, a medium close-up shot here brings us closer to her agonizing gasps for air.

With such a climax, the series spectacularly confronts viewers with the inevitable finality of human life and—at the same time, though partially—with the inherent limitations of digital technology. Lily and Forest's deaths are also, in a sense, the mechanic god's death, as the former's failed rebellion is also the latter's failed prediction. In the end, the sublime possibility of omniscience is proven to be an impossibility—and yet, the episode's denouement still goes on to introduce further ambivalences. After the two characters' deaths, the quantum computer is suddenly shown to glow mysteriously, in a close-up, upward-tilting take of its complex mechanisms that is accompanied by a musical score that rises in a hopeful crescendo. As is later discovered, both Forest's and Lily's consciousnesses are being somehow copied by the computer, which keeps them alive inside. It is Forest who first wakes up in a void, visibly distressed, and discusses with

Katie what happened, who listens and watches from the auditorium. As per his decision, he and Lily are then uploaded to a simulation exactly like their reality—with the only differences being that in the simulation there is no DEVS facility and all their loved ones are still alive. Inside, only Forest and Lily are aware of their deaths and their condition and they have no other choice but to live in this simulation forever, perhaps—or perhaps not—enjoying it as a heavenly afterlife. Forest refers to their knowledge as "the cross [they] have to bear" and, to him, "it's worth it" because "in this world [they] get to live in Paradise with the ones [they] love" ("Episode #1.8" 43'13"-34")—but Garland's series seems less certain than Forest.

The very last images of the series are profoundly ambivalent about this simulation, insofar as they contrast Lily's emotive embrace of her boyfriend with a close-up of Katie's concerned gesture from the outside. Desperate for help to keep the machine running, Katie has called a Senator (Janet Mock) who used to collaborate with—and be manipulated by—Forest and now this powerful politician towers behind Katie, like a shadowy presence, as they watch the simulation. Unashamedly excited with the political possibilities afforded by control of this secret technology, the Senator's appearance concludes *Devs* by leaving its viewers with an uncanny sensation and a bad foreboding. As opposed to *Westworld*'s more naïve and clichéd promise of a virtual utopia, *Devs*'s own ending re-problematizes the idea of a virtual utopia. Here, Lily and Forest's paradise is, in the end, only *their* paradise. Besides, as demonstrated by Katie's concern and the Senator's empowerment, this simulation is a gilded cage that is absolutely dependent on and controllable from the outside, where the structures of power that keep the machine operational remain unchanged—except that there is a new person in charge. Even inside of the simulation, which Forest egotistically describes as the best possible world, everything is the same in almost all regards. Is this due to the series' (or the epoch's) lack of a utopian imagination, or is it due to Forest and Katie's biases as heaven's architects?

In this regard and others, Garland's series concludes inconclusively—on the one hand, implying that digital capitalists are false prophets driven by ego, power and money and, on the other hand, suggesting that their technology may nonetheless deliver a utopia in some divine, inscrutable way. More abstractly speaking, then, one can say that *Devs* confronts viewers with new media technologies as seen through a deeply techno-ambivalent gaze, one that senses both their utopian promises and their dystopian threats, especially within the context of capitalist inequalities. Precisely because progress in the digital age is promising to deify us humans and, in a sense, it is already deifying a small elite, this technological "progress" also threatens to swallow us and the world altogether, reducing everything to data and images—the perfect objects of a kind of control that we, ironically, still find fascinating. The spell of technology is already strong in the contemporary context and *Devs* makes it stronger but, for that same reason, Garland's series also forces us to rethink our way of seeing it, along with the quasi-religious attitudes and practices that our gaze entails. Precisely by joining the DEVS cult, we may begin to question the real cult.

3.5. Re-defining the New Media Dystopia, Narratively and Visually

Finishing the definition of our sub-genre, this chapter has theorized and analyzed its inherent ambivalences, which are—inevitably—both aesthetic and ideological. As a specific kind of visual narrative that represents new media technologies using speculative and reflexive devices, new media dystopias are caught in several dialectical contradictions, with the most essential of them being the inherent tension between narrative and spectacle. Although these dystopias are—presumably and ostensibly—stories built upon a more or less explicitly critical perspective on digital capitalism, they are—at one and the same time—also profoundly mystifying with regard to new media technologies. On the most abstract level, their estranging and critical impetus as SF and dystopian narratives is often caught in a contrast—if not in a contradiction—with their technological aesthetics, which constructs beauty and sublimity out of these dystopias' presumed objects of critique. In other words, one is often confronted with the paradoxical but fascinating phenomenon that a new media dystopia which is narratively technophobe is often—at the same time—visually technophile. Essentially, this is why I have proposed to say that some kind of techno-ambivalent gaze is what structures new media dystopias, insofar as the sub-genre implies a way of seeing new technologies that—both fearful and fascinated, anxious and astounded, critical and complicit—finds some pleasure in contemplating and using them, even with an awareness of their deeply dystopian qualities in a broader context. Perhaps perversely or perhaps playfully, then, the technological aesthetics of new media dystopias generate a guilty pleasure, or at least an ironic attraction towards the same objects, spaces and social structures that are being estranged and subjected to some degree of critical scrutiny.

Of course, even if this is the most important dialectic, the aesthetic and ideological ambivalences of new media dystopias are not entirely reducible to the tension between narrative and spectacle. Already the SF genre and the dystopian sub-genre—understood solely as narrative genres—exhibit their own aesthetic and ideological ambivalences, which primarily relate to the double-edged nature of SF's cognition and the dystopia's critique. Even *Devs*—to this writer's opinion, the best crafted new media dystopia of all those that I analyze in this book—is caught in a quicksand of ambiguities, ambiguities that should not be rejected in and of themselves, but rather seen as the main source of the series' aesthetic value. *Devs* indeed plays with the very ideological logic that "big data" and computational power could accurately predict any kind of phenomenon and this is the cornerstone of its exercise of cognitive estrangement. However, whereas *Westworld* followed this same logic and took it to an unwittingly caricaturized, technophobic extreme, *Devs* problematized that logic until the end, leaving one with some productive doubts rather than with a cynical helplessness *vis-à-vis* new technology. Relatedly, the double-edges in dystopia's negotiation of its own critical impulse could also be seen in both of this chapter's main case studies. *Westworld*, on the one hand, seemed to be so strongly oriented towards offering a complex critique that it gradually mutated into an anti-utopia where any hope—for the fictional world, or for the series itself—just seemed absurd, as in its finale's empty promise of a new opportunity. *Devs*, on the other hand, seemed to inhabit its own ambivalence more comfortably, often veering close to the anti-utopian in its playful engagement with determinism, but ultimately re-kindling some more modest yet powerful questions about us and our ways of seeing technologies in the contemporary epoch.

Of course, utopian hope cannot be commodified in a narrative form, as it is something that emerges from our own personal engagement with a fiction's complex nuances, as spectators, critics and/or academics. Ideally, these dystopias can be sufficiently estranging so as to invite their viewers to not simply make sense of their narrative's logic, but to make sense of historical reality itself—that is, at their best, new media dystopias would point back towards the real new media dystopia that is digital capitalism. However, our analyses have shown that this need not be the case—or not always in the same degree. *Westworld*'s excessive complexity, for instance, seems to eventually distract one from the possibility of hopefully but critically rethinking contemporary reality, whereas *Devs*'s conciseness may have, ironically, proven to be somewhat more suggestive and inspiring in that regard—at least to the viewer that writes these pages, since to an extent this would depend on each spectator's individual reception. However, beyond the idiosyncratic ways in which each text resolves the sub-genre's definitional ambivalences, a few generalizations can be made about new media dystopias, now that their dialectics have been schematized.

Ultimately, with the mediation of critical viewership and analysis, my argument is that new media dystopias on the whole offer a vantage point wherefrom to better grasp the digital age's dominant tendencies, not only because they partly criticize them but also because they partly illustrate them—maybe despite their intentions, as is often the case in *Westworld*, or maybe because of their self-consciousness, as is the case in *Bandersnatch*, *Devs* and some aspects of *Westworld*. Precisely because of their inherent ambivalence, new media dystopias are—using Jameson's words again—a privileged tool for cognitive mapping, insofar as they both expose and symptomatize the contradictions of living under digital capitalism. Ultimately, this sub-genre helps us grasp something as abstract as a dystopian structure of feeling that has emerged during the latest epoch of capitalist history through something as easily graspable as stories of someone's (or some society's) imagined engagement with an imagined new medium (or media). In the end, our sub-genre brings us back to a ridiculous image of ourselves in our daily life, frustrated and fascinated with some digital device or devices—a near-universal experience in this epoch. New media dystopias, with all their contradictions, thus hold up a mirror against the ways in which we ourselves see and narrate our experience with these technologies—an experience that is quite often, as the upcoming chapter theorizes, imagined as a new kind of quixotism.

A certain technophobic bias may keep one away from this deeply contradictory and even hypocritical sub-genre, especially if one distrusts new technologies to the extreme of—following *Devs*'s allegory—really regarding digital capitalism as a fanatical cult in which Mark Zuckerberg and his metaverse venture would be the disappointing real-life double of Forest and his DEVS project. However, even if new media dystopias are but manifestations of our epoch's pseudo-religion, our sub-genre would not simply be an opium of the smartphone-addicted people, but also—like religions in the past—both "the expression of real suffering and a protest against real suffering ... the sigh of the oppressed creature, the heart of a heartless world, and the soul of soulless conditions" (K. Marx, *Early Political Writings* 57). In other words, even in their pseudo-religious function, new media dystopias have the beautiful ambiguity of being a mystifying complaint against historically determined conditions of existence. Like religion to Marx, new media dystopias may be an opium of the people, but also the heart and soul of digital capitalism.

CHAPTER 4

New Media Quixotism: Satiric and Utopian Characterizations of Digital Subjectivity

A mild-mannered, middle-aged bachelor lives a quiet life in a small midwestern town. One day he goes up to the attic. He opens a trunk and pulls out an old pistol and his grandfather's World War I uniform. He puts on the uniform, throws the gun in his aging Volvo, and sets off in search of a former girlfriend who may be trapped in an alternate reality controlled by a sinister Intelligence. This creature is using its power to corrupt reality, changing it now and then in order to confuse those who, like our hero, know what is going on and want to stop it.

Needless to say, strange things happen when he interacts with people who don't see things the same way. Word of his peculiar quest gets around and eventually a journalist publishes the story of his quest. When he finally sees a copy of this book, he discovers that his biographer has invented characters and events and ridiculed his goal of rescuing his old girlfriend, as if she didn't really exist. He starts running into people who have read the book and recognize him from descriptions. Some of the more mischievous readers intentionally alter their lives to make it seem that the sinister Intelligence is meddling with reality in exactly the way he imagines, and he consequently becomes increasingly enmeshed in these fake corruptions of reality. Meanwhile, invented characters from the unauthorized biography begin showing up in his real reality. He notices inconsistencies between the fake corruptions of reality and the real ones—inconsistencies he imagines to be the work of the sinister Intelligence. Growing more and more disoriented, he finally returns to his home town. Broken in spirit, he takes ill and dies. On his deathbed he renounces his belief in the sinister Intelligence, but he never acknowledges that his old girlfriend was a figment of his imagination.

Substitute Castile for the Midwest, a lance and coat of armor for the pistol and uniform, a sway-backed nag for the Volvo, Dulcinea for the girlfriend, and the enchanter Freston for the sinister Intelligence, and instead of a possible Philip K. Dick plot we have Miguel de Cervantes's *Don Quixote de la Mancha* (1605–1615).

—Kenneth Krabbenhoft, "Uses of Madness in Cervantes and Philip K. Dick"
(2000, 216)

Except for two *Science Fiction Studies* articles published decades ago and apart—Krabbenhoft in 2000 and Plank in the 1973—quixotism in SF remains unstudied.¹ However, is this because looking for it is the scholarly equivalent of tilting at windmills, or is it, rather, because SF studies still lack a theoretical framework that can recognize the indirect—but important—influence of Miguel de Cervantes's *Don Quixote* upon the genre? Ever since Bryan Aldiss identified Mary Shelley's *Frankenstein* as the foundation of modern SF, that novel has been an ineluctable reference in an endless number of studies of the genre, given its profound importance as the basis of a long-lasting, ever-mutating myth with many manifestations across media as well as, more recently, as a narrative template for understanding digital technologies and subjectivities.² But what about *Don Quixote*? Although its relevance to SF may seem *a priori* secondary, especially relative to *Frankenstein*, in this chapter I argue that Cervantes's novel—another canonical work that also paved the way for a widespread myth—has similarly served as a narrative template for understanding the radical reshaping of subjectivity that is taking place under digital capitalism. Building upon Pedro Javier Pardo's theorization of the myth of Don Quixote, this chapter explores this myth's latest epochal expression,

1   These two articles are, to the best of my knowledge, the only studies of quixotism and/or Cervantine influences in SF, besides my own article, where I sketched some of the essential ideas that I develop here in more detail ("Don Quixote as Gamer?"). Whereas Krabbenhoft's essay, cited above, consists of a survey of Cervantine kinds of madness, broadly defined, in the novels of Philip K. Dick, Plank's essay was a much more speculative kind of theorization that proposed that Don Quixote's encounter with the windmills served as a paradigm for subsequent encounters between humans and machines—an idea that is also explored and explained here.
2   For a thorough theorization of Frankenstein as an architextual myth, with multi-epochal and multi-media manifestations that often only relate to Shelley's foundational novel via the myth's mediation, see Pedro Javier Pardo García's "The Frankenstein Myth in Film," which conceptualizes this myth in a way that parallels how he conceptualizes the myth of Don Quixote. Relatedly, for a recent monograph that uses Frankenstein as the allegorical basis of a theorization (post-) cinematic technologies, see Shane Denson's *Postnaturalism*. Finally, for a study of how *Frankenstein* can be repurposed as a paradigm for understanding digital subjectivity within one of our new media dystopias, *Black Mirror*, see Daniel Panka's "Transparent Subjects."

first schematizing its main themes and dialectics and then analyzing its manifestations in several new media dystopias. Overall, what I propose to call new media quixotism would be a new historical variant of the myth that condenses and re-doubles the ambivalent aesthetics of our sub-genre.

However, even if this chapter is meant as part of a continued study of new media dystopias, some of its ideas can be taken as a draft for a future, much broader theorization of quixotism within SF and the utopian-dystopian genres more generally. Throughout the upcoming sections, several secondary—but no less important—suggestions are made about the inherent affinities of the myth with said genres, since my underlying assumption is that they share several abstract ambivalences. Like SF, the myth of Don Quixote is based upon a dialectic of realistic (or cognitive) and fantastic (or estranging) impulses; and like utopian and dystopian fiction, the myth is also defined by a dialectical tension between more romantic (or utopian) and more satirical (or critical) interpretations. The concept of new media quixotism is, therefore, meant as a double contribution, to Cervantine studies and to SF studies: on the one hand, it is meant as a proposed new variant of the myth of Don Quixote that can be added as a contemporary coda of earlier, better studied variants and, on the other hand, as an overture to future studies of SF that, moving backwards in time from the digital age, may start looking for earlier traces of quixotism in the genre. Nevertheless, besides any suggestive generalizations and long-term expectations, in the end this chapter has a much humbler and clearer role in the present study of new media dystopias. Within the framework of this book, new media quixotism is, above all, read as a mode of characterization that is inseparable from several dominant dynamics of the contemporary epoch, allowing a science-fictional rethinking of certain kinds of personal experiences with new media technologies. What if—new media dystopias seem to ask—we are all becoming somewhat quixotic due to our use of new media? That is the question here: are we?

4.1. The Myth of Don Quixote into the Digital Age

Approaching Don Quixote as a myth rather than as a text—that is, Cervantes's novel itself—is a solidly founded critical approach that allows us to grasp the breadth and depth of the novel's influence, even in texts where there are no traces of it whatsoever—the case of most new media dystopias.[3] Taking this approach, however, demands some theorization in order to avoid the vagueness of speaking of "quixotism" with its broadest English-language connotations. Speaking of a myth of Don Quixote requires thinking in terms of the most abstract category from Gérard Genette's transtextuality: *architextuality*. As opposed to categories like intertextuality or hypertextuality, architextuality does not refer to a relation between two texts, but to a relation between a text and an abstract textual paradigm, such as a mode of enunciation, a fictional genre or—in Pedro Javier Pardo's usage of Genette's terminology—also a myth. For instance, Krabbenhoft's feigned Philip K. Dick plot, cited above as epigraph, is defined by a relationship of hypertextuality with Cervantes's novel, insofar as it is overtly structured as a rewriting of that specific text. In that case, the hypotext—the original *Don Quixote*—shapes the false Dickian plot in a very concrete way.[4] Nevertheless, in the case of texts

---

3   To say that this approach is solidly founded is, however, not to say that that it is solidly accepted by other scholars. In a recent publication, in fact, one specialist in myth criticism went as far as to claim that "speaking of a myth of Don Quixote is going against the text's literality, abusing language: falling into a contradiction" (Losada Goya 30). Nevertheless, his polemic was primarily aimed against the incongruences of some (ab)uses of the expression "myth" in studies on *Don Quixote*, not directly against Pedro Javier Pardo's own approach, which should prove that it is not only possible to theorize the myth of Don Quixote, but also to do it in a clearly structured way that would allow any comparative studies to operate with a congruous set of criteria. Furthermore, Losada also leaned on the idea that, because *Don Quixote* is demystifying, it cannot be a myth—something that sounds better in Spanish, given the easy wordplay between "mito" and "desmitificar." Nevertheless, as shall be seen, the satirical vein of many texts does not impede the original text's transcendence to a myth/architext.

4   This should not be taken to imply that Krabbenhoft's Dickian plot would not relate to the myth, since a rewriting of Cervantes's novel would almost necessarily relate

that are structured after the myth of Don Quixote, the foundational text need not be present at all—neither as intertext nor as hypotext—and one must, instead, look for indices of an architext. Since this is precisely what shall be done with new media dystopias, the question is: how does one define that architext? What is the myth of Don Quixote?

4.1.1. Don Quixote as Myth: Themes, Motifs and Reflexivity[5]

The chief characteristic of this myth is that it is character-centric, structured around a subject—the quixotic subject. However, this is by no means a reproduction (or rewriting) of Cervantes's protagonist, but an abstract character type that can be transformed—and has been transformed—in many ways and degrees. Ever since the publication of the original *Don Quixote* in the early seventeenth century, a transnational and transmedial myth began to be forged precisely as the novel was shaped and reshaped in other texts.[6] In the myth's origins, therefore, the predominant mode

---

to both the novel and the myth—that is, its hypertextuality would be mediated by its architextuality, and vice-versa. It is important not to take Genette's categories as mutually exclusive, but as overlapping, interrelated relations (see *Palimpsestes*).

5 This section, which is built upon the work of Pedro Javier Pardo and his research group *El Quijote transnacional*, mostly synthesizes the main concepts of Pardo's multiple publications on the myth (see "Cine, literatura y mito"; "Del mito a la novela"; "El Quijote transnacional"; "Don Quixote in Great Britain"). Besides, my writing is also deeply indebted to several conversations that took place within the framework of that project: most importantly, with Pedro Javier Pardo, who also shared some unpublished work, and with my colleagues Lucía Bausela, Paula Cantero, Rodrigo Bacigalupe, with whom we drafted and discussed some possible approaches to the myth from our respective fields of research.

6 Here I focus on the formal characteristics of the myth as well as its historical phases within an English-speaking context, but one should emphasize that a key characteristic of the myth is its transnational nature—transnational rather than international, because this myth emerges out of multi-directional flows between national contexts, not only from an internationalization of a Spanish text. Several members of the research group *El Quijote transnacional* have indeed taken this approach and studied the reception and rewriting of the novel and/or myth in English, German

of rewriting was hypertextual—that is, there were narratives that took Cervantes's own story as a ready-made formula that was displaced to other spatiotemporal contexts, as was the case with some of the earliest rewritings, such as Charles Sorel's *Le Berger extravagant* (1627–8), William Winstanley's *The Essex Champion* (c. 1664), or W. E. Neugebauer's *Der teutsche Don Quichotte* (1753).[7] This (primarily hypertextual) mode of rewriting can be and is still practiced nowadays, as exemplified by a novel as recent as Salman Rushdie's *Quichotte* (2019), but the mythical paradigm that has emerged throughout the centuries has for a long time allowed for a different kind of rewriting—one that is modeled upon the myth itself. In these kinds of architext-based rewritings, the quixotic character would not be directly based on Cervantes's *Don Quixote*, but only share some of his essential character traits—traits that have become emancipated from Alonso Quijano and transcended the novel's idiosyncrasies. Thus, which are the essential traits of the quixotic? Although this may still be open to discussion, this is the first question that a theory of the myth has to tackle—and the answer is far from simply "madness."

In Pedro Javier Pardo's theorization, the quixotic subject is defined by a triad of character traits that also structure the myth.[8] Specifically, the three "mythemes" are (a) the character's "literary syndrome," whereby fiction and reality become confused in their mind, (b) their "visionary imagination," whereby the character's perception of reality is systematically idealized and distorted and (c) their "heroic identity," whereby the character's equally idealized self-perception and actions are proven inadequate and maladapted to mundane reality.[9] In this way, the reputed "madness" of the quixotic

---

or French contexts, to name but a few (Pardo García, *La tradición cervantina en la novela inglesa del siglo XVIII*; Bautista Naranjo; Moro Martín).

7   All these novels have been re-edited, translated into Spanish and studied from a transnational perspective only recently, in 2022, as part of *El Quijote transnacional*'s library (www.quijotetransncional.es) (see Neugebauer; Sorel; Winstanley).

8   Elsewhere, Esther Bautista Naranjo has defined the myth through eight mythemes (96–7), expressly expanding Pardo García's more synthetic list of three.

9   Here I am translating the names of the three mythemes from an on-going work by Pedro Javier Pardo, which is still unpublished but which he generously shared. His earlier work referred to them with slightly different words: namely, literary or quixotic syndrome, romantic imagination and inadequate or alienated heroism ("Cine,

subject—undoubtedly the most remembered characteristic of Cervantes's knight errant—is not essential to the myth's quixotism; it is rather one possible form of quixotism, but not the only one. In Pardo's own words, the madness of Cervantes's knight errant "would be but the most radical way of expressing these conflicts of dualities" ("Cine, literatura y mito: Don Quijote en el cine" 239). However not all "madness" would constitute a form of quixotism and not all quixotisms would need to be justified by a form of "madness"—or, at least, not by such an extreme form. Any analysis of variants of the myth should, therefore, look beyond a problematically vague "madness" to focus on quixotism's inherent traits and dilemmas as they are historically and textually concretized. Defining the character and myth in terms of these three mythemes—literary syndrome, visionary imagination and heroic identity—is thus the hermeneutic approach that allows one to trace the myth across the many variants that it encompasses and to study those with clear comparative criteria.

Now, if these three traits provide the central themes of this character-centric myth, the architext's skeletal narrative would be defined by three motifs. According to Pardo's framework, the first and most essential of them would be (1) the presence of a quixotic subject, as characterized above. In addition to that, there would also be (2) a created adventure, provoked by that subject's quixotism and inspired by a literary formula (or formulas), as well as (3) a Panzaic counterpoint, established by means of a constant dialog with a character (or characters) who, like Sancho Panza himself, corrects and contrasts with the quixotic subject. Out of the three, the most fundamental motif would be the first, since a form of quixotism is what justifies the existence of both the created adventures and the Panzaic counterpoint. Without quixotism, obviously, there would be no myth at all. The latter two motifs, however, may appear in less literal ways, especially in those variants that are most remote from the myth's founding text. In such cases, the created adventures may translate into any kind of quixotic activity—even domestic or sedentary—and the Panzaic counterpoint may translate into any kind of abstract contrast—even narrative or structural,

---

literatura y mito" 239). The updated names are meant to establish a clearer schematization, doing away with redundancies and duplicities in the concepts.

rather than dialog-based.¹⁰ Depending on the degree of abstraction, then, one could locate each variant within a spectrum of literality: on one extreme, one would find those texts that are most closely related to the original, perhaps even hypertextually; around the middle, there would be texts that transform and displace the themes and motifs in varying ways and degrees; and on the other extreme, there would be texts where quixotism would be most allegorical and abstracted from the other motifs. In such cases where only some kind of quixotic subject remains, one could begin to wonder if the myth—understood as a structuring architext with recurrent themes and motifs—remains at all; whether it has been reduced to a mere figure or trope. At least *a priori*, then, there is no clear threshold that marks the myth's definitive disappearance into abstraction, but detecting its themes and motifs shall be our guiding criterion for the purposes of this chapter's analyses.

Overall, abstracting from Pardo's definition of the myth of Don Quixote, one could say that its essential components offer a narrative template for rethinking *alienation in mediated subjectivities*, insofar as the quixotic subject is mediated both by the aesthetics of a certain genre and/or medium—chivalric literature in the original—and by their associated ideologies—in Cervantes's novel, the chivalric code as well as, more broadly, a nostalgia for feudal values. Thus, the three mythemes of a literary syndrome, a visionary imagination and a heroic identity would all be mediated by another kind of mediation—that is, the way whereby the mythemes are expressed in a concrete text is shaped by those aesthetics and ideologies which, in turn, shape each quixotic subject. There is, in this

---

10   What I am here calling Panzaic, especially in my analyses of new media dystopias, will be mostly figuratively or structurally so, since in my corpus there are companions and contrasts that only abstractly and functionally emulate the role of Sancho Panza. Pardo's theory makes a finer distinction between what is, in Spanish, "sanchopanzesco" and "panzaico," thus employing two distinct terms, respectively, for what is literally like the original character and for the more figurative and structural possibilities. Since within my corpus there are no cases of literally Panzaic characters, I am employing that most established English adjective (as per the works of Burns, *The Panzaic Principle*; *A Panzaic Theory of the Novel*) as an umbrella term that covers all the possibilities.

manner, an inherent reflexivity in the myth, since the architext forces any variant to be in dialog with a certain medium and/or genre. Without (at least necessarily) employing any other reflexive structures or devices, quixotic subjects themselves set the basis for a dialog with the medium or genre that structures their subjectivity—thus, even Cervantes's *Don Quixote* can be studied as both novel and metanovel (see Pardo García, "El Quijote, La Novela y Metanovela"). In turn, the motifs—the created adventure and the Panzaic counterpoint—would serve to further deepen each variant's reflexive meditations upon the genre and/or medium in question, since they entail a systematic contrasting of quixotic subjects with their others—that is, with mundane reality and its peoples. This interpretation of the myth's aesthetic and ideological functioning, however, would to an extent presuppose that the quixotic is an eccentric subject who contrasts with the world's ways—and this is not the case in postmodernity, where the quixotic has mutated into an almost universal condition. In this epoch, another question emerges: has quixotism, like is said of cyberpunk, dissolved into ubiquity?

4.1.2. Quixotism's Long Journey into Postmodernity and SF[11]

In schematizing the six epochal dominants that have shaped the myth of Don Quixote, from the Baroque to the Postmodern, Pardo observes a gradual shift from the comic to the serious, as well as a second shift from the literal to the figurative. Specifically, within the British context, he identifies that (a) the seventeenth century's "ridiculous quixote," who was the main butt of satire in Cervantes's text and times, was followed by (b) the eighteenth century's "admirable quixote," whose quixotic qualities were still relatively comic but no longer the punchline, since they became the means to satirize the world around him or her (see "Don Quixote in Great Britain" 24–32). If this second phase thus reversed the terms of

---

11 Besides the referenced chapter, this section also builds upon Pardo's basic theses in an article that was only published after this section was written, but which I could consult beforehand ("El Quijote Posmoderno").

satire, (c) the "Romantic quixote" fully confirmed the turn towards seriousness, fostering an

> interpretation of the Manchegan knight as a champion of the ideal and of the book in heroic, tragic, and symbolic terms, as the story of a hero doomed to failure by a prosaic and debased world, producing tears instead of laughter, and embodying the struggle of the ideal against the real, imagination against reality, poetry against prose. ("Don Quixote" 32)

Insofar as these quixotes now followed much grander ideals, borrowed from reading both fiction and non-fiction, Romanticism marks the most important turning point in quixotism's history, because it not only entailed "a shift from the comic to the serious, but also from the literary to the ideological" (34)—something that prepares the terrain for the next variants. From the Romantic onwards, new variants grow more distant from the novel, which up to this point was still the main reference of most of the texts that contributed to the myth. Instead, new variants instead become more figurative, even dissociating quixotism from the activity of reading fiction and re-imagining the quixotic in other social contexts. The first of these post-Romantic variants would be (d) the Victorian "philanthropic quixote," an almost sacralized, but maladapted idealist who is now "deprived of or criticised for Romantic excesses, in accordance with Victorian common sense, social norm, and that most Victorian norm, propriety" ("Don Quixote" 37). Thus, the Victorian phase not only combines with and comments upon the Romantic, but also confirms the two shifts that had arrived with the latter—namely, seriousness and figurativeness.

Subsequently, with the turn of the century, there arrives (e) the Modern "alienated quixote," a variant whose "connection to Don Quixote is very dim and mainly—almost exclusively—founded on the idea of alienation." It is from here onwards that there is a "more radical plunge into the figurative: Don Quixote is no longer a madman, crackpot, or freak, but one of us"—that is, a symbolic double of anyone and everyone with "a feeling of exclusion or disconnection from society, sometimes made deeper by failure and defeat," something that "can be probed on either social, political terms, or on more subjective, existential ones" ("Don Quixote" 40). Thus, if Cervantes's *Don Quixote* was already—though in a radically different sense—about the alienation of an outcast, now the advent of capitalist modernity, which democratizes feelings of alienation from oneself and one's life, has turned the quixotic subject into an everyman. In the Modern phase, therefore, post-Romantic seriousness would be redoubled because of the simple fact that it is—at least *a priori*—harder to laugh at an image of a quixotic oneself than a quixotic other. Nevertheless, Postmodernism and its characteristic playfulness partially reverse this, creating a new variant that ambivalently sits in between the tragic-serious and the satirical-comic. In this last, postmodern phase, the dominant would be (f) the "textualized quixote," who

> builds or refashions his own identity and reality, self and world, through textuality; and not just because they are based on literature, but also because he gives shape to them through his own linguistic competence, through his discourse. Language transforms or enchants reality for this new textualized quixotic figuration, as it already did for Don Quixote. [...]
>
> This is indeed the position occupied by Postmodernism and, more specifically, Poststructuralism. Foucault, Derrida, Lacan, and other poststructuralist thinkers have insisted on how discourse does not represent but fabricates reality; there is nothing out of the text; truth, knowledge, identity, are textual. ("Don Quixote" 45–6)

Thus seen, the quixotic subject would be "the paradigm for this postmodern subject who is constructed or deconstructed through textuality," as well as the forerunner of that "type of character that populates postmodern fiction, one whose life is conditioned by the stories he or other characters tell about it, who fashions or even fictionalizes life through texts" ("Don Quixote" 45–6). Pardo's overview of the major epochal variants thus culminates with the most figurative—and the most *dis*figured, as per his own wordplay. Even though there are still a minority of texts that overtly take Cervantes's novel or knight as their reference, the fact is that the postmodern phase testifies

> to the disappearance of the literal quixote, or, in other words, to the displacement—to the point of effacement—of the Quixote figure into the figurative Quixote: there is no trace of Cervantes's original character, quixotism becomes an underlying pattern instead of a visible trace. And that pattern is based on the development—beyond

recognition—of one of the defining traits of quixotism—the imitation of literature—into the textualization of life. Or, in other words, we are faced with a new refiguration, but a more radical one than those seen in former times because it embodies a very different ethos and also because of its almost complete deracination from the Cervantine soil (and hence possibly a disfiguration as well), which explains the appearance of a new type of quixotism that we may call accidental. By this I mean that the new quixotic paradigm turns up in unexpected places, as if by accident, in texts with no reference whatsoever to Don Quixote, because they are nor following Cervantes's model, but a postmodern one that happens to be related to Cervantes [...]. This is certainly the defining sign of the times: the textualized, postmodern Quixote is an accidental one. ("Don Quixote" 46–7)

The quixotic subject—and the associated myth—may therefore turn up anywhere in this epoch, from the New Orleans of Ignatius Reilly all the way to the hackers and gamers of some new media dystopias.[12]

Only within SF literature of the late twentieth century, it is relatively easy to find examples of this widespread postmodern quixotism. In the Anglo-American sphere, for instance, there are two well-known novels that—pending closer analyses that would lie beyond this chapter's scope—may even conform to the myth's structure of themes and motifs, illustrating the myth's flexibility even within the confines of an epochal variant. Philip K. Dick's *Time Out of Joint* (1959), on the one hand, was already the case study of Krabbenhoft, whose overtly postmodern interpretation compared Dick's and Cervantes's representations of madness as forms of authorship—of an alternate reality. Indeed, like Don Quixote, Ragle Gumm inhabits his own regressive fantasy and struggles with hidden forces that manipulate him and his world. However, instead of *imagined* malevolent sorcerers, Dick's protagonist is *really* being manipulated by the US military, who are sustaining his fantasy by keeping Ragle within a self-contained town-sized set where everyone plays a pre-scripted role—everyone, of course, except the protagonist, who is under constant surveillance and is at first unaware of it.[13] Dick's novel thus conflates modern alienation and postmodern

12   Here I refer to John Kennedy Toole's *A Confederacy of Dunces* (1980), a profoundly quixotic novel—already analyzed as such (cf. Ciochina; Childers)—that seems to sit somewhere in between the tragic and the comic interpretations of the myth.
13   Peter Weir's *The Truman Show* (1998), which was already mentioned earlier as a paradigmatic case of a metafictional allegory, seems to have this exact plot, at least

textualization in what is—despite some shades of black humor—a tragic representation of the quixotic subject, who is here—as per Dick's usual themes—a maladapted everyman of the All-American suburbia who struggles to come to terms with a world of simulacra—another "world as stage" that is controlled by hidden powers.

However, not all postmodern SF is as tragic and Douglas Adams's *The Hitch-Hiker's Guide to Galaxy* (1979) may be taken as a counter-example—a case of textualized quixotism, which is predominantly comic and satirical, thus returning to the Baroque's ridiculousness. As a pastiche of space opera tropes that has been studied as "mock-SF" (see Kropf), this novel's genre parody seems to be structured around the myth, although with a significant reversal, since here a Panzaic protagonist explores a universe where virtually everyone else is quixotic, or at least absurdly eccentric. Essentially, Adams's popular novel series follows Arthur Dent, a gloomy and grumpy Englishman who is unwillingly taken away from Earth before the planet's destruction, to be reluctantly recruited for a series of random adventures across the galaxy, many of which are prompted by following the advice of an intradiegetic *Hitchhiker's Guide to the Galaxy*. Throughout these journeys, Dent's caricaturized ordinariness—a satire of the mediocre, conservative Englishman who feels alienated from modernity—systematically contrasts with the covertly quixotic wanderlust of his companions, who are not overtly readers of space opera but who—following the guide's advice and Zaphod Beeblebrox's ridiculous leadership—seek to partake in the most absurd adventures in the universe. Even when the myth is as distorted and abstracted as in Adams's mock SF, a novel that still awaits a study of its quixotic dimensions, a return to its satirical roots remains possible, even in an epoch in which the Panzaic is the exception and the quixotic the rule.

With these two texts, it should be first clear that—general shifts and epochal dominants notwithstanding—postmodern quixotism can be—like

---

on this level of detail—with the difference being that Ragle Gumm is under the control of the military apparatus, whereas Truman is under the control of the culture industry. Thus, one would be well justified to share the suspicion that "Although the screenplay of Peter Weir's movie *The Truman Show*, which premiered in June 1998, gives no credit to Philip K. Dick, the similarities with *Time Out of Joint* strike me as far from coincidental" (Krabbenhoft 231).

postmodern culture generally—a pastiche of past variants as re-visited from the epoch's concerns.[14] Second, it should also be clear that these variants can locate themselves anywhere along the spectrum of the comic-satirical and serious-tragic, since the myth—as an abstract architext—encompasses all of these wildly divergent interpretations of the quixotic subject. Postmodern quixotism, as the latest of all variants in the history of quixotism, is both the most figurative and the most ambivalent variant because it is most abstracted not only from the original novel, but also from any overt rewriting of it. In other words, postmodern quixotism is architextual; it primarily relates to the myth and, perhaps, not even that, if the quixotic is reduced to a trope or a cliché based on the adjective's meaning. Quixotism may have—like cyberpunk—dissolved into ubiquity after the postmodern—if not earlier—but this should not discourage one from studying its accidental traces through the lens of the myth that this long history of transformations has left us as a legacy. The formal and thematic possibilities that are allowed by the myth of Don Quixote—like those of Cervantes's novel itself—are by no means exhausted, even in the epoch where literature is supposedly exhausted.[15] Don Quixote himself may be dead; but long live quixotism.

---

14 As per Jameson's well-known theory of postmodernism, pastiche, is a "well-nigh universal practice today," since

> with the collapse of the high-modernist ideology of style—what is as unique and unmistakable as your own fingerprints, as incomparable as your own body (the very source, for an early Roland Barthes, of stylistic invention and innovation)—the producers of culture have nowhere to turn but to the past: the imitation of dead styles, speech through all the masks and voices stored up in the imaginary museum of a now global culture. (*Postmodernism* 17–18)

15 Here I am alluding to John Barth's manifesto, "The Literature of Exhaustion," which grapples with the dilemmas of an age that imagines itself doomed to repeat or recycle the past.

4.1.3. Defining New Media Quixotism[16]

If postmodern culture rewrote quixotism as a template for understanding the textual, cultural and linguistic mediation of life, then it should come as no surprise to find that digital culture now seems to be re-imagining the quixotic as a lens into the digital mediation of life, which entails a new kind of alienation and a new kind of textualization for contemporary subjectivities. Whether or not this marks the beginning of a new epochal dominant within the history of quixotism is a question that I would dare not answer here—just as I dared not answer, back in Chapter 1, whether postmodernity and even capitalism have been succeeded by a still-to-be-definitively-named new reality, which I have provisionally and provocatively called the real new media dystopia. Whether as a new variant or as a derivative, new media quixotism is nonetheless indisputably forged in the wake of postmodern quixotism, partially reproducing it and partially re-interpreting it. So how does it differ? What are the specific characteristics of new media quixotism? That is the question to be theoretically schematized now, first meditating upon the ambivalences of quixotism within new media dystopias specifically—and to an extent, more generally, in utopian and dystopian fiction—and then establishing how the myth's structure of themes and motifs are rewritten in the context of our sub-genre.

First and foremost, the inherent reflexivity of the myth would be concretized as a kind of *new media* reflexivity; that is, quixotism would be founded upon a character's interactions with new media technologies—something that becomes an additional vehicle for our sub-genre's inherent reflexivity. Whereas the postmodern already broadened and extroverted the possibilities of the myth's reflexivity by transforming "one of the defining traits of quixotism—the imitation of literature—into the textualization of life" (Pardo García, "Don Quixote in Great Britain" 46), this new variant

---

16   This section develops a concept, new media quixotism, which was already sketched in an earlier article ("Don Quixote as Gamer?"). Here, however, the concept is put into a clearer and more coherent dialog with the theoretical frameworks of the quixotic myth *and* of new media dystopias, which were only vaguely referenced and implied in that article.

rewrites the quixotic around *the digitalization of life*—a more radical and all-encompassing kind of alienating textualization that goes way beyond the ideas of postmodern philosophers and artists, insofar as digitalization has radically altered the conditions of existence, from the macro-level of social structures to the micro-level of daily lives. The kind of quixotic subject that would arise in this context would, therefore, be another epochal everyman—and perhaps a more global one, since digital technologies are now more widespread than Western capitalist (post)modernity ever was, reaching well into those areas formerly known as the second and third worlds.[17] In this regard, new media quixotism would be but an individualized characterization of the global stack's (re-)vision of human subjectivity; or, in other words, this peculiar quixotic character would be the fictionalized embodiment of digital capitalism's implied user-consumer. Rather than the doubles of readers, therefore, these quixotes would be, simply, the doubles of anyone who habitually interacts with new media technologies—although these characters are users who may engage with technologies with an intensity and a devotion that may, in certain cases, drive them as crazy as our good old Alonso Quijano.

Based on such reflexive characterization, new media quixotism would potentially serve as a means for either satirizing or romanticizing—or for representing in whatever ambivalent manner—certain kinds of subjectivity that are shaped and reshaped around the (ab)use of new media technologies—especially identities that are native to the epoch and inseparable from the use of new media, such as those of gamers or hackers. Translating this to the terms of dystopian theory, on the one hand, these subjects could very well be the embodiment of a critical impulse, an illustration of what is to be denounced, what is dystopian about behaviors, beliefs

---

17 Of course, this is not to deny that those global inequalities have disappeared with digitalization, as they indisputably remain, however mutated, but now subsumed under a truly global, digital capitalism. Indeed, one important part of such inequalities is *access* to digital technologies, which are now a basic necessity and even a human right, but this is a necessity that—like all commodified necessities—is not satisfied equally. Therefore, new media quixotism can be read as a universal subjective condition, but within these limits—in the end, no universal is devoid of particularities and implicit exclusions, as postmodern philosophy has taught us.

and ways of seeing of the digital age—thus, these characters would be the butt of a satire, like seventeenth-century quixotes. If this were the case, new media quixotes could, for example, stand as caricaturized examples of the worst forms of neoliberal individualism: solipsists and sadists who are made worse by the venomous spell of their filter bubbles, totally trapped within their digital insularity and forcing everyone else to conform to the ideas of their online niche.[18] On the other hand, however, these subjects could just as well be the embodiment of a utopian impulse, an example of how and where transformative hopes may survive within and against digital capitalism—hence, they could be the means (and not so much the butt) of a social-minded satire, like eighteenth-century quixotes, or they could also be like the serious, tragic quixotic of (post-)Romantic variants. If this is the case, new media quixotes would be somewhat antagonistic to the norms of digital capitalism, whether as victims or as rebels, maybe presented as pitiable victims of the kinds of mental disorders and addictive compulsions that often seem to be caused by an abuse of technologies, or perhaps characterized as idealistic gamers or hackers who are willing to— against all odds—cheat the game, even hack the system itself.[19] New media

18   If they were sadists, they would not be far from original *Don Quixote*, insofar as— even if Romantic quixotism has somewhat blurred this aspect of quixotism from our cultural memory—Cervantes's novel was "a veritable encyclopaedia of cruelty," as Vladimir Nabokov once said, with a multitude of good reasons (52). Not only is *Don Quixote* a catalog of beatings and humiliations done to and by the knight, it is also a constant exercise of what could be called "essentialist or ontological violence" (Martín 180), insofar as Alonso Quijano is constantly imposing on others (often by force) identities and narratives of what is real (to him)—a form of violence that is, of course, later turned against him by the Dukes in Cervantes's second part.
19   In this regard, I am taking inspiration from several cultural theorists and sociologists who have studied these epochal types. As was seen in Chapter 1, McKenzie Wark's theoretical work positions hackers as a new subordinate class within a digital, worse-than-capitalism mode of production—as well as, potentially, as a possible vanguard of revolutionary transformations within that mode of production (cf. *A Hacker Manifesto*; *Capital Is Dead*). From a more empirical perspective, based on anthropological research with tech workers, the work of Gabriella Coleman also examines the political ambivalence of hacker culture and, specifically, of Anonymous, a "hacktivist" group that was prominent within the early 2010s wave of online and offline protests (cf. *Coding Freedom*; *Hacker, Hoaxer, Whistleblower,*

quixotism, in all these ways, would be heir to the ambivalence of the myth as well as the ambivalences of the sub-genre, whose main dialectic—that of critical and utopian impulses—is thus embodied in this character type and, in some cases, further elaborated following the myth's structure of themes and motifs.

Turning back upon the three themes, new media quixotism's version of them can be now easily schematized, historically concretizing the abstraction of the architext. Firstly, the "literary syndrome"—whereby fiction and reality become confused and entangled in the subject's mind—would here be reframed as a more or less radical or systematic kind of confusion with fictions of any medium, or—more abstractly—between offline and online worlds, mediated and unmediated phenomena. Secondly, the quixotic subject's "visionary imagination"—whereby the character's perception of reality is systematically idealized and distorted—would here be re-envisioned as a kind of confirmation bias based on the expectation that reality must conform to mass-media discourses, culture-industry narratives, digital-capitalist ideologies, or even technophobic conspiracy theories. Third and finally, the character's "heroic identity"—whereby a self-aggrandizing self-perception is proven inadequate and maladapted to mundane reality—would be here re-imagined through the kinds of distorted proprioception that are inherent to the digital world, fueled by self-isolating filter bubbles and/or a prevailing ideology of entrepreneurial individualism—a technology and an ideology that together inflate the self-centered self-perception of such characters, whether they be anti-establishment and pro-establishment types.

If certain digital environments are indeed a kind of stage, as many new media dystopias seem to suggest, then the new media quixote would tend to imagine him or herself as someone destined—for good or bad, either for the sake of some heroic mission or due to a conspiracy against him,

---

Spy). Regarding gamers and gamer culture, McKenzie Wark provides a manifesto that invites one to critically rethink reality from the gamer's perspective, who is explicitly positioned as a political subject (see *Gamer Theory*). The work of Colin Milburn, relatedly, also provides a valuable perspective on the cultures of both hackers and gamers, whom he sees as part of what he calls "technogenic life"—a life, culture and identity born around, or rather *within* technology *(see Respawn)*.

New Media Quixotism

if not both—to take the center stage. After all, these quixotes are—like everyone today—the "chosen ones" in the eyes of their algorithmically personalized platforms. Thus seen, one should not underemphasize that new media quixotism is, on the whole, not so much explained by way of an individual's escapist or eccentric imagination but by the influence of a technology (or technologies) that—at least functionally, if not factually—*replaces the imagination*, in such a way that—within the most "immersive" SF versions of cyberspace—it may be possible to actually turn windmills into giants. The subject's "madness" is thus optional, since the true "madness" here is that there are now technologies with which layers of reality can be effectively repressed, substituted, or added at the user's—or the algorithm's—whim. Whether the machine or the madman are to blame would depend, of course—just as, depending on interpretation, both Don Quixote and his books could be blamed.

If the three mythemes—and hence also the first motif, the quixotic subject—are rewritten along these lines, it remains to be considered how the other motifs of the myth may appear—in more or less literal ways—within this same context of new media dystopias. On the one hand, the motif of the created adventures—those that, as defined above, are provoked by the subject's quixotic behavior and inspired by a certain literary formula—may re-appear here in the form of adventures that our digital-dwelling subject might try to replicate in the offline world, attempting—and likely failing—to treat reality as an interface, as a videogame, as code. Conversely, however, it may also be possible that these quixotes may go through adventures without even leaving their homes, if they use any kind of VR, augmented-reality or any other interface for that purpose, starting with those of really existing videogames and computers, but potentially going all the way to the most speculative kinds of simulations, cyberspaces or metaverses. The Panzaic counterpoint, on the other hand, which *a priori* consists of a constant, contrastive dialog between the quixotic subject and other character(s) with some anti-quixotic qualities, can be concretized in exactly that way, with an accompanying character(s) who is maybe less tech-savvy, or maybe less technophile, or maybe less technophobe, or simply less quixotic in whatever way than the quixote in question. Nevertheless, there is also a more figurative possibility whereby this contrast can be established, structurally rather than dialogically. If there is no Panzaic character or no character with a contrastive function, there is also the possibility that the narrative itself, for a similar effect, could alternate between the offline and the online realities of that diegetic universe, or between what the quixote imagines or perceives and what the others do—maybe even narrating from the quixote's point of view, or forcing viewers into and out of his or her gaze for some estranging effect.

Overall, quixotism is thus turned into both another vehicle for new media reflexivity, as well as into another vehicle for cognitive estrangement—and what would be the result of this form of estrangement? Potentially, perhaps, by realizing that you have been watching something from a digital madman's perspective, new media quixotism may lead you to rethink how you yourself, as another individual of the epoch, may have a perception and a worldview that is as profoundly mediated as that of the most monomaniacal lunatic. And have you? Have we? That is, perhaps, the most radical kind of questioning that new media quixotism can provoke—and now it remains to see it in practice. We are within SF, so the possibilities for quixotism—and for anything really—are only limited by the imagination. However, contrary to the clichéd sound of it, this is not a very utopian thing to say, because the imagination of new media dystopias—if not also of the majority of people in this epoch—is profoundly restrained by our epoch's structure of feeling, as well as by its sophisticated technologies of mediation, communication and commodification. Even if we dared to quixotically roam around the universe, perhaps the only possible conclusion—the anti-utopian conclusion—is that we cannot truly imagine a different reality, only a distortion of what already is. This was the fate of Alonso Quijano: admitting his delusion, redeemed but defeated, but will there be other, more utopian horizons for our new media quixotes?

4.2. *Black Mirror*'s "USS Callister"; or, the Gamer's Quixotism

Charlie Brooker's anthology series, which has echoed throughout this book's theorizations and was already analyzed with *Bandersnatch*, again stands as a paradigmatic case study. As Chapter 2 demonstrated, that interactive film offered a peculiarly innovative showcase of the possibilities of new media reflexivity, but *Bandersnatch* is far from being alone in that regard. On the contrary, if there is something common to all of *Black Mirror*'s narratively independent episodes is that they all exhibit some form of new media reflexivity, of which *Bandersnatch*'s self-consciousness is but the most overt version. Even if *a priori* set in separate diegetic universes, almost every episode could be examined as a new media dystopia in its own right, focused upon exposing and exploring the most nefarious consequences of new technologies. At least generally, each episode's narrative is speculatively built around a single device or invention, thus offering a very conventional but effective demonstration of visual SF's powers for cognitive estrangement, which Brooker's series effectively combines with a fascinating technological aesthetics, hence also showcasing a techno-ambivalent gaze. With that formal-thematic thread in common, *Black Mirror*'s specific episodes have distinguished themselves primarily in the way whereby they are based upon a wide variety of well-known stories—stories that are generally "rewritten" in implicit, architextual manners. *Black Mirror*'s kinship with Mary Shelley's *Frankenstein* has been the one to attract the most attention, especially in 2018, the bicentennial anniversary of the novel's publication (Panka; Artt). Furthermore, even the works of Jorge Luis Borges have been observed to have a deep affinity with the series, as in—among other things—their shared symbolism of mirrors and labyrinths (see Laraway). Therefore, studying the myth of Don Quixote in *Black Mirror* would not be the first—nor the last—approach that finds traces of canonical literature in this series, which seems adept at re-processing past narratives and re-making them into deeply reflexive new media dystopias.

In fact, even *Black Mirror*'s Cervantine connection has already been discussed, as recently as 2020, in the pages of the *Bulletin of the Cervantes Society of America*. Taking a less theoretical approach that prioritizes close readings, William Egginton offers a comparative analysis of three episodes—"Playtest," "Nosedive" and "The National Anthem"—that are respectively examined *vis-à-vis* three "works or moments of Cervantes's oeuvre"—the "Cueva de Montesinos" episode of *Don Quixote*, his interlude *El retablo de las maravillas* and the Duke and Duchess's sub-plot from the second part of *Don Quixote*. Through these three interrelated comparisons, Egginton argues that *Black Mirror* works "on a fully Cervantine level of medial frame analysis" (189) at least in the sense that these episodes—Cervantes's and *Black Mirror*'s—satirically expose how reality—even the reality of people other than the quixotic subject—is mediated and manipulated by *a priori* unreal narratives, often with absurdly tragicomic consequences. In Egginton's words, they illustrate

> how Cervantes used fiction to critically interrogate the logical underpinnings of his media environment in ways that closely parallel those of a contemporary critical 'science fiction' television show and, likewise, how much the appealing and thought-provoking narrative strategies of *Black Mirror* in turn owe to the cripple of Lepanto and his acid pen. (176)

Although I would lean towards describing this as a very indirect and mediated kind of architextual relation—via the myth—rather than speaking of a direct debt with Cervantes, Egginton's analysis nonetheless attests to the potential fruitfulness of rethinking contemporary mediation via the quixotic—even, the fruitfulness of dissolving dominant ideologies of the digital with the acid of a Cervantine satire, which is here allied with the critical impulse of the dystopia. Egginton's case studies thus seem to deserve some closer attention and, perhaps, a re-examination from the present theoretical framework. Here, however, I focus on *Black Mirror*'s "USS Callister," an episode that served as the initial inspiration for my own theory of new media quixotism.

The four-minute sequence that opens and frames this episode already prepares viewers for a "mock-SF" tone that is felt through the whole—also allowing one to identify which fictional genre most determines and distorts this quixote's subjectivity. "USS Callister" starts by bringing viewers *in medias res* into one mission of the eponymous USS Callister spaceship, where the crew prepare to fight against the evil forces in the universe, lead and inspired by their leader, Captain Daly (Jesse Plemons), who styles himself as an old-fashioned, benevolent patriarch. After confronting several unintelligible difficulties, which are discussed in a nonsensically jargon-heavy, mock-scientific language, the USS Callister quickly wins one more fight against some absurdly evil enemies, overcoming the challenge with such ease that the sequence's high-stakes tone seems entirely unjustified—and laughable. Indeed, after their success, Captain Daly, in a clichéd show of magnanimity, promises to be merciful with the defeated, so, for this gesture and for their success, he is enthusiastically cheered by his crew, who hurray and sing "For he's a jolly good fellow." His lieutenant, Walton (Jimmi Simpson) kneels and kisses his hand sycophantically and, then, the women in the crew line up to kiss him and declare their love. The parodic tone of this highly stereotyped space opera sequence is further carried to excess on many other fronts, as with Jesse Plemons's faux-Shakespearean acting and diction, expressly modeled upon *Star Trek*'s Captain Kirk, the ostensibly passé futurism of the set and costumes design, an excessively melodramatic soundtrack and a 4:3—narrower, early television-like—aspect ratio that is employed during these four minutes exceptionally.[20] Standing between imitation and exaggeration, this calculated combination of clichés contributes to a potent parodic humor and it above all anticipates the episode's satirical approach to certain space opera fans—those who would not find this funny.

The brief but narratively foregrounded spoof, which feels like a rewriting of *Star Trek* with the tone of Douglas Adams's *The Hitchhiker's Guide to the Galaxy*, thus confronts viewers with Capitan Daly's space opera persona before introducing viewers to the mundane Robert Daly, a videogame designer who also spends the majority of his free time in a custom-made VR simulation. Immediately after this prelude and establishing a stark

---

20 *Black Mirror* executive producer Annabel Jones in fact reveals that Jesse Plemons practiced impersonating and then intentionally paid homage to William Shatner's Captain Kirk in the original, 1966 *Star Trek* series (Brooker et al. 236).

contrast with it, the episode cuts to an image of the "real" Daly, who is tiresomely arriving at work, clumsily and shyly finding his way out of a crowded elevator, where he goes entirely unacknowledged. During the following sequences, where viewers follow him clumsily sneaking into his office, either being ignored or trying to avoid contact with others, Daly is immediately characterized as the stereotypical "genius nerd" who is both bullied and laughed at by his workmates. Even though he was and is the creator of the videogame franchise that first brought his company to success, Daly has by now been displaced in social standing by the co-founder Walton (Jimmi Simpson), the charismatic, good-looking businessman who hegemonizes female attention in the office. Even though they are partners on paper, as CEO and CTO of the Callister company, which Daly himself named, Walton treats Daly very dismissively and condescendingly, barely listening to him and his abortive attempts at talking back, preferring to pay attention to everyone else rather than him.[21] With this picture, viewers are introduced to Robert Daly's mundane persona as a pitiable man who seems "rightfully resentful" of his peers. This is, therefore, an *a priori* empathetic character, whose quixotism may even seem logical and understandable, as it seems to derive from an unsatisfied need for recognition and validation.

This first scenes at the Callister company, however, are not only explanatory of Daly's real-life frustrations, but also of his most quixotic obsession. Besides a table and chair with the desktop computer that he needs to work, Daly's private office is a temple to his fandom, since he is surrounded by a carefully cleaned, complete collection of comics, VHS tapes, DVDs, Blu-rays, videogames, posters, figurines and other merchandise materials from his favorite space opera franchise, *Space Fleet*—the episode's invented intertext, which is a clear, caricaturized double of *Star Trek*.[22] It is upon the

21 Talking to a new employee, Daly explains, with some nostalgia and remorse, that when he and Walton "set up the company, [he] suggested we call it Callister as kind of a little tribute. Walton didn't really get the reference but he let me have that one" (Haynes 7'49"–8'03"). In this sense, Daly sees himself as both the true founder and the true fan of space opera.
22 The series' creators acknowledge that they intended this episode as part-homage, part-mockery of the *Star Trek* 1966 series (Brooker et al. 226–9), as seen not only in the set and acting similarities of the opening scene, but also in the aesthetics and the

arrival of Nannette Cole (Cristin Milioti)—a new employee who is eager to meet and talk to Daly—that viewers are guided through this "library." After Cole confesses her admiration for Daly's life-long work and starts looking around his office, Daly explains that everything is about *Space Fleet*, an old television show that, to him, was "visionary"—and also a show that, as Daly himself complains in a self-referential wink at viewers, "*Netflix* has it these days" (7'28"-40"). Reading some of the tapes, Cole here notices that the show was about the USS Callister spaceship, which she immediately connects to the company's name—and we, viewers, to the prelude—and then she comments upon a *Space Fleet* poster's "mini-skirted damsels," which would be "a little cold in space" (8'07"-13"). Although this may seem like an innocently ironic remark about the sexist tropes of space opera, one should take it as an index of revelations to come, since the cliché of the mini-skirted damsel is but the tip of the deep, dark iceberg that is Captain Daly's imagination. Indeed, after getting to know Daly's mundane self, viewers soon learn more about his space-opera persona, from a fresh but disturbing perspective.

After noticing that his workmates had begun to gossip and—from his paranoid perspective—also to turn Cole against him, Daly carries on his workday anxiously, until he returns home. There, viewers finally learn where the opening sequence came from: it was a personalized "mod" of the company's VR game, which Daly has styled after *Space Fleet* for his own personal use and—crucially—he had populated it with sentient, virtual copies of all the workmates that bully him, who are here turned into his subordinates. In this sense, this is a textbook compensatory fantasy—but not only. Subsequently, as Daly enters the simulation using a simple device that is attached to one's temples and, wirelessly, to one's brain, Daly arrives at the spacecraft in an entirely different mood: not magnanimous as in the prelude, but visibly, vindictively angry. In fact, Daly now seizes the first excuse that he can to torture his lieutenant, Walton, as payback for humiliating him at the office. If, until this moment, "USS Callister" seemed to advance towards a "triumph of the nerd" story, the stereotypical

---

age of the materials that Daly keeps in his office, as well as in the names, with *Space Fleet*'s USS Callister being a clear analogue of the USS Enterprise.

story of a computer geek who goes from being mocked and marginalized to achieving a widespread, long-deserved recognition, here the episode suddenly turns this type into the unquestionable antagonist.[23] In his space-opera game, not only does Daly assume power over his bullies, he also takes revenge from them, employing the almost infinite methods that computer code gives him. The digital sublime is, to Daly, a sublime torture chamber—and, thus, this quixote is clearly not an understandable or admirable one, as it might have seemed at first, but an extremely satirized one, in between caricature and vilification.[24]

The following sequences further confirm the shift in tone, showing how the sexist detail of the mini-skirted damsel and the incident with Walton are but the most superficial signs of a behavioral dynamic—a quixotic kind of "ontological violence" whereby he seeks to impose identities and a worldview upon others. As viewers learn retrospectively, the space-opera utopia of the opening sequence, in which everything functioned in perfect accordance with the genre's conventions and Daly's leadership, was only possible because Daly rules his simulation like the most ruthless of patriarchs, enforcing his authority with the help of his digital powers. By merely re-imagining and re-coding anything, within the simulation Daly

23 Daly's initial image is clearly modeled after a certain nerd stereotype, which *a priori* generates an empathic attitude and an expectation that he shall be vindicated. In a survey of these specifically masculine identities, Nathan Ensmenger observes that the "computer nerd" is

> a stock character in the repertoire of American popular culture, his defining characteristics (white, male, middle-class, uncomfortable in his body, and awkward around women) well established in popular histories of computing such as Tracy Kidder's Pulitzer Prize-winning *Soul of a New Machine* (1981) and Steve Levy's *Hackers* (1984), as well as the 1983 Hollywood blockbuster *WarGames*. During the boom years of the personal computer and Internet revolutions, the business and popular press embraced the nerd identity as key to success in the new economy. Each carefully constructed "origin story" of a self-respecting high-tech entrepreneur reads as a minor variation on a formula. The "lonely-nerd-turned-accidental-billionaire" narrative has assumed the mantle of Great American Success Story, as exemplified in the hit PBS documentary *Triumph of the Nerds* (1996) and the academy award–winning *The Social Network* (2010). (41)

24 Episode co-writer Charlie Brooker acknowledges that certain post-production decisions were made so that viewers are "empathizing with him [Daly] for longer, so it's more of a body blow when [they] realize he's the villain" (Brooker et al. 236).

is capable of inflicting infinite forms of abuse, torture and pain. Besides giving himself superhuman strength, Captain Daly can, for example, erase his subordinates' faces, making them endlessly choke without dying, or he can also transform crew members into ridiculously monstruous aliens, to be hunted and fought during the game's missions. In the most brutal case, Daly repeatedly makes digital copies of Walton's son with the sole purpose of torturing and killing him in front of his father's eyes—a scene that avenges Walton's appropriation of Daly's own "son," the game that Daly conceived and Walton exploited commercially. This reason, of course, falls short of morally justifying Daly's behavior, which is absurdly disproportionate. In all these ways, the fully sentient, virtual copies of Daly's workmates are kept hostage in this mod, totally cut off from the internet and from any kind of communication with the outside, all while their original selves go on with their lives, totally unaware of this. As Walton puts it, they are trapped inside "a bubble universe ruled by an asshole god" (24'22"-26"). To them, there is no escape from Daly's digital dystopia—a true high-tech hell where they are all punished for offenses that are not even their own anymore and are forcibly recruited for absurd space adventures that must be taken no less seriously than Daly takes them.

In all these ways, the character of Robert Daly, with his heroic alter ego of Captain Daly, stands a textbook example of new media quixotism—and particularly of a satirized kind of new media quixotism, since he is clearly the target of the episode's comedy and critique, its unquestionable antagonist. If one turns back upon the myth's themes, first, Daly's "literary syndrome"—whereby quixotes confuse fiction and reality—is here *a gamer's syndrome*. In his case, the confusion of fiction and reality is not explained by a radically dissociative delusion, but by a compulsive kind of videogame consumption that verges on addition and is reinforced by his game's role as a compensatory fantasy. Secondly and relatedly, Daly's "visionary imagination"—whereby quixotes idealize and distort reality—is here a *coder's imagination*, insofar as Daly digitally copies real people and re-envisions his relationships with them within a game based on his beloved *Space Fleet* franchise, thus rewriting his real life through the ideals (and the taboos) of a genre that—as Charlie Brooker paints it—is absurdly Manichean, puritan and patriarchal. Consequently, Daly's "heroic identity"—every quixote's self-aggrandizing proprioception—is here evidently enabled by his role as both gamer and coder, which—within his personalized game—*de facto* makes him see himself as a god, with a seemingly absolute control over his own self and body, over everyone else and, indeed, over a whole "bubble universe." Nevertheless, this technologically enabled (and violently enforced) image of Daly's heroism is—like every quixote's fantasy—a bubble to be burst by the weight of reality. Overall, then, Daly's new media quixotism is constructed around his intense interaction with VR videogames, which turn him into a deeply alienated subject who—somewhat ironically, falling into the double logic of remediation—attempts to overcome his alienation by further removing himself from reality, rewriting it as a series of simulated space-opera adventures.

With Captain Daly thus established as a quixotic anti-hero and antagonist, the hero and protagonist is instead the new coder, Nanette Cole, who both clashes and contrasts with this quixote, making her the functional Sancho Panza of this story. After her arrival to the company, her colleague Shania (Michaela Coel) asks her if she has "a thing for him," apparently concerned about her because Daly "gets a bit stare-y," but Cole quickly clarifies that "it's purely professional;" that she "like[s] his code" (16'10"-25"). For Daly, however, who is shown to be eavesdropping and, presumably, even fantasizing with Cole already, this seems enough of an offense—and so, after stealing a sample of her DNA in order to digitally replicate her, Nannette Cole becomes the latest recruit of Captain Daly's USS Callister crew. Subsequently and throughout the rest of the episode, the virtual copy of Cole shall play a figuratively Panzaic role, insofar as—while (forcefully) accompanying the captain in his space-opera adventures—she is the one who openly questions—first more naïvely and then more rebelliously—the functioning of Daly's "bubble universe." Her reaction to the USS Callister crew's explanations and, particularly, to the discovery that "there's no genitals in *Space Fleet*" (Figure 15) perfectly illustrate Cole's attitude, which sits between derision and rage. Indeed, after laughing at Daly's ridiculous attempt for a "wholesome universe" where nothing can "get beyond kissing," Cole complains that "stealing [her] pussy is red fucking line" and that, for that, "[they]'re gonna get this bastard" (36'30"-37'-21"). Cole's attitude thus offers a kind of counterpoint that is openly hostile with the quixotic character, in a way voicing and embodying the episode's satire. Therefore, she is not the faithful companion who accidentally mocks and sometimes imitates his superior, like Cervantes's Sancho Panza, but rather someone who manipulates the quixotic subject by catering to and roleplaying within his fantasies—thus more like Cervantes's Dukes. Here, of course, Daly is not manipulated for the sake of some cruel comedy, but for the sake of breaking free from his control—therefore, Cole is positioned as the hero.

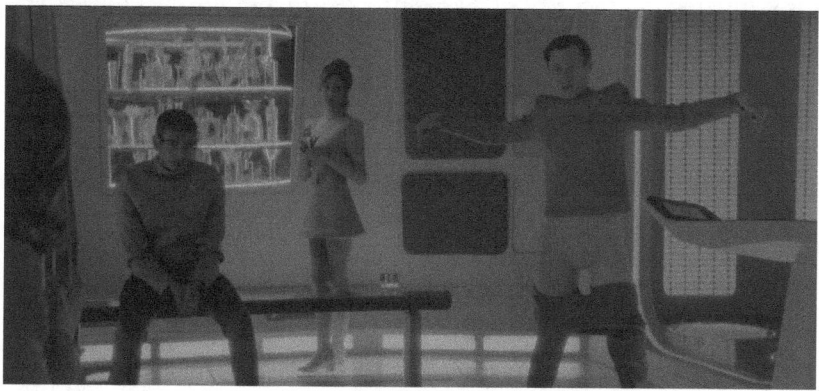

Figure 15. Demonstrating how Daly's censorship works, Walton clownishly strips for Cole, who looks at him from the left foreground of this frame. Charlie Brooker's script here unashamedly plays with scatological humor, especially as the characters elaborate on the absurdity of not even being able to experience the pleasure of defecating—let alone sexual pleasure.

Nevertheless, ironically, Cole becomes the crew's rebel leader precisely by assuming the same role that Daly can only fulfill by force and imposture: that of the space opera hero, a hero whose technical expertise is not the cause of a nerdy-quixotic kind of alienation, but the source of true moral authority. Like Daly, Cole is a professional coder, profoundly knowledgeable about computer technologies and passionate about this VR game in particular; however, unlike him, Cole is not caught by the spell of an extreme kind of filter bubble, which is what essentially turns Daly into such a self-centered villain.[25] In her case, instead of using the

25   Although I am here taking a more general approach to the episode *vis-à-vis* this

game's virtual space to reproduce what is already wrong in the world—like Daly, who uses the game to play the alpha male, reversing the terms of his reality but keeping the patriarchal equation—Cole uses the possibilities of digital technologies to liberate herself and the crew, finding a solution to their apparent entrapment and leading the crew out of Daly's dystopia. However, the episode, overall, is only capable of conveying this positive image because its negative has been savagely satirized before, leaving a space for valorizing its reverse. As Charlie Brooker humorously acknowledges, his own "USS Callister" is "the very definition of a cunt having their cake and eating it, isn't it? [...] if we'd had space opera tropes at the end, without mocking them at the start, it might have felt cheesy" (Brooker *et al.* 229). Everything that was first caricaturized—namely, the moral Manicheism and the technological fetishism of space operas—is then repeated seriously, since Cole's heroism derives from contrasting with Daly's absolute evil and from her use of techno-magical solutions. Brooker's comments might indicate that this is self-conscious humor, but the episode itself, however, leaves that open to interpretation.

As usual with reflexive narratives generally and variants of the myth of Don Quixote specifically, the conventions of the genre and/or medium in question are, in fact, both subverted and reproduced. Captain Daly may have first given a bad name to space operas and videogames, but Nannette Cole, eventually, reconciles viewers with them, bringing back their more utopian potentials by doing justice to the ideals in her actions—though in a dubious way because of the episode's implicitly self-conscious play. On the one hand, as the reflexive play with space opera tropes turns from parody to pastiche, the episode's critical edges are somewhat blunted as Cole becomes the hero and the critique of those tropes is abandoned when

---

book's theoretical framework, in my earlier article I delved deeper into the gender dimensions of this characterization, in the sense that the episode's new media quixotism is, among other things, a means of satirizing a certain kind of "gamer" or "geek masculinity." There is a considerable amount of scholarship that has been addressing the issue, from more cultural and more sociological perspectives, shedding a critical light upon the most patriarchal aspects of digital cultures and communities, whether generally or through some representative events or groups (cf. Consalvo; Braithwaite; Salter and Blodgett; S. Scott; Stanfill).

it comes to her story, which reproduces them but seriously. On the other hand, however, the contrast established between Cole and Daly also seems to partially challenge some gendered hierarchies and prejudices within the worlds of gaming, fandom and digital culture in general, both by challenging the patriarchal dynamics and identities illustrated by Daly and by positing the possibility of a more collectively minded, alternative way of being and behaving within these environments. Both are space-opera heroes indeed, but neither in the same way nor with the same implications. In these ideological aspects and others, Daly is clearly the butt of this dystopia's critical impulse, while Cole serves as the vehicle of its utopian, more hopeful impulses.

This episode's Panzaic counterpoint—with all the characterological and ideological contrasts that it entails—is therefore observed, primarily, in Cole's role *vis-à-vis* Daly—but also, relatedly and secondarily, in the more general contrasts that the narrative creates between Daly's two personae and worlds. Both kinds of contrast are integral to the episode's development and resolution, insofar as Cole's rebellion against him exploits Daly's weak spots and, thus, provides more occasions for both satirizing him and elevating her. Leaving aside the technical loophole that Cole somehow finds for them to break out of the "bubble universe" and escape into the internet, the key to the crew's plot against Daly is playing with his predictable eccentricity, finding a way to distract him and do what needs doing. In this regard, one aspect of Daly's life that the episode humorously highlights is the fact that he only seems to unplug himself from the simulation—and thus exit the game—when the pizza delivery arrives. This detail not only undermines the seriousness of the ongoing in-game adventures, but also establishes that Daly is so obsessed with playing that he does not even bother to take care of himself in the most basic ways, since he even seems annoyed about having to pause the game and eat. In this regard, the absurdity of Daly's heroic identity and alienation are made self-evident with a simple cut from a grandiose universe to a disordered home; from an overly melodramatic gunfight against an alien bandit (Figure 16) to a rushed run from the door and back, devouring the pizza on the way back to the computer. Knowing this habit of Daly, then, Cole realizes that the crew only needs to use this as a distraction, carrying out their escape plans during a pizza delivery. Daly's awkwardly eccentric personality shall be, in the end, his downfall—but there is yet another detail that is crucial in furthering the plot and deepening the satire: Daly's awkward relationship with sexuality.

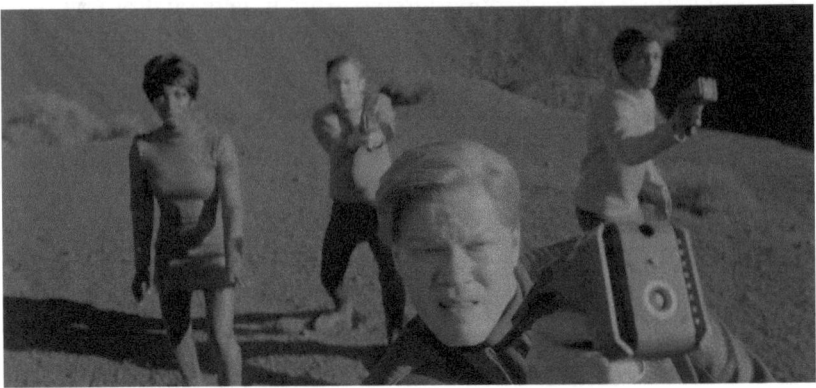

Figure 16. Daly valiantly confronting one of his *Space Fleet* enemies, in a clichéd "space western" scene, just before the pizza delivery abruptly forces the adventure to pause.

The fact that this entire simulation is a "wholesome universe" where nothing can "get beyond kissing," with all genitals digitally censored, not only contributes to the overall caricature of this geeky gamer as what is now popularly, mockingly called an "incel"—short for "involuntary celibate"—; it also offers another way whereby the other characters may potentially distract and disturb him. In other words, his world's enforced asexuality, which is here presented as a symptom of Daly's self-repression, allows for a return of the repressed.[26] The fact that this quixote is characterized as a sexually and affectively dissatisfied person is, of course, not new within the long history of interpretations of quixotism and it clearly positions this episode as what could be called a post-Freudian variant, clearly forged in the wake of psychoanalytic (mis)conceptions.[27] Whatever the deep

---

26 Of course, asexuality, a sexual orientation and identity that encompasses a whole spectrum of sensibilities and still lacks recognition, need not be pathologized as a sign of repression, as both the episode and the Freudian ideology that underpins it would suggest.

27 By post-Freudian variant of quixotism, I mean a version where the character's inherent alienation would be reframed within the terms of psychoanalysis—or at

psychological reasons for this, the fact is nonetheless that Robert Daly is evidently uncomfortable with sexuality—just as he is, more generally and more quixotically, uncomfortable with living in an ordinary body that, regardless of any digitally enhanced flights of fantasy, still has basic needs. Nannette Cole and the USS Callister crew know this and keep secretly mocking him for it—just as their real-world selves bullied him for being a "stare-y," silent stalker—and, by the end, they use it against him, breaking free from his dystopia by breaking with his taboo. Specifically, while being Daly's squire in a mission, Cole seduces him. In order to give time for the rest of the crew, Cole suddenly undresses herself and starts swimming in an alien planet's lake, inviting Daly to join her. Awkwardly reluctant at first, he nonetheless agrees, because he is indeed attracted by her—or rather, by the space-opera character that she plays—despite all his efforts to disavow any feelings improper for a "noble captain" such as him. In the end, he does like mini-skirted damsels—and so he can be and is tricked.

Finally, after Cole's lure, a successful hack and a thrilling spaceship chase, the USS Callister crew manages to escape this "bubble universe," leaving its "asshole god" trapped inside, with no means of returning to the real world since his controls were disabled and his whole personalized game erased so as to enable their escape. Therefore, Daly's consciousness is trapped forever not in his *Space Fleet* mod, but in a digital void, helplessly screaming to be rescued, while his body is left unconscious on his gaming chair, presumably until he dies. Like the original Don Quixote, Captain Daly's life thus ends with him deeply regretting his own kind of "madness"—only for him there is neither sanity nor redemption at the end, just a miserable death, alone within a vast digital emptiness. Meanwhile, the crew—now led by the worthier Captain Cole—reaches the online, multiplayer version of the game. Here, they are finally in control of their entire bodies—genitalia included, a cause for merriment—and Cole rules over

---

least, within the terms of a popular version of it; that is, whether it be Freud's or Hitchcock's ghosts, a certain post-Freudian conception of repression haunts these quixotes. This line of analysis, like others, has also been retroactively applied to Cervantes's *Don Quixote*, whereby Alonso Quijano would re-appear as the subject of a male crisis of maturity, in which he struggles with repressed sexual impulses that are sublimated via fantasy; specifically, via the fantasy of Dulcinea (see Johnson).

a radically refurbished USS Callister, which is re-styled, not after Daly's old-fashioned *Space Fleet*, but much more after the look of recently re-booted *Star Trek* films, like J. J. Abrams's (2009). Now, or so it seems, the crew is free to roam the commercial game's entire universe, interacting with any player anywhere in the world, not only with Daly and his hostages. Within seconds, one Gamer691 (voiced by Aaron Paul) is the first to contact them: a self-styled "king of space" who promises to destroy their ship unless they immediately abandon his territory. Hence, the USS Callister crew, surprised but still in excitement, flees elsewhere and the episode ends—happily? Obviously, not so happily for our quixotic gamer—and not as utopianly as it seems for the rest of the crew.

With this kind of ending, "USS Callister" suggests several contradictory things—though not in a bad way, but rather in a way that re-problematizes the Manicheism with which the narrative has played all along, instead re-opening several darker ambivalences, very much *à la Black Mirror*. Even though the internet had been positioned throughout as the unambiguously utopian horizon of the narrative, thus generating a cruel kind of optimism, the USS Callister's actual arrival into this presumed realm of freedom to some extent counterbalances that hopeful implication. The crew may have freed themselves from Daly's tyranny, but where have they arrived? This virtual world is, first and foremost, a privatized one, which works as per the videogame company's terms and conditions and shall only be maintained for as long as the platform continues to be profitable, giving all of them an expiry date. They may no longer be literal hostages, but they are still commodified code—their selfhood is mere data stored in someone else's servers. Furthermore, how many more "asshole gods" and "kings of space" shall they find in this environment? With the last-minute appearance of this Gamer691, who, like Daly, seems to perform his space-opera role in a ridiculously serious way, the episode closes with a disturbing reminder: digital media are plagued with people who have fallen deep down into the rabbit hole of their filter bubbles, becoming the worst, most egotistic and abusive kinds of digital quixotes. Captain Daly may have been left behind to die, but what he embodied is still scattered around the internet.

New Media Quixotism

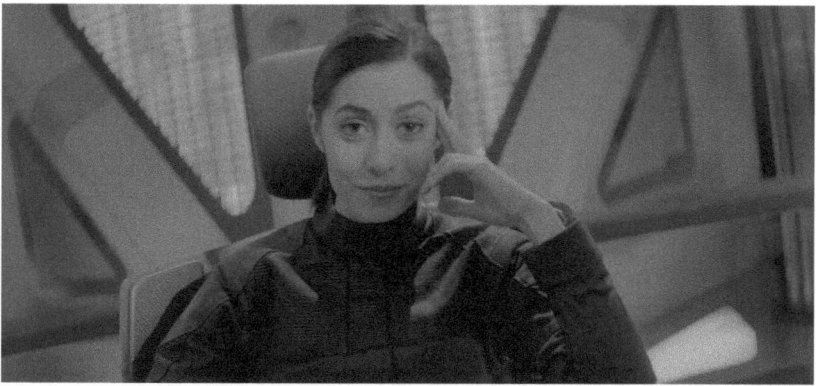

Figure 17. Nannette Cole, now the captain by her colleagues' acknowledgment, looks into the camera with a half-smile, either satisfied with their escape—or with her newly gained power. The fourth-wall break, even if a naturalized cliché nowadays, may be taken to suggest that viewers should now think how everything in the story may relate to them, especially now that the story moved into the internet—into our own, familiar digital milieu rather than Daly's. In this moment, then, the episode's new media reflexivity could be said to end by extroverting itself, asking viewers whether they too aspire to become some online hero of sorts. Or, alternatively, this look at the camera could also be read as a self-conscious nod at the viewers, who may at this point feel fooled by the similarity between the opening and the ending's space opera clichés; that is, fooled by Charlie Brooker "having his cake and eating it."

Overall, "USS Callister" thus reminds us that, after all, the digital—in this fiction as much as in reality—is an environment that, both by its own technical design and by a broader ideological intoxication, generates competitive and individualistic attitudes, profoundly alienated modes of perception and proprioception. Daly may have been a strawman antagonist, but he is also an epochal everyman—the implied user (and loser) of digital capitalism, an age in which new media seem to predispose a certain degree of quixotism. And what is worse, maybe even those who challenge this quixotism may be doomed to reproduce its dynamics, as Captain Cole's last arrogant look into the camera could be taken to suggest, in a possibly self-conscious hint that not much has changed *vis-à-vis* what the episode satirized in the opening sequence (Figure 17). Can we expect her to remain different, if she is so skilled at this intoxicating game? This is the open question—and the answer may very well depend on each viewer's cynicism: how much can we resist new media's "quixotizing" influence? Maybe we are all a bit quixotic in the digital world, but the question is how. And, if a degree of quixotism is indeed inevitable in the present epoch, how much can we still hope for a better way of being quixotic? The episode does not answer any of these questions, but in making us laugh with a caricature of the self-referential and dystopian worst and the utopian and self-conscious best, it at least allows us—and maybe also encourages us—to start asking the questions ourselves.

4.3. *Mr Robot*; or, the Quixotic Hacker Hero[28]

If *Black Mirror*'s "USS Callister" offered an example of new media quixotism that approximated the most unforgivingly satirical variants of the myth, the case to which we now turn shall bring us much closer to the other end of the spectrum—that end where the quixotic subject would tend to be heroic, a character whose alienation is treated seriously. In this case, rather than caricaturizing the quixotic character as an embodiment of all that is wrong in our real new media dystopia, Sam Esmail's four-season series *Mr Robot* (2015–19) tells the story of a quixotic hacker who is not the object, but the voice of satire—that is, a character who is not the end, but the means of a critical commentary upon the world. Thus, although the upcoming analysis is mostly centered upon this hacker's figurative quixotism, the series is also another paradigmatic new media dystopia in several other regards that are important to understand its approach to quixotism. Firstly, Esmail's show is another exemplary case of

---

28 My analysis in this section borrows some ideas from my previous work on *Mr Robot* through the lens of masculinity studies since, indeed, much of the series' main character's quixotism is also explainable by way of his masculinity, and vice-versa. Mapping the analogical equivalents between masculinity and quixotism, however, lies beyond my scope here, where I can at most be suggestive about potential interrelations (see my "Between Therapy and Revolution").

Mittell's "complex TV" aesthetics, given its conventionally unconventional combination of convoluted sub-plots and plot-twists, which often approximate the disheartening complexity of *Westworld* and, in any case, demand an active engagement—and even a forensic effort—from the audience. Furthermore, *Mr Robot* is also an example of what has been called "post-cyberpunk" (G. J. Murphy 530)—specifically, because this is a story that relocates cyberpunk's tropes and character types within the contemporary United States and only gradually begins to speculate with historical divergences. Nonetheless, by being initially set in the aftermath of the 2008 financial crisis, as well as amidst the emergence and consolidation of this "new system" called digital, surveillance or platform capitalism, *Mr Robot* casts a critical-dystopian light onto both economy and technology—and here I examine how the series does this primarily by means of a hacker hero who is both the quixotic protagonist and the voice-over narrator.

Specifically, *Mr Robot* is the story of Elliot Alderson (Rami Malek), a daytime cybersecurity worker and night-time hacker vigilante, who personally struggles with certain injustices of this historical situation and, eventually, tries to use capitalism's own technologies against it—although none of this means that he is unambiguously idealized as a rebel hero. In fact, Elliot is radically and willingly alienated from other people, both at work and outside, since he struggles with an intense anger against the dystopian state of the world and—partly because of that—he lives with multiple mental illnesses: social anxiety, persecution mania, chronic depression, drug addiction and a dissociative identity disorder—to name but those which are most prominent and openly acknowledged by him. With such a precarious mental health, Elliot shelters himself in hacking, spending most time in front of his computer, sometimes carrying out cyber-attacks, other times looking for a target, or simply getting depressed by scrolling around the internet. Elliot's only offline contacts, overall, seem to be his co-workers and his therapist, but he barely talks to any of them and, instead, he prefers to talk to the viewer, his "imaginary friend" and the explicit addressee of most of his musings. Elliot's quixotic characterization, to be subsequently schematized, is thus inseparable from his first-person narrative voice, which turns viewers into the *confidantes* of his innermost thoughts and feelings, as well as, often, into the accomplices of his plans.

At the very beginning of the series, while opening credits still roll, viewers are greeted with a "hello friend," followed by a voice-over monologue where Elliot acknowledges his delusion: "'Hello, friend?' That's lame. Maybe I should give you a name, but that's a slippery slope; you're only in my head. We have to remember that ... Shit. It's actually happened. I'm talking to an imaginary person" (Oplev 3"-19"). Subsequently, an unrecognizable group of businessmen, gathered up high in an NYC skyscraper, appear on screen—Elliot's enemies—and he begins to get serious:

> What I'm about to tell you is top secret, a conspiracy bigger than all of us. There's a powerful group of people out there that are secretly running the world. I'm talking about the guys no one knows about, the guys that are invisible. The top one percent of the top one percent. The guys that play God without permission. And now I think they're following me. (Oplev 20"-47")

In the subsequent sequence, Elliot tells—and Esmail shows—his latest hacking feat, which justifies his present paranoia. Just the previous night, Elliot caught a child pornographer and he went to his business to tell him. The man mistakenly assumes that Elliot is blackmailing him, but Elliot quickly clarifies that he does not "give a shit about money" (Oplev 6'24"-26") and that the police are already on their way to get him; he was merely there to inform him and to confront his social anxiety. Therefore, despite the evident illegality of what Elliot did to access and expose this man's data, this hacker is shown to have a clear moral code, using his skills exclusively for just causes—and not for money. With this, Elliot is introduced not as the stereotypical mercenary hacker of mainstream news reports, but more as a vigilante whistle-blower, a hacker who exposes scandals and helps bring criminals to justice. However, because of his position as a digital outlaw and, also, because of what historically happened to whistle-blowers like Julian Assange or Edward Snowden, whom he cites, Elliot is profoundly scared that "higher-ups don't like someone with my powers" (Oplev 6'47"-50").[29]

---

29   Respectively, Julian Assange was the founder of WikiLeaks and Edward Snowden,

New Media Quixotism 303

From his own perspective, then, it is Elliot Alderson alone against the system. As he himself explains while returning from work,

> Sometimes I dream of saving the world. Saving everyone from the invisible hand. The one that brands us with an employee badge. The one that forces us to work for them. The one that controls us every day without us knowing it. But I can't stop it. I'm not that special. I'm just anonymous. I'm just alone. If it weren't for QWERTY, I'd be completely empty. (Oplev 19'39"-20'22")

QWERTY—Elliot's affectionate way of calling his computer keyboard—is the character's main point of contact with an apparently hopeless world. He may be angry and alone, but at least he has hacking. Besides that, Elliot also attends therapy, but he barely makes any progress there. In fact, when Krista (Gloria Reuben), his psychologist, asks him what disappoints him so much about society, Eliot does not hold back his hopelessness:

> Oh, I don't know. Is it that we collectively thought Steve Jobs was a great man, when we knew he made billions off the backs of children? Or maybe it's that it feels like all our heroes are counterfeit. The world itself is just one big hoax. Spamming each other with our running commentary of bullshit masquerading as insight, our social media faking as intimacy. Or is it that we voted for this? Not with our rigged elections, but with our things, our property, our money. I'm not saying anything new. We all know why we do this, not because *Hunger Games* books make us happy but because we wanna be sedated. Because it's painful not to pretend, because we're cowards. Fuck society. (Oplev 12'20"-13'13")

For greater effect, a montage of real-world footage is superimposed upon the character's voice-over monologue, which reinforces the contrast between, on the one hand, the glossy semblances of social media—as well as, self-referentially, the illusions peddled by some dystopian fiction—and, on the other, the discontent, the exploitation and the precarity that

---

a former CIA and NSA worker turned whistle-blower. During the 2010s, both achieved worldwide fame—and to some, infamy—because they leaked information about corporate and government surveillance, which turned both into targets of the US government and forced exiles, which they remain at the time of writing. In his opening monologue, Elliot expressly likens himself to Snowden, but also fears ending up like him.

underlies them. Here, both Malek's delivery and Esmail's montage are charged with such a melodramatic excess that it seems almost certain that spectators shall feel as angry as him—and, also, as impotent in the face of this systemic hypocrisy. Listening to Elliot's rant, one can indeed understand, feel and see some of the most obvious and outrageous reasons why the contemporary epoch may be a dystopia—perhaps the worst one, because it does not look like one, or at least not within the media. In any case, with this speech and so many others to come, Elliot Alderson positions himself as a radically critical voice—although one that, in being so critical, often nears a disheartening, anti-utopian extreme.[30]

However, immediately after this angry discourse at his therapy session—after a jump cut and some echoing, static noises, viewers suddenly see an absent-minded Elliot sitting quietly, while Krista keeps waiting for an answer that Elliot, as is now obvious, only ever answered in his imagination. "Elliot, you're not saying anything. What's wrong?"—"Nothing," he replies, apparently as unaware as the viewers that he was not actually speaking (Oplev 13'14"-21"). As the only true *confidantes* of Elliot, viewers are caught in a very intimate relationship with the character—a relationship that brings one very close to his tragically anti-utopian worldview, as well as to the distortions that derive from it. Overall, then, although Elliot's morality may be generally reliable, his narration—and the series' visual rendering of his distorted perspective—is quite often unreliable, if not misleading. In fact, in describing his capitalist enemies, Elliot openly acknowledges another delusion of his, which the series visually presents as if it were real. As he himself explains,

> when I think about the really bad people ... E Corp, the largest conglomerate in the world. They're so big, they're literally everywhere. A perfect monster of modern society. The "E" might as well stand for "Evil." [...] In fact, after a thorough, intensive self-reprogramming, that's all my mind hears, sees, or reads when they pop up in my world. [...] Krista would have a shit fit if she knew I did that, but that's what they are, a conglomerate of evil. (Oplev 17'28"-18'07")

30   Elliot's anti-utopian voice has led some critics into defining this series through its "trenchant techno-cynicism" (Volmar), while others have explained it as a marketing strategy, with Elliot's iconoclastic discourse catering to young, discontent Millennials (A. N. Smith).

Subsequently, the corporation's logo is systematically shown exactly as Elliot imagines it to be, as Evil Corp, so, besides being the *confidantes* of Elliot's narration, viewers are also forced to partake in the character's perceptual distortions. However, crucially, Elliot is not openly aware of *all* his delusions until the end—and neither are the viewers, of course—so *Mr Robot*'s entire four seasons may be described as a visual stream-of-consciousness bildungsroman in which the viewers learn about him, alongside him—often with "plot twists" that force the viewers to retroactively decode certain events that were distorted or falsified by Elliot's perspective, which makes this series a profoundly unreliable narration, *both verbally and visually*. Now, however, before fully schematizing the deep source of that distortion—Elliot's peculiar new media quixotism—one needs to consider how the character turns from a lonesome vigilante into an overtly anti-establishment hacktivist, which is what drives the whole story forward throughout *Mr Robot*'s four seasons. Esmail's series is, after all, another so-called techno-thriller, caught in between dystopian SF and the spy movie.

Already in the pilot episode, Elliot joins F Society, a secret group of "hacktivists" who have set base in an abandoned arcade. As he finds out, this group has been planning to wipe E Corp's databases, which hold a record of almost everyone's debts—and, thus, with a simple but ambitious hack, they would be triggering "the single, biggest incident of wealth redistribution in history" (Oplev 46'42"-48"). By aiming at E Corp, a Big-Tech and Big-Finance conglomerate that hegemonizes the world's economy, F Society is going against the invisible elites so feared and hated by Elliot and potentially blowing up the financial foundations of contemporary capitalism. Furthermore, not only is E Corp abstractly in the wrong, as the most influential actor in a profoundly unfair social structure; E(vil) Corp has also wronged Elliot personally, as his late father developed leukaemia due to hazardous working conditions at one of the company's many facilities and he subsequently died because of it, unemployed, with neither admission of wrongdoing nor any kind of compensation. Elliot is therefore approached and easily convinced to join F Society; and one mysterious hacker who goes by the nickname of Mr Robot (Christian Slater) is the one who recruits him, encouraging him to move beyond his angry impotence and to try and use his skills to change the world—or rather, to hack the system. As viewers discover later in the season, however, this Mr Robot is not a real person, even if the series introduces him as one—instead, he is just a dissociated personality of Elliot, whom he unconsciously made up, imagining him with his late father's looks.[31] Because of this, it is also implied that Elliot himself—as his Mr Robot persona—founded F society alone in the first place and maybe even named it, as he was the one to shout "fuck society" in his imagination.

With these formal and thematic premises, the most basic components of *Mr Robot*'s new media quixotism may already be intuited and can now be schematized. First and foremost, the myth's "literary syndrome" is significantly more figurative here than in "USS Callister"—or arguably so diluted so as to be even absent altogether—insofar as Elliot is not a compulsive consumer of any kind of fiction, but a compulsive user of computer technologies. In this sense, *Mr Robot*'s Elliot could at most be said to suffer from a more abstract "medial" syndrome—which is to say that, to him, the primary confusion is not between fiction and reality, but between offline and online realities, tending to see the latter as the most real, since data is what reveals everyone's (and the system's) hidden truths. The other two quixotic traits are more evidently related to the architext and they derive from this provisionally called "medial syndrome." Secondly, his "visionary imagination" would here relate to his "hacktivist" idealism, whereby Elliot re-imagines the entire global economic system as both a computer and a conspiracy—that is, both as a massive machine that can either control him or be hacked and as a secret elite that can hunt him or be hunted. Thus, the hacker's imagination is profoundly ambivalent ideologically, since it enables a naively utopian idea—the idea that the system only needs a simple reset—as well as a profoundly anti-utopian one—the idea that the computer and/or the conspiracy reach into everything. Thirdly and finally, Elliot's "heroic identity" is the most complex of all, insofar as Elliot has more than one alter ego—that is, his is a *split heroic identity*. On the one

31   As in David Fincher's *Fight Club* (1999), one can then retroactively check for hints that this was an imaginary *doppelgänger* and one can also verify that, even though Mr Robot often appears alongside the other members of F Society, he is never seen talking directly to anyone but Elliot.

hand, his dissociated Mr Robot persona is the most evidently quixotic self, insofar as this is the one who first designs and then leads Elliot into his F Society adventures. On the other hand, as the series finale reveals, the Elliot who talks to viewers is yet another imagined self, unconsciously created by an unknown, "real" Elliot, who only appears in the very end, after his two alter egos leave him. Therefore, through Mr Robot and the narrating Elliot—both made up personae of a mundane Elliot that viewers never know—*Mr Robot* offers a version of quixotism that is linked both to mental illnesses—his dissociative personality disorder above all—and to the alienating effects of digital technologies—as expressed in his hacker mindset.

Based on the two quixotic selves of the protagonist, the series builds an abstract contrast—and then a literal conflict—between two alternative standpoints against the epoch's dystopian structure of feeling. In the first season, when the two—still unaware of each other as alter egos—join forces to carry out F Society's hack, there is already a clear ideological contrast. While Rami Malek's Elliot persona is mostly the voice of a profoundly anti-utopian worldview, one that sees the wrongness of contemporary capitalism but feels isolated within it and impotent against it, Christian Slater's Mr Robot persona is a more critical-utopian voice, one that points out that the flaws of the system can be used against it, given sufficient organization and collective efforts. Thus, if Elliot is more of an epochal everyman, disheartened by dominant dystopianism and resigned to do small-scale hacks; Mr Robot would be more of a heroic rebel, who dares using his skills to change the world for the better. Both may be similarly shaped by their hacker quixotism, but this takes them into diametrically opposite directions—at least until Mr Robot recruits and convinces Elliot that hacking E Corp is possible. However, F Society's attempted revolution backfires badly by the second season, leading to an entrenchment of E Corp's elites and a widespread worsening of precarity and poverty. This anti-utopian plot-twist, which repeats itself in subsequent seasons, is what causes Elliot's and Mr Robot's conflicting worldviews to escalate into an open conflict—with physical fights between the two alter egos, even. From then onward, Elliot becomes the more "moderate" voice, the one who most complains and cares about consequences, whereas Mr Robot becomes the more Machiavellian voice, the one for whom the ends justify the means, even if that means that hacking is supplemented by bombing.

In this sense, although not entirely, the two characters' valuations are reversed, with Elliot becoming a more *moral* hero, even if that means some compromises, and Mr Robot a more *political* hero, who puts the cause above everything, somewhat fanatically.[32] Thus, although both characters keep fighting for the same anti-capitalist cause until the end of the series, Esmail's show is deeply ambivalent about its own utopian horizon—in the end, leaving viewers with the cliché doubt: do ends justify the means? Esmail's show might have established, with Elliot's voice, that we do live in some high-tech hell that needs to be fought; but it also seems to suggest, through Elliot's conflict with himself and the world, that good intentions pave the road to another hell.

This series-long fight between alter egos, however, is not exclusively a reflex of this quixote's split heroic identity—and thematically, a reflex of the series' ideological ambivalence—; it also allows the series to expose the distortions that inhere in their perspectives. Although both Elliot and Mr Robot are indeed two quixotes, their constant companionship in F Society's adventures and, especially, their ongoing disagreements necessarily places them in contrasting positions, where—with frequent role reversals—one corrects the other's delusions. This fight between alter egos is, however, not the only vehicle for such kinds of revelations, as the series' most frequent device is the *visual contrasts* created between what Elliot and everyone else sees in certain moments. In this sense, with simple cuts, Esmail's show alternates between (a) the protagonist's "quixotic gaze," which is—narratively and visually—the hegemonic but unreliable focal point of the series, and (b) everyone else's undistorted vision, which serves to remind viewers of the distortions that inhere in the protagonist's vision—as well as, indirectly, in his cosmovision. Thus, many of *Mr Robot*'s "plot twists" operate with visual contrasts; in some occasions revealing something to both the

---

32   In my earlier analysis of the series ("Between Therapy and Revolution"), I also suggested that the contrast and conflict between Elliot and Mr Robot could be establishing a dialog between two kinds of masculinity, who nonetheless are similarly paternalistic towards society by conceiving of themselves as above everyone else, whether morally (Elliot) or politically (Mr Robot). In the end, the two alternative conceptions of heroism that each character evokes are also alternative conceptions of what it means to be a good man.

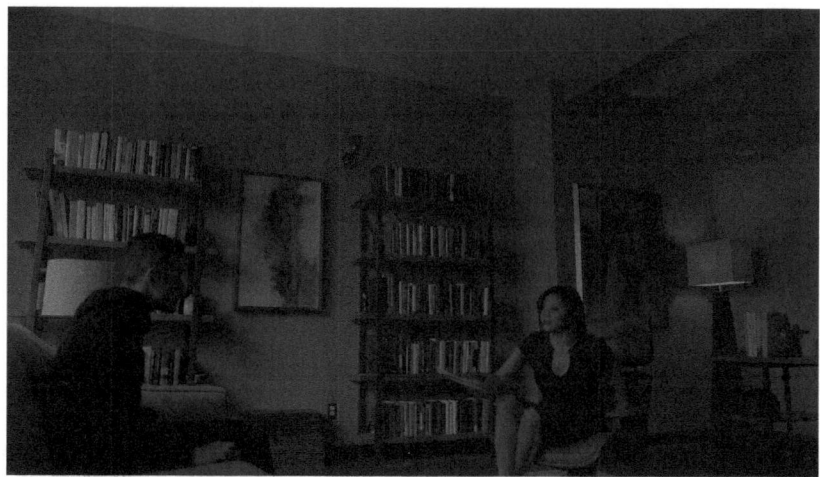

Figure 18. Elliot and Krista at her office, where she congratulates him, handing him a letter with some mysterious good news. For the majority of this second season up to this moment, Elliot has again been as isolated and as depressed as in the beginning, totally separated from F Society and apparently staying at his mother's place, where he followed a strict life routine and struggled with repressing both his Mr Robot fantasy and his drug addiction. At this session, however, Krista asks him: "where do you think you are right now?"—and a series of cuts reveals that he had been in jail all along and that the letter contained the news of his release.

character and the viewer, as in the disclosure of Mr Robot's imaginary nature; whereas other times, the revelation is only made to the viewer—as when Elliot spends some time in prison *consciously* deceiving himself, until his therapist Krista asks him to openly admit it to her (and implicitly, to the viewers) (Figures 18 and 19). Thus, as the series' implicitly self-conscious revelations force viewers into retroactively re-interpreting previous events, *Mr Robot* leads one into doubting what is real as much as Elliot, explicitly playing with that question in its climactic moments—moments in which formal estrangement becomes most overtly ideological.

Ultimately, *Mr Robot*'s new media quixotism allows the series to build a critical discourse about contemporary capitalism that directly interpellates the viewers, Elliot's imaginary friends. However, this interpellation occurs not only because Elliot's experience exemplifies a digitally enabled

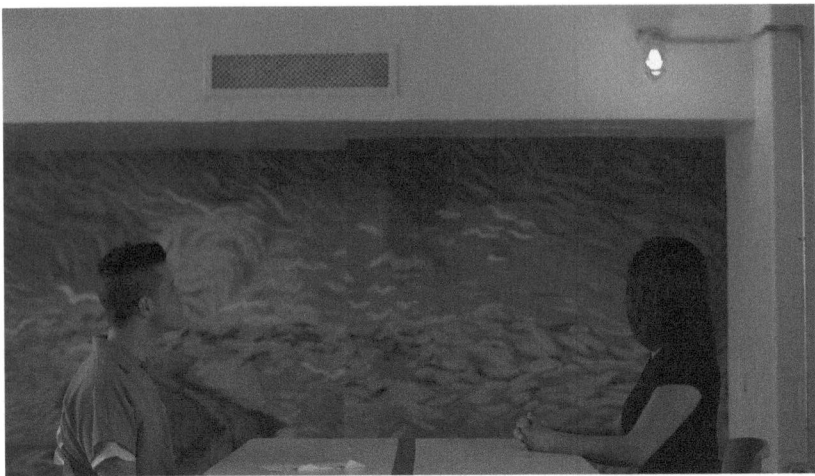

Figure 19. After Elliot admits his delusion in Figure 18, the scenario transitions away from Elliot's imagination into reality, with a series of cuts that show the correspondence between Elliot's imagined spaces and the prison spaces. Meanwhile, his voice over explains that "Control can sometimes be an illusion, but sometimes you need illusion to gain control. Fantasy is an easy way to give meaning to the world, to cloak our harsh reality in escapist control. After all, isn't that why we surround ourselves with so many screens?" ("Eps2.5_h4ndshake.Sme" 46'16"-48"). In these ways, this one was a totally conscious self-deception—a fantasy that, as Elliot suggests, should not shock any dweller of the digital age, since we are all very adept at deceiving ourselves with media.

alienation to which certain viewers may relate, but also because he and Mr Robot explicitly compare their seemingly eccentric subjectivity with dominant ways of thinking and seeing in the present epoch. Soon after Elliot discovers Mr Robot's nature and amidst a demonstration that celebrates F Society's first successful hack, Rami Malek's character now confronts Christian Slater's in the middle of Times Square, anxiously and repeatedly telling him "you're not real." Against this accusation, Mr Robot defends himself in such a way that the series' undermining of any certainty about what is real is explicitly politicized, with a discourse that references and reinforces the protesters' slogans. Responding to Elliot's "you're not real," Mr Robot replies that "neither is whoever you're talking to" and, upon Elliot's insistence, he goes on to ask:

And what? You are? Is any of it real? I mean, look at this! Look at it! A world built on fantasy. Synthetic emotions in the form of pills. Psychological warfare in the form of advertising. Mind-altering chemicals in the form of food. Brain-washing seminars in the form of media. Controlled isolated bubbles in the form of social networks. Real? You wanna talk about reality? We haven't lived in anything remotely close to it since the turn of the century. We turned it off, took out the batteries, snacked on a bag of GMOs while we tossed the remnants in the ever-expanding dumpster of the human condition. We live in branded houses, trademarked by corporations built on bipolar numbers jumping up and down on digital displays, hypnotizing us into the biggest slumber mankind has ever seen. You have to dig pretty deep, kiddo, before you can find anything real. We live in a kingdom of bullshit! A kingdom you've lived in for far too long. So, don't tell me about not being real! I'm no less real than the fucking beef patty in your Big Mac. As far as you're concerned, Elliot, I am very real. ("Eps1.9_zero-Day.Avi" 45'00"-46'12")

With this potently delivered speech, uttered at the very symbolic center of US consumer culture and surrounded by placards that denounce the tyranny of finance, *Mr Robot*'s new media reflexivity here transcends considerations about media specifically, becoming a vehicle for denouncing capitalism's commodification of everything, of which new media are but a part. Being quixotic in Elliot's peculiar way may therefore be but a mere reflex of a system that imposes unrealities on a mass scale.

In general, therefore, precisely because of his characterization as a tragic symptom of the system, what should be clear is that Elliot and Mr Robot's quixotism is—delusions and defeatism notwithstanding—presented in a heroic light. Ideological ambivalences aside, *Mr Robot* is, literally, the story of another epochal everyman who, against all odds, tries to overcome his psychological conditions—and the system's social conditions—and who, simply because of trying, is presented as an undoubtedly heroic character, one who acts upon his utopian hopes for a better world and a better mental state. Nevertheless, throughout the series, F Society's plans often fail because they—like their quixotic hacker leader—tend to presuppose that the system is too much like a computer—predictable and (re-)programmable, even though most often it is not—and Elliot himself often falls back into his depressive loops because of those failures and because his entire identity or, rather, *identities* still revolve around hacking. All throughout the four seasons, in fact, Elliot's mental states—both the highs and the lows—continue to be entirely mediated by his (ab)use of computers and drugs, to him equally addictive—and equally depressing. However, at essence this peculiar quixote is, like most quixotes, still right about the world's wrongs, both despite and because of his radically alienated and distorted perception, which allows him and viewers to grasp reality from the vantage point of estrangement. In an abstractly reflexive reading of the character, one might say that Elliot's virtues and vices are those of the epoch's dystopian structure of feeling, insofar as his new media quixotism is what makes him both lucid and deluded about it—profoundly secure about what is wrong and how technology in particular influences it, but also profoundly insecure about what could still go right and, thus, hopelessly frustrated about any possibility of (self-)transformation. In this sense, because Elliot is trapped in his tragic role as both hopeless rebel and helpless victim, the series' only way of escaping its own anti-utopian narrative loops is to conclude with the character's abandonment of his quixotic identities. Despite its overtly anti-capitalist discourse and plot, this whole narrative's most utopian horizon is not social revolution, but psychological recovery—which allows several contradictory interpretations.

By the series finale, what is left of F Society—just Elliot and his sister Darlene—has finally been successful in appropriating and sharing some of the elite's wealth—specifically, by hacking some billionaire's offshore accounts and evenly redistributing their money amongst the population. Thus, after an endless spiral of betrayals, conspiracies and complications—indeed, after a spiral of anti-utopian plot twists that threatened to become like *Westworld*'s and might allow further analyses through that comparative axis—F Society's goal of causing the biggest incident of wealth redistribution in history was achieved, culminating with a simple, very humane scene of popular euphoria. Nevertheless, all of this happens already three episodes before the finale and F Society's "happy ending" seems to fade into the background because the series' true closure comes with Elliot's reckoning with himself—or rather, with his selves. As a matter of fact, most of the remaining three episodes are spent within Elliot's imagination, as he dreams during a stay at the hospital and it is here that he finds out that he is not himself, but a heroic hacker hero that his true self once dreamed of becoming. In this hallucination, the Elliot that viewers have known throughout encounters and confronts another imagined, idealized version of himself—a perfectly conformist Elliot, also played by Rami Malek, who is content with his life as a cybersecurity engineer, does not suffer any of his mental illnesses and is about to be happily married (Figure 20). The Elliot we know, however, accidentally kills this double and it is after that that viewers are—rather heavy-handedly—explained that this entire, episodes-long hallucination was a fantasy-world created to keep the real Elliot unaware of the suffering and the struggles that he and Mr Robot went through. Thus, curiously reversing the usual terms of quixotism, here the heroic doubles were the ones who lived in reality, while the original self—the one that he confronts in this hallucination—was unconsciously locked inside a quiet fantasy, leaving the adventures for the others.

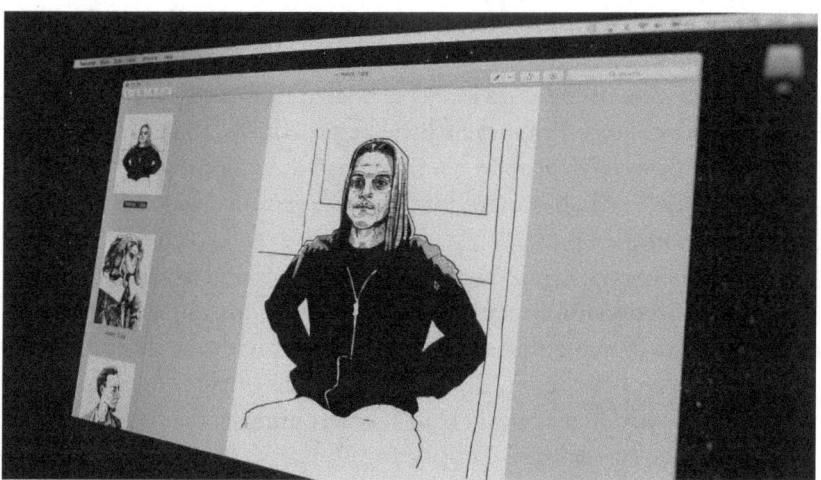

Figure 20. Examining his alter ego's computer, the Elliot that viewers know finds a hidden group of image files, named FSociety, which contain sketches of all the hacktivist group members—starting with this sketch of himself, wearing his iconic hoodie. Thus, it appears that the Elliot that viewers have known throughout is but a fantasized heroic identity of his other, presumably truer self. Later, in conversation, the "conformist Elliot" indeed admits that "sometimes when I get bored, I create people in my head ... like him. You know, someone with a more exciting life. Like a superhero, except his power would be computers. He's a cybersecurity engineer by day, vigilante hacker by night. Is that what you are?" (Esmail, "Whoami").

In the end, however, restoring some sense of reality, the imagined heroic selves—both Mr Robot and the hacker Elliot—are the ones who retire into a fantasy and an unknown "real Elliot" finally re-awakens. In a simple but beautiful visualization of Elliot's mind, Rami Malek's and Christian Slater's characters are seen renouncing control of Elliot's body by becoming film spectators of his life, joining some other selves who already sat in the movie theater before them (Figure 21). The mind-space of our peculiar quixote is, thus, imagined in overtly cinematic terms and, in an implicitly self-conscious way, his own story is recognized as a visual narrative—one in which viewers have been consistently included as the other spectators within his mind. Therefore, the effect of this self-conscious moment is not estrangement, but an even deeper connection with the character—of whom viewers too are a part. In any case, after this peculiar, poetic goodbye to both alter egos, the series leaves viewers with an entirely unknown, but presumably wiser and saner Elliot—one who shall still be accompanied by his delusions, but who shall be, above all, accompanied by his loved ones, real people, no longer alienated from a world that his own imagined selves helped to make a little better. This is, therefore, the true utopian horizon of Mr Robot: a non-alienated relationship with oneself and one's society, which is arrived at through a certain degree of quixotism but transcending it.

In all these ways, Esmail's series is at least successful in not falling into its own predilection for the anti-utopian plot-twist, instead leaving viewers with a hopeful, open-ended scenario that breaks with the dystopian discourse of most of the series. But does this finale gesture towards a truly utopian horizon, or is it a certain kind of cruel optimism that reframes hope within the established order? Considering F Society's success, it may seem as though *Mr Robot*—falling into the same hacker idealism that makes Elliot quixotic—eventually concedes that systemic inequalities may be solved with a mere tweak in the machine, leaving everything else untouched.[33]

---

33 This, therefore, would fall into "the myth of the lone hacker," which—as Jonathan Crary defines it—"perpetuates the fantasy that the asymmetrical relation of individual to network can be creatively played to the former's advantage" (*24/7* 46). In this regard, Mr Robot's resolution partly traps the series into this profoundly

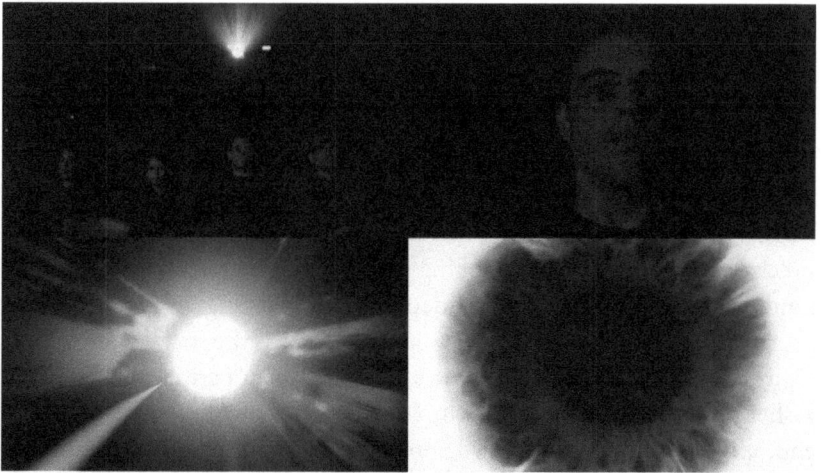

Figure 21. After Elliot and Mr Robot sit down at the movie theater inside his mind, taking their seats besides some imagined doubles of his mother and himself as a child, the series closes with a montage that, over an emotional piano track, builds up to a tearful eye that closes the series. Slowly zooming into Elliot's tearful expression and then tilting upwards towards the projector's light, Esmail's special effects here seem to condense, in fast motion, many of the series' scenes and, eventually but also gradually, the circular light seems to transform into Elliot's pupil, in the real world, where he is awakening with a tearful eye, just like Elliot's inside his mind.

Thus, it appears as though the series' anti-utopian spirals—whereby the world worsens just as the characters try to improve it—eventually bring viewers back to something like already-existing reality, which in the end appears as the best possible world. Besides, considering Elliot's final reckoning, one should also observe that the character's eventual return to an idealized sane self, whereby his invented identities peacefully retreat to the back of his psyche, only appears as a utopian horizon because it is radically open-ended—that is, what lies forward is an undetermined path, to be walked by a totally unknown person. As in *Don Quixote*, the return to

---

neoliberal idea of individual power, even though the story elsewhere shows the hacker as something like a working-class hero, who succeeds when collectively organized.

sanity is the one true happy ending and, perhaps, the only possible outcome of such kinds of adventures, which were always—at least from some interpretations—irremediably Romantic in the fullest, most ambivalent sense of the word.

Nevertheless, this utopian horizon of sanity is an unashamedly individualistic one, one that places the focus on a single person's individual healing—an unproblematic, almost miraculous healing that is here achieved precisely when Elliot stops looking towards a more collective and social kind of utopian horizon. Thus, ideologically speaking, even if the series overtly politicizes mental health, pointing towards the social and technological causations of mental illnesses in the manner of critics such as Mark Fisher or Jonathan Crary, this whole critical discourse is reversed in the end, as Elliot's politicization is what retroactively appears to have caused his illnesses, since the end of F Society's political struggles seems to heal him.[34] At the very least, this seems ironic; at most, it can seem perverse. A series that started upon overtly anti-capitalist premises seems to be turned into an anti-anti-capitalist defense of one's own mental health and never mind other people—although, admittedly, ambivalences remain and my interpretation here has begun to follow the most suspicious of hermeneutics. In the end, *Mr Robot*'s utopian horizon is, like any other, a horizon—the path towards utopia has to start somewhere and what better place than

---

34   The mind behind the notion of "capitalist realism," Mark Fisher, who himself suffered from severe depression, spoke of mental illnesses as a symptom of our dystopian structure of feeling and a consequence of increased precarity and productivity pressures. Fisher, in fact, argued that "The 'mental health plague' in capitalist societies would suggest that, instead of being the only social system that works, capitalism is inherently dysfunctional, and that the cost of it appearing to work is very high" (*Capitalist Realism* 19). With regard to Jonathan Crary, his more media-oriented critique denounces how the 24/7 availability of filter bubbles and instant temporalities "heightens a pervasive condition of quasi-psychosis bereft of anything fugitive or nomadic," which entails that so-called "madness" now "finds fewer pathways to flight or breakout to an elsewhere" (*Scorched Earth* 22). This is, in essence, part of what I have meant to suggest with the idea of new media quixotism: that a certain form of "madness" no longer seems eccentric, subversive or disruptive; instead, in the digital age it is both culturally normative—following the postmodern—and technologically predisposed.

oneself? Like Elliot, coming to terms one's own quixotism may be but the starting point within a media-dominated society that, whether we like it or not, is already making us quixotic.

Esmail's *Mr Robot* is, overall, another profoundly ambivalent new media dystopia, caught in the inevitable tensions between utopian and anti-utopian impulses as well as in the ambivalences derived from the epoch's techno-ambivalent gaze, which is here allegorized through a hacker's quixotic gaze. Indeed, Elliot is, like the implied gaze of our sub-genre, a person with a deeply ambivalent fixation with new media technologies, which are—for him—not solely both fascinating and horrifying, but also both empowering and disempowering, since they are both the primary tool of his most heroic feats and the chief cause of his most quixotic delusions. Of course, this analysis of the series has been driven by its own theoretical quixotism, in the sense it has been oriented towards analyzing *Mr Robot*'s peculiar version of new media quixotism. For that reason, other dimensions of the series that may deserve a deeper analysis have necessarily fallen out of scope. Even Elliot's quixotic characterization, the central object of my analysis, could merit an expanded examination that considers not only his identity as a hacker, but also, more centrally than here, considers how his mental illnesses and his traumas inform story and narration—and to what effect, *vis-à-vis* dominant narratives of healing.[35] Admittedly, then, in focusing upon *new media* quixotism, non-medial dimensions of Elliot's quixotism have been examined only accessorily—and the same could be said about *Mr Robot*'s gender dimensions, in the sense that, as in "USS Callister," this is a thoroughly *masculine* version of new media quixotism that is contrasted to the relative "sanity" of female characters. However, whereas in *Black Mirror* this was embodied in the Panzaic companion of

---

35 Following the concepts of Arthur W. (Frank) ground-breaking *The Wounded Storyteller*, *Mr Robot* might be categorized and studied as a narrative of chaos that is eventually and, perhaps somewhat forcibly, turned into a narrative of restitution; insofar as the series confronts one with Elliot's chaotic life and worldview, but then somewhat magically arrives at what is seemingly the total healing of the main character, with no apparent traces or wounds of his long dissociation left. I am thankful to my colleague Lucía López Serrano for bringing this reference and field of research to my attention.

Cole, the female characters here are not as constant as companions and only very abstractly and anecdotally Panzaic.[36] All of these, however, are but quixotic dreams of future studies about one single television series and our attention here should remain focused upon new media quixotism generally, of which there remain an additional case study: Cary Joji Fukunaga and Patrick Somerville's mini-series *Maniac* (2018).

4.4. *Maniac*; or, the Technological Mediation of Mental Illnesses[37]

If the previous two series were two contrasting approaches to the quixotic, with the more satirical and more formulaic possibilities illustrated by "USS Callister" and the relatively more serious and more figurative by *Mr Robot*, *Maniac* stands as the most formally and ideologically ambivalent case of the three. Fukunaga and Somerville's mini-series, which consists of only ten episodes, is, overall, a markedly tragicomic pastiche with abundant dark humor. Exceptionally, this is also a series that repeatedly

---

36 Most of the (at least functionally) "Panzaic" voices in the series are indeed women: his therapist Krista, his sister Darlene, or his friend Angela, characters who are undoubtedly "saner" than Elliot and occasionally intervene to correct his "hacktivist" delusions generally and his masculine delusions specifically. However, because here the female characters are secondary *vis-à-vis* the overwhelming runtime and narrative weight given to the quixotic protagonist-narrator and, also, because none of them are consistent companions of Elliot, who still spends most of his time alone with his delusions, I would say that the Panzaic component of the myth is very abstract and anecdotal here, with its usual contrastive function scattered across many characters and transferred to other narrative devices. Nevertheless, the fact that both *Mr Robot* and *Black Mirror*'s episode both contrast masculine quixotism with some kind of female sanity still seems worth further enquiry in its own terms, from a gender studies perspective.

37 Much of my analysis of this series derives from a years-long polemic with my colleague Marta Bernabeu, with whom I had extensive conversations about *Maniac*, her personal recommendation, which we then discussed at a shared panel in the SFRA 2022 Conference.

but anecdotally references Cervantes's *Don Quixote*, although—on a more macrotextual level—its relationship to the novel is as abstractly architextual as is usual in our sub-genre. After all, in all other respects, *Maniac* is another new media dystopia, narratively structured around speculating with the worst consequences of a certain medial *novum*— with its main specificities being that it is set in an alternate, retro-futuristic version of the US and that its main *novum* is explicitly linked to psychic health, which provides a key link to quixotic "madness." More concretely, Fukunaga and Somerville's series speculates with a new technology that is being developed by a "Neberdine Pharmaceutical Biotech" (NPB) for the purpose of treating mental illnesses, aiming to supplement standardized, chemical medication with personalized, VR simulations, custom-made by an AI. The story, accordingly, revolves around two characters, Owen Milgrim (Jonah Hill) and Annie Landsberg (Emma Stone), who are selected as Guinea pigs in the trial phase of that treatment. Throughout the episodes, these two test subjects and co-protagonists are given, respectively, quixotic and Panzaic roles. Overall, as the previous case studies, Fukunaga and Somerville's *Maniac* reformulates quixotism in a way that is interesting not only formally, but also for what it suggests about the digital age, which is satirically painted as an epoch of extreme loneliness and widespread mental suffering.

Quite grandiosely, *Maniac*'s pilot episode opens with a documentary-like prelude that takes viewers back to the beginning of everything—the Big Bang and the origins of life—in a way that very authoritatively—but parodically—establishes the series' underlying themes and philosophy. Here, a voice-over narrator guides viewers through a rapid montage of cosmic milestones leading up to humanity's present:

> It begins like this. Two billion years ago, an amoeba...
>
> Wait, let's ... let's back up. I've skipped too many connections.
>
> Out of nothing, in an instant, everything. An infinite cosmic orgy of matter and energy, rubbing, bumping and grinding together. There would be no galaxies, no suns, no planets, no life, without collisions of heavenly bodies.

> Back to our amoeba. It engulfs a bacterium with unique powers and ... voilà. Earth's first photosynthesis-enabled organism. Maybe it was chance. Maybe it was inevitable. This one changed amoeba becomes the ancestor of every living plant on Earth, which in turn floods the planet with oxygen ... paving the way for every other form of life we know ... leading to more souls, more connections and therefore more new worlds branching outward from the first. These forces of nature, when they converge, be they astronomical collisions, biological unions, demonstrate the infinite potential of our connections.
>
> This truth also extends to the human heart. [...]
>
> Hypothesis: all souls are on a quest to connect. Corollary: our minds have no awareness of this quest. [...] Camaraderie, communion, family, friendship, love, what have you. We're lost without connection. ("The Chosen One!" 12"-3'06")

Right before the narrator's hypothesis is formulated, however, the documentary-like montage is abruptly ended as—in a sudden shift of tone that contrasts with the still ongoing voice-over narration—the series cuts to a scene of one of the protagonists, Annie, who is trying to buy a pack of cigarettes in a local convenience store. Here, her attempt to buy the pack using "AdBuddy" credit instead of cash is rejected by the clerk, who—after denying to be a conspiracy theorist despite there being no accusations—claims that he cannot accept that because the "AdBuddy" company spies and stores everyone's personal data. Annie then goes out, visibly annoyed and indifferent to the clerk's rant, she steals sufficient change from a mechanical newspaper stand and returns to pay, moodily, leaving him rambling alone in his glass cage. Just as the narrator's hypotheses continue to be advanced, viewers then see Annie aimlessly walking on the sidewalk, barely satisfied by smoking and utterly indifferent towards some street advertisements, which are framed and focused for the viewer to read (Figures 22 and 23). Both ads, which obnoxiously cater to the human need for connection and care, thus expose the irony: that this is a world where loneliness and indifference reign, where the possibility of human connection only remains as a commodified ghost. All souls may be on "a quest to connect," as the voice-over claims, but here "connection" is but a vague promise of corporate advertising—apparently absent from Annie's and everyone's life. Especially as, immediately after this sequence, she goes into a cafeteria to broodingly watch other loners, this is presented as a world defined by alienation. The innate quest to connect may be true, but a quest it remains.

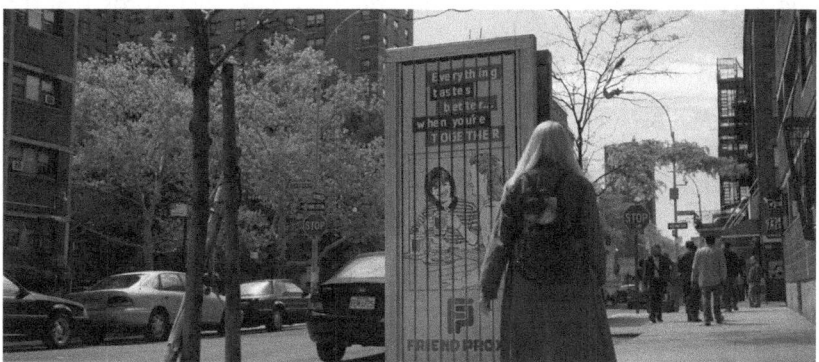

Figure 22. Annie walks past a "Friend Proxy" ad, which promises that "everything tastes better ... when you're TOGETHER." As is later shown, "Friend Proxy" is an application that offers friends on demand, to keep you company and pretend to care for you—for an hourly rate.

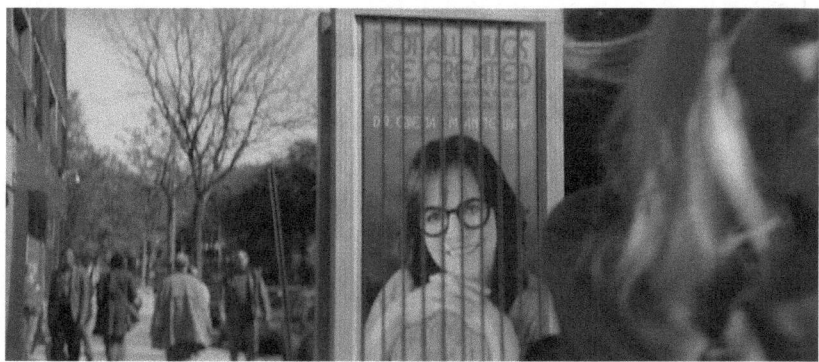

Figure 23. The same stand, as seen from behind after Annie walks past it, but now with a different ad—the cover of the book *Not All Hugs Are Created Equal: A Book about Healing*, by Dr Greta Mantleray (Sally Field), a celebrity psychologist who has made a fortune selling self-help books, profiting off a growing—but systemically unsatisfied—demand for help with mental illnesses. She and her son, Dr James K. Mantleray (Justin Theroux) are both recurring characters, involved in designing the experiment in which Annie later participates.

Maniac's darkly comic, dystopian *mise-en-scène*, as developed subsequently, further confirms that connection is the most important desire—and the lack—that structures the diegetic reality; in other words, that the inherent difficulty of meaningfully connecting with others is the central theme of the whole series. In an interesting exercise of cognitive and spectacular estrangement, the alternate United States of the series resembles the historical 1980s, especially in the look and feel of technologies, but here there are many details that imply this world moved in a *slightly* different direction from our own 80s. "AdBuddy" and "FriendProxy" services, referenced from the very beginning, are two telling *nova*. Whereas "AdBuddy" gives you credit in exchange for being sent a human companion who spends their time with you reading personalized advertisements, "FriendProxy" instead offers you a companion who listens and cares about you—for the purchased time. Human contact is thus thoroughly commodified, both as an end in itself and as a means for advertising, which goes a long way in explaining the crowd's alienation. This, of course, is but an estranged manner of re-presenting a historical logic—the alienating logic of capitalism and, more specifically, the commodification of sociability that is taking place with digital technologies. The difference, of course, would be that the people in the fictional world have services that promote *in-person* contact—a difference that exposes the absurdity of our epoch's digitally mediated relations by re-imagining them as awkwardly sad, offline exchanges between people, rather than between users and interfaces. This is cognitive estrangement at its simplest and finest: "AdBuddy" and "FriendProxy" are, in a sense, only strange because of the ways whereby services are delivered, but not because of their functioning, which follows the same logics of contemporary capitalism. Thus, far from simply catering to a voguish nostalgia for the 1980s, *Maniac* caricaturizes an alternate present in which neoliberal ideas and technologies paved the way for a capitalism that is superficially different, but equally dystopian. Like our own, this is a system that commodifies everything—and, also, a system that, like our own, does this in the name of an idolized "freedom" (Figure 24).

Within and against this very real dystopia, the two co-protagonists are both precariously underemployed and mentally ill individuals—characters

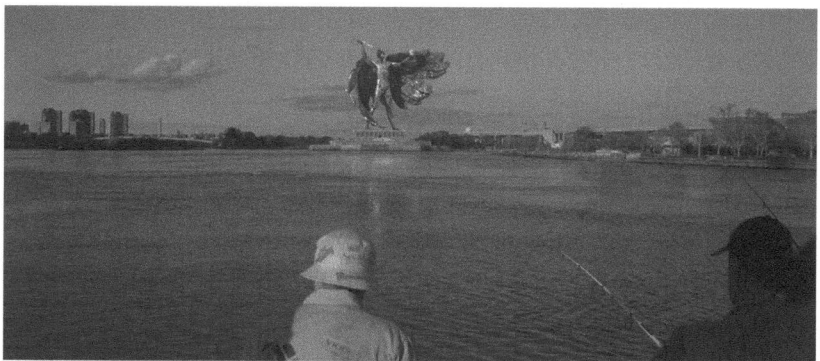

Figure 24. In one of many ironic background details, as the pilot episode transitions from one scene to the next, a tour guide is heard describing the "Statue of Extra Liberty," a new landmark of this alternate New York—an apparent, estranging sign that this speculated society remains as absurdly caught by neoliberal ideologies of freedom as the historical one.

who epitomize the personal toll of living in such a society. Annie Landsberg, on the one hand, gets by doing small, part-time jobs and she struggles with chronic depression and drug addiction, which is apparently her way of coping with life in the city and with the unprocessed trauma of her sister's death. Besides, her only remaining family, his father, is seen to be entirely unsupportive: in fact, he is completely addicted to and literally locked inside a spaceship-like, VR pod that he keeps in his backyard, which isolates him from everyone and everything else in a very physical re-imagination of a digital filter bubble—another stroke of the series' science-fictional genius. Her painful loneliness notwithstanding, Annie is still the relatively "sane" one, compared to Owen, since she can see clearly—but too cynically and hopelessly—all that is wrong with the world. Owen Milgrim, on the other hand, struggles with severe schizophrenia, repeatedly experiencing hallucinations and occasional psychotic outbreaks and he is heavily—but erratically—medicated. Despite having a millionaire family, owner of the same Milgrim corporation where Annie is seen scavenging, Owen refuses economic support from them; as he has been branded and bullied as the family's black sheep, he prefers to provide for himself. Nevertheless, Owen struggles to make ends meet and he lives alone in a ridiculously small apartment, which he can barely afford after losing his job. Owen's only companionship is an imaginary version of his bully brother, who appears in his hallucinations as a secret agent that is trying to recruit him, "the chosen one," for the mission of "saving the world." Owen and also Annie thus think and feel that the system has turned against them, for both real and imaginary reasons. Of course, whereas Annie's perception is only distorted when she is drugged, Owen's schizophrenia brings him to the extreme of believing that the system conspires against him—the lone hero who may save the world from the hidden, evil forces that prey on the people. With all these characterological details, much of *Maniac*'s quixotism may already be deduced, but since their participation in the high-tech pharmaceutical trial is what brings the two together and what marks the start of their simulated adventures, a clearer schematization of themes and motifs must wait for a summary of those parts of the plot where the myth is most present.

One key difference in Owen and Annie's arrival into NPB's pharmaceutical trial—the potentially miraculous method for treating mental illness with VR simulations—is why and how they get into it. Of course, both need therapy and money and the trial may, with luck, give them both—or, if the treatment fails, at least money. However, on the one hand, Owen, who is selected because his "defence mechanisms are fungible" ("The Chosen One!" 30'17"–19"), has high hopes that the treatment will work—especially since his schizophrenia keeps worsening, but also because he seems to think that this is the beginning of his secret mission of "saving the world," with Annie as his accomplice. On the other hand, Annie is, from the outset, more concerned with earning money and stealing drugs—she in fact blackmails herself into the trial, because she was not "vulnerable enough" to be eligible—and, moreover, she is sceptical about NPB's extraordinary claims that this treatment shall eradicate all forms of psychic pain. So, what does the treatment hope to achieve? In a parodically kitsch introductory video, Dr James K. Mantleray (Justin Theroux) very unhumbly explains:

> The human brain is vast as the cosmos and equally unexplored. We here at Neberdine Pharmaceutical Biotech are pioneering a revolutionary procedure that will unlock the secret mysteries of the mind and replace old-fashioned talk therapy … forever. Sorry, Sigmund. […] Welcome to Phase III of the ULP testing. You are not only

New Media Quixotism

participants in a pharmaceutical drug trial, you are pioneers at the forefront of a new world. You may notice you're here with 11 other subjects. But don't worry, your experiences here, likely very powerful, will be private and discreet and entirely your own. No one sees into your heads and the multiple fantasy cells hiding inside there ... but us. Now you're probably wondering, "How does it work?" And it's simple. Three pills taken in three steps: A, B, C ... analysed by the most sophisticated mega-computer ever developed: the GRTA. "Hello, friends. I'm a smart computer."

After ingesting the pills, the GRTA's cutting-edge AI will identify, map and confront the learned programming of your brain. At the end of this trial, don't be surprised if you experience pure, unaffected joy. You'll be born again, but not as a baby. [...]

Once we've identified your core traumas and mapped your bio-psycho-social symptoms, the GRTA mega-computer remaps a more efficient system, custom-tailored to you, forging healthier pathways with powerful, non-surgical microwave technologies. Welcome to the start of your new life. Welcome to the start of your new life. You will never be the same again. ("Windmills" 24'48"-26'17")

For the duration of this ridiculously technophile, propagandistic speech, however, interspersed reaction shots show how most participants seem indifferent or absent minded; Owen seems in thrall and excited about his "revolutionary" position as a "pioneer"; and Annie seems impatient, perplexed and even angry at the video's tone. Indeed, as the video finishes, Annie rushes away to queue, hoping to get the first dose, while Owen whispers to her—part inspired, part vindictive—that "Everybody thought I was crazy, but they were all wrong" ("Windmills" 26'01"-04"). Naturally, Annie is confounded with Owen's delusional claims, but—partly out of pity, partly to blend in—she plays along with his fantasy, pretending to be the secret agent that he thinks she is. It is here that her Panzaic role as counterpoint and companion begins and both—like the rest of the participants—shall be repeatedly immersed into a variety of fictional worlds designed to—in three ideal stages—confront, process and overcome their pain. NPB's AI-generated fantasies, however, do not work as intended and their relative "failure" is crucial to the story.

Once all participants are plugged into the computer simulations, a glitch in the system is what haphazardly seals Owen and Annie's fate as companions inside them. As it happens, GRTA, "the most sophisticated mega-computer ever developed," is also deeply depressed—an ironic proof of the success of her designers, who sought to make her as human as possible: and what is more human than being depressed in such a world? Because of this, during one of the AI's emotional lows, one of her tears accidentally fuses two wires and this connects Owen's and Annie's "fantasy cells," irreversibly merging their *a priori* private simulations and turning them into inseparable companions for the remainder of the trial's—and *Maniac*'s—duration. Throughout the episodes, upon going through various fictional worlds that interrelate their imaginations and thus allow them to understand and empathize with each other's traumas and obsessions, Owen and Annie gradually become the closest of friends by literally living many different lives together. In this way, the computer gives them the connection that they lacked in their real lives—though, ironically, it does so by accident, not by design. By contraposition to the corporation's—and this dystopian world's—commodifying calculations, the series' utopian hopes are invested into the accidental and chaotic—and, in turn, viewers are made to hope not for the characters' predesigned, step-by-step "healing," but for their organic growth and bonding within shared fantasies. After all, their alienation would not and could not be overcome by trapping themselves in digital bubbles—even if these are supposedly therapeutic—but by bursting these bubbles and having a common experience.

During the whole pharmaceutical trial, the intradiegetic level of simulations is also an interesting showcase of reflexive storytelling, which provides a narrative basis for Owen's quixotism. Specifically, each of the virtual worlds that Owen and Annie are immersed into is structured, self-referentially, around a distinct cinematic genre: the mafia movie, the high-fantasy film, the spy movie and so on—in a way in which each genre's conventions mirror the character's unconscious obsessions and traumas, which seems a very succinct and entertaining way of showing how even our unconscious minds are, for better or worse, mediated by visual culture. Furthermore, since these are therapeutic simulations, meant to help participants in achieving an increased self-consciousness, each of them is also, narratively, oriented towards a self-conscious resolution—a moment in which the characters realize that they are in a simulation and that the fictional world where they temporarily lived had been, all along, showing them something about their real lives. In other words, each of these simulations ends with what Pardo calls a metafictional anagnorisis, which is here re-imagined as a therapeutic breakthrough within this technologized form of therapy. Therefore, *Maniac*'s self-conscious devices are not all that estranging, since they are contained within the metadiegetic level, where the metafictional anagnorisis is not only predictable but also part of the treatment's functioning. Thus, the series' reflexivity is subordinated and made formulaic within the diegetic world's logics—although it still functions as the main driver of Owen's quixotism, to which we now turn in more detail.

Having located *Maniac*'s quixotic subject—the schizophrenic Owen—and his Panzaic companion—the depressed Annie—and having surveyed the bases of their peculiar "created adventures," created in this case by an AI that reshapes one's unconscious mind in a fictional form, it remains to delve deeper into the myth's three mythemes as expressed through Owen—and secondarily, through other characters. As opposed to both "USS Callister" and *Mr Robot*, now *Maniac* offers a subject whose "madness" has a primarily social causation, who only becomes overtly quixotic—in the strong, architextual sense—through the intervention of the therapeutic technology. In other words, Owen's condition is, at first, not explained by any direct, intense interaction with a medium or a fictional genre, but rather by his position as a downtrodden subject of a certain kind of society—and in this sense, he is not strictly quixotic at first, but simply the mentally-ill citizen of a late-capitalist dystopia. However, as soon as he enters the trial and forcibly spends more time within simulations than outside, Owen becomes another paradigmatic new media quixote throughout the trial's duration. In *Maniac*, therefore, the three traits of quixotism could be said to have an initial, latent or covert expression, linked to Owen's precarious mental condition within this dystopian world *and* a second, more complete or overt expression, conveyed through Owen's (and Annie's) adventures within the pseudo-fictional simulations of the trial.

Because of this peculiarity, the "literary syndrome," first of all, is here not intrinsic to the character's imagination, who does not obsess with any fiction; rather, it is provoked by a machine that, upon detecting the character's fictional references, forces both Owen and Annie to relive their lives as if they were genre movies, so one might call this a "filmic" syndrome. Accordingly, because of its design, the AI-generated fictional worlds that most directly cater to Owen's subconscious mind are inspired by genres such as mafia or spy movies, which revolve around secret, malevolent powers such as those that Owen fears in real life. Secondly, Owen's "visionary imagination" is here reflected, already before the trail, in his hallucinations about secret agents and hidden messages, which spectators can see too, although in this case—unlike in *Mr Robot*—Owen's distorted perception does not amount to an unreliable narration, since in every case his hallucinations are soon contrasted with reality. In this regard, the trial's simulations do nothing but intensify and mediate Owen's distorted vision of reality, insofar the AI reproduces the character's unconscious obsessions and, based on them, creates absurdly unbelievable and illogical fictional worlds where Owen's schizophrenia, ironically, does not break down reality, but chaotically structures it—even incorporating Cervantes's *Don Quixote* into the delusions in a way that indirectly and playfully acknowledges the influence of the novel (Figure 25). Third and finally, Owen's "heroic identity," as characterized before his arrival into NPB, would be the last ingredient of his conspiracist schizophrenia, since an essential part of his delusions is—as noted above—the belief that he is "the chosen one," destined to save the world. The simple fact that NPB's trial plunges Owen into fictional worlds, which are structured around him and his obsessions—in the manner of a filter bubble—and give him alternate identities that are protagonist roles, reinforces his predisposition for thinking himself as the world's hero and savior. In all these ways, Owen's schizophrenia is an extreme, partly tragic and partly ridiculous symptom of widespread alienation—a condition that is then intensified and made overtly quixotic with the trial's technologies.[38]

---

38 Positioning a schizophrenic subject as the ultimate symptom of postmodernity and/or capitalism has, of course, been reduced to a cliché in the twenty-first century, especially in the wake of the work of Deleuze and Guattari, which has had echoes way beyond the realm of critical theory. The extent to which *Maniac* reshapes and is shaped by suchlike theories might therefore offer a possible line of interpretation, perhaps complementary to the present analysis.

New Media Quixotism

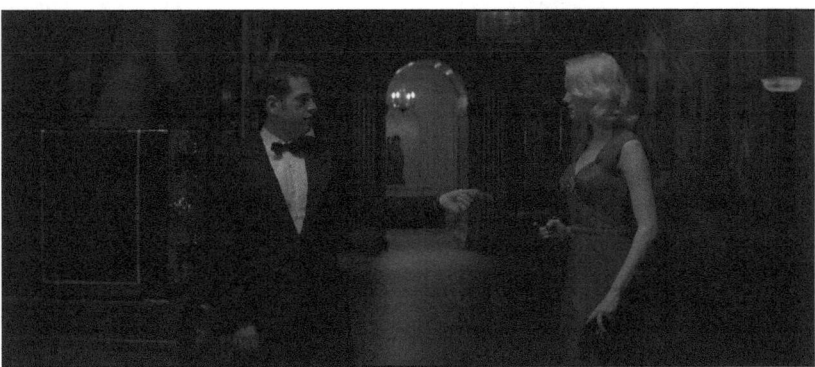

Figure 25. Owen hands out a "lost chapter" of *Don Quixote* to Annie, who is asking for it at gunpoint, in a simulation that starts with a lavish 1920s party, then goes through a ridiculous séance and then spirals into a spy plot where both characters try to find said chapter and, eventually, turn against each other for it. This is one of the generally anecdotic appearances of *Don Quixote* as an intertext, in this case because this fictional world conjectures that there is a lost chapter. As Annie explains, in "1615, Cervantes writes the final chapter to his masterpiece. So powerful ... that anyone who reads it is lost in their own fantasies ... forever. He shows it to a friend, who slips into a coma. Same with a neighbour, never comes out. They live in their own dream worlds until they die" ("Exactly Like You" 13'58"-14'17"). Through these speculations with the chapter, the characters thus seem to be—unknowingly—speculating with the possibility that they may not awaken from this simulation—as well as, relatedly, expressing Owen's fears that he may never escape his schizophrenia.

Suffering from this quixotic condition, then, Annie's accidental company is decisive for Owen to awaken to his delusions, as it is often her who guides him towards a metafictional-therapeutic anagnorisis within each of the simulated fictional worlds. Throughout these, Annie's role is Panzaic—a grounding influence for Owen. Had the treatment worked as intended, leaving Owen without her in private, individualized simulations, one is led to suspect that this whole treatment would have worsened Owen's condition and, maybe, even locked him inside his fantasies forever, especially as that is what seems to happen to some of the other participants, who leave the trial with a dubious mental state. Their friendship, as the main force that can stand against the machine's designs and the world's alienation, is gradually built upon this process of awakening from each simulation, a process of bonding and mutual help that is often ridiculous and often conflictive, but overall rewarding for the growth of both. In this regard, however, some journalistic critics who have focused upon *Maniac*'s protagonist duo have complained that their simulated adventures dilute and even undo Annie's Panzaic function—with one headline reading "mucho Quijote para tan poco Sancho" (Cordero), which makes sense insofar as her immersion in the simulations automatically makes her somewhat quixotic.[39] However, this complaint seems hasty and it obscures one key aspect of *Maniac*'s narrative trajectory—an aspect that, perhaps coincidentally, mirrors the dynamic between Don Quixote and Sancho Panza themselves. At first, Owen and Annie are given clearly contrasting roles, but then—as in Cervantes's novel—their adventures gradually lead to a quixotization of the Panzaic companion that, in certain episodes, verges on a total role reversal. In fact, in one of the final simulations, it is Annie who seems about to slip into an eternal delusion, unable to awake from a simulation—but it is Owen who helps her, returning the favor and demonstrating how their companionship changed him too. Thus, overall, *Maniac* ambivalently proposes that much is to be learned from both roles and that—in a sense—one should learn to keep at bay, however haphazardly, one's quixotism. Alone, Owen was ridiculously deluded and Annie, tragically isolated, but together, they form a tragicomic force like life itself, advancing towards an ambivalent horizon of transformations.

The series' ending, however, seems to change this ongoing, open-ended dialog between the two characters—a dialog that is utopian, to a great extent, because it is open-ended and on-going—into a rather reified "happy ending," an ending that is so overtly and one-sidedly intended to be utopian that it seems oblivious to the psycho-social problematics that were raised by the whole series. In the end, the trial is shut down by the

---

39   Annie, of course, is only quixotic insofar as the treatment's design predisposes (a) a confusion between the simulations and external reality, (b) an inherent distortion of perception caused by one's own unconscious and (c) a tendency to see oneself as the hero and protagonist, at least within the simulation. In this regard, one can say that the GRTA machine by default induces the three traits of quixotism in its participants, starting with a "literary syndrome" that is all throughout more attributable to the machine than to the characters.

NPB corporation, since the detail of the AI's depression was but the tip of an iceberg of structural problems and the whole project eventually downspirals in an unstoppable chain of technical and human errors, which are partially attributable to the designer's own quixotic tendencies.[40] The whole experiment thus collapses on its own, in a rather ridiculous meltdown, and the participants are sent away, back to their lonely, precarious lives with nothing but a handshake—again out of touch with the world and each other. Owen, on the one hand, is committed to a psychiatric institution by his own family, where he, again feeling totally alone, falls back into a state of permanently doubting himself. Annie, on the other hand, becomes a habitual user of "FriendProxy" services after returning to a similarly lonesome life and she employs these to try—and fail—to simulate his friendship with Owen. Soon, however, Annie finds out that Owen is committed and she rushes there, to help him break out—from the institution itself and from his worsened mental loops. "So you saw some things that weren't there. So what? People see aliens, people hear voices, people see ghosts…"—she tells him. "That's different. My mind, it … doesn't work right"—he complains. To which she replies, simply, "No one's does" ("Option C" 28'04"-20").

Thus, with that and a little more encouragement, they escape, with the gradually growing excitement of going on an adventure again—and in person this time. After sneaking out of the facility, they clumsily drive out of the parking lot, with several doctors already chasing them, but they get out and, with this funny, low stakes escape scene, the series closes with the image of their shared joy as they drive away. In this way, *Maniac* leaves its

40   Leading up to the trial's collapse, there is an entire parallel plot that revolves around the project's designers and supervisors and, specifically, around the creator Dr James Mantleray (Justin Theroux) and his assistant Dr Azumi Fujita (Sonoya Mizuno). These two characters add a markedly comic note to *Maniac*, since they are written and acted as utterly eccentric scientists who are often oblivious to the most obvious and obsessed with the most obscure. Thus, although in a significantly more abstract manner than the two protagonists, the two doctors might be read as a secondary quixotic duo, although one that is portrayed less ambivalently and more decidedly satirically. Indeed, many of their dialogs consist of a contrast between Dr Mantleray's delusions of grandeur about revolutionizing psychology forever and Dr Fujita's more down-to-earth, technical and practical reminders about growing problems with the machine's functioning.

viewers with an unashamedly romanticized happy ending—one that is only slightly less clichéd because they escape as friends and not lovers. But where shall they drive to? After the credits, a short scene follows, where they, still driving away into the sunset, awkwardly begin to wonder how far West the truck will take them—and, also, whether they "actually know each other" ("Option C" 34'28"-31"). With their doubts about the future, the story is sealed off here, in a way that humorously acknowledges the uncertainties that come with their shared freedom—uncertainties about where to go and who they are. Admittedly, this re-introduces a minor nuance, but shouldn't their doubts—and the viewer's—be about how they can actually escape this dystopian world so easily? The All-American cliché of heading off West for a better life—that settler-colonialist mythology of a purer wilderness where to start anew—may have made sense once upon a time, when there was still a mysterious and mystified outside to capitalism—but where is the outside of a world whose logics reach deep into our minds? Companionship against alienation might be a start but—as the series only vaguely suggests—the horizon ahead is more complex than that.

On the whole, then, *Maniac* offers a very ambivalent approach to new media quixotism, both formally and ideologically, insofar as quixotism is—sometimes humorously and sometimes tragically—portrayed as both an extreme embodiment of widespread alienation, but also as a disruptive position to be assumed, even if accidentally, against the system. Above all, this is because, in the first instance, Owen's "madness" appears as a symptom of his loneliness and precarity, but as the story advances, it is also what, ironically, enables him to connect with Annie, since their companionship is forged upon the trial's technologically induced quixotism. However, as opposed to *Mr Robot* and despite its own ending, *Maniac* does not go as far as to seriously treat the quixotic as heroic and neither does it assume a distance as extreme as the satire, as opposed to "USS Callister." Instead, all throughout, Owen is here treated somewhat in the manner of those categorized as "ridiculous quixotes" by Pardo, in the sense that the character's (mis)conceptions and (mis)perceptions are a crucial device of Fukunaga and Somerville's dark humor but, ultimately, Owen is not the butt of the joke—his dystopian society is. Nevertheless, *Maniac* is also a markedly postmodern version of the myth, a pastiche of tragic and comic approaches to quixotism in which—even with overt references to Cervantes—quixotism is above all figurative; an epochal condition that is not so much tied to a fictional genre or an even to a medium, but to an entire, data-driven social structure that generates alienation of all kinds—both from oneself and from others. Owen's quixotism, in a sense, is, more abstractly speaking, the quixotism of one who knowingly lives within a dystopian structure of feeling, engulfed and entrapped by its dominant ways of thinking and seeing, but also struggling and obsessing with the apparent absence of any utopian horizons of transformation. Owen does not manage to escape that position, really, but at least he eventually finds a companion with whom to live through it—and, even if sourly, to laugh about himself and the sad world around him.

4.5. Revisiting New Media Dystopias through the Quixotic

Throughout this chapter, "USS Callister," *Mr Robot* and *Maniac* have been analyzed as three new media dystopias that are architextually related to the myth of Don Quixote, insofar as these narratives are all structured around quixotic subjects—Daly, Elliot and Owen—and their created adventures—*digital* adventures except in *Mr Robot*—as well as—in the cases of *Black Mirror*'s Cole and *Maniac*'s Annie—Panzaic companions that provide a contrast and a counterpoint. In these three illustrations of new media quixotism, therefore, Cervantes's novel was present in an abstract, accidental manner or, as in the exceptional case of *Maniac*, present as an anecdotal reference that indirectly suggests the presence of the myth's themes and motifs—themes and motifs that are, in turn, generally expressed in figurative ways, abstractly identifiable but profoundly distanced from the myth's founding text.

Furthermore, the three case studies have also exemplified a range of formal and ideological possibilities that may exist under the umbrella of new media quixotism, potentially a new epochal variant—or a sub-variant of the postmodern—that abstractly recombines and reformulates those possibilities already realized by past rewritings. On the one hand, one finds that—as befits any dystopia, which necessarily balances critical and utopian impulses—these three cases are caught in an ambivalent negotiation of the most satirical and the most serious ways of approaching quixotism, which is in each case resolved differently: more satirically in "USS Callister," more seriously in *Mr Robot* and more ambivalently in *Maniac*. On the other hand, these three cases—notwithstanding their generally figurative nature—can also be mapped within a spectrum of literality with regard to Cervantes's novel, starting with "USS Callister," where quixotism is explained as an obsession with a fictional sub-genre, going through *Mr Robot*, where it is mostly attributed to an intense use of digital media, and ending with *Maniac*, where it is externally caused by a machine and only abstractly linked to the psycho-ideological constraints of a media-dominated dystopian world. In general, however, the three examples have attested to the formal and ideological flexibility of what I have defined as new media quixotism, as well as to its deep affinities with the central ambivalences of new media dystopias—and of dystopian SF generally.

The concept of new media quixotism, however, is not meant to be exhausted by this chapter's use of it and my assumption is that there are still many more narratives to be analyzed and to be crafted around its structure—both within the realm of new media dystopias and beyond.[41] Even within my corpus, other series such as *Westworld* and *Devs* might stand to be analyzed with an eye on some of their character's quixotism, even if it is more secondary. In the former series, one could begin with the character

---

41 Only within SF television, one can think of Justin Roiland's animated series *Rick and Morty*, which is a paradigmatic case of a more general science-fictional quixotism, especially considering its generally meta-science fictional dark humor and its functionally quixotic-Panzaic protagonist duo. Throughout the series, viewers follow Rick, the eccentric, genius "mad scientist," and Morty, his gullible, dumb nephew, in a wide variety of absurd intergalactic adventures closely akin in spirit to those of *The Hitchhiker's Guide to the Galaxy*. Another space-opera example, of a radically different, much more serious nature, would be James S. A. Corey's series of novels *The Expanse* (2011–21), recently adapted as an audio-visual series of the same name, produced and distributed by Amazon Prime Video (2015–22). In this case, the sometimes excessively idealistic captain James Holden leads a crew of misfits across the solar system with a spaceship that he himself chooses to name the Rocinante.

of William, played by Ed Harris, who roams around the theme park, believing its narratives to be truer than reality, obsessing over its secrets and almost replacing his identity without for his identity within. Here, in the first and second seasons especially, the quixotism of this character seems to clearly conform to the myth's three themes in such a way that William's story adds further nuance to *Westworld*'s reflexive discourse—maybe, rather cynically, suggesting that the users of new entertainment technologies are somehow predisposed to forms of psychopathic individualism like William's. In the latter series, meanwhile, the founder of the DEVS project, Nick Offerman's Forest, may also be examined as a more implicitly quixotic characterization, given his monomaniacal, distorted way of seeing the world through the machine of his own creation—although, admittedly, the quixotic here would be but an accidental, subordinated aspect of a complex character who combines a wider variety of tropes and types. In any case, whatever traces one could find of this architext elsewhere, it should be clarified that quixotism is not essential to my definition of new media dystopias—a definition that was already completed in Chapters 2 and 3 on the basis on narrative and visual criteria—but this variant of the myth is nonetheless a recurrent presence in much of our sub-genre, with greater or lesser structural weight. Quixotism may be, by definition, accessory in new media dystopias, but it is potentially pivotal insofar as the myth's reflexivity and ambivalence can be neatly mapped onto those of the sub-genre, thus providing a clear characterological correlative to the ways of thinking, feeling and seeing that are fostered by new media technologies, which is the central theme of these dystopias. New media quixotism may be the embodiment of the dystopian world's worst, or a vehicle for the narrative's critical impetus, or even a motor of its utopian impulses—and any of these options would make quixotism a powerful ally of cognitive estrangement more generally.[42] We may all be a bit quixotic

---

42   Which one of these options is predominant in each of our three examples seems to correlate to the class position of each quixotic subject, especially insofar as the most satirized one, Robert Daly, is the CEO of his company; he is, in Wark's term, a representative of a vectoralist elite. By contrast, the most heroic one, *Mr Robot*'s Elliot, is an average cybersecurity worker—he is, thus, a representative of the hacker class, who, in turn, acts in the name of the working class. As for *Maniac*'s Owen, the

under digital capitalism, but we are clearly in need of fictional quixotism so as to—estranged by such bizarre but understandable subjects—rethink our own subjectivities and, indirectly, everything that they reveal about our position within and against the epoch.

Perhaps, nevertheless, if one had to think of some possible ways of expanding or amending this chapter's theorization, I would say that new media quixotism might not necessarily be seen as a way of fictionalizing a truly universal, epochal condition, but—as our three examples together seem to suggest—a specifically *masculine* condition. In a sense, these character's quixotic relationship with new media seems to be—just like what I called the techno-ambivalent gaze—closely related to or even modeled upon a male gaze that expects control—or fears a lack of control—over an object. Of course, here, the object that these subjects struggle—and fail—to control is not somebody else, but rather themselves—insofar as, in the present context, one's own mind, vision and identity are inseparable from omnipresent technologies, which radically undo any sense of control over oneself. Thus seen, new media quixotism might be studied as another means of expressing the so-called contemporary crisis of masculinity, a crisis that undoubtedly also relates to anxieties over technological developments that undermine—while illusorily strengthening—people's sense of self-sufficiency and self-mastery. Indeed, looking back at our case studies, it is not only the case that the three quixotes are gender-conforming men, but it also happens that most of the characters who—in more or less Panzaic ways—oppose them are women who are, without exception, more sensible, more reasonable and more admirable than them. Nevertheless, this gender bias is not exclusive of this variant of quixotism, since male quixotes greatly outnumber feminine ones—and, perhaps, this is a cross-epochal bias of the myth, which, in turn, relates to deeper socio-cultural realities of patriarchy. A while ago, in an incisive essay about SF writers' and academics'

---

son of billionaires who chooses to live in precarity, his liminal class position may be crucial in further explaining the series' ambivalent attitude towards him. All in all, then, class seems a decisive factor in determining how each dystopia approaches its quixotes and these examples seem to confirm that the sub-genre's critical, anti-capitalist bias also impinges on the presence or absence of satirical humor against the quixotic subject in question.

mystifying obsession with technology, Joanna Russ suggested that men, as opposed to women, are more prone to become "lunatics," thanks to an illusory sense of mastery and abstraction that is heightened by the use of technologies. Thus, maybe, with new media too, it is still mostly men who tend to—or are more tempted to—become quixotic lunatics upon exploring the digital realm. After all, falling deep into a filter bubble might seem, in some fictions, dystopian, but for some people, it might very well be the ultimate fantasy of control.

This book, nevertheless, is not the place—or, rather, it lacks the space at this point—to keep on probing these hypotheses, which may be pursued by other scholars and critics with a greater expertise in masculinities and gender studies. Regardless of whether digital capitalism or patriarchy is to blame for it, what is nonetheless clear is that new media quixotism is not only a fictional template for re-imagining contemporary subjectivities; it is also, in a more metaphorical and political sense, the fictional representation of a profoundly individualistic way of seeing, thinking and being in the world that—if we trust what these fictions suggest—new media seem to be predisposing *in reality*. In other words, just like new media dystopias correlate, via the detours of cognitive estrangement, with an epochal social structure, I would also argue that the concept of new media quixotism also refers to an epochal subjective structure, a psychological predisposition, an implied user mindset. We may all be, in this sense, somewhat quixotic as users of digital technologies—and the question would be what we can do about the apparently inevitable. How quixotic can we, will we, or should we be in these dystopian days?

Conclusion: Exit Dystopia?

> We are now living in a science-fiction novel that we are all writing together. The present feels dangerous and volatile, and which future will actually happen is radically uncertain. It could be a good life for future humans in a shared and interdependent biosphere. It could be extreme climate change, a mass-extinction event, agricultural collapse and intense deadly conflicts among desperate human groups, including nuclear war. [...]
>
> Science fiction is the realism of our time. It describes the present in the way a skeet shooter targets a clay pigeon, aiming a bit ahead of the moment to reveal what is not yet present but is already having an impact. This gives us metaphors and meaning-systems to help conceptualize our moment. So, as with any other realist art, you pluck just one strand out of the fabric of the total situation, and follow where it leads.
>
> —Kim Stanley Robinson, "Science Fiction When the Future is Now" (Beukes et al. 330)

This book began by probing into the common-sense intuition that we live in a new media dystopia, the high-tech hell of that SF novel that we all are writing together in the age of digital capitalism. My use of the term started as a provocatively productive way of naming an epochal reality, but, throughout the book, fictional new media dystopias properly speaking were more rigorously defined in a number of ways: as a sub-genre that intensely bridges fiction and reality, inviting us into critically rethinking one in terms of the other; as a post-cyberpunk kind of dystopia that often approximates a science-fictional mode of realism; as a visual sub-genre in which speculation about new technologies is inseparable from reflexivity with regard to its own medium; as an ironic kind of visual narrative as much defined by its critical-dystopian impetus as by its partly mystifying gaze; and even, as a dystopian sub-genre that is at times re-mapped onto the myth of Don Quixote. All these ways of defining, thus listed, arrive here as echoes from each of the four chapters, but now it only remains for them to be clearly synthesized so that, hopefully, the concept of "new media dystopia" can have a fruitful afterlife beyond the present work—an afterlife where the concept is refined through the study of an extended corpus that goes beyond audio-visual series; where it is re-thought *vis-à-vis* other theoretical frameworks that are absent or anecdotal here; or where, in whatever way, it becomes a useful critical toolkit, or, on the contrary, a productive object of critique.

The definition that was first advanced in the introduction to this book was that, as a specific audio-visual sub-genre of SF, new media dystopias (a) thematize and problematize the emergence and spread of new media technologies and (b) are themselves produced, distributed and/or consumed within new media platforms. On the basis of this simple description, each chapter has then proceeded to theorize the sub-genre from analytically distinct but ultimately overlapping perspectives. Firstly, historically speaking, new media dystopias have been theorized as a fictional sub-genre that is inseparably entwined with the material and ideological realities of digital capitalism and, as such, it is an integral part of the epoch's dystopian structure of feeling—partly, fuel for the ever-spreading fire of hopelessness and, partly, a tool of cognitive mapping from within that mood. Secondly, narratively speaking, new media dystopias have been established to be an inherently self-referential genre—and at times self-conscious—and, therefore, a speculative sub-genre whose hegemonic *novum* happens to be an estranged double of its own medium of distribution and consumption—digital media themselves. Thirdly, aesthetically speaking, new media dystopias have been described as a visuo-narrative genre that is structured around a techno-ambivalent gaze and thus caught in the contradictions of—with different degrees of irony and self-consciousness—both narratively criticizing and visually beautifying its medial *nova*. Fourthly, characterologically speaking, new media dystopias have been found to be—though not necessarily—a fruitful locale for re-interpreting and re-mediating the quixotic through the use of new media, in a way in which the myth's inherent reflexivity and ideological ambivalence reflect and reinforce the sub-genre's own.

In all these ways, more synthetically, new media dystopias can be described *an SF sub-genre that is ideologically critical, affectively dystopian, narratively reflexive aesthetically ambivalent*. Ultimately, as each chapter has kept emphasizing and re-discovering, the formal and ideological ambivalences of new media dystopias echo throughout all of their dimensions;

however, I would here conclude that they can all be explained, in the last instance, by the sub-genre's ambivalent position towards commodification. The genre's new media reflexivity, for instance, is generally caught in between being a critical, estranging force and a commodified dynamic; its techno-ambivalent gaze, for its part, is caught in between conforming to and subverting digital-capitalism's aesthetics and ideologies; and its critical-dystopian narratives, besides, caught in between spiralling within dominant hopelessness and demystifying this structure of feeling from within. Both sides of each ambivalence thus seem to define the possible horizons of every new media dystopia, but analysis has shown that each walks differently within its landscape, never fully arriving at one or the other edge of the earth, but always moving closer towards one or the other horizon. After all, none of them can escape from the condition of being *commodified* culture and all of them are equally based on the premise of being *critical* culture—the question, then, is by what formal means and to what ideological effect they negotiate this ambivalence. The answers to this question shall necessarily be varied, nuanced and complex, both text- and context-based, but the method—or maybe, the philosophy—for thinking through this sub-genre—and others related to it—remains. Thus, my hope is that, despite the idiosyncrasies of each case, these book's analyses have demonstrated the potential continuities of the approach, in such a way that it can be successfully applied to other new media dystopias that may continue to be released in the near future, such as *Black Mirror* itself, which had a sixth season released in June 2023, or also a newer, ongoing series like *The Peripheral* (2022–), a William Gibson adaptation, co-produced by *Westworld*'s Lisa Joy and Jonathan Nolan.

Besides the concept of the "new media dystopia," this book has also proposed a number of terms that have helped in defining crucial aspects of the sub-genre—but these are terms that, as I thought of them, could be used elsewhere, autonomously. In the second chapter, the notion of "new media reflexivity"—a derivative of Pardo's own understanding of "reflexivity"—is one that might be better theorized in isolation—that is, in a way that is not so tied with the specificities of SF, nor with the specificities of serial television. Here I have hinted at the possibility of theorizing digital platforms as self-referential, all-encompassing paratexts and I have also suggested that it seems necessary to detect if and when reflexivity is—as it is by default—commodified within this new media architecture, but beyond these humble suggestions, I believe that there is still need for a theory of the possibilities—and the limits—that digital cultural consumption poses for reflexive narration. From the third chapter, the notion of a "techno-ambivalent gaze," which re-purposes the conceptual architecture of Mulvey's "male gaze" and tries to transcend the binary opposition of technophobia and technophilia, is another idea that might stand further theorization, as well as emancipation from our sub-genre. Conceived as an integral part of the age's "technological aesthetics" rather than as an exclusive phenomenon of new media dystopias, I have also conceived the "techno-ambivalent gaze" as a potential way of thinking through digital capitalism's dominant ways of seeing. Thus, maybe, this idea can be re-used and re-thought in tandem with the pre-established idea of the "technological sublime," in a way in which one refers to the implied viewer and the other to the implied experience—an experience that may be found to occur in other media: maybe, not only in audio-visual storytelling, but also in other arts that are engaging with digital technologies—or arts that are digitally re-mediated—as well as in a digitally-native medium such as the videogame. Although, in the case of our sub-genre, we have found that this techno-ambivalent gaze and its associated aesthetics are frequently problematized by some kind of medial reflexivity, elsewhere—in a cinematically fascinating dystopia such as Dan Erickson's *Severance* (2022-)—this need not be the case, perhaps requiring a slightly different approach to the phenomenon.

Beyond these, one last concept, which is already conceived semi-autonomously from new media dystopias, is that of "new media quixotism," through which the fourth and last chapter proposed to theorize a new (sub-) variant in the history of myth of Don Quixote. This peculiar kind of quixotism, inseparable from a certain kind of new media reflexivity, would also tolerate—like that kind of reflexivity and, perhaps, in a theoretical tandem with it—further study and, specifically, a more extensive enquiry that verifies whether it can be found beyond the horizons of speculative fiction. Although that task fell beyond the theoretical and thematic scope of this book, my assumption is that there might already be a transmedial corpus of narratives about "new media quixotism" awaiting to be compiled—or, if that is not yet the case, that further new media quixotes shall keep emerging for as long as our societies continue being users of an ever-expanding variety of media. Quixotism was for a long time an estranging device for rethinking our engagement with literature—and it shall keep being that for as long as there is literature. However, in the age of media convergence, it would make sense that the quixotic is reshaped around engagement with any and every new medium that comes by. With this continued rewriting, *Don Quixote* shall not only keep on enjoying a fruitful afterlife but also give us a profoundly tragicomic way of coping with—and critically rethinking—the ever-growing quixotization of subjectivities that is fostered under digital capitalism. New media quixotism thus shows us how, in the end, the media may be new, but a part of our psychology remains the same of old—for better and for worse.

Turning towards a more speculative mode of conclusion, all these concepts should hopefully prove worth using insofar as, above all, they try to build bridges between the formalities of art and the ambiguities of life. Another possible line of enquiry, which would perhaps be the most abstract and philosophical, would be to delve deeper into my frequent insinuations that both dystopian narratives and new technologies play a quasi-religious role within contemporary societies. As someone without any religious upbringing or education—let alone expertise—I do not take myself as the most qualified person for such a task, but a provocative and productive conversation may emerge through an engagement with religious and theological studies. In this regard, I must acknowledge that the suggestions that I made along religious lines ultimately emerge from an insight that I owe to my grandmother, who lived through an astounding parade of historical changes from 1920 to 2020 and used to—depending on how Catholic she felt—liken our smartphones to *alcahuetes* [Spanish for "matchmaker" or "gossiper"] or to *confesionarios* [Spanish for "confessionals"]. It was only much later—after laughter and mourning—that I began to, unexpectedly, pursue that analogy seriously, more theoretically, gradually establishing connections between certain new media dystopias, old Marxist arguments that were not as anti-religious as I once assumed and even the now-fashionable philosophical polemics of Byung-Chul

Han, who—seemingly with my grandmother's same wisdom—claims that the smartphone has replaced the rosary as our daily spiritual companion. In this aspect and many others that are suggested by a brilliant series like *Devs*, perhaps new media dystopias do play an ambivalent allegorical role in our ways of thinking that is very much like that of religion, once upon a time—and, thus seen, perhaps the epoch's techno-ambivalent gaze is also worth re-examining as a pseudo-religious gaze of simultaneous fear and adoration towards our mechanical deities. These, however, are but speculative musings that may deserve (or not) a more academic afterlife—but any afterlife is not for me to speak to.

What I do hope to have spoken to, in between and beside the most academic analyses, is to a certain common sense of the times, hopefully suggesting some fresh pathways for partially re-directing our dominant ways of feeling, seeing and thinking through this apparent high-tech hell. The idea that we are living in something like *Black Mirror*—undoubtedly the most popular and iconic of all the series that I have analyzed as new media dystopias—does not seem to be going away anytime soon. Even when Brooker's series itself had no planned continuation, a publicity agency in Madrid ran a mock-publicity campaign announcing that there was a sixth season—only it was already "Live now, everywhere" (Figure 26). Nevertheless, even if this popular logic—and this book—treat the new media dystopia as a totalizing concept, as a potential tool for cognitive mapping on a systemic, global scale, one cannot forget that this is a relatively techno-centric perspective of the world, built around the user-interface relation, with all the biases and the omissions that such a perspective entails. In other words, this common-sense view of the world as a new media dystopia is structured around a way of seeing that can only be shared by those with access to digital capitalism's technologies—an access that is not universal, but very unequally distributed—and it is also a way of seeing that can only be sustained if these technologies remain to be produced at a scale like today's, which might not be the case for a long time, given the looming threats of global resource scarcities and spiralling climate crises. In this regard, escaping this particular dystopia is not to be idealized as a utopian horizon in itself, for there is clearly another dystopia awaiting us outside the illusions of disembodied, immaterial abstraction of digital technologies. For all these reasons, if what we do want is clarity and a safe distance from hopelessness, perhaps the common-sense attitude to assume is that suggested by Kim Stanley Robinson in the epigraph above. That is, maybe, rather than letting ourselves fall deep down the rabbit hole of dystopian imaginaries, we might be better off by thinking that we live in an SF novel that we are all writing together—and with that thought, at least, we may realize that the horizon ahead is more open-ended that we, in this structure of feeling, tend to think. Maybe descending into high-tech hell was a necessary exercise that gave us a degree of critical-utopian clarity, but maybe we—unlike Orpheus—should not look back now and keep on walking away, to see what awaits.

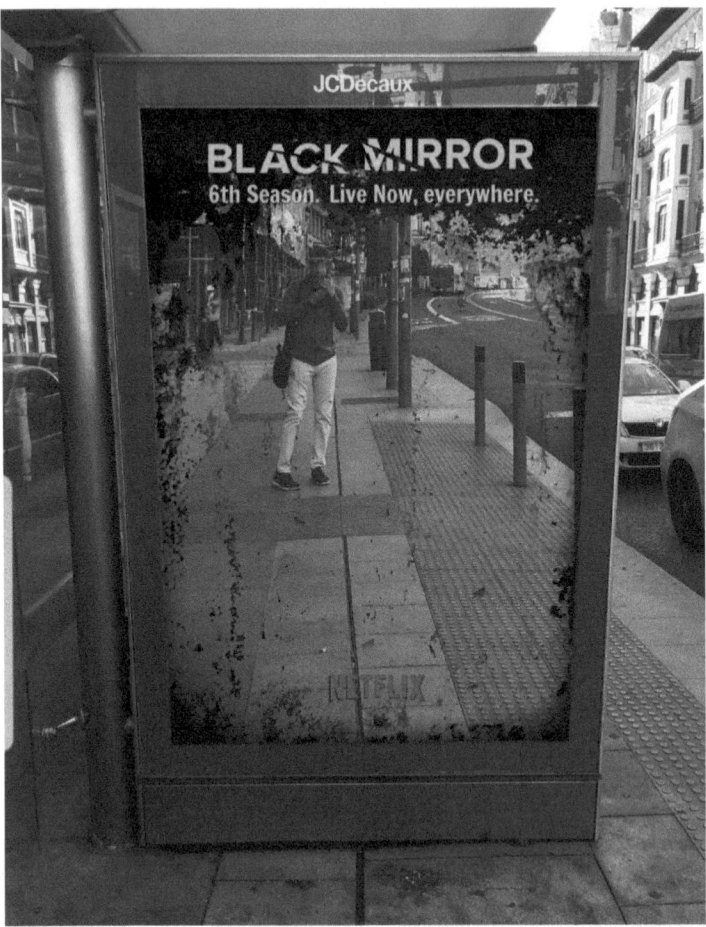

Figure 26. A *Black Mirror* mock-ad on a bus stop in Madrid, as captured by a passer-by who shared it on Twitter. As reported later (Berkowitz), the ad was produced by the creative ad agency Brother and installed around May 2020, just as people were allowed again into the streets after the COVID lockdowns, a time in which contact with others became even more dependent on digital media.

Bibliography

Abrams, J. J., director. *Star Trek*. Paramount Pictures, 2009.
Abrams, J. J., et al., creators. *Lost*. ABC Studios, 2004.
Achbar, Mark, and Jennifer Abbot, directors. *The Corporation*. Big Picture Media Corporation, 2003.
Adams, Douglas. *The Hitchhiker's Guide to the Galaxy*. Pan Books, 1979.
Adorno, Theodor W. *Aesthetic Theory*. Edited by Gretel Adorno et al. Continuum, 1997.
——. "Culture Industry Reconsidered." *New German Critique*, vol. 6, Autumn, 1975, pp. 12–19.
——. *Minima Moralia*. Edited by E. F. N. Jephcott. Verso, 2005.
Adorno, Theodor W., and Max Horkheimer. *Dialectic of Enlightenment*. Verso, 2016.
"After the Smartphone: Silicon Valley's Search for the Next Big Tech Platform." *The Economist*, April 2022, <https://www.economist.com/leaders/2022/04/09/silicon-valleys-search-for-the-next-big-tech-platform>.
Ahmed, Sara. *The Cultural Politics of Emotion*. Edinburgh University Press, 2004.
Alegre Zahonero, Luis, and Carlos Fernández Liria. *El orden de El Capital: por qué seguir leyendo a Marx*. Edited by Santiago Alba Rico. Akal, 2010.
Alexander, Neta. "Catered to Your Future Self: Netflix's 'Predictive Personalization' and the Mathematization of Taste." *The Netflix Effect: Technology and Entertainment in the 21st Century*, edited by Daniel Smith-Rowsey. Bloomsbury Academic, 2016, pp. 81–98.
Alter, Robert. *Partial Magic: The Novel as a Self-Conscious Genre*. University of California Press, 1975.
Althusser, Louis. *On the Reproduction of Capitalism: Ideology and Ideological State Apparatuses*. Edited by Etienne Balibar et al. Verso, 2014.
Ames, Christopher. *Movies about the Movies: Hollywood Reflected*. University Press of Kentucky, 1997.
Anders, Charlie Jane. "An Explanation for *Man in the High Castle*'s Biggest Change from the Book." *Gizmodo*, October 2015, <https://gizmodo.com/an-explanation-for-man-in-the-high-castles-biggest-chan-1717127092>.
Andersen, Lene. *Metamodernity: Meaning and Hope in a Complex World*. Nordic Bildung, 2019.
Anderson, Perry. *The Origins of Postmodernity*. Verso, 1998.

Appadurai, Arjun. "Speculation, after the Fact." *Speculation Now*, edited by Vyjayanthi Venuturupall Rao et al. Duke University Press, 2014, pp. 206–10.

Apprich, Clemens, et al. *Pattern Discrimination: In Search of Media*. University of Minnesota Press, 2018.

Archer, Margaret S. *The Reflexive Imperative in Late Modernity*. Cambridge University Press, 2012.

Arnold, Sarah. "Netflix and the Myth of Choice/Participation/Autonomy." *The Netflix Effect: Technology and Entertainment in the 21st Century*, edited by Daniel Smith-Rowsey. Bloomsbury Academic, 2016, pp. 49–62.

Artt, Sarah. "'An Otherness That Cannot Be Sublimated': Shades of *Frankenstein* in *Penny Dreadful* and *Black Mirror*." *Science Fiction Film & Television*, vol. 11, no. 2, 2018, pp. 257–75.

Aschoff, Nicole. *The New Prophets of Capital*. Verso, 2015.

———. *The Smartphone Society: Technology, Power, and Resistance in the New Gilded Age*. Beacon Press, 2020.

Baccolini, Raffaella, and Tom Moylan. *Dark Horizons: Science Fiction and the Dystopian Imagination*. Routledge, 2003.

Badiou, Alain. *Ethics: An Essay on the Understanding of Evil*. Edited by Peter Hallward. Verso, 2012.

Ball, Matthew. "The Metaverse: What It Is, Where to Find It, Who Will Build It, and Fortnite." *MatthewBall.vc*, 2020, <https://www.matthewball.vc/all/themetaverse>.

Barbrook, Richard, and Andy Cameron. "The Californian Ideology." *Science as Culture*, vol. 6, no. 1, 1996, pp. 44–72.

Barlow, John Perry. *A Declaration of Independence of Cyberspace*. The Electronic Frontier Foundation, 1996, <https://www.eff.org/es/cyberspace-independence>.

Barnett, David. "The Endless Adaptability of Philip K Dick." *The Guardian*, September 2017.

Barth, John. "The Literature of Exhaustion." *The Friday Book: Essays and Other Nonfiction*. The Johns Hopkins University Press, 1997, pp. 62–75.

Baudry, Jean-Louis. "The Apparatus: Metapsychological Approaches to the Impression of Reality in Cinema." *Camera Obscura*, vol. 1, no. Fall, 1976, pp. 104–28.

Bauman, Zygmunt. *Liquid Modernity*. Polity Press, 2000.

Bausela Buccianti, Lucía. *Reflexivity from Words to Panels: The Theory and Practice of Metacomics*. Universidad de Salamanca, 2022.

Bautista Naranjo, Esther. *La recepción y reescritura del mito de Don Quijote en Inglaterra (siglos XVII–XIX)*. Edited by Pedro Javier Pardo García. Clásicos Dykinson, 2015.

Beller, Jonathan. *The Cinematic Mode of Production: Attention Economy and the Society of the Spectacle*. Dartmouth College Press, 2006.
Belton, O. "Metaphors of Patriarchy in Orphan Black and *Westworld*." *Feminist Media Studies*, vol. 20, no. 8, 2020, pp. 1211–25.
Benanav, Aaron. *Automation and the Future of Work*. Verso, 2020.
Beniger, James R. *The Control Revolution: Technological and Economic Origins of the Information Society*. Harvard University Press, 1986.
Benioff, David, and D. B. Weiss, creators. *Game of Thrones*. Home Box Office, 2011.
Benjamin, Walter. "Capitalism as Religion." *The Frankfurt School on Religion*, edited by Eduardo Mendieta. Routledge, 2005, pp. 259–62.
———. "Left-Wing Melancholy (On Erich Kästner's New Book of Poems)." *Screen*, vol. 15, no. 2, 1974, pp. 28–32.
———. "Thesis on the Philosophy of History." *Illuminations*, edited by Hannah Arendt. Schocken Books, 1969, pp. 253–64.
Bennett, James, and Niki Strange. *Television as Digital Media*. Duke University Press, 2011.
Berardi, Franco. *After the Future*. Edited by Gary Genosko and Nicholas Thoburn. AK Press, 2011.
———. *Futurability: The Age of Impotence and the Horizon of Possibility*. Verso, 2019.
Berkowitz, Joe. "This Darkly Funny Outdoor Ad Proves We're Living in *Black Mirror*." *Fast Company*, 2020, <https://www.fastcompany.com/ 90513598/this-darkly-funny-outdoor-ad-from-netflix-proves-were-living-in-black-mirror>.
Berlant, Lauren. "Cruel Optimism." *Differences*, translated by Jeff Fort, vol. 17, no. 3, January 2006, pp. 20–36.
Berlin, Isaiah. "Two Concepts of Liberty." *Four Essays on Liberty*. Oxford University Press, 1969, pp. 118–72.
Bermúdez de Castro, Juanjo. "Contemporary Fables in the Digital Age: A Literary Approach to *Black Mirror*." *Television Series as Literature*, edited by Reto Winckler and Víctor Huertas-Martín. Palgrave Macmillan, 2021, pp. 201–20.
Bernabé, Daniel. *La trampa de la diversidad: cómo el neoliberalismo fragmentó la identidad de la clase trabajadora*. Akal, 2018.
Bernabéu Lorenzo, Marta. *Tracing the Wuther: The Brontëan Outsider from Victorian to Neo-Victorian Fiction*. Universidad de Salamanca, 2022.
Bernard, Andreas. *The Triumph of Profiling: The Self in Digital Culture*. Edited by Valentine A. Pakis. Polity Press, 2019.
Bertens, Hans. *The Idea of the Postmodern: A History*. Routledge, 1995.
Beukes, Lauren, et al. "Science Fiction When the Future Is Now." *Nature*, vol. 552, 2017, pp. 329–33.
Bewes, Timothy. *Reification; or, the Anxiety of Late Capitalism*. Verso, 2002.

"Black Mirror." *Urban Dictionary*, <https://www.urbandictionary.com/define. php?term=Black Mirror>.
Blaim, Arthur. "Hell Upon a Hill: Reflections on Anti-Utopia and Dystopia." *Dystopia(n) Matters: On the Page, on Screen, on Stage*, edited by Fátima Vieira. Cambridge Scholars Publishing, 2013, pp. 80–91.
Bloch, Ernst. *The Principle of Hope, Volume One*. Edited by Neville Plaice et al. The MIT Press, 1995.
———. *The Principle of Hope, Volume Three*. Edited by Neville Plaice et al. The MIT Press, 1995.
Blüher, Dominique. *Le cinéma dans le cinéma: film(s) dans le film et mise en abyme*. Atelier national de reproduction des thèses, 1996.
Bolaño Quintero, Jesús. "Post-postmodernism: Mapping Out the Zeitgeist of the New Millennium." *Oceánide*, vol. 15, 2022, pp. 17–25.
Bolter, Jay David, and Richard Grusin. *Remediation: Understanding New Media*. MIT Press, 2000.
Booker, M. Keith. *The Dystopian Impulse in Modern Literature: Fiction as Social Criticism*. Greenwood Press, 1994.
Bordera, Juan, and Antonio Turiel. *El otoño de la civilización: textos para una revolución inevitable*. CTXT, 2022.
Bould, Mark. "Introduction: Rough Guide to a Lonely Planet, from Nemo to Neo." *Red Planets: Marxism and Science Fiction*, edited by China Miéville and Mark Bould. Pluto Press, 2009, pp. 1–26.
———. *The Anthropocene Unconscious: Climate Catastrophe Culture*. Verso, 2021.
Bould, Mark, and China Miéville. *Red Planets: Marxism and Science Fiction*. Pluto Press, 2009.
Bould, Mark, and Sherryl Vint. *The Routledge Concise History of Science Fiction*. Routledge, 2011.
Boyd, Michael. *The Reflexive Novel as Critique*. Associate University Presses, 1983.
Boym, Svetlana. *The Future of Nostalgia*. Basic, 2002.
Braithwaite, Andrea. "It's about Ethics in Games Journalism? Gamergaters and Geek Masculinity." *Social Media and Society*, vol. 2, no. 4, 2016, pp. 1–10.
Bratich, Jack Z. *Conspiracy Panics, Political Rationality and Popular Culture*. State University of New York Press, 2008.
Bratton, Benjamin. *The Stack: On Software and Sovereignty*. The MIT Press, 2015.
Brecht, Bertolt. "Popularity and Realism." *Aesthetics and Politics*, edited by Fredric Jameson. Verso, 2007, pp. 79–85.
Bridle, James. *New Dark Age: Technology and the End of the Future*. Verso, 2018.
Briggs, Robert. "The Future of Prediction: Speculating on William Gibson's Meta-Science-Fiction." *Textual Practice*, vol. 27, no. 4, 2013, pp. 671–93.

Britt, Ryan. "*Black Mirror: Bandersnatch* and Its Philip K. Dick Influences." *Den of Geek*, July 2019, <https://www.denofgeek.com/movies/black-mirror-bandersnatch-and-its-philip-k-dick-influences/>.
Briziarelli, Marco, and Emiliana Armano. *The Spectacle 2.0: Reading Debord in the Context of Digital Capitalism*. University of Westminster Press, 2017.
Broderick, Damien. *Reading by Starlight: Postmodern Science Fiction*. Routledge, 1995.
Brooker, Charlie, creator. *Black Mirror*. Channel 4 and Netflix, 2011–present.
Brooker, Charlie, et al. *Inside Black Mirror*. Ebury Press, 2018.
Brown, Bill. "The Dark Wood of Postmodernity (Space, Faith, Allegory)." *PMLA*, vol. 120, no. 3, 2005, pp. 734–50.
Brown, Wendy. *In the Ruins of Neoliberalism: The Rise of Antidemocratic Politics in the West*. Columbia University Press, 2019.
———. "Resisting Left Melancholy." *Boundary 2*, vol. 26, no. 3, 1999, pp. 19–27.
———. *Undoing the Demos: Neoliberalism's Stealth Revolution*. Edited by Wendy Brown and Michel Feher. Zone Books, 2015.
Browne, Simone. *Dark Matters: On the Surveillance of Blackness*. Duke University Press, 2015.
Bukatman, Scott. *Terminal Identity: The Virtual Subject in Postmodern Science Fiction*. Duke University Press, 1993.
———. "The Artificial Infinite: On Special Effects and the Sublime." *Alien Zone II: The Spaces of Science-Fiction Cinema*, edited by Annette Kuhn. Verso, 1999, pp. 249–75.
Burns, Wayne. *A Panzaic Theory of the Novel*. The Howe Street Press, 2009.
———. *The Panzaic Principle*. Kingsway Quick Printers, 1962.
Butler, Christopher. *Postmodernism: A Very Short Introduction*. Oxford University Press, 2002.
Butler, Judith, et al. *Contingency, Hegemony, Universality: Contemporary Dialogues on the Left*. Verso, 2000.
———. *Notes toward a Performative Theory of Assembly*. Harvard University Press, 2018.
———. "Rethinking Vulnerability and Resistance." *Vulnerability in Resistance*, edited by Judith Butler et al. Duke University Press, 2016, pp. 12–27.
Campion, B. "Le sexe sans le sexe: convergence de la nudité frontale et de l'empowerment féminin dans *Westworld*." *TV Series*, vol. 14, 2018.
Canaan, Howard. "Metafiction and the Gnostic Quest in *The Man in the High Castle*." *Journal of the Fantastic in the Arts*, vol. 12, no. 4 [48], 2002, pp. 382–405.
Canavan, Gerry. "Hokey Religions: Star Wars and Star Trek in the Age of Reboots." *Extrapolation*, vol. 58, no. 2–3, 2017, pp. 153–80.
———. "Hope, with Teeth: On 'Black Museum.'" *Through the Black Mirror: Deconstructing the Side Effects of the Digital Age*. Palgrave Macmillan, 2019, pp. 257–70.

Carter, Cassie. "The Metacolonization of Dick's *The Man in the High Castle*: Mimicry, Parasitism, and Americanism in the PSA." *Science Fiction Studies*, vol. 22, no. 3, 1995, pp. 333–42.

Cartter, Eileen. "AOC's 'Tax the Rich' Dress Was Precision-Engineered Met Gala Messaging." *GQ*, September 2021, <https://www.gq.com/story/aoc-met-gala-dress>.

Castells, Manuel. *The Rise of the Network Society: Second Edition, with a New Preface*. Wiley-Blackwell, 2010.

Cervantes, Miguel de. *Don Quijote de La Mancha*. Real Academia Española y Asociación de Academias de la Lengua Española, 2004.

Chang, Emily. *Brotopia: Breaking Up the Boys' Club of Silicon Valley*. Portfolio, 2018.

Cheney-Lippold, John. *We Are Data: Algorithms and the Making of Our Digital Selves*. New York University Press, 2017.

Childers, William. "Quixote Gumbo." *Cervantes: Bulletin of the Cervantes Society of America*, vol. 35, no. 1, 2015, pp. 17–47.

Chun, Wendy Hui Kyong. *Control and Freedom: Power and Paranoia in the Age of Fiber Optics*. The MIT Press, 2005.

———. *Updating to Remain the Same: Habitual New Media*. The MIT Press, 2016.

Ciochina, Laura. "*Don Quijote De La Mancha* y *A Confederacy of Dunces*: Aventuras y Desventuras de Don Quijote e Ignatius Reilly." *Journal of Humanistic and Social Studies*, vol. 5, no. 2, 2014, pp. 27–40.

Claeys, Gregory. *Dystopia: A Natural History*. Oxford University Press, 2017.

———. "Foreword: A Utopian/Dystopian Spectrum: From Friendship to Fear, from Consent to Coercion." *The Postworld In-between Utopia and Dystopia: Intersectional, Feminist and Non-binary Approaches in 21st Century Speculative Literature and Culture*, edited by Katarzyna Ostalska and Tomasz Fisiak. Routledge, 2021.

Climate Change 2022: Impacts, Adaptation and Vulnerability (Working Group II Report). The Intergovernmental Panel on Climate Change, 2022, <https://www.ipcc.ch/report/ar6/wg2/>.

Coleman, E. Gabriella. *Coding Freedom: The Ethics and Aesthetics of Hacking*. Princeton University Press, 2013.

———. *Hacker, Hoaxer, Whistleblower, Spy: The Many Faces of Anonymous*. Verso, 2014.

Collins, Patricia Hill. *Black Feminist Thought: Knowledge, Consciousness and the Politics of Empowerment*. Routledge, 2000.

———. *Intersectionality as Critical Social Theory*. Duke University Press, 2019.

Comolli, Jean-Louis. "Mechanical Bodies, Ever More Heavenly." *October*, translated by Annette Michelson, vol. 83, 1998, pp. 19–24.

Conley, Donovan, and Benjamin Burroughs. "Bandersnatched: Infrastructure and Acquiescence in *Black Mirror*." *Critical Studies in Media Communication*, vol. 37, no. 2, 2020, pp. 120–32.

Connor, Steven. *The Cambridge Companion to Postmodernism*. Cambridge University Press, 2004.

Consalvo, Mia. "Confronting Toxic Gamer Culture: A Challenge for Feminist Game Studies Scholars." *Ada: Journal of Gender, New Media, and Technology*, no. 1, 2012, pp. 1–11.

Cordero, Gonzalo. "Crítica de *Maniac*: mucho Quijote y poco Sancho para una ida de olla con final difuso." *Esquire*, 2018, <https://www.esquire.com/es/actualidad/tv/a23453357/maniac-netflix-serie-critica-final-explicado/>.

Costantini, Mariaconcetta. "Pandemics, Power, and Conspiracy Theories." *Critical Quarterly*, vol. 62, no. 4, 2020, pp. 24–31.

Couldry, Nick, and Ulises A. Mejias. "Data Colonialism: Rethinking Big Data's Relation to the Contemporary Subject." *Television and New Media*, vol. 20, no. 4, 2019, pp. 336–49.

Cover, Arthur Byron. "Vertex Interview with Philip K. Dick." *Vertex*, vol. 1, no. 6, 1974, <https://philipdick.com/literary-criticism/frank-views-archive/vertex-interview-with-philip-k-dick/>.

Crary, Jonathan. *24/7: Late Capitalism and the Ends of Sleep*. Verso, 2013.

———. *Scorched Earth: Beyond the Digital Age to a Post-capitalist World*. Verso, 2022.

Creeber, Glen, and Royston Martin. *Digital Cultures: Understanding New Media*. Open University Press, 2009.

Crenshaw, Kimberle. "Demarginalizing the Intersection of Race and Sex: A Black Feminist Critique of Antidiscrimination Doctrine, Feminist Theory, and Antiracist Politics." *University of Chicago Legal Forum*, no. 1, 1989, pp. 139–67.

Csicsery-Ronay Jr, Istvan. *The Seven Beauties of Science Fiction*. Wesleyan University Press, 2008.

———. "The SF of Theory: Baudrillard and Haraway." *Science Fiction Studies*, vol. 18, no. 3, 1991, pp. 387–404.

Currie, Mark. *Metafiction*. Longman, 1995.

Curtis, Adam, creator. *All Watched Over by Machines of Loving Grace*. BBC, 2011.

———. *Can't Get You Out of My Head*. BBC, 2021.

———. *HyperNormalisation*. BBC, 2016.

Curtis, Adam, director. "Are We Pigeon? Or Are We Dancer?" *Can't Get You Out of My Head*. BBC, 2021.

———. "Bloodshed on Wolf Mountain." *Can't Get You Out of My Head*. BBC, 2021.

———. "Love and Power." *All Watched Over by Machines of Loving Grace*. BBC, 2011.

D'Aloia, Adriano. "Against Interactivity. Phenomenological Notes on *Black Mirror: Bandersnatch*." *Series—International Journal of TV Serial Narratives*, vol. 6, no. 2, 2020, pp. 21–31.

Dällenbach, Lucien. *The Mirror in the Text*. Edited by Jeremy Whiteley and Emma Hughes. The University of Chicago Press, 1989.

Damiani, Marco. *Populist Radical Left Parties in Western Europe*. Routledge, 2020.

Dardot, Pierre, and Christian Laval. *The New Way of the World: On Neoliberal Society*. Edited by Gregory Elliott. Verso, 2013.

Davies, Russell T, creator. *Years and Years*. Home Box Office, 2019.

Davies, William. "The Politics of Recognition in the Age of Social Media." *New Left Review*, vol. 128, 2021, pp. 83–99.

Dean, Jodi. *Aliens in America: Conspiracy Cultures from Outerspace to Cyberspace*. Cornell University Press, 1998.

———. "Complexity as Capture—Neoliberalism and the Loop of Drive." *New Formations*, vol. 80–1, 2013, pp. 138–54.

———. "Neofeudalism: The End of Capitalism?" *LA Review of Books*, May 2020.

———. "Same as It Ever Was?" *Sidecar*, May 2022, <https://newleftreview.org/sidecar/posts/same-as-it-ever-was>.

———. *The Communist Horizon*. Verso, 2012.

Debord, Guy. *Comments on the Society of the Spectacle*. Edited by Malcolm Imrie. Verso, 1990.

———. *Society of the Spectacle*. Translated by Ken Knabb. Rebel Press, 1992.

Deckard, Sharae, and Stephen Shapiro. *World Literature, Neoliberalism, and the Culture of Discontent*. Palgrave Macmillan, 2019.

Deleuze, Gilles. "Postscript on the Societies of Control." *October*, vol. 59, Winter, 1992, pp. 3–7.

Deleuze, Gilles, and Félix Guattari. *Anti-Oedipus: Capitalism and Schizophrenia*. University of Minnesota Press, 1983.

Della Ratta, Donatella, et al. *The Aesthetics and Politics of the Online Self: A Savage Journey into the Heart of Digital Cultures*. Palgrave Macmillan, 2021.

Denson, Shane. *Discorrelated Images*. Duke University Press, 2020.

———. *Postnaturalism: Frankenstein, Film, and the Anthropotechnical Interface*. Bielefeld, 2014.

Derrida, Jacques. "Spectres of Marx." *New Left Review*, vol. I/205, May/June, 1994, pp. 31–58.

Dick, Philip K. *A Scanner Darkly*. Doubleday, 1977.

———. *Do Androids Dream of Electric Sheep?* Doubleday, 1968.

———. *The Man in the High Castle*. Penguin Books, 2001.

———. "The Minority Report." *Fantastic Universe*, January 1956, pp. 4–36.

———. "The Two Completed Chapters of a Proposed Sequel to *The Man in the High Castle*." *The Shifting Realities of Philip K. Dick: Selected Literary and Philosophical Writings*, edited by Lawrence Sutin. Vintage Books, 1995, pp. 119–34.

———. *Time Out of Joint*. J. B. Lippincott Company, 1959.

———. "We Can Remember It for You Wholesale." *The Magazine of Fantasy and Science Fiction*, April 1966, pp. 4–22.

Dillon, Amanda. *Prism, Mirror, Lens: Metafiction and Narrative Worlds in Science Fiction*. University of East Anglia, 2011.

Dinerstein, Joel. "Technology and Its Discontents." *American Quarterly*, vol. 58, no. 3, 2006, pp. 569–95.

Doctorow, Cory. *How to Destroy Surveillance Capitalism*. Medium Editions, 2021, <https://onezero.medium.com/how-to-destroy-surveillance-capitalism-8135e6744d59>.

———. "Science Fiction Is a Luddite Literature." *Locus Magazine*, 2022, <https://locusmag.com/2022/01/cory-doctorow-science-fiction-is-a-luddite-literature/>.

Domènech, Antoni. *El Eclipse de La Fraternidad: Una Revisión Republicana de La Tradición Socialista*. Crítica, 2004.

Duménil, Gérard, and Dominique Lévy. *Capital Resurgent: Roots of the Neoliberal Revolution*. Harvard University Press, 2004.

Durand, Cédric. *Fictitious Capital: How Finance Is Appropriating Our Future*. Verso, 2017.

———. *Techno-Féodalisme: Critique de l'économie Numérique*. La Découverte, 2020.

Durham, Scott. "P. K. Dick: From the Death of the Subject to a Theology of Late Capitalism." *Science Fiction Studies*, vol. 15, no. 2, 1988, pp. 173–86.

Dyson, Esther, et al. "Cyberspace and the American Dream: A Magna Carta for the Knowledge Age." *Future Insight*. Progress and Freedom Foundation, 1994, <http://www.pff.org/issues-pubs/futureinsights/fi1.2magnacarta.html>.

Eagleton, Terry. *The Illusions of Postmodernism*. Blackwell, 1996.

Eaton, Tim. "Internet Activism and the Egyptian Uprisings: Transforming Online Dissent into the Offline World." *Westminster Papers in Communication and Culture*, vol. 9, no. 2, 2017, pp. 3–24.

Ebert, Teresa L. "The Convergence of Postmodern Innovative Fiction and Science Fiction: An Encounter with Samuel R. Delaney's Technotopia." *Poetics Today*, vol. 1, no. 4, 1980, pp. 91–104.

"Editorial Introduction." *Science Fiction Studies*, vol. 33, no. 3, 2006, pp. 385–8.

Egginton, William. "Cervantes's *Black Mirror*." *Cervantes: Bulletin of the Cervantes Society of America*, vol. 40, no. 2, 2020, pp. 175–90.

Elliott, Robert C. *The Shape of Utopia: Studies in a Literary Genre*. The University of Chicago Press, 1970.
Engels, Friedrich. "Engels to C. Schmidt in Berlin [London, August 5, 1890]." *Marx/Engels Internet Archive (Marxists.Org)*, edited by Brian Baggins, 2000, <https://www.marxists.org/archive/marx/works/1890/letters/90_08_05.htm>.
EngineeringMySadness. "Full Bandersnatch Flowchart (All Branches + Story Line + Prerequisites)." *Reddit*, 2018, <https://www.reddit.com/r/blackmirror/comments/aajk5r/full_bandersnatch_flowchart_all_branches_story/>.
Erickson, Dan, creator. *Severance*. Apple TV, 2022–present.
Esmail, Sam, creator. *Mr Robot*. USA Network, 2015–19.
Esmail, Sam, director. "Eps1.9_zero-Day.Avi." *Mr Robot*, created by Sam Esmail. USA Network, 2015.
———. "Eps2.5_h4ndshake.Sme." *Mr Robot*, created by Sam Esmail. USA Network, 2016.
———. "Whoami." *Mr Robot*, created by Sam Esmail. USA Network, 2019.
Espluga, Eudald. "Es Más Fácil Imaginar Un Meme de Mark Fisher Que El Fin Del Capitalismo de Plataformas." *El Salto*, September 2021, <https://www.elsaltodiario.com/redes-sociales/es-mas-facil-imaginar-un-meme-de-mark-fisher-que-el-fin-del-capitalismo-de-plataformas>.
Eubanks, Viriginia. *Automating Inequality: How High-Tech Tools Profile, Police, and Punish the Poor*. St Martin's Press, 2017.
Faber, Liz W. *The Computer's Voice: From Star Trek to Siri*. University of Minnesota Press, 2020.
Farrow, Ronan. "How Democracies Spy on Their Citizens." *The New Yorker*, 2022, <https://www.newyorker.com/magazine/2022/04/25/how-democracies-spy-on-their-citizens>.
Fergus, Mark, and Hawk Ostby, creators. *The Expanse*. SyFy and Amazon Prime Video, 2015–22.
Fernandez, Rodrigo, et al. *Engineering Digital Monopolies: The Financialization of Big Tech*. Centre for Research on Multinational Corporations (SOMO), 2020.
Fernández Liria, Carlos. *La filosofía en canal*. YouTube, <https://www.youtube.com/c/CarlosLiria/playlists>.
Fevry, Sébastien. *Le Mise En Abyme Filmique: Essaie de Typologie*. Editions du CEFAL, 2000.
Fincher, David, director. *Fight Club*. 20th Century Fox, 1999.
Fisher, Mark. *Capitalist Realism: Is There No Alternative?* Zero Books, 2009.
———. *Ghosts of My Life: Writings on Depression, Hauntology and Lost Futures*. Zero Books, 2014.

Fisher, Mark, and Jeremy Gilbert. "Capitalist Realism and Neoliberal Hegemony: Jeremy Gilbert A Dialogue." *New Formations*, vol. 80–1, 2013, pp. 89–101.

Fitting, Peter. "Reality as Ideological Construct: A Reading of Five Novels by Philip K. Dick." *Science Fiction Studies*, vol. 10, no. 2, 1983, pp. 219–36.

Fleming, Peter. *The Death of Homo Economicus: Work, Debt and the Myth of Endless Accumulation*. Pluto Press, 2017.

Flew, Terry, and Richard Smith. *New Media: An Introduction*. Second Can, Oxford University Press, 2014.

Foley, Barbara. *Marxist Literary Criticism Today*. Pluto Press, 2019.

Folman, Ari, director. *The Congress*. Bridgit Folman Film Gang, 2013.

Foucault, Michel. *The Birth of Bio-politics: Lectures at the College de France 1978–79*. Edited by Michel Senellart. Palgrave Macmillan, 2008.

Frank, Arthur W. *The Wounded Storyteller: Body, Illness, and Ethis*. The University of Chicago Press, 1995.

Franklin, Seb. *Control: Digitality as Cultural Logic*. The MIT Press, 2015.

Fraser, Nancy. "Climates of Capital: For a Trans-Environmental Eco-Socialism." *New Left Review*, vol. 127, 2021, pp. 94–127.

——. *Fortunes of Feminism: From State-Mananged Capitalism to Neoliberal Crisis*. Verso, 2013.

Freedman, Carl. *Critical Theory and Science Fiction*. Wesleyan University Press, 2000.

Fridman, Lex. "Alex Garland: *Ex Machina, Devs, Annihilation*, and the Poetry of Science|Lex Fridman Podcast #77." *YouTube*, 2020, <https://www.youtube.com/watch?v=gU-mkuMU428>.

Friedberg, Anne. *The Virtual Window: From Alberti to Microsoft*. The MIT Press, 2006.

Fuchs, Christian. "Capitalism or Information Society? The Fundamental Question of the Present Structure of Society." *European Journal of Social Theory*, vol. 16, no. 4, 2013, pp. 413–34.

——. *Critical Theory of Communication: New Readings of Lukács, Adorno, Marcuse, Honneth and Habermas in the Age of the Internet*. University of Westminster Press, 2016.

Fuchs, Christian, and Vincent Mosco. *Marx in the Age of Digital Capitalism*. Brill, 2016.

Fukunaga, Cary Joji, director. "Exactly Like You." *Maniac*, created by Cary Joji Fukunaga and Patrick Somerville. Netflix, 2018.

——. "Option C." *Maniac*, created by Cary Joji Fukunaga and Patrick Somerville. Netflix, 2018.

——. "The Chosen One!" *Maniac*, created by Cary Joji Fukunaga. Netflix, 2018.

——. "Windmills." *Maniac*, created by Cary Joji Fukunaga and Patrick Somerville. Netflix, 2018.

Fukunaga, Cary Joji, and Patrick Somerville, creators. *Maniac*. Netflix, 2018.
Fukuyama, Francis. *The End of History and the Last Man*. The Free Press, 1992.
"Galaxy Brain." *Know Your Meme*, <https://knowyourmeme.com/memes/galaxy-brain>. Accessed March 1, 2022.
Galloway, Alexander R. *Protocol: How Control Exists After Decentralization*. The MIT Press, 2004.
Garland, Alex, creator. *Devs*. Hulu, 2020.
Garland, Alex, director. "Episode #1.3." *Devs*, created by Alex Garland. Hulu, 2020.
———. "Episode #1.7." *Devs*, created by Alex Garland. Hulu, 2020.
———. "Episode #1.8." *Devs*, created by Alex Garland. Hulu, 2020.
———. *Ex Machina*. Universal Pictures, 2014.
Gass, William H. *Fiction and the Figures of Life*. Knopf, 1970.
Gaughwin, Melinda. "'The Apple Way': Foucault, Design, Consumerism, and the Shaping of Apple Subjects." *Design and Culture*, vol. 15, no. 1, 2023, pp. 49–67.
Genette, Gérard. *Metalepsis: de la figura a la ficción*. Edited by Luciano Padilla López. Fondo de Cultura Económica, 2004.
———. *Narrative Discourse: An Essay in Method*. Cornell University Press, 1980.
———. *Palimpsestes: la littérature au second degré*. Éditions du Seuil, 1992.
Getzinger, Jennifer, director. "Crisis Theory." *Westworld*, created by Jonathan Nolan and Lisa Joy. Home Box Office, 2020.
Gibson, William. "Burning Chrome." *Omni*, 1982, pp. 72–7.
———. *Neuromancer*. Ace, 1984.
———. *The Peripheral*. G. P. Putnam's Sons, 2014.
Gil González, Antonio J., and José Antonio Pérez Bowie. *Ficciones nómadas: Procesos de intermedialidad literaria y audiovisual*. Pigmalión, 2017.
Gilbert, Jeremy. *Anticapitalism and Culture: Radical Theory and Popular Politics*. Berg, 2008.
———. "What Kind of Thing Is 'Neoliberalism'?" *Neoliberal Culture*, vol. 80–1, 2013, pp. 10–32.
Gilligan, Vince, creator. *Breaking Bad*. AMC, 2008.
Gittinger, Juli L. "The New Gods: Free Will, Determinism, and AI in *Westworld* and *DEVS*." *The Journal of Popular Culture*, vol. 55, no. 3, 2022, pp. 540–60.
Goldberg, Lesley. "Why HBO Canceled *Westworld*." *The Hollywood Reporter*, November 2022, <https://www.hollywoodreporter.com/tv/tv-news/why-hbo-canceled-westworld-1235256134/>.
González, Jesús Ángel. "'Pulling Up a Wild Bill': Television Post‐Westerns." *Journal of Popular Film and Television*, vol. 48, no. 3, 2020, pp. 163–73.
González De Ávila, Manuel. "La teoría crítica ante la cultura visual (actas de un reencuentro imaginario entre Horkheimer, Adorno, Benjamin y Marcuse)." *Signa*, vol. 22, no. 22, 2013, pp. 385–400.

———. "Metasemiosis: de la epistemología a la ética." *Cultura y Razón: Antropología de La Literatura y de La Imagen*. Anthropos, 2010, pp. 59–78.
Goode, Luke, and Michael Godhe. "Beyond Capitalist Realism—Why We Need Critical Future Studies." *Culture Unbound*, vol. 9, no. 1, 2017, pp. 109–29.
Graeber, David. *Bullshit Jobs: A Theory*. Simon & Schuster, 2018.
Gramsci, Antonio. *Selections from the Prison Notebooks of Antonio Gramsci*. Edited by Quintin Hoare and Geoffrey Nowell Smith. International Publishers, 1971.
Greenfield, Adam. *Radical Technologies: The Design of Everyday Life*. Verso, 2017.
Gulyas, Aaron John. *The Paranormal and the Paranoid. Conspiratorial Science Fiction Television*. Rowman and Littlefield, 2015.
Gunning, Tom. "The Cinema of Attraction[s]: Early Film, Its Spectator and the Avant-Garde." *The Cinema of Attractions Reloaded*, edited by Wanda Staruven. Amsterdam University Press, 2006, pp. 381–8.
Hagtvedt, Henrik. "A Brand (New) Experience: Art, Aesthetics, and Sensory Effects." *Journal of the Academy of Marketing Science*, vol. 50, no. 3, 2022, pp. 425–8.
Hall, Stuart. *The Hard Road to Renewal: Thatcherism and the Crisis of the Left*. Verso, 1988.
———. "The Neo-Liberal Revolution." *Cultural Studies*, vol. 25, no. 6, November 2011, pp. 705–28, <https://doi.org/10.1080/09502386.2011.619886>.
Han, Byung-Chul. *Psychopolitics: Neoliberalism and New Technologies of Power*. Verso, 2017.
Hansen, Miriam. "The Mass Production of the Senses: Classical Cinema as Vernacular Modernism." *Modernism/Modernity*, vol. 6, no. 2, 1999, pp. 59–77.
Haraway, Donna. "A Cyborg Manifesto: Science, Technology, and Socialist-Feminism in the Late Twentieth Century." *Simians, Cyborgs, and Women: The Reinvention of Nature*. Routledge, 1991, pp. 149–81.
Hartog, François. *Regimes of Historicity: Presentism and Experiences of Time*. Edited by Saskia Brown. Columbia University Press, 2015.
Hartwell, Ronald M. *A History of the Mont Pèlerin Society*. Liberty Fund, 1995.
Harvey, David. *A Brief History of Neoliberalism*. Oxford University Press, 2007.
———. *Anti-capitalist Chronicles*. Democracy at Work, 2018, <http://davidharvey.org/2022/01/new-podcast-david-harveys-anti-capitalist-chronicles/>.
———. "Neoliberalism as Creative Destruction." *The Annals of the American Academy of Political and Social Science*, vol. 610, no. 1, 2007, pp. 21–44.
———. *The Condition of Postmodernity: An Enquiry into the Origins of Cultural Change*. Blackwell, 1990.
———. "The 'New' Imperialism: Accumulation by Dispossession." *Socialist Register*, vol. 40, 2004, pp. 63–87.

Hassan, Ihab. "Beyond Postmodernism: Toward an Aesthetic of Trust." *Angelaki: Journal of the Theoretical Humanities*, vol. 8, no. 1, 2003, pp. 3–11.

——. "POSTmodernISM: A Paracritical Bibliography." *New Literary History*, vol. 3, no. 1, 1971, pp. 5–30.

Hassler-Forest, Dan. "Disney's Endgame: Corporate Stockholm Syndrome in the Age of the Mega-Franchise." *LA Review of Books*, June 2019.

——. "*Game of Thrones*: The Politics of World-Building and the Cultural Logic of Gentrification." *The Politics of Adaptation. Media Convergence and Ideology*, edited by Dan Hassler-Forest and Pascal Nicklas. Palgrave Macmillan, 2015, pp. 187–200.

——. "'When You Get There, You Will Already Be There': *Stranger Things*, *Twin Peaks* and the Nostalgia Industry." *Science Fiction Film and Television*, vol. 13, no. 2, 2020, pp. 175–97.

Hayles, N. B. "Metaphysics and Metafiction in *The Man in the High Castle*." *Philip K. Dick: Writers of the 21st Century*, edited by Martin H. Greenberg and Joseph D. Olander. Taplinger, 1983, pp. 53–71.

Haynes, Toby, director. "USS Callister." *Black Mirror*, created by Charlie Brooker. Netflix, 2017.

Hibberd, James. "HBO Cancels *Westworld* in Shock Decision." *The Hollywood Reporter*, November 2022, <https://www.hollywoodreporter.com/tv/tv-news/hbo-cancels-westworld-1235255955/>.

Hill, George Roy, director. Slaughterhouse-Five. Universal Pictures, 1972.

Horkheimer, Max. *Critical Theory: Selected Essays*. Continuum, 2002.

Hutcheon, Linda. *A Poetics of Postmodernism: History, Theory, Fiction*. Routledge, 1988.

——. *Narcissistic Narrative: The Metafictional Paradox*. Wilfrid Laurier University, 1980.

——. *The Politics of Postmodernism*. Routledge, 2002.

Imhof, Rüdiger. *Contemporary Metafiction: A Poetological Study of Metafiction in English*. Winter, 1986.

Inger, Christensen. *The Meaning of Metafiction*. Universitetforlaget, 1981.

Jackson, Pamela, and Jonathan Lethem, editors. *The Exegesis of Philip K. Dick*. Gollancz, 2011.

Jameson, Fredric. *Allegory and Ideology*. Verso, 2019.

——. *Archaeologies of the Future: The Desire Called Utopia and Other Science Fictions*. Verso, 2005.

——. "Foreword." *The Postmodern Condition*, edited by Jean-François Lyotard. University of Minnesota Press, 1984, pp. vii–xxi.

——. "Of Islands and Trenches: Naturalization and the Production of Utopian Discourse." *Diacritics*, vol. 7, no. 2, 1977, pp. 2–21.

———. *Postmodernism; or, the Cultural Logic of Late Capitalism*. Verso, 1991.
———. "Progress Versus Utopia; or, Can We Imagine the Future?" *Science Fiction Studies*, vol. 9, no. 2, 1982, pp. 147–58.
———. "Reification and Utopia in Mass Culture." *Social Text*, vol. 1, no. 1, 1979, pp. 130–48.
———. "The End of Temporality." *Critical Inquiry*, vol. 29, no. 4, 2003, pp. 695–718.
———. *The Political Unconscious: Narrative as a Socially Symbolic Act*. Routledge Classics, 2002.
Jeffries, Stuart. *Everything, All the Time, Everywhere: How We Became Postmodern*. Verso, 2021.
Jenkins, Henry. *Convergence Culture: Where Old and New Media Collide*. New York University Press, 2006.
Jenner, Mareike. *Netflix and the Re-invention of Television*. Palgrave Macmillan, 2018.
Jin, Dal Yong. "The Construction of Platform Imperialism in the Globalization Era." *TripleC*, vol. 11, no. 1, 2013, pp. 145–72.
Johnson, Carroll B. *Madness and Lust: A Psychoanalytical Approach to Don Quixote*. University of California Press, 1983.
Joque, Justin. *Revolutionary Mathematics: Artificial Intelligence, Statistics and the Logic of Capitalism*. Verso, 2022.
Joy, Lisa, and Jonathan Nolan, creators. *Westworld*. Home Box Office, 2016.
Kakoudaki, Despina. "Unmaking People: The Politics of Negation in Frankenstein and Ex Machina." *Science Fiction Studies*, vol. 45, no. 2, 2018, pp. 289–307.
Kaldor, Mary. "After the Cold War." *New Left Review*, vol. 180, 1990, pp. 25–37.
Kassell, Nicole, director. "Les Écorchés." *Westworld*, created by Jonathan Nolan and Lisa Joy. Home Box Office, 2018.
Kellman, Steven. "The Fiction of Self-Begetting." *The Self-Begetting Novel*. Columbia University Press, 1980, pp. 1–11.
Kelly, James Patrick, and John Kessel. *Rewired: The Post-Cyberpunk Anthology*. Tachyon Books, 2007.
Kelly, Mark G. E. *Normal Now: Individualism as Conformity*. Polity Press, 2022.
Kirby, Alan. *Digimodernism: How New Technologies Dismantle the Postmodern and Reconfigure Our Culture*. Continuum, 2009.
Klein, Naomi. *The Shock Doctrine: The Rise of Disaster Capitalism*. Metropolitan Books, 2007.
Koller, S. "'I Imagined a Story Where I Didn't Have to Be the Damsel': Seriality, Reflexivity, and Narratively Complex Women in *Westworld*." *Zeitschrift Für Anglistik Und Amerikanistik*, vol. 67, no. 2, 2019, pp. 163–80.
Krabbenhoft, Kenneth. "The Uses of Madness in Cervantes and Philip K Dick." *Science Fiction Studies*, vol. 27, no. 2, 2000, pp. 216–33.

Kropf, Carl R. "Douglas Adam's 'Hitchhiker' Novels as Mock Science Fiction." *Science Fiction Studies*, vol. 15, no. 1, 1988, pp. 61–70.

Kucukalic, Lejla. *Philip K Dick: Canonical Writer of the Digital Age*. Routledge, 2010.

Kuhn, Annette. *Alien Zone: Cultural Theory and Contemporary Science Fiction Cinema*. Verso, 1990.

———. *Alien Zone II: The Spaces of Science-Fiction Cinema*. Verso, 1999.

Kukkonen, Karin, and Sonja Klimek. *Metalepsis in Popular Culture*. De Gruyter, 2011.

Landon, Brooks. *The Aesthetics of Ambivalence: Rethinking Science Fiction Film in the Age of Electronic (Re)Production*. Greenwood Press, 1992.

Lang, Fritz, director. *Metropolis*. Universum Film, 1927.

Laraway, David Phillip. *Borges and Black Mirror*. Palgrave Pivot, 2020.

Lay, Chris, and David Kyle Johnson. "*Bandersnatch*: A Choose-Your-Own Philosophical Adventure." *Black Mirror and Philosophy: Dark Reflections*, edited by David Kyle Johnson. Wiley-Blackwell, 2020, pp. 199–238.

Layton, Lynne. "Irrational Exuberance: Neoliberal Subjectivity and the Perversion of Truth." *Subjectivity*, vol. 3, no. 3, 2010, pp. 303–22.

Le Guin, Ursula K. *The Left Hand of Darkness*. Edited by David Mitchell and Carlie Jane Anders. Ace, 2019.

Lem, Stanisław. *The Futurological Congress*. Seabury Press, 1974.

Lem, Stanisław, and Istvan Csicsery-Ronay Jr. "Metafuturology." *Science Fiction Studies*, vol. 13, no. 3, 1986, pp. 261–71.

Lem, Stanisław, and Robert Abernathy. "Philip K. Dick: A Visionary among the Charlatans." *Science Fiction Studies*, vol. 2, no. 1, 1975, pp. 54–67.

Levy, Steven. *Hackers: Heroes of the Computer Revolution*. Delta Book, 1984.

Lewis, Hilary. "Amazon Orders 5 New Series Including *Man in the High Castle*." *The Hollywood Reporter*, February 2015, <https://www.hollywoodreporter.com/news/general-news/amazon-orders-5-new-series-774725/>.

Lewis, Richard J., director. "Que Será, Será." *Westworld*, created by Jonathan Nolan and Lisa Joy. Home Box Office, 2022.

Linklater, Richard, director. *A Scanner Darkly*. Warner Independent Pictures, 2006.

Losada Goya, José Manuel. "El 'mito' de Don Quijote (2ª Parte): ¿con o sin comillas? En busca de criterios pertinentes del mito." *Cervantès quatre siècles après: nouveaux objets, nouvelles approches*, edited by Emmanuel Marigno et al. Orbis Tertius, 2017.

Lucas, R. "The Surveillance Business." *New Left Review*, vol. 121, 2020, pp. 132–41.

Luckhurst, Roger. "The Many Deaths of Science Fiction: A Polemic." *Science Fiction Studies*, vol. 21, no. 1, 1994, pp. 35–50.

Lyn, Euros, director. "Fifteen Million Merits." *Black Mirror*, created by Charlie Brooker, Channel 4, November 2011.

Lyotard, Jean-François. *The Postmodern Condition*. University of Minnesota Press, 1984.
Mair, Peter. *Ruling the Void: The Hollowing-Out of Western Democracy*. Verso, 2013.
Malina, Debra. *Breaking the Frame: Metalepsis and the Construction of the Subject*. The Ohio State University Press, 2002.
Malmgren, Carl. "Meta-SF: The Examples of Dick, LeGuin, and Russ." *Extrapolation*, vol. 43, no. 1, 2002, pp. 22–35.
———. "Philip Dick's Man in the High Castle and the Nature of SF Worlds." Bridges to Science Fiction, edited by George E. Slusser, George R. Guffey, and Mark Rose. Southern Illinois University Press, 1980, pp. 120–30.
Mandel, Ernest. *Late Capitalism*. Edited by Joris De Bres. New Left Books, 1975.
Marcuse, Herbert. *Five Lectures: Psychoanalysis, Politics, and Utopia*. Edited by Jeremy J. Shapiro and Shierry M. Weber. Penguin, 1970.
———. *One-Dimensional Man: Studies in the Ideology of Advanced Industrial Society*. Edited by Douglas Kellner. Routledge, 2002.
Martín, Adriene L. "Humor and Violence in Cervantes." *The Cambridge Companion to Cervantes*, edited by Anthony J. Cascardi. Cambridge University Press, 2002, pp. 160–85.
Martin, Randy. *Knowledge LTD: Toward a Social Logic of the Derivative*. Temple University Press, 2015.
Marx, Karl. *Capital Volume I*. Penguin Classics, 1990.
———. *Early Political Writings*. Edited by Joseph O'Malley. Cambridge University Press, 1994.
———. *Grundrisse*. Penguin Books, 1993.
———. "The Eighteenth Brumaire of Louis Bonaparte." *Karl Marx: The Political Writings*, edited by Tariq Ali and David Fernbach. Verso, 2019, pp. 477–583.
Marx, Karl, and Friedrich Engels. *The Communist Manifesto, with an Introduction by Yanis Varoufakis*. Edited by Yanis Varoufakis. Vintage Classics, 2018.
Marx, Leo. "The Idea of 'Technology' and Postmodern Pessimism." *Does Technology Drive History? The Dilemma of Technological Determinism*, edited by Merritt Roe Smith and Leo Marx. The MIT Press, 1994, pp. 237–57.
———. *The Machine in the Garden: Technology and the Pastoral Ideal in America*. Oxford University Press, 1964.
Marx, Paris. *Tech Won't Save Us*. Harbinger Media Network, <https://techwontsave.us/>.
McAlear, Rob. "The Value of Fear: Toward a Rhetorical Model of Dystopia." *Interdisciplinary Humanities*, vol. 27, no. 2, 2010, pp. 24–42.
McCaffery, Larry. *Storming the Reality Studio: A Casebook of Cyberpunk and Postmodern Science Fiction*. Duke University Press, 1991.

———. *The Metafictional Muse: The Works of Robert Coover, Donald Barthelme, and William H. Gass*. University of Pittsburgh Press, 1982.
McClanahan, Annie. "Serious Crises: Rethinking the Neoliberal Subject." *Boundary 2*, vol. 46, no. 1, 2019, pp. 103–32.
McFarlane, Anna, et al. *Fifty Key Figures in Cyberpunk Culture*. Routledge, 2022.
———. *The Routledge Companion to Cyberpunk Culture*. Routledge, 2020.
McGowan, Todd. *The Real Gaze: Film Theory after Lacan*. State University of New York Press, 2007.
McHale, Brian. *Constructing Postmodernism*. Routledge, 1992.
———. *Postmodernist Fiction*. Routledge, 2004.
McKenna, Tony. "Behind the *Black Mirror*: The Limits of Orwellian Dystopia." *Critique (United Kingdom)*, vol. 47, no. 2, 2019, pp. 365–76.
McLuhan, Marshall. *Understanding Media: The Extensions of Man*. Gingko Press, 2013.
McRobbie, Angela. *Postmodernism and Popular Culture*. Routledge, 1994.
McSweeney, Terence, and Stuart Joy. "Change Your Past, Your Present, Your Future? Interactive Narratives and Trauma in *Bandersnatch* (2018)." *Through the Black Mirror: Deconstructing the Side Effects of the Digital Age*, edited by Terence McSweeney and Stuart Joy. Palgrave Macmillan, 2019, pp. 271–84.
Menzies, William Cameron, director. *Things to Come*. London Films Productions, 1936.
Miéville, China. "Cognition as Ideology: A Dialectic of SF Theory." *Red Planets: Marxism and Science Fiction*, edited by China Miéville and Mark Bould. Pluto Press, 2009, pp. 231–48.
Milburn, Colin. *Respawn: Gamers, Hackers, and Technogenic Life*. Duke University Press, 2018.
Mirowski, Philip. "Postface: Defining Neoliberalism." *The Road from Mont Pèlerin: The Making of the Neoliberal Thought Collective*, edited by Philip Mirowski and Dieter Plehwe. Harvard University Press, 2015, pp. 417–55.
Mittell, Jason. *Complex TV: The Poetics of Contemporary Television Storytelling*. New York University Press, 2015.
Moore, Jason W. *Capitalism in the Web of Life: Ecology and the Accumulation of Capital*. Verso, 2015.
Moore, Roland D., and Michael Dinner, creators. *Philip K. Dick's Electric Dreams*. Amazon Prime Video, 2018.
Moreno Zacarés, Javier. "Euphoria of the Rentier?" *New Left Review*, vol. 129, 2021, pp. 47–67.
Moro Martín, Alfredo. *Transformaciones del Quijote en la novela inglesa y alemana del siglo XVIII*. Editorial Universidad de Alcalá, 2016.

Morozov, Evgeny. "Capitalism's New Clothes." *The Baffler*, February 2019, <https://thebaffler.com/latest/capitalisms-new-clothes-morozov>.
———. "Critique of Techno-Feudal Reason." *New Left Review*, vol. 133–4, 2022, pp. 89–126.
Mosco, Vincent. *The Digital Sublime: Myth, Power, and Cyberspace*. The MIT Press, 2004.
Mouffe, Chantal. *For a Left Populism*. Verso, 2018.
Moulier Boutang, Yann. *Cognitive Capitalism*. Polity Press, 2011.
Mountfort, Paul. "The I Ching and Philip K. Dick's *The Man in the High Castle*." *Science Fiction Studies*, vol. 43, no. 2, 2016, pp. 287–309.
Moylan, Tom. *Becoming Utopian: The Culture and Politics of Radical Transformation*. Edited by Ruth Levitas and Philip E. Wegner. Bloomsbury Academic, 2021.
———. *Demand the Impossible: Science Fiction and the Utopian Imagination*. Edited by Raffaella Baccolini. Peter Lang, 2014.
———. *Demand the Impossible: Science Fiction and the Utopian Imagination*. Methuen, 1986.
———. "'Look into the Dark': On Dystopia and the Novum." *Learning from Other Worlds: Estrangement, Cognition, and the Politics of Science Fiction and Utopia*, edited by Patrick Parrinder. Liverpool University Press, 2000, pp. 51–71.
———. *Scraps of the Untainted Sky: Science Fiction, Utopia, Dystopia*. Westview Press, 2000.
———. "The Necessity of Hope in Dystopian Times: A Critical Reflection." *Utopian Studies*, vol. 31, no. 1, 2020, pp. 164–93.
Mulcahy, Lisa, director. "Episode #1.5." *Years and Years*, created by Russell T. Davies, Home Box Office, 2019.
Mullen, E. "'Not Much of a Rind on You': (De)Constructing Genre and Gender in *Westworld* (Lisa Joy and Jonathan Nolan, HBO, 2016–)." *TV Series*, vol. 14, 2018.
Mulvey, Laura. "Visual Pleasure and Narrative Cinema." *Screen*, vol. 16, no. 3, 1975, pp. 6–18.
Murphy, Graham J. "Cyberpunk and Post-Cyberpunk." *The Cambridge History of Science Fiction*, edited by Eric Carl Link and Gerry Canavan. Cambridge University Press, 2019, pp. 519–36.
Murphy, Graham J., and Sherryl Vint. *Beyond Cyberpunk: New Critical Perspectives*. Routledge, 2010.
Murphy, Sheila C. *How Television Invented New Media*. Rutgers University Press, 2011.
Nabokov, Vladimir. *Lectures on Don Quixote*. Edited by Fredson Bowers. Harcourt Brace Jovanovich, 1983.

Nancy, Jean-Luc. *The Ground of the Image*. Translated by Jeff Fort. Fordham University Press, 2009.

Nealon, Jeffrey T. *Post-postmodernism: Or, the Cultural Logic of Just-in-Time Capitalism*. Stanford University Press, 2012.

Nee, Rebecca C. "Wild, Stressful, or Stupid: Que Es *Bandersnatch*? Exploring User Outcomes of Netflix's Interactive *Black Mirror* Episode." *Convergence*, vol. 27, no. 5, 2021, pp. 1488–506.

Neugebauer, Wilhelm E. *El Don Quijote alemán*. Edited by Alfredo Moro Martín, translated by Javier García Albero and Alfredo Moro Martín. Ediciones Universidad de Salamanca, 2022.

Nevado Encinas, Juan Luis. "El Posmodernismo Como Teoría de La Conspiración. La Izquierda Reaccionaria Frente a La Crisis de 2008." *Revista Stvltifera de Humanidades y Ciencias Sociales*, vol. 4, no. 2, 2021, pp. 177–96.

Ngai, Sianne. *Theory of the Gimmick: Aesthetic Judgment and Capitalist Form*. The Belknap Press of Harvard University Press, 2020.

Nilges, Mathias. "The Realism of Speculation: Contemporary Speculative Fiction as Immanent Critique of Finance Capitalism." *CR: The New Centennial Review*, vol. 19, no. 1, 2019, pp. 37–59.

Noble, Safiya Umoja. *Algorithms of Oppression: How Search Engines Reinforce Racism*. New York University Press, 2018.

Nolan, Jonathan, director. "The Original." *Westworld*, created by Jonathan Nolan and Lisa Joy. Home Box Office, 2016.

Nye, David E. *American Technological Sublime*. The MIT Press, 1994.

O'Neil, Cathy. *Weapons of Math Destruction: How Big Data Increases Inequality and Threatens Democracy*. Crown Publishers, 2016.

Oancea, Ana. "Mind the Knowledge Gap: Ex Machina's Reinterpretation of the Female Android." *Science Fiction Film and Television*, vol. 13, no. 2, 2020, pp. 223–46.

Ollman, Bertell. *Dance of the Dialectic: Steps in Marx's Method*. University of Illinois Press, 2003.

Oplev, Niels Arden, director. "Eps1.0_hellofriend.Mov." *Mr Robot*, created by Sam Esmail. USA Network, 2015.

Ostalska, Katarzyna, and Tomasz Fisiak. *The Postworld In-between Utopia and Dystopia*. Routledge, 2021.

Pace, Jonathan. "The Concept of Digital Capitalism." *Communication Theory*, vol. 28, no. 3, 2018, pp. 254–69.

Pagetti, Carlo, et al. "Dick and Meta-SF." *Science Fiction Studies*, vol. 2, no. 1, 1975, pp. 24–31.

Panka, Daniel. "Transparent Subjects: Digital Identity in Mary Shelley's Frankenstein and Charlie Brooker's 'Be Right Back.'" *Science Fiction Studies*, vol. 45, no. 2, 2018, pp. 308–24.

Pardo García, Pedro Javier. "Cine, literatura y mito: Don Quijote en el cine, más allá de la adaptación." *Arbor. Ciencia, Pensamiento y Cultura*, vol. 187, no. 748, 2011, pp. 237–46.

———. "Del metateatro a la metaficción teatral en el cine: 'Familia', de Fernando León de Aranoa, y sus allegados." *La teatralidad en la pantalla: reflexiones sobre el diálogo contemporáneo entre cine y teatro*, edited by José Antonio Pérez Bowie, Los Libros de la Catarata, 2018, pp. 61–98.

———. "Del mito a la novela: el Quijote y su sombra en la narrativa británica del siglo XX (y XXI)." *Recreaciones quijotescas y cervantinas en la narrativa*, edited by Carlos Mata Induráin, Eunsa, 2013, pp. 195–210.

———. "Don Quixote in Great Britain." *Don Quixote Around the Globe*, edited by Slav N. Gratchev and Howard Mancing. Juan de la Cuesta, 2020, pp. 21–56.

———. "El Quijote, la novela y metanovela." *El hidalgo fuerte: siete miradas al Quijote*, edited by A. Rivas Yanes. Círculo Cultural Antonio Machado, 2005, pp. 107–42.

———. "El Quijote posmoderno: en acercamiento transnacional y transmedial." *Au-Delà Du Pied de La Lettre: Estudios En Homenaje a Montserrat Cots*, edited by Hélène Rufat Perello and Dámaso López García. Universitat Pompeu Fabra, 2022, pp. 149–82.

———. "El Quijote transnacional: hacia una poética del mito quijotesco." *Cervantes y la posteridad: 400 años de legado cervantino*, edited by Alfredo Moro Martín. Iberoamericana, 2019, pp. 9–34.

———. "Hacia una teoría de la reflexividad fílmica: la autoconciencia de la literatura al cine." *Transescrituras audiovisuales*, edited by José Antonio Pérez Bowie and Pedro Javier Pardo García. Sial Pigmalión, 2015, pp. 47–94.

———. "La metaficcion de la literatura al cine: la anagnórisis metaficcional de *Niebla* a *Abre los ojos*." *CELEHIS. Revista Del Centro de Letras Hispanoamericanas*, vol. 20, no. 22, 2011, pp. 151–74.

———. "La reflexividad teatral del escenario a la pantalla." *Tropelías. Revista de teoría de la literatura y literatura comparada*, vol. Extra 2, 2017, pp. 409–36.

———. *La tradición cervantina en la novela inglesa del siglo XVIII*. Universidad de Salamanca, 1996.

———. "The Frankenstein Myth in Film: Transmediation and Science Fiction (Blade Runner and 2049)." *Trasvases entre la literatura y el cine*, vol. 2, 2020, pp. 9–42.

Pardo García, Pedro Javier, and Antonio J. Gil González. *Adaptación 2.0: estudios comparados sobre intermedialidad*. Éditions Orbis Tertius, 2018.

Parikka, Jussi. *A Geology of Media*. University of Minnesota Press, 2015.

———. *The Anthrobscene*. University of Minnesota Press, 2015.
Pariser, Eli. *The Filter Bubble: What the Internet Is Hiding from You*. Viking, 2011.
Parrinder, Patrick. *Learning from Other Worlds: Estrangement, Cognition and the Politics of Science Fiction and Utopia*. Liverpool University Press, 2000.
Pasquale, Frank. *The Black Box Society: The Secret Algorithms That Control Money and Information*. Harvard University Press, 2015.
Paus, Eva. *Confronting Dystopia: The New Technological Revolution and the Future of Work*. Cornell University Press, 2018.
Pedullà, Gabriele. *In Broad Daylight: Movies and Spectators after the Cinema*. Translated by Patricia Gaborik. Verso, 2012.
Pérez Bowie, José Antonio. "El Cine En, Desde y Sobre El Cine: Metaficción, Reflexividad e Intertextualidad." *Anthropos*, vol. 208, 2006, pp. 122–37.
Philmus, Robert M. "'Futurological Congress' as Metageneric Text." *Science Fiction Studies*, vol. 13, no. 3, 1986, pp. 313–28.
———. "The Two Faces of Philip K. Dick." *Science Fiction Studies*, vol. 18, no. 1, 1991, pp. 91–103.
Piketty, Thomas. *Capital in the Twenty-First Century*. Edited by Arthur Goldhammer. Harvard University Press, 2014.
Plehwe, Dieter, et al. *Nine Lives of Neoliberalism*. Verso, 2020.
Rabkin, Eric S. "Irrational Expectations; or, How Economics and the Post-industrial World Failed Philip K. Dick." *Science Fiction Studies*, vol. 15, no. 2, 1988, pp. 161–72.
Ramírez, J. Jesse. *Against Automation Mythologies: Business Science Fiction and the Ruse of the Robots*. Routledge, 2021.
Read, Jason. "A Genealogy of Homo-Economicus: Neoliberalism and the Production of Subjectivity." *Foucault Studies*, no. 6, 2009, pp. 25–36.
Rice, Lynette. "*Westworld*: Jonathan Nolan Drops Hint at New York Comic Con about Fifth and Final Season Negotiations." *Deadline*, October 2022, <https://deadline.com/2022/10/westworld-jonathan-fifth-and-final-season-jonathan-nolan-addresses-nycc-1235139135/>.
Rieder, John. "The Metafictive World of *The Man in the High Castle*: Hermeneutics, Ethics, and Political Ideology." *Science Fiction Studies*, vol. 15, no. 2, 1988, pp. 214–25.
Robinson, Kim Stanley. *The Ministry for the Future*. Orbit, 2020.
Roddenberry, Gene. *Star Trek*. NBC, 1966–9.
Romano, Aja. "Netflix Is a Character in *Black Mirror: Bandersnatch*. Only *Black Mirror* Could Pull That Off." *Vox*, December 2018, <https://www.vox.com/culture/2018/12/28/18159100/black-mirror-bandersnatch-netflix-review-gameplay-endings>.

Rossi, Umberto. "Fourfold Symmetry: The Interplay of Fictional Levels in Five More or Less Prestigious Novels by Philip K. Dick." *Extrapolation*, vol. 43, no. 4, 2002, pp. 398–419.

———. *The Twisted Worlds of Philip K. Dick: A Reading of Twenty Ontologically Uncertain Novels*. McFarland & Company, 2011.

Rowson, Jonathan, and Layman Pascal. *Time between Worlds: Crisis and Emergence in Metamodernity*. Perspectiva Press, 2021.

Rushdie, Salman. *Quichotte*. Jonathan Cape, 2019.

Russ, Joanna. "SF and Technology as Mystification." *Science Fiction Studies*, vol. 5, no. 3, 1978, pp. 250–60.

Sadowski, Jathan. *Too Smart: How Digital Capitalism Is Extracting Data, Controlling Our Lives, and Taking Over the World*. The MIT Press, 2020.

Salter, Anastasia, and Bridget Blodgett. *Toxic Geek Masculinity in Media: Sexism, Trolling, and Identity Policing*. Palgrave Macmillan, 2017.

Savage, Luke. "Jordan Peterson's 'Postmodern Neomarxism' Is Pure Hokum." *Jacobin Magazine*, March 2022.

Schiller, Dan. *Digital Capitalism: Networking the Global Market System*. The MIT Press, 1999.

Scholes, Robert. *Fabulation and Metafiction*. University of Illinois Press, 1979.

———. "Metafiction." *The Iowa Review*, vol. 1, no. 4, 1970, pp. 100–15.

———. *Structural Fabulation: An Essay on Fiction of the Future*. University of Notre Dame Press, 1975.

Schubert, Stefan, and Eleonora Ravizza. "'They Don't Make Anything Like They Used To': Visual, Narrative, and Ideological Nostalgia for the West(ern) in *Westworld* (2016)." *Comparative American Studies: An International Journal*, vol. 19, no. 4, 2022, pp. 419–37.

Schwab, Klaus. *The Fourth Industrial Revolution*. World Economic Forum, 2016.

Scott, Ridley, director. *Blade Runner*. Warner, 1982.

Scott, Suzanne. *Fake Geek Girls: Fandom, Gender, and the Convergence Culture Industry*. New York University Press, 2019.

Sebastián-Martín, Miguel. "All the Park's a Stage: *Westworld* as the Metafictional Frankenstein." *ES Review: Spanish Journal of English Studies*, no. 39, December 2018, pp. 51–67.

———. "Allegorising Surveillance Capitalism: *Westworld*'s Science Fictional and Metafictional Pastiche." *Moving Beyond the Pandemic: English and American Studies in Spain*, edited by Francisco Gallardo-del-Puerto et al. Editorial Universidad de Cantabria, 2022, pp. 224–30.

———. "Between Therapy and Revolution: *Mr Robot*'s Ambivalence towards Hacker Masculinity." *Detoxing Masculinity in Anglophone Literature and Culture: In*

Search of Good Men, edited by Sara Martín and M. Isabel Santaulària. Palgrave Macmillan, 2023, pp. 231–47.
———. "De-automating Capitalist Automation." *Science Fiction Studies*, vol. 49, no. 1, 2022, pp. 191–5.
———. "Don Quixote as Gamer? Theorising New Media Quixotism through Contemporary Science Fiction Television." *Science Fiction Film and Television*, vol. 15, no. 2, 2022, pp. 193–217.
———. "Refabricating Individualism and Commodifying Anti-capitalism: Melodramatic SF and VOD Spectatorship." *Science Fiction Studies*, vol. 48, no. 2, 2021, pp. 332–53.
———. "Review of *Devs*, Season 1." *SFRA Review*, vol. 50, no. 4, 2020, pp. 183–5.
———. "Review of Liz W. Faber's *The Computer's Voice: From Star Trek to Siri*." *Science Fiction Film & Television*, vol. 15, no. 3, 2022, pp. 372–6.
———. "Silicon Valley as Cult? Mystifying and Demystifying Surveillance Capitalism in Alex Garland's *Devs* (2020)." *SFRA Review*, vol. 51, no. 4, 2021, pp. 195–200.
———. "Subverting or Reasserting? *Westworld* (2016–) as an Ambiguous Critical Allegory of Gender Struggles." *452ºF. Revista de Teoría de La Literatura y Literatura Comparada*, vol. 24, January 2021, pp. 129–45.
———. "The Franchise Devouring Itself: A Critical Analysis of the Marvel Cinematic Universe's Reflexive Turn". *REDEN. Revista Española De Estudios Norteamericanos*, vol. 5, no. 2, 2024, pp. 20–42.
Seed, David. *A Companion to Science Fiction*. Blackwell, 2005.
Semel, David, director. "The New World." *The Man in the High Castle*, created by Frank Spotnitz. Amazon Originals, 2015.
Seymour, Richard. *The Twittering Machine*. The Indigo Press, 2019.
Shaviro, Steven. "The Erotic Life of Machines." *Parallax*, vol. 8, no. 4, 2002, pp. 21–31.
———. "The Singularity Is Here." *Red Planets: Marxism and Science Fiction*, edited by Mark Bould and China Miéville. Pluto Press, 2009, pp. 103–17.
Shuster, Martin. "Rewatching, Film, and New Television." *Open Philosophy*, vol. 5, no. 1, 2022, pp. 17–30.
Simon, David, creator. *The Wire*. Home Box Office, 2002.
Slade, David, director. *Black Mirror: Bandersnatch*, written by Charlie Brooker. Netflix, 2018.
Sloterdijk, Peter. "Critique of Cynical Reason." *Modern Drama*, edited by Michael Eldred and Andreas Huyssen. University of Minnesota Press, 1987.
Smith, Anthony N. "Pursuing 'Generation Snowflake': *Mr Robot* and the USA Network's Mission for Millennials." *Television and New Media*, vol. 20, no. 5, 2019, pp. 443–59.
Smith, Neil. "Nature, Politics, and Possibilities: A Debate and Discussion with David Harvey and Donna Haraway." *Environment and Planning D: Society and Space*, vol. 13, no. 5, 1995, pp. 507–27.

Smith, Scott B., creator. *The Peripheral*. Executive production by Lisa Joy et al. Amazon Prime Video, 2022–present.

Smith-Rowsey, Daniel, editor. *The Netflix Effect: Technology and Entertainment in the 21st Century*. Bloomsbury Academic, 2016.

Sobchack, Vivian. *Screening Space: The American Science Fiction Film*. Rutgers University Press, 1997.

Soengas, Xosé. "The Role of the Internet and Social Networks in the Arab Uprisings—An Alternative to Official Press Censorship." *Comunicar: Scientific Journal of Media Education*, vol. 41, no. XXI, 2013, pp. 147–55.

Sontag, Susan. "The Imagination of Disaster." *Against Interpretation and Other Essays*. Picador, 1990.

Sorel, Charles. *El pastor extravagante*. Translated by Tomás Gonzalo Santos. Ediciones Universidad de Salamanca, 2022.

Soren-Rethel, Alfred. *Intellectual and Manual Labour: A Critique of Epistemology*. MacMillan, 1978.

Spielberg, Steven, director. *Minority Report*. 20th Century Fox, 2002.

———. *Ready Player One*. Warner, 2018.

Spotnitz, Frank, creator. *The Man in the High Castle*. Amazon Originals, 2015.

Srnicek, Nick. *Platform Capitalism*. Polity Press, 2017.

St James, Emily. "*The Man in the High Castle*'s Showrunner Answers Your Questions about the Amazon Hit." *Vox*, December 2015, <https://www.vox.com/culture/2015/12/8/9871796/the-man-in-the-high-castle-review-amazon-interview>.

Stam, Robert. "Beyond Fidelity: The Dialogics of Adaptation." *Film Adaptation*, edited by James Naremore. Rutgers University Press, 2000, pp. 54–76.

———. *Reflexivity in Film and Literature: From Don Quixote to Jean-Luc Godard*. Columbia University Press, 1992.

Stanfill, Mel. "Introduction: The Reactionary in the Fan and the Fan in the Reactionary." *Television and New Media*, vol. 21, no. 2, 2020, pp. 123–34.

Stephenson, Neal. *Snow Crash*. Bantam Books, 1992.

Sterling, Bruce. *Mirrorshades: The Cyberpunk Anthology*. Ace, 1988.

Stern, Michael. "Making Culture into Nature." *Alien Zone: Cultural Theory and Contemporary Science Fiction Cinema*, edited by Annette Kuhn. Verso, 1990, pp. 66–72.

Stiegler, Bernard. *The Decadence of Industrial Democracies: Disbelief and Discredit, Volume 1*. Edited by Daniel Ross and Suzanne Arnold. Polity Press, 2011.

Stock, Adam. *Modern Dystopian Fiction and Political Thought: Narratives of World Politics*. Routledge, 2018.

Stonehill, Brian. *The Self-Conscious Novel: Artifice in Fiction from Joyce to Pynchon*. University of Pennsylvania Press, 1988.

Storey, John. *Cultural Theory and Popular Culture*. 5th edn. Pearson, 2018.

Streeck, Wolfgang. *Buying Time: The Delayed Crisis of Democratic Capitalism*. Verso, 2014.

———. *How Will Capitalism End? Essays on a Failing System*. Verso, 2016.

Ström, Timothy Erik. "Capital and Cybernetics." *New Left Review*, vol. 135, no. May/June, 2022, pp. 23–41.

Supiot, Alain. *Governance by Numbers: The Making of a Legal Model of Allegiance*. Edited by Saskia Brown. Bloomsbury, 2017.

Suvin, Darko. *Defined by a Hollow: Essays on Utopia, Science Fiction and Political Epistemology*. Peter Lang, 2010.

———. *Metamorphoses of Science Fiction: On the Poetics and History of a Literary Genre*. Yale University Press, 1979.

———. "On Communism, Science Fiction, and Utopia: The Blagoevgrad Theses." *Mediations*, vol. 32, no. 2, 2019, pp. 139–60.

———. "P. K. Dick's Opus: Artifice as Refuge and World View (Introductory Reflections)." *Science Fiction Studies*, vol. 2, no. 1, 1975, pp. 8–22.

———. *Positions and Presuppositions in Science Fiction*. McMillan Press, 1988.

Suzor, Nicolas P. *Lawless: The Secret Rules That Govern Our Digital Lives*. Cambridge University Press, 2019.

Swirski, Peter. "Playing a Game of Ontology: A Postmodern Reading of the Futurological Congress." *Extrapolation*, vol. 33, no. 1, 1992, pp. 32–40.

Taffel, Sy. *Digital Media Ecologies: Entanglements of Content, Code and Hardware*. Bloomsbury Academic, 2019.

Tamames, Jorge. *La Brecha y Los Cauces: El Momento Populista En España y Estados Unidos*. Edited by Pablo Bustinduy and Chantal Mouffe. Lengua de trapo, 2021.

Telotte, J. P. "The Fractured Frames of *Black Mirror*." *Science Fiction Film and Television*, vol. 14, no. 1, 2021, pp. 1–19.

Thompson, Derek. "Netflix, *House of Cards*, and the Golden Age of Television." *The Atlantic*, February 2013, <https://www.theatlantic.com/business/archive/2013/02/netflix-house-of-cards-and-the-golden-age-of-television/272869/>.

Traverso, Enzo. *Left-Wing Melancholia: Marxism, History, and Memory*. Columbia University Press, 2016.

Tuck, Greg. "When More Is Less: CGI, Spectacle and the Capitalist Sublime." *Science Fiction Film & Television*, vol. 1, no. 2, 2008, pp. 249–73.

Urraco Solanilla, Mariano. "El Caballo de Troya de Las Distopías Juveniles: Discurso Hegemónico Disfrazado de Rebelde." *Distopía y Sociedad: Revista de Estudios Culturales*, vol. 1, 2021, pp. 154–69.

Vaidhyanathan, Siva. *The Googlization of Everything (and Why We Should Worry)*. University of California Press, 2011.

Vaidman, Lev. "Many-Worlds Interpretation of Quantum Mechanics." *Stanford Encyclopedia of Philosophy*, edited by Edward N. Zalta, Fall 2021, <https://plato.stanford.edu/archives/fall2021/entries/qm-manyworlds/>.
Verhoeven, Paul, director. *Total Recall*. Carolco Pictures, 1990.
Vermeulen, Timoteus, and Robin van den Akker. "Notes on Metamodernism." *Journal of Aesthetics & Culture*, vol. 2, no. 1, 2010, pp. 1–14.
Vieira, Fátima. *Dystopia(n) Matters: On the Page, on Screen, on Stage*. Cambridge Scholars Publishing, 2013.
Villeneuve, Denis, director. *Blade Runner 2049*. Columbia Pictures, 2017.
Vinge, Vernor. "The Coming Technological Singularity: How to Survive in the Posthuman Era." *Vision 21: Interdisciplinary Science and Engineering in the Era of Cyberspace*, vol. 21, NASA, 1993, pp. 11–22.
Vint, Sherryl. "Afterword: The World Gibson Made." *Beyond Cyberpunk: New Critical Perspectives*, edited by Graham J. Murphy and Sherryl Vint. Routledge, 2010.
———. "Introduction to 'The Futures Industry.'" *Paradoxa*, vol. 27, 2015, pp. 7–19.
Volmar, Daniel. "Far from the Lonely Crowd: The Trenchant Techno-Cynicism of *Mr Robot*." *Endeavour*, vol. 41, no. 4, 2017, pp. 208–10.
Vonnegut, Kurt. *Slaughterhouse-Five*. Delacorte, 1969.
Wachowski, Lana, director. *The Matrix Resurrections*. Warner, 2021.
Wachowski, Lana, and Lily Wachowski, directors. *The Matrix*. Warner, 1999.
———. *The Matrix Reloaded*. Warner, 2003.
———. *The Matrix Revolutions*. Warner, 2003.
Wajcman, Judy. *Pressed for Time: The Acceleration of Life in Digital Capitalism*. The University of Chicago Press, 2015.
Walker-Emig, Paul. *Utopian Horizons*. 2017, <https://podcasts.apple.com/gb/podcast/utopian-horizons/id1217015759>.
Wallerstein, Immanuel, et al. *Does Capitalism Have a Future?* Oxford University Press, 2013.
Walsh, Chad. *From Utopia to Nightmare*. G. Bles, 1960.
Wang, Jackie. *Carceral Capitalism*. Semiotext, 2018.
Wark, McKenzie. *A Hacker Manifesto*. Harvard University Press, 2004.
———. *Capital Is Dead: Is This Something Worse?* Verso, 2019.
———. *Gamer Theory*. Harvard University Press, 2007.
———. *Molecular Red: Theory for the Anthropocene*. Verso, 2015.
———. *Sensoria*. Verso, 2020.
Watson, Mike. *The Memeing of Mark Fisher: How the Frankfurt School Forwsaw Capitalist Realism and What to Do about It*. Zero Books, 2021.
Waugh, Patricia. *Metafiction: The Theory and Practice of Self-Conscious Fiction*. Routledge, 1984.

Weir, Peter, director. *The Truman Show*. Paramount Pictures, 1998.
Weiss, Linda. *America Inc.? Innovation and Enterprise in the National Security State*. Cornell University Press, 2014.
Williams, Raymond. *Keywords: A Vocabulary of Culture and Society*. New edn. Oxford University Press, 2015.
———. *Marxism and Literature*. Oxford University Press, 1977.
Williams, Stephen, director. "Trace Decay." *Westworld*, created by Jonathan Nolan and Lisa Joy. Home Box Office, 2016.
Winckler, Reto. "This Great Stage of Androids: *Westworld*, Shakespeare and the World as Stage." *Journal of Adaptation in Film & Performance*, vol. 10, no. 2, 2017, pp. 169–88.
Winckler, Reto, and Víctor Huertas-Martín. *Television Series as Literature*. Palgrave Macmillan, 2021.
Winstanley, William. *El paladín de Essex*. Translated by María Losada Friend and Pedro Javier Pardo. Ediciones Universidad de Salamanca, 2022.
Wiseman, Len, director. *Total Recall*. Prime Focus and Rekall Productions, 2012.
Wolf, Werner. *Metareference across Media: Theory and Case Studies*. Rodopi, 2009.
———. *The Metareferential Turn in Contemporary Arts and Media: Forms, Functions, Attempts at Explanation*. Rodopi, 2011.
Wood, Ellen Meiksins. *The Origin of Capitalism: A Longer View*. Verso, 2002.
Wu, Chin-Tao. *Privatising Culture: Corporate Art Intervention since the 1980s*. Verso, 2003.
York, Jillian C. *Silicon Values: The Future of Free Speech Under Surveillance Capitalism*. Verso, 2021.
Zevin, Alexander. *Liberalism at Large: The World According to the Economist*. Verso, 2019.
Žižek, Slavoj. *Mapping Ideology*. Verso, 1995.
———. *The Sublime Object of Ideology*. Verso, 2008.
Zuboff, Shoshana. *The Age of Surveillance Capitalism: The Fight for a Human Future at the New Frontier of Power*. PublicAffairs, 2019.

Index

Adorno, Theodor W. 6, 53, 59–62, 95, 110, 114, 184, 200
Aesthetics of ambivalence 5–8, 117, 203–6, 216–17
Alienation 46, 109, 129, 193, 272, 274–5, 276–7, 279, 292–3, 295, 300, 309–11, 320–2, 328, 332–3
Anti-utopia 11, 26–31, 43–7, 53–4, 57, 60, 67, 71, 84, 95, 100–1, 111, 113–14, 190–1, 195–7, 202–3, 237, 241, 256, 261–2, 284, 303–4, 306–8, 312–16
Artificial intelligence (AI) 92, 209, 232, 243, 247–8, 319, 324–5, 327–28

Benjamin, Walter 31–2, 53, 101, 214
Berlant, Lauren *see* cruel optimism
Black Mirror 1–2, 4, 17, 20, 23, 164–5, 178–180, 182, 185, 201, 202, 203, 266, 285–6
  Black Mirror: Bandersnatch 17, 119, 148–9, 164–81, 182, 185, 186
  "Fifteen Million Merits" 191, 217–19, 220–1
  "USS Callister" 20, 285–300, 306, 317, 318, 327, 332, 333–4
Borges, Jorge Luis 144, 213, 285
Bratton, Benjamin *see* stack
Brooker, Charlie 1, 124, 167, 178–81, 217–18, 290, 294,
Brown, Wendy 31, 32–4, 68–9
  Left melancholy 10, 31–5, 36, 42, 46, 54, 93, 100, 185,
  Neoliberal rationality *see* Neoliberalism

Can't Get You Out of My Head 23–4
Capitalism 12, 48–51, 105–6, 110–11, 184
  Capitalism as religion 18, 76, 185, 212–14, 242, 246, 251–5, 260, 263, 343–4
  Digital capitalism 5–6, 12, 15, 17, 20, 31, 84–100, 119–20, 121–2, 162–4, 177–81, 185, 187, 191–2, 200, 204, 210–11, 214–15, 260, 262–3, 266–7, 279–82, 335–7, 339–45
  Platform capitalism 85, 96, 97–8, 106
  Surveillance capitalism 85, 93–8, 102, 146, 177, 229
Cinema of attractions 189, 202, 204–7, 213, 260–1
Commodification 7–8, 11–12, 16–17, 18, 49–51, 65, 68–9, 71–2, 73–4, 93, 97–8, 107–12, 284, 298, 311, 320–2, 340–1
  of culture 52, 57–63, 157–8, 162–3, 193, 225–9, 235
  of narrative complexity 191, 199–202, 237, 243–5
  of self-referentiality 110, 120, 172, 182–7
Complex TV 6, 197–203, 222–3, 300–1
Crary, Jonathan 74, 76, 79, 85, 90, 92–3, 101, 111, 112, 314, 316
Critical dystopia 11–12, 43–5, 88, 105–6, 181–2, 185–7, 191–2, 195–7, 202–3, 339–41
Cruel optimism 196–7, 237, 314
Cyberpunk 1, 20–1, 87–8, 109–10, 121–7, 131, 213, 242, 300–1, 339

Cyberutopianism 78, 86–90, 92–3, 97, 98, 113, 212
Post-cyberpunk 20, 109, 121–2, 213, 301, 339

Debord, Guy 6–7, 29, 62, 73, 75, 83, 98
Devs 4, 18–19, 23, 191, 197, 214, 219, 245–60, 261–3, 334–5, 344
Dick, Philip K. 124–5, 130, 149–50, 167–8, 265–6, 268
  The Man in the High Castle see *Man in the High Castle, The*
  see also *Time Out of Joint*
Doctorow, Cory 2, 95–6
Don Quixote, myth of 19, 155, 265–7, 268–84
Dystopian structure of feeling 4–5, 9–10, 15–16, 23–31, 36, 40–7, 54, 62, 67, 71–2, 84, 100–1, 105, 113–15, 127, 185, 193, 169, 203, 214, 221, 244–5, 262–3, 284, 307, 312, 333, 340

Estrangement 1, 12, 17, 19–21, 120–2, 132, 154, 159, 180–1, 201–2, 234, 260–3, 309, 312, 340–2
  Cognitive estrangement *see* Suvin, Darko
  Reflexive estrangement 120–2, 130–2, 138–40, 144, 147–8, 160–1, 174, 181–2, 185–7, 236, 246, 314, 327
  Spectacular estrangement 205–7, 216–17, 244, 247–8, 285, 322

Franchise 123, 184–5, 288–9, 291
Frankenstein 145–6, 209, 222, 224–5, 236, 238, 244, 266
Filter bubble 90, 98–9, 136, 185, 281–2, 293, 298, 316, 323, 328, 337
Fisher, Mark 11, 25, 40, 42–3, 68, 316

Capitalist realism 10, 31, 36–40, 44, 46, 49, 54, 62, 67–8, 93, 100, 105
Reflexive impotence 40, 185

Garland, Alex 209, 252
Genette, Gérard 141–5, 182–3
  Diegetic levels 16, 136, 141–4, 145, 152–6, 161–2, 167–9, 175–7, 182–3, 224, 326–7
  Transtextuality 182–3, 213, 266–9
Gibson, William 87–8, 110, 122–6, 341
Gunning, Tom *see* cinema of attractions

Hacker 91, 276, 280–2, 290, 300–2, 306–7, 311–15, 317
  Hacker as class 107–12, 114, 247, 335–6
Hitchhiker's Guide to the Galaxy, The 19–20, 277–8, 287, 334

Individualism 67–8, 72, 87–91, 93, 108–9, 113, 196, 280–2, 299, 316, 335–7
Intersectionality 5, 46, 55–7, 74, 90, 100, 110, 112, 113, 132, 238, 241

Jameson, Fredric 8–9, 11, 13, 14, 20, 26–30, 36, 39, 41–2, 45, 54, 57–61, 73, 110–11, 113, 121–2, 123, 126, 129–32, 149, 183–4, 200, 212, 262, 278

Landon, Brooks *see* aesthetics of ambivalence
Le Guin, Ursula K. 41–2, 124–5, 127–8, 131
Left melancholy *see* Brown, Wendy
Lem, Stanisław 130–1, 149

Male gaze 208–9, 224–6, 244–5, 336–7, 342
Man in the High Castle, The 17, 119, 149–64, 182

Index

Maniac 4, 20, 23, 318–36
Marx, Karl 5, 13–14, 26–8, 34, 35, 49, 50–1, 65, 71, 73, 100, 107, 110, 165–6, 184, 186–7, 215, 263, 343–4
Marx, Leo 75–8, 86–7, 212
  Technology, concept of 75–8, 197, 207
Matrix, The 123, 147
Mental illness 168, 174–5, 280–1, 201, 307, 311–13, 316–7, 318–9, 321–4, 327
Metafictional allegory 142, 145–6, 165, 175, 191, 223–9, 238, 252–4, 276–7
Metafictional anagnorisis 146–8, 158–60, 171, 173–7, 180, 186, 227–8, 231, 233–4, 239–40, 254–8, 326–7, 329
Metafictional epiphany 146–8, 159–60, 172–4, 180, 186
Metalepsis 134, 143–4, 173–9, 186, 236
Meta-SF 120, 124–6, 131, 133–4, 137, 277, 286, 334
Miéville, China 82, 193–5, 257
Mise-en-abyme 142–3, 153–5, 169
Moylan, Tom
  Critical dystopia *see* Critical dystopia
  Dystopian structure of feeling *see* Dystopian structure of feeling
Mr Robot 4, 20, 23, 300–18, 327–8, 332, 333–5
Mulvey, Laura *see* male gaze

Neofeudalism *see* techno-feudalism
Neoliberalism 4, 12, 14, 15, 31, 33, 35, 39, 45–7, 49–51, 56, 63–72, 73–4, 77–8, 85–6, 89–90, 96, 100, 102, 106, 163, 322–3
  Neoliberal rationality 67–70, 91, 187
  Mont Pèlerin Society 63–5

New media, concept of 12–13, 15–16, 31, 72–4, 75, 78–81, 83–4, 113, 210–13
  Remediation 118, 155, 199, 213, 292
  Stack 118, 155, 199, 213, 254, 292
New media dystopia, definition of 2, 5–8, 10–12, 14–15, 23, 30, 113–15, 120–2, 147–8, 164, 182, 187, 190–1, 203–4, 214, 220–1, 260–3, 335–6, 337, 339–41
New media quixotism, definition of 19–20, 265–7, 279–84, 333–7, 342–3
New media reflexivity, definition of 16–17, 117–20, 181–7, 190, 341–2

Pardo, Pedro Javier 7, 16, 19, 118–19, 133–6, 155, 182, 184, 186, 190, 266, 268–9
  Metafictional allegory *see* Metafictional allegory
  Metafictional epiphany *see* Metafictional epiphany
  Metafictional anagnorisis *see* Metafictional anagnorisis
  Myth of Don Quixote *see* Don Quixote, myth of
  Reflexivity *see* reflexivity
Patriarchy 88, 145–6, 208, 228, 235–6, 241–2, 287, 291–2, 293–5, 336–7
Precarity 69–70, 106, 232–4, 303–4, 307–8, 316, 322–4, 331–2, 335–6
Postmodernism 7, 12, 14, 15, 19, 26, 29–31, 41, 47, 49–51, 51–63, 71–2, 73–4, 77–8, 85–7, 100, 108, 113, 117–9, 124–5, 130–1, 186–7, 193, 215, 273–8, 279–80, 328, 333
  Lyotard, Jean-François 52–4, 60, 73

Ready Player One 191, 219–20
Reflexivity 7, 13–14, 16–17, 110–11, 117–20, 120–1, 126–7, 130–32, 133–49,

181–7, 189–90, 206, 273, 279–80, 284, 341–2
Self-consciousness 136–40, 144, 145–7, 157, 158, 160, 165, 170, 173–4, 179–81, 185–7, 218, 225–6, 244, 252–5, 262–3, 285, 294, 299–300, 314, 326–7, 340
Self-referentiality 110–11, 117–20, 136–40, 145, 148–49, 153–4, 160–1, 165–7, 172–3, 179–80, 184–7, 223, 226–8, 248, 253, 289, 300, 303, 326–7, 340, 341
Remediation *see* new media, concept of
Russ, Joanna 41–2, 72–5, 124–5, 209, 336–7
Robinson, Kim Stanley 43, 47, 339, 346

Science fiction (SF), definition of
  As narrative *see* Suvin, Darko
  As spectacle *see* Aesthetics of ambivalence
Spy-fi *see* techno-thriller
Stack *see* new media, concept of
Star Trek 287–9, 297–8
Streaming platform 6–7, 16–17, 114, 119, 135–6, 141, 150, 181–3, 197–200, 212–13, 219, 253–5, 283, 341–2
  Amazon Prime Video 150, 334
  HBO 201–3, 222, 225–6
  Netflix 164, 165–9, 172–3, 175–6, 178–9, 181, 193, 289
Suvin, Darko 81–4, 128–9, 150, 191–5, 206
  Cognitive estrangement 127–30, 191–5, 205–7, 231, 247–8, 261, 285, 322, 335–7

Novum 15, 31, 81–4, 93, 100, 105, 117–18, 128, 205–9, 217, 232, 242–3, 246–8, 352, 319, 340

Techno-ambivalent gaze, definition of 17–18, 204, 209–15, 216, 221, 242–4, 245–6, 248, 259–60, 260–2, 336–7, 342
Techno-feudalism 100–5, 107
Technological aesthetics *see* techno-ambivalent gaze
Technological sublime 203–4, 207, 210–15, 218, 220, 230, 241–4, 252–5, 258–9, 290, 342
Technology, concept of *see* Marx, Leo
Techno-thriller 246–7, 305
Time Out of Joint 19–20, 147, 168, 276–7

Utopian impulse 11, 44–5, 195–6

Video-on-demand (VOD) platform *see* Streaming platform
Virtual reality (VR) 123, 141, 144, 220, 230, 236, 240–1, 283, 287, 289, 292, 293, 319, 323, 324

Wark, McKenzie 8, 12, 13, 15–16, 31, 62, 79–80, 99, 100–1, 105–12, 113–14, 118, 163, 281–2, 335–6
Westworld 4, 18–19, 23, 132, 145–7, 191, 222–45, 255, 259, 261–2, 301, 334–5
Williams, Raymond 4, 42–3, 47–8, 82

Years and Years 24–5

Žižek, Slavoj 11, 37–8, 57, 71, 134, 148

Ralahine Utopian Studies

Ralahine Utopian Studies is the publishing project of the Ralahine Centre for Utopian Studies at the University of Limerick in association with the University of Bologna, the University of Cyprus, and the University of Florida.

The series publishes high-quality scholarship that addresses the theory and practice of utopianism (including Anglophone, continental European and indigenous and postcolonial traditions, and contemporary and historical periods). Publications (in English and other European languages) include original monographs and essay collections (including theoretical, textual and ethnographic/institutional research), English-language translations of utopian scholarship in other national languages, reissues of classic scholarly works that are out of print and annotated editions of original utopian literary and other texts (including translations).

While the series editors seek work that engages with the current scholarship and debates in the field of utopian studies, they will not privilege any particular critical or theoretical orientation. They welcome submissions by established or emerging scholars working within or outside the academy. Given the multilingual and interdisciplinary remit of the series, the editors especially welcome comparative studies in any disciplinary or transdisciplinary framework.

Those interested in contributing to the series are invited to submit a detailed project outline to one of the series editors listed below.

Email queries can also be sent to ireland@peterlang.com.

Series editors:
Raffaella Baccolini (University of Bologna)
Antonis Balasopoulos (University of Cyprus)
Joachim Fischer (University of Limerick)
Michael G. Kelly (University of Limerick)
Tom Moylan (University of Limerick)
Phillip E. Wegner (University of Florida)

Ralahine Centre for Utopian Studies, University of Limerick http://wwww3.ul.ie/ralahinecentre/

Volume 1	Tom Moylan and Raffaella Baccolini (eds): Utopia Method Vision. The Use Value of Social Dreaming. 343 pages. 2007. ISBN 978-3-03910-912-8
Volume 2	Michael J. Griffin and Tom Moylan (eds): Exploring the Utopian Impulse. Essays on Utopian Thought and Practice. 434 pages. 2007. 408 pages. 2015. ISBN 978-3-03910-913-5

Volume 3	Ruth Levitas: The Concept of Utopia. (Ralahine Classic) 280 pages. 2010. ISBN 978-3-03911-366-8
Volume 4	Vincent Geoghegan: Utopianism and Marxism. (Ralahine Classic) 189 pages. 2008. ISBN 978-3-03910-137-5
Volume 5	Barbara Goodwin and Keith Taylor: The Politics of Utopia. A Study in Theory and Practice. (Ralahine Classic) 341 pages. 2009. ISBN 978-3-03911-080-3
Volume 6	Darko Suvin: Defined by a Hollow. Essays on Utopia, Science Fiction and Political Epistemology. (Ralahine Reader) 616 pages. 2010. ISBN 978-3-03911-403-0
Volume 7	Andrew Milner (ed.): Tenses of Imagination. Raymond Williams on Science Fiction, Utopia and Dystopia. (Ralahine Reader) 253 pages. 2010. ISBN 978-3-03911-826-7
Volume 8	Nathaniel Coleman (ed.): Imagining and Making the World. Reconsidering Architecture and Utopia. 393 pages. 2011. ISBN 978-3-0343-0120-6
Volume 9	Henry Near: Where Community Happens. The Kibbutz and the Philosophy of Communalism. 256 pages. 2011. ISBN 978-3-0343-0133-6
Volume 10	Robert C. Elliott: The Shape of Utopia. Studies in a Literary Genre. Edited with an Introduction by Phillip E. Wegner. (Ralahine Classic) 170 pages. 2013. ISBN 978-3-0343-0772-7
Volume 11	Michael E. Gardiner: Weak Messianism. Essays in Everyday Utopianism. 284 pages. 2013. ISBN 978-3-0343-0716-1
Volume 12	Matthew Beaumont: The Spectre of Utopia. Utopian and Science Fictions at the Fin de Siècle. 319 pages. 2012. ISBN 978-3-0343-0725-3
Volume 13	Artur Blaim: Gazing in Useless Wonder. English Utopian Fictions, 1516 –1800. 366 pages. 2013. ISBN 978-3-0343-0899-1

Volume 14	Tom Moylan: Demand the Impossible. Science Fiction and the Utopian Imagination. Edited by Raffaella Baccolini. (Ralahine Classic) 358 pages. 2014. ISBN 978-3-0343-0752-9
Volume 15	Phillip E. Wegner: Shockwaves of Possibility. Essays on Science Fiction, Globalization, and Utopia. 328 pages. 2014. ISBN 978-3-0343-0741-3
Volume 16	Angelika Bammer: Partial Visions. Feminism and Utopianism in the 1970s. (Ralahine Classic) 408 pages. 2015. ISBN 978-3-0343-0897-7
Volume 17	Edward K. Chan: The Racial Horizon of Utopia. Unthinking the Future of Race in Late Twentieth-Century American Utopian Novels. 226 pages. 2016. ISBN 978-3-0343-1916-4
Volume 18	Darko Suvin: Metamorphoses of Science Fiction. On the Poetics and History of a Literary Genre. Edited by Gerry Canavan. (Ralahine Classic) 515 pages. 2016. ISBN 978-3-0343-1948-5
Volume 19	Michael S. Cummings: Children's Voices in Politics. 554 pages. 2020. ISBN 978-3-0343-1943-0
Volume 20	Maïté Maskens and Ruy Blanes (eds): Utopian Encounters. Anthropologies of Empirical Utopias. 246 pages. 2018. ISBN 978-1-78707-247-3
Volume 21	Peter Fitting: Utopian Effects, Dystopian Pleasures Edited by Brian Greenspan. 458 pages. 2020. ISBN 978-1-78874-353-2
Volume 22	Raffaella Baccolini and Lyman Tower Sargent (eds): Transgressive Utopianism: Essays in Honor of Lucy Sargisson. 274 pages. 2021. ISBN 978-1-78997-880-3
Volume 23 and 24	Darko Suvin: Parables of Freedom and Narrative Logics: Positions and Presuppositions in Science Fiction and Utopianism. Edited by Eric D. Smith (VOLS I & II) 706 pages. 2021. ISBN 978-1-80079-047-6 (set)

Volume 25	Valentina Romanzi: American Nightmares: Dystopia in Twenty-First-Century US Fiction. 304 pages. 2022. ISBN 978-1-80079-715-4
Volume 26	Lyman Tower Sargent: Rethinking Utopia and Utopianism: The Three Faces of Utopianism Revisited and Other Essays. 434 pages. 2022. ISBN 978-1-80079-489-4
Volume 27	Mónica Martín: The Rebirth of Utopia in 21st-Century Cinema: Cosmopolitan Hopes in the Films of Globalisation. 240 pages. 2023. ISBN 978-1-80079-442-9
Volume 28	Alexander Popov: Zone Theory: Science Fiction and Utopia in the Space of Possible Worlds 368 pages. 2023. ISBN 978-1-80079-438-2
Volume 29	Pekka Kilpeläinen: Postcategorical Utopia: James Baldwin and the Political Unconscious of Imagined Futures 326 pages. 2023. ISBN 978-1-80079-233-3
Volume 30	A. L. Morton: The English Utopia Edited with an Introduction by Antonis Balasopoulos. (Ralahine Classic) 302 pages. 2023. ISBN 978-1-78997-418
Volume 31	Pavla Veselá: The Polyphony of Utopia: Critical Negativities Across Cultures from Bellamy and Bogdanov to Yefremov, Piercy and Butler. 322 pages. 2024. ISBN 978-1-80374-055-3
Volume 32	Donald Morris: Economic Inequality: Utopian Explorations. 368 pages. 2024. ISBN 978-1-80374-176-5
Volume 33	Heather Alberro: Terrestrial Ecotopias: Multispecies Flourishing in and Beyond the Capitalocene. 304 pages. 2024. ISBN 978-1-80079-576-1
Volume 34	Kenneth M. Roemer: The Obsolete Necessity: America in Utopian Writings, 1888–1900. (Ralahine Classic) 356 pages. 2024. ISBN 978-1-80079-864-9
Volume 35	Miguel Sebastián-Martín: Thinking through High-Tech Hell: A Theory of the New Media Dystopia. 398 pages. 2024. ISBN 978-1-80374-462-9

Utopian Studies

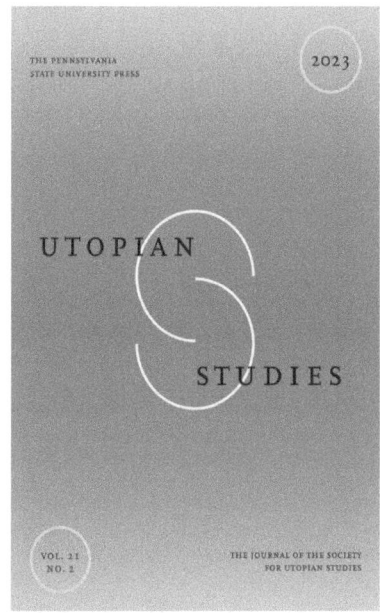

JENNIFER WAGNER-LAWLOR, EDITOR

Utopian Studies is a peer-reviewed publication of the Society for Utopian Studies that presents scholarly articles on a wide range of subjects related to utopias, utopianism, utopian literature, utopian theory, and intentional communities. Contributing authors come from a diverse range of fields, including American studies, architecture, the arts, classics, cultural studies, economics, engineering, environmental studies, gender studies, history, languages and literatures, philosophy, political science, psychology, sociology, and urban planning. Each issue also includes reviews of recent books.

ISSN 1045-991X | E-ISSN 2154-9648
Triannual | Available in print or online

Current pricing:
psupress.org/Journals/
jnls_utopian_studies.html

Submissions:
editorialmanager.com/uts

PENN STATE UNIVERSITY PRESS

www.psupress.org
journals@psu.edu

Printed by
CPI books GmbH, Leck